NEW RULES TRILOGY

BIANCA SOMMERLAND

Also by Bianca Sommerland

Untamed (Feral Bonds)

Solid Education

Street Smarts

Upper Class

Polished

Chapter One

The face in the reflection couldn't be me. So pale, with deep shadows under my big blue eyes, lips almost the same shade. My damn hair, a golden shade that had my brothers calling me 'pretty boy' reached the collar of my faded blue T-shirt. I was a pathetic mess.

And my situation wasn't getting better any time soon.

"Do it, Alec! Hurry up!"

Pressing my eyes shut, I inhaled sharply and smashed in the reflective window of the 1966 Chevelle LS3. The car was a beauty, modified with black windows that had to be illegal, its gleaming red paint job glowing even in the dim lighting of the parking garage. Too bad the owner was an idiot. Who left a car like this sitting around, with no alarm, in downtown Dallas?

You were asking for this, pal.

I stepped aside so my oldest brother, Erik, could climb in and hotwire the car. Christian, the second oldest, headed around to claim shotgun.

They stole cars all the time, so they looked completely relaxed, but I couldn't stop shaking and searching the garage for any sign of security. No way were we gonna get away with this. I was gonna end up with the same criminal record every male in my family earned by the time they sprouted their first facial hair. Fine, I was a late bloomer, but when I'd hit nineteen and managed to stay out of trouble, I should have seen it coming.

And then I saw *him* coming.

His skin was so dark, I couldn't make him out at first, but as he started running towards us there was no missing how freakin' *huge* he was. The black suit didn't hide his impressive build. And the dim light didn't conceal the rage hardening his features as he cut across the parking deck.

"Hey! Get the fuck away from that car!"

Christian's hand rammed into the center of my chest and I fell back, hitting the pavement hard. A sharp, burning pain spread over my palms, but I hardly felt it as I stared at the closed door. Then watched the car speed away.

They'd left me behind. Left me to take the fall.

A firm grip on my arm dragged me to my feet. The big black man's huge hand wrapped around my wrist like a shackle as he glared at me, his brown eyes dark with rage.

"Who are they, boy?" He shook me hard when my lips parted, but not a word came out. "Come on, they abandoned you. If you tell me, I'll put in a good word for you with the cops."

Bowing my shoulders, I pressed my tongue into my bottom lip. Should I just tell him? I didn't owe them anything. The only reason I'd agreed to steal the car in the first place was because I was fucking starving. And I'd run out of alleys to sleep in. All the good places had been cleared out by the police. If I could just find a real place, with an address to put on applications, maybe I could get off the street and build myself a life.

But I'd spent the last three years struggling to find enough to eat and steer clear of my brothers. Desperation led to me going back home.

And ended with me in this wonderful predicament.

"They're my brothers." I twisted my wrist, suddenly needing to get free. "Look, Mister, I won't rat them out. They might have screwed me over, but they're still family. And if they find out, they'll kill me. Just…just turn me in."

Prison might not be too bad. Erik and Christian had survived it a few times. I'd get food anyway. And a bed to sleep in. Damn luxury compared to what I'd had to look forward to before.

The money would've changed everything. You would've had enough to get an apartment. Maybe even get the hell out of Dallas and start fresh somewhere new.

Assuming they'd had any intention of giving me a cent.

I'd known the risks. Considered them for days as we scoped out the car, which was here every night until around midnight. I'd known it was wrong, but I did it anyway.

So I deserved to pay for my crime.

The big guy sighed and shook his head. "Come on."

I nodded and let him lead me to the elevator at the far side of the garage. They all went up to the new high rises erected over the last few years. The lower levels were full of expensive cars, owned by executives of the fashion and media corporations that filled the high rises, but this level was for the underlings. During the day cheap cars surrounded the beautiful classic. There was no security, no cameras. Almost as though the Cheville was here just to tempt someone to take it.

Giving in to temptation has a price.

Standing beside the giant, who'd let go of my wrist once the elevator door closed, leaving me with no chance of escape, I watched him push a button. Then blinked as the elevator began to rise.

"Aren't you taking me to the lobby? The cops will probably be a lot happier if they don't have to come fetch me." I chewed at my bottom lip when he glanced over at me as though I was a slightly irritating puppy performing a neat trick. Then I cleared my throat. "You know, I could probably talk my brothers into bringing the car back. And…and I could work off the cost of the broken window."

He gave me his full attention, lips slanted in amusement. "What happened to accepting your fate?"

My fate of a prison term. Yeah, sounded like a good time, but if I could avoid it? I shrugged. "Probably be easier to get a job without a criminal record."

"Probably." He snorted, nudging me forward as the elevator slid open. "I've decided to let Mr. Ashburne figure out what he wants to do with you."

The *Mr. Ashburne?* My mouth went dry and I dug the heels of my word sneakers into the charcoal colored carpet under my feet. "How about we just let the cops deal with me?"

"How about you don't piss me off, kid? It's been a long day, I'm tired, and I want to get this over with." He took a key card from his pocket and swiped it down the reader by one of the many large, steel doors lining the hall. With his hand on my shoulder, he propelled me into the reception area of the Ashburne Style and Media Company.

The place was damn impressive. Everything was shining, from the crisp, white walls, the weird, black art deco chairs around a round table in the corner, to the black glass reception desk in the center of the room. The wall-to-wall carpet was thick, with circles of black, white, and steel grey.

I didn't get much time to check out the rest of the room, because Mr. Manhandling-Giant was guiding me to a short hall past the desk. He stepped up to a pair of dark wood doors and rapped his knuckles on them.

No answer, but he opened the door anyway.

"Mr. Ashburne, I'm sorry to bother you." The giant tugged me to his side, his attention on the man sitting behind a big, black desk. "I thought you'd be interested to know your car has been stolen."

The man didn't look up from whatever he was writing in the notepad set between a huge desktop screen to his left, and the laptop off to his right. "Oh?"

"Yes." The giant sounded annoyed. "I'll have Jasper bring the limo, but—"

"Have him bring the town car if you must, but you know I hate the limo." Mr. Ashburne flipped the page and continued writing. "Is that all?"

I glanced up at the giant when he went quiet. He ground his teeth. "No. I caught one of the thieves. I thought you'd like to meet him."

The pen in Mr. Ashburne's hand was set softly down on top of the notepad. He sat up, lifting his head slowly, a bored smile on his lips as his eyes met mine.

Fuck me, this dude is scary. I swallowed as those piercing green eyes trapped me. Even from this distance, they were stunning, and frightening with their intensity. Not like emeralds, but more like a rainforest. Deep and wild, full of so much danger, but beautiful from a safe distance.

Which could describe every inch of him. He stood and I realized he was almost as big as the giant beside me. Or maybe I was just ridiculously small. I felt small as he stepped around the desk and came toward me. His expensive, dark blue suit was tailored perfectly to emphasize his broad shoulders and solid build. A five o'clock shadow darkened his jaw, making him look even more intimidating. Calling him handsome would have been an understatement. He probably made the men who modeled for his clothing line feel inferior.

The only thing that didn't fit with his perfectly put together appearance was his hair, which was unconventionally long. Men like him usually had short, styled hair, but his was slicked back and tied low. It looked so soft, I had the strangest urge to reach out and touch it as he circled me.

Not being completely stupid, I kept my hands to myself.

He stopped at my left side, his gaze on my face as I stared straight ahead. "Are you hungry?"

I blinked. *Am I what?*

Why in the world would he ask me that?

"Simple question. You will answer."

My stomach growled, answering for me. My cheeks heated as I folded my arms over my chest and ducked my head.

"Luther, please bring us something to eat." Mr. Ashburne walked away from me, returning to his seat behind his desk. "Take a seat, boy. What is your name?"

"Alec." I frowned at the giant, Luther, as he pressed his hand against my shoulder, pushing me toward one of the two metal and leather chairs in front of the desk. As I sat I heard the door open and close.

Elbows on the desk, fingers steepled, Mr. Ashburne studied me like I was a new specimen he'd discovered, and he was trying to decide what to call me. "Alexander?"

I nodded. "Yes."

"Last name?"

"Tremaine." Might as well tell him. The cops probably would once he filled out the police report. "Look, Mr. Ashburne, I'm sorry about your car. You have no reason not to call the cops, but like I told the giant—I mean, Luther—"

"'The giant'? Really, boy, he's not that big." Mr. Ashburne chuckled, picking up his pen again. He pulled out a drawer and lifted a stack of papers to his desk, writing on them as he continued. "What do you do for a living, Alexander?"

"It's just Alec. I mean, that's what people call me." I hunched my shoulder as his eyes narrowed. Right. He could call me whatever he wanted. "Uh…I don't do anything."

"Aside from stealing cars?"

"Yeah…that's new."

"Good." He jotted down a few more things on the papers. "What's your address?"

Shit. The only one I had to give was my brothers' address, but I didn't live there. Not since I ran away when I was sixteen. Giving him their address was the same as turning them in. He would send the cops there and I'd be spending the next five to ten trying not to be murdered by my own blood.

"I don't have one." The truth.

He slammed the pen down on his desk and stood. "Alexander, don't lie to me. I am feeling generous. I would like to offer you an opportunity. One you do not deserve." He approached me, his voice lowering as he leaned over me, one hand on the back of the chair by my shoulder. "Make no mistake. I will know everything about you very soon. This will be more pleasant for you if you are as honest with me as possible."

More pleasant sounded good, and I wished I could give him the answer he wanted, but he wouldn't believe me. The story was fucked up and pathetic and what would a guy like him know about having absolutely nothing? About *choosing* to have nothing when the alternative was staying where you were treated like dirt and could only prove your worth in abandoning your conscience and any hope for a future?

I had abandoned all those pretty ideals today. I'd become all I'd tried to escape.

My chin jutted up and my eyes burned as I met his hard gaze. "I'm fucking homeless, all right? I dropped out of school when I was sixteen. Ran away from home so I wouldn't be forced to steal or sell drugs. But I was tired of being hungry, so I gave up being good and figured if I did one bad thing, maybe my life would change."

Mr. Ashburne inclined his head, his eyes softening slightly. The brilliant green almost seemed to glow as he straightened and his lips curved. "I believe you."

He moved to his desk, staying on this side, resting his hip on the edge as he continued to study me.

Which was driving me nuts. I was starting to be a bit less scared of the cops, and a bit more scared of *him*. He hadn't called them yet, so what exactly were his plans for me?

Not gonna lie, the guy was hot, so the idea of him wanting *me* wasn't an issue. Living on the street, I'd considered whoring myself out just to get enough money for a meal. I was gay and men paid good money for a pretty boy. But that idea had been shelved along with the one where I'd sell drugs with my brothers to get a roof over my head.

I'd met some of the guys who dealt with pimps, and they

weren't much better off than I'd been when I'd lived with my brothers. They weren't as skinny as me, well, except for the ones on hard drugs, but the constant bruises were a reminder of why a sleeping bag and a ball cap at my feet on the curb was preferable to a nice, warm bed.

If Mr. Ashburne wanted to fuck me, I'd be cool with that. Hell, just the thought had blood rushing to my dick, but I couldn't peg him as a gay man. I was pretty sure I'd seen him in the paper before with chicks. Hot chicks. Models and actresses and girls with rich daddies.

So whatever he wanted from me, it probably wasn't to get in my torn, grungy blue jeans.

"Try to relax, Alexander." Mr. Ashburne spoke softly, and for the first time, I noticed he didn't have the Texan drawl absolutely everyone I knew—including myself—had. His voice was deep. Refined. And I couldn't detect an accent at all. It was like his voice was fine-tuned to sound dark, strong, alluring and perfect as the rest of him. "I have a few questions for you. Answer them truthfully and your situation may improve in ways you've never imagined. We will have something to eat. Not here though. You don't seem comfortable."

I wasn't, but I hadn't been paying much attention to comfort. The chair was stiff, like whoever he made sit here shouldn't want to stay long. He must have investors meet him somewhere else. Otherwise, the chairs alone would have his company going bankrupt.

He stepped up to me and held out his hand.

Without thinking, I placed my hand in his. My heart stuttered as he pulled me to my feet. All my blood surged down to my balls. He was so close the fresh aroma of whatever soap he used, the spice of his cologne, and the mint on his breath, flooded my senses. The heat of his body had me leaning toward him. Careful not to touch, but...damn, I was cold. The room was cold and his body lured me in like a fireplace with soft fur laid out on the floor, just close enough to soak in all the warmth without getting burned.

"Your hands are cold. Stay right here." He released my hand and headed to the wall, which looked solid, but when he pressed his hand to it, a door slid open, revealing a small closet. He grabbed a black, wool sweater, the kind a man would wear over a shirt and tie, and handed it to me.

The thing *felt* expensive. I was dirty. I couldn't wear his nice stuff.

Before I could object, he caught my wrist and met my eyes. "You can keep it. Alexander, I need to make one thing very clear. This will be the last time I see you looking like...*this*." His lips curled as he looked me over. "We'll eat as we discuss my plans for you. Is there anything else you need first?"

I shook my head, completely humiliated. I still didn't have a clue what his 'plans' were, but I got it. I didn't belong here. He was being nice, and I'd take what I could get.

Going to prison was still a possibility. If there was an alternative?

At this point, I wouldn't question the why or how.

I was feeling something I hadn't in so long, I didn't recognize it at first.

Hope.

There was so much food in front of me; I didn't know where to start. Home fries, burgers, pizza, fried chicken, fried pickles, fried cheese curds...Oh my god, was that fried strips of steak? I grabbed a few pieces, burning my fingers and letting out a yelp.

Luther laughed at me, then handed me a napkin. "Careful, it's hot."

I nodded, but dumped some on the fine china plate he'd set in front of me. Murmured thanks as Luther set three cans of Pepsi by my plate. Why they were feeding me so well after catching me helping steal Mr. Ashburne's car was a mystery, but I hadn't had a solid meal in...hell, it had been a week, hadn't it? My stomach was ready to eat itself. It hurt just to look at the food and know I couldn't inhale it all. If I ate too fast, I'd probably make myself sick.

But I took some of everything. Including the pickles, which I didn't even like. Who knew when I'd get to eat again? Hopefully, I could keep enough down to last.

"Thank you, Luther. If you could give us a few moments alone?" Mr. Ashburne was very polite to his...damn, I didn't know what Luther was to him. A bodyguard, probably. Anything less would be a waste of his obvious talents.

Luther inclined his head and stepped out into the hall.

Mr. Ashburne watched me eat whatever didn't burn my tongue, not touching the food himself. After I'd downed a few mouthfuls, he leaned forward, putting his hand over the back of mine.

"Don't stop eating, but let me explain your situation to you." His lips curved when I nodded. My mouth was full, so it was all I could do. "I could call the police, but I'm curious as to why Luther brought you to me. He's not only my head of security but my partner. He knows me better than anyone, and he's aware that I have one position I've failed to fill."

I finished chewing, swallowed, then ran my tongue over my teeth to make sure I didn't have any food stuck there. "What's that?"

"I need an assistant. A secretary." He smirked when I made a face. "I'm sure you have much more appealing prospects, but hear me out. In my business, it's difficult to find a man I can trust."

"Aren't secretaries usually women?" I wasn't trying to be sexist, but a man like him could have eye candy, like most rich men did. A pretty blond chick willing to serve him in every way.

He laughed. At me. I was sure of it. "Traditionally, yes. But I'm not traditional. The women who work for me are capable of the same level of control I manage. Ruthless businesswomen who can face their male counterparts in the boardroom. They all have male secretaries who are more than capable of...submitting to them. I envy the relationships they have and I've been looking for someone to fill that place for me."

"And you're gonna choose the guy that stole your car?"

"You don't have my car, Alexander. Your brothers do." He gave me a stiff smile when I blinked at him. "Luther gave me a brief summary while you were washing up. I believe your circumstances forced your hand. And either misplaced loyalty, or fear, has you protecting your siblings. I will get my car back, but what's more important to me right now is the unique opportunity to fill this vacant position. Are you interested?"

"Hell yes!" This couldn't be happening. A job offer? The man had to be crazy, but I'd be crazier to say no. Except…well, could I be a secretary? I was a high school dropout. Willing to learn whatever he needed from me, but why should he put up with a man without skills when he could find a hundred guys who had plenty to offer? "I can't type. I'm willing to learn, but I have to ask. Why me? I'm the last person you should even consider for the job. Not that I'm saying you shouldn't hire me. I'll work harder than anyone. I'm desperate and I won't fuck you over. No one else would want me, but these other guys could find work anywhere."

You just answered your own question, idiot.

"I can see you understand. Your desperation is actually appealing, Alexander. And you may not know this, but I do have cameras in the parking garage. None so obvious as those on the lower levels. I park my car with the employees because they are all gone by five. I have management and fellow board members who work as late as I do. When I finish my day—or night, as happens more often than not—I prefer to avoid interacting with any of them." He folded his hands on the table. "I can identify both your brothers with surveillance. I will use it to retrieve my car. It is not one of my most expensive, but I am fond of it."

Damn, he didn't need to make me an offer at all. My 'loyalty' was irrelevant. If Mr. Ashburne wanted them, they were done for.

And so was I. He had me breaking his window on video. Probably high definition, because why the hell not? I didn't have a leg to stand on. He had me by the balls.

But instead of using that, he was informing me of the facts as though giving me options. Options that no sane person would consider. Except…he was taking away fear as my only motivation for taking the job.

Or…maybe he wasn't? I didn't have to turn my brothers in for them to get caught. He didn't need me for that. If I turned him down, we could still go to jail. All of us.

"What *exactly* do you want from me, Mr. Ashburne?" I used the napkin Luther had given me to wipe my mouth. Despite him having caught me and dragged me up here, I kinda liked the guy. He was cool. Didn't play around. Unlike his boss, I had a good idea of where he was coming from. "If all you want is someone who can do the job, but can't be grabbed up by a rival, I can do that. I'll sign whatever you want. I don't know anyone, and you've got shit on me, so not like I'd even consider a better offer."

"I will expect more than you can even imagine, Alexander. What you sign will not be in blood, but it might as well be. You will never find another job anywhere if you breech our contract." Mr. Ashburne rested his hands on the table. Completely relaxed. But I sensed my answer was important to him. That he wanted me to say yes. "You will learn things about me that may make you reconsider your answer. As of tonight, so long as you work for me, you may not go back to the place you consider 'home'."

No big loss there. I wouldn't miss sleeping on a park bench. "Where am I gonna go then?"

"We will work on your language. You're not a stupid boy, Alexander. Please don't let your speech have people believing otherwise."

"Fine. Where would you like me to stay?"

"With me."

Holy fuck! I stared at him. Was he joking? He'd just met me and he was gonna take me home with him?

He laughed again. "I do enjoy your reactions. Luther lives with me as well. My house is not small. You will have your space and you will be watched until you've earned our trust. Which will be a bit easier with Luther, since he found you worthy enough to bring to me. Show him he wasn't wrong to do so, and you may earn yourself a very good friend."

"But…" I wasn't sure what to make of all he'd said. What would happen after I signed his papers? "When does all this happen? I look at the contract and bring it back to you and then—"

"You'll look at it now, Alexander. I'm a busy man. If you don't accept my offer, we'll be having a very different conversation. It's almost midnight. I trust you'll make up your mind before then." He stood and gestured to the food. "Please enjoy your meal. Luther will bring you the contract. He will answer any questions you have about it. I will see you again once it's signed."

Okay, I didn't like how fucking confident he was that I'd go along with what he expected me to do. My pride wasn't dead, even though it might look like it was when I begged for spare change on the corner.

I fisted the napkin in my hand. "What if I don't sign?"

Hand on the doorknob, he glanced back at me, his sharp features completely relaxed. "As I said, I don't believe you're a stupid man. Young, but not stupid. Proving me wrong would be a mistake."

A not so subtle threat. I stared at the door long after he was gone. For some reason, I didn't think he was threatening to turn me in to the police. I had a feeling he could do so much worse.

The contract was fucking weird. I read every single word of it as I tested my stomach's ability to hold down more food than I'd eaten in a month. Chewing the last bite of my burger, savoring the bacon and cheese, I wiped my greasy fingers on my jeans then turned the page.

A few things stuck out:

*Employee will sign a non-disclosure agreement (hereby referred to as NDA) pertaining to all aspects of company and personal relationships involving the employer.

I guess he doesn't want me spilling his business to the press. Makes sense.

*Employee will submit to a physical exam, as well as a blood test, every three months. All results will be fully disclosed to the employer.

Little weird, but he probably wants to make sure I'm not on drugs.
I had to read the next section over twice because...what the hell?

*Discipline for any infractions will be handled by the employer or the head of security. All aspects of discipline fall under the NDA.

What the actual fuck?
I kept reading, wondering if there would be any details about the 'discipline'. Was I gonna be writing lines? Kneeling in the corner like a five year old? What kind of company used the word 'discipline' in their contracts?

I struggled not to laugh as I considered Luther signing something like this. Did Mr. Ashburne spank him when he was bad?

Luther shot me a curious look. "Any questions?"

Shaking my head, I glanced down at the word 'discipline' again. And cleared my throat. "Did you sign this contract?"

Letting out a sharp laugh, Luther sat back in his chair and folded his arms over his massive chest. "No."

"Oh..." I frowned when he smirked at me, like he knew something I hadn't figured out yet. "What sort of discipline are we talking about here?"

"That will be discussed after you sign the NDA."

"But Mr. Ashburne told me you'd answer any questions I asked."

"Yes." Luther sounded amused. "I just did."

Great. Well, if that was the kind of answer I was gonna get, why bother?

I continued on to the forms, which took up the last three pages. The first page was easy enough. Education, experience, former employment. Didn't have much to write there. I used to take out the trash for the old lady next door when I was a kid. She paid me a buck a week. I didn't think Mr. Ashburne would consider that a job.

My lips parted as I started on the next page.

* Number of sexual partners, past and present.

He couldn't legally ask that, could he? What the hell did who I'd slept with have to do with being a secretary?

Not that I had anything to hide…well, except that I was lame for a guy my age. I jotted down a number that I thought would look good. Five was a nice number.

Luther made a low sound of disapproval. "Lying on your application is a very bad idea, Alec."

"How do you know I'm lying?"

His brow rose.

I sighed, crossed out the five, and wrote the truth.

Zero.

He leaned forward and grinned. "That's what I thought."

Glaring at him, I pulled the form closer to me. "Why the fuck do I have to answer all these personal questions? What does my sex life have to do with the job?"

"That will be discussed after—"

"After I sign the NDA. Fuck, you're useless."

As I moved to continue filling out the insanely invasive form, Luther latched onto my wrist. "A little advice, boy. Do not swear at me. And if you have any brains in that cute little head of yours, you won't *ever* swear at Mr. Ashburne."

Heat spread across my cheeks even as goosebumps rose all over my skin. Out of all the rules and questions, not swearing at my boss was probably the most reasonable request so far, but there was no mistaking the warning in Luther's tone. It reached some primal instinct within, one that had wolves baring their throat to the leader of the pack, admitting defeat because defiance would cost them their life.

I finished filling out all the papers, signed and initialed where indicated, and handed them over.

Luther set the neatly stacked papers in front of him and gave me a level look. "I know this isn't easy, Alec. And I know there's a lot you don't understand. It will be overwhelming, but I promise you one thing."

Nibbling on a fry, because I was full, but I had to try to test my limits a little, I met his eyes.

"I will do my best to get you through this. I decided you'd be worth my time, and Mr. Ashburne's, when you refused to turn your brothers in even after they ditched you. When you were willing to pay for their crimes. You're a good kid." His lips thinned. "I hope you're strong enough to get through the next few days. If you are, you'll look back and consider this the best thing that ever happened to you."

"And if I'm not?" I had to ask. I had no idea what I'd really signed on for. He wasn't painting any pretty pictures for me.

He lifted his shoulders and sighed. "Then you'll probably be hoping it's all a nightmare, and one day you'll wake up. You're not the first young man I've had this conversation with, Alec." His lips curved slightly. "But you're the first one I'd be willing to put money on. And I might do so, so don't let me down."

Chapter Two

The mansion was just as insanely huge as I expected, but I couldn't make out much of it in the dark. Luther pulled up in front of a large, dark wood door at the far end of the right wing of the massive, light grey stone building and got out, opening the back door of his SUV for me before I could regain my senses enough to move. I swallowed hard as he reached out and offered me his hand.

What am I doing here? What if they're both serial killers and this is where I die?

With all the landscape, the tall trees and hills surrounding us, it was easy to imagine bodies hidden away out there. Bodies of stupid guys like me who'd tried to mess with Xavier-fucking-Ashburne.

But Luther, tough as he was, didn't seem like the depraved-murderer-type. Sure, he'd probably take someone out if he thought Xavier was in danger, that was his job. But looking into his warm brown eyes, patient even as I kept him waiting, I wasn't afraid. Not really. Nervous? Damn right I was. I had no idea what they planned to do with me.

Whatever it was, I'd live through it.

I took his hand.

"Very good." Luther's lips slanted as he pulled me to his side, then placed his hand on the small of my back to lead me to the door. "But don't expect me to put up with you keeping me waiting very often. Once you learn to trust me, that is."

"Will I?" I bit into my cheek, cursing myself for voicing the question out loud. Telling the guy who'd saved me from prison that I didn't trust him was stupid.

He didn't seem to mind. Opening door, he motioned me forward. "When I've earned it? Yes. And don't be afraid to speak your mind, Alec. Not with me. I can't train you if I don't know what you're thinking."

"Train me?"

"I took on the job when I brought you to Xavier." Luther flicked on the lights in the small kitchen and went directly to the fridge. "This is my kitchen, by the way. Since you'll be staying in my wing, you may use it whenever you want. But please leave a note on the fridge if you finish anything. Would you like a beer?"

"I'm not old enough to drink."

"But you're old enough to serve in the military or be tried as an adult." Luther arched a brow as he pulled out a beer, standing in the door of the fridge, and regarding me with interest. "If you don't drink, that's fine. But you may do so here within reason."

I hadn't had a beer since I was sixteen. At a friend's house, celebrating his birthday. Just a few months before I'd left home. It had been nice. We didn't get stupid drunk, just buzzed and relaxed.

A feeling which would be more than welcome right now.

"Yes, please." I looked around the kitchen, sleek with stainless steel and gleaming white accents. Never in my life had I been somewhere so expensive looking and clean. Even when my parents had been alive things were always grungy, half the appliances barely functioning, only one lightbulb working if there were any at all sticking out of the one outlet in the ceiling.

This room had so many inlaid lights not a single corner was dark. Which was somehow…comforting. Even in the middle of the night, I was somewhere bright. There were no sounds of trashcans being kicked. People screaming. Sirens blaring.

Just the soft sound of the wind outside. Luther's steady steps and he came to join me at the kitchen island, pulling out a stool and motioning for me to sit in the other as he set down both our beers.

"Alec, I don't want you under the impression that this will be easy. Now that you've signed the agreement, I will give you one chance to back out. Only one. After this, there will be negotiations, but I won't let you go so easily." Luther motioned for me to drink, took a gulp from his own beer, then continued. "The job itself will be easy. Filing paperwork, typing out Xavier's notes, taking phone calls. You can do that."

"But he wants more from me?"

"You have an idea of what he wants. What we both want." Luther licked a drop of beer off his bottom lip, giving me a hooded look that sent a shiver down my spine, sweet and cool and speeding up my pulse. "What I saw in you wasn't for him alone."

I wasn't sure if that should scare me. Xavier seemed to be the one with all the power, but there was something in Luther…a presence I couldn't define. With that last look, I couldn't breathe. Couldn't speak.

He watched me. Waited as I finished my beer. Kept waiting until I couldn't stand the silence anymore.

"What do *you* want from me?"

"Everything." Luther finished off his beer. Set it aside. "I want to see that beautiful body exposed. I want to have you kneeling at my feet. I want to reach that moment when I tell you to come and you don't hesitate." Pushing off his stool, Luther went back to the fridge, grinning when I nodded at his offer for another beer. "You won't ever have to guess with me, Alec. I don't play those kinds of games."

"So…" I accepted the beer. Gulped it down. Would he let me get drunk before I had to answer?

His steady look told me no.

I chose my words carefully. "So I won't just be answering phone calls."

"No."

"He wants to fuck me."

Luther spat out a laugh. "Not yet. You're too innocent."

"So he want you to…" This was harder. I saw Luther as larger than life, strong and…and my hero. How else could I see him? I'd be talking to cops right now if not for him. I lowered my gaze and took a deep breath. "You have to get me ready for him?"

"Yes and no." Luther cocked his head, studying me for a moment. "You'll always have a choice. I'm not asking you to whore yourself out for the things we'll give you. Being Xavier's secretary won't be easy and you'll more than earn your keep. You'll be paid a salary as well, like every other employee." He paused to take another gulp of beer. "We chose you for this specific task because, not only are you appealing, you have more reason than anyone to keep his secrets."

"And what secrets are those?"

"He'll let you know himself when he's ready. The trust needs to be mutual."

"Fair enough." I hadn't expected Luther to be so forthcoming with me, but I was grateful for it. Even though I still wasn't sure I got how this was gonna work. "So I'll be his secretary, and if I'm into it, his…boy toy? And yours?"

Luther let out a startled laugh. "'Boy toy'? I wouldn't put it quite that way." His tone took on a deep, dark edge as he leaned in. He took my half full beer and set it aside, leaving nothing between us. "But if you're willing, we will play with you."

Blood pulsed down to my dick and I swallowed hard against a spill of lust I couldn't ignore. There was a reason Luther didn't sound concerned that I *wouldn't* be willing. He wasn't even trying to seduce me yet and I was ready to say yes to whatever he wanted. If he actually turned on the heat?

I was a goner. And I wasn't even upset about it.

But I still had questions. Or more…one. I licked my lips. "Together?"

"At times. We enjoy sharing. Xavier has terrible taste in men — he's been burned in the past, so now he trusts me to find lovers who might enjoy our lifestyle." Luther's tone had returned to the conversational one he'd used earlier, which made it easier to breathe. He shot me a knowing smile. "Don't look so nervous. This won't happen overnight. And not until you're ready."

"What if I never am?" My dick throbbed as though protesting my words, but I had to know he meant it about me having a choice.

Standing, Luther held out his hand, much like he had at the car. When I placed mine in his, he pulled me to my feet. Close to him, but not so close that my personal space felt invaded. Still holding my hand, he met my eyes.

"I will do everything in my power to tempt you, Alec. Not with money, or safety. When you submit to me for the first time you will come to me. You will tell me what you're ready for." There was a soft, lulling edge to his voice, one that had me wanting to stay right where I was, feeling his hand around mine, his thumb stroking my knuckles in a way that was much more erotic that it should have been.

His lips curved and I couldn't help staring at them, wondering what they'd feel like on mine. Damn it, no one had ever been this gentle with me. This patient. Maybe that was why his touch felt so good. I was starved for any contact that didn't end with pain.

"So fucking desperate for it, aren't you?" Luther shook his head and sighed. "I could have you tonight, but it's much too soon. Make me work for it a little, pup."

"You're making it very hard." Heat covered the back of my neck and I pressed my eyes shut. I hadn't meant to sound like I was talking about my dick, but I kinda was. He was right, it was too soon, but after everything he'd said, I didn't want to walk away without a taste of what he was teasing me with.

A big, strong, incredibly sexy guy telling me he wanted me was almost as much of a dream come true as having a full stomach and a roof over my head. Sure, in my fantasy the guy wouldn't be sharing me with his boss. And the romantic side of me, I'd never given too much attention, imagined dates and sweet words and falling in love.

But I hadn't been holding on to my virginity until I found 'The One'. I just hadn't had any good opportunities.

This one was pretty damn good.

"You're as precious as I knew you'd be." Luther let out a soft laugh. "Look at me, Alec."

I opened my eyes. He hadn't moved any closer, but I could tell he wanted to.

The lust in his eyes gave me such a rush the room seemed to be swaying a little, like I'd stood up too fast and the ground was unsteady.

"I won't fuck you tonight. But I will give you one thing." His lips curved slightly. "Just ask."

Shifting closer to him, I inhaled slowly. "I want you to touch me. To kiss me. And it's fucking weird, but—"

He pulled me against him, bringing his lips to mine and smiling. "That's two things."

Before I could respond, his lips covered mine, the heat of them consuming me whole. I didn't have a second to wonder if I was a good kisser, he guided me effortlessly, teasing the seam of my lips with his tongue, his hand in my hair tilting my head as my lips parted and he claimed my mouth. There was a sweetness as his tongue touched mine, then grazed a sensitive spot behind my teeth before drawing out, using the pressure of his lips to massage mine in a sensual way that had my whole body moving, as though I could feel him everywhere.

And I could. Every nerve lit up, as the hardness of his body sent shivers of pleasure to the base of my spine. My dick was so hard, painfully confined pressed tight against my jeans, but the ache of it grinding his through the material was the most erotic thing I'd ever experienced.

His free hand slipped under my shirt at the base of my spine, his fingers stroking lightly, just above the waist of my jeans. I let out a rough, desperate sound and lowered my head to his chest. Holding still so he wouldn't stop. Too fucking turned on to manage getting any air into my lungs.

"Soon." He nudge my head with his chin and brought his lips to my throat. "Very soon."

He held me for a moment, kissing my neck gently before easing me away from him.

I whispered an incoherent protest, but he shook his head.

"Let me show you to your room. There's a shower. Use it and then get some sleep." He caught my elbow when I stumbled, his eyes warm, not laughter in them when I'd expected there to be. Just the same patience he'd shown all night. "If you're still feeling this way tomorrow…"

Chewing on my bottom lip, I stared up at him.

"I'll let you ask two things of me." He brought me to his side and whispered in my ear. "And ask for one in return."

Chapter Three

The next morning I expect to feel drained and disoriented, but everything about me was light and fresh and alive. Maybe being clean and surrounded by soft blankets and sleek sheets, my stomach not tight with pain forcing me to crawl out of whatever shelter I'd manage to find to hunt down anything even slightly edible…

Yeah, that probably made a difference.

I'd also jerked off in the shower thinking about Luther, and came so hard I'd almost passed out right there. And did pass out in the wonderful bed seconds later.

Still naked.

I looked around for the black silk pajamas Luther had left for me, guilt tainting my happy buzz a little when I spotted them on the floor. After pulling them on quickly, I headed to the bathroom to take a piss, then wash my hands and face and brush my teeth. I even used floss and mouthwash.

Thinking of Luther's kiss, the state of my mouth was embarrassing. Sure, I tried to brush my teeth at least once a day when I lived on the streets, but finding somewhere with a sink that would let me in wasn't always easy. And I hadn't been to a dentist since I was ten.

But he hadn't seemed to notice my teeth weren't as perfectly white as his. Or that my hair wasn't groomed and my clothes were grungy and worn.

I looked in the mirror at the 'pretty' face I'd always hated, one that was too weak, too smooth, lacking the strength in my brothers' hard jaws and even harder eyes.

Aside from the shadows under my eyes and the slight gauntness of my cheeks, I looked...good. My hair had dried a little fluffy, with the overgrown light blond waves touching my collar, but it was a nice color, shiny now that it had been washed. My lips had more color to them, probably from the kisses that I could still feel whenever I closed my eyes.

A soft knock at the door drew my attention away from staring at the new, less pathetic me. I hurried across the room, grinning when I saw Luther standing there, arms folded over his chest.

He smiled back. "You look good, Alec. No regrets?"

"Nope." I pressed my tongue into my bottom lip. "Do you want to come in?"

Laughing, he shook his head, unfolding his arms and stepping back. "No. You're coming down to the kitchen to have breakfast with me. We can discuss your orientation so you can start work on Monday."

"Right. Work." I tried not to sound disappointed. Work was good. Needed. I wasn't some charity case they'd taken off the streets. I was a thief who'd been handed a damn golden ticket. One with terms and conditions, all of which I'd agreed to.

But part of my mind was still stuck in the fantasy Luther had given me. One where desire meant not having to think too hard that this was all too good to be true.

There had to be a catch.

"You are going to be very easy to spoil." Luther reached out and took my hand. "I have you to myself for the next two days. Behave and you will enjoy every minute. I'm generous with my rewards."

"Yeah?" I glanced down at our hands, loving how easy it was to be touched by him. That contact was so natural, maybe because he did it as though there was no reason not to. As if it wasn't a big deal.

Which it might not be to him, but his hold anchored me. Made this all seem real.

Real enough not to think too hard about what I was getting myself into.

The kitchen smelled like absolute heaven. Syrup and coffee and blueberry muffins. Two plates stacked with pancakes sat on the table, along with fresh strawberries, oranges, a pitcher of orange juice, another of milk, and a carafe of coffee. There was a slab of butter, a tray piled high with muffins, and two covered, silver dishes.

Luther lifted the tops of the trays, revealing bacon in one, and scrambled eggs in the other. "I wasn't sure what you'd like."

"*Everything.*" My mouth watered as I approached the table. "Did you make all this?"

"All but the muffins. The cook, Ms. Lacey, heard we had a new guest and brought them over from the main kitchen." He pulled out a chair and waited for me to join him before handing me a muffin. "They're her specialty. And Xavier's favorite."

I nodded, opening the muffin, groaning at the steam that rose and taking a second just to breathe it in. I placed it on the white and blue trimmed plate in front of me and reached for the butter. "Does Mr. Ashburne eat alone?"

Brow furrowing slightly, Luther inclined his head. "More often than not, in his office while he's working. He's always been a bit of a workaholic—you don't make your first million before twenty-five without some insane dedication."

Damn, I couldn't manage enough money to feed myself, never mind even imagine somehow making millions. I'd heard enough about Xavier to know he hadn't come from a wealthy family. He'd gotten scholarships to one of the best art schools in the world and used his talents to design dresses that ended up on runways when he was just a bit older than I was now.

Then he'd invested every cent and watched his money grow. He owned his own fashion line and magazine and he couldn't be more than thirty. In his place, I'd probably be chilling, just enjoying all the hard work that got me rich and famous.

Which was probably why I'd never be in his place.

But I would get somewhere. I'd be the best damn secretary he'd ever had.

Maybe start with letting Luther teach you and not obsessing over how much you want to kiss him again.

I cleared my throat as I buttered my muffin. "Maybe when I'm working for him, he won't have to do that so often."

Luther shot me an amused look. "It's cute that you think that."

Wrinkling my nose, I took a big bite of muffin before I could say something regrettable. Like 'I'm not cute' or 'Isn't that the point of me doing the damn job?'

"What was that thought?" Luther grabbed my wrist before I could take another bite. "You'll have to get used to me thinking you're adorable. You're not used to this world and you have an idealized outlook. I appreciate that. It's refreshing."

"I won't always be. Aren't I supposed to become part of this world?"

"Yes, but I think you'll keep the best qualities that you've earned through survival." He released my wrist. "Xavier's survival turned into obsession. He's a good man, but he rarely sees beyond how dark the world could be again if he loses control of the power he's gained. Remember that when you're with him. He'll fill every free moment you give him with work he doesn't trust anyone else to do. And there's always plenty of that. If you can offer him some distraction, it'll help, but don't count on it."

"What if he wants to be distracted?" I couldn't forget where this might lead if Xavier was interested in me. It wasn't a hardship to imagine myself on my knees under his desk, the man was fucking gorgeous.

But I didn't see him taking his time like Luther was. He probably wouldn't seduce me.

Maybe *that* was part of my job. The part that remained unsaid.

It would be up to me to seduce him.

Luther was watching me, a sly smile on his lips. "Him *wanting* to be distracted would be very good. But it won't be easy to get him there."

"Which is why you're going to teach me how." I licked a crumb off my thumb, grinning around it as Luther's gaze dropped to my mouth. "You must be good at it."

"I like to think so." He inhaled slowly. "But he keeps me too busy to tempt him as often as I'd like."

I sucked on my finger. "Is that why you found him a new toy?"

Shaking his head, Luther laughed. "You're cheeky when you're well fed. I like that. Now finish eating and stop teasing me. Unless you want the one thing I ask of you is to bend over my knee?"

My lips part. I gulped. "You'd do that?"

"I will, eventually." He lifted his shoulders. "Pass me the syrup, please?"

The rest of the meal was spent discussing my duties, which didn't sound too difficult—except for the repeated warnings about how specific Xavier was about his files, how many times the phone was allowed to ring, and under which conditions I was allowed to enter the office.

We spent the most time on the latter. Luther seemed to want me to find plenty of reasons to be around Xavier. To 'get to know him', of course.

He frowned for the first time when I repeated the words with air quotes. "Yes, you actually do need to get to know him, Alec. If he doesn't feel close to you, no amount of flirting will draw his interest. He may find you attractive, but he's indulging *me* by having you around. The job, the contract…he will give you a chance, but he's not convinced you're any different than the last boy."

"Oh…" I looked down at my empty plate. "What did he do wrong?"

"He was fake. A very good actor, but once we started getting deeper into our favorite…*games*, the act slipped." Luther glared at his plate. "He'd been playing along, trying to get close to Xavier for his money. Xavier got attached to him before I did. I was happy to see him relax again, so I wasn't as careful as I should have been. It created issues between us. We've spent the last year rebuilding what we once had."

"Then why involve me? Why risk ruining your relationship again?" I wrapped my arms across my chest, feeling a little sick. Here I was, lusting after a man who was with someone else. Beginning what had almost destroyed their relationship before. "Are these 'games' really that important?"

Lifting his head, Luther smiled. "Damn it, Alec, you're something else. I told you that so you'd understand why Xavier will have a hard time trusting you. Don't feel guilty, this is something we both need."

"I don't understand."

"You don't have to. Not yet." Luther took my hand. "Come here."

Inhaling roughly, I slipped out of my chair.

Turning his, he pulled me down to straddle him. His big, muscular thighs spread my legs wide and my heart pounded as he framed my jaw with his warm, calloused hand. "Two things."

There were so many things I wanted. Being in this position, I wondered if 'Do whatever you want' would be considered one thing. His body was hard everywhere. The musky aroma, mixed with a hint of coconut oil and shea butter made me hungrier than the food had. He grazed his thumb over my bottom lip and it took every ounce I had not to suck it into my mouth.

"I can't." The words were little more than a whisper, but I could tell he'd heard me. I couldn't relax like I had last night. Not knowing what I did. "Maybe once I've been doing my job for a bit and I'm sure he's okay with this."

Nodding slowly, Luther rubbed my thighs. "That's fair. This is a very...different kind of arrangement. I won't have you feeling uncomfortable." He placed his hands on my hips. "Do you want to get up?"

No. I bit into my cheek as I nodded and he closed his thighs so I could regain my balance and stand.

Slow clapping came from behind us and I jumped.

Xavier spared me a glance when I spun around, then turned his focus to Luther, his tone dry. "I'm impressed. You already have such a soft spot for the boy, I expected to find him in your bed."

"I won't rush him." Luther rose from the chair, moving to my side and folding his arms over his chest. "You know that."

"He's willing." Xavier lifted his shoulders and leaned against the doorframe, hands in the pockets of his black slacks, looking much more relaxed than he had at the office, but no less intimidating. "In any case, his proposal is intriguing. He wants to prove he's fit for the job and that I can trust him before you fuck him? This should be entertaining, at the very least."

Stepping forward, Luther lowered his voice. Not as though he didn't want me to hear, but as though he was fighting not to shout. "Don't start being a cold hearted asshole. I love you, but I can't stand you when you're like this."

Eyes narrowing, Xavier pushed away from the doorframe. "You brought him to me like some kind of gift and now you're coddling him. Look at him, he'll never fit into our world. He's innocent and unrefined. To make him ours, we'd have to destroy the very things about him you enjoy so much."

"What are you suggesting?"

"Keep him for yourself." Xavier shrugged and checked the gold watch on his wrist, looking bored now. "He'll make the perfect pet for you." He shot me a slanted smile. "Luther is an amazing lover. A little too dominant for my tastes at times, but having you should temper those urges."

All right, I was getting pretty tired of them arguing about me like I was an ugly vase they couldn't agree where to keep. Walking out and telling them both to fuck off was tempting, but I had nowhere else to go.

And I'd signed a damn contract. I wasn't losing the job before I'd started, not even for a chance to be with Luther. Mind-blowing sex wouldn't keep me from ending up back on the streets.

"You said you liked my suggestion." I folded my arms over my stomach when both men stared at me like they'd just remembered I was capable of speaking for myself. "I can do the job. I'll be discreet and I'll work hard. Isn't that what you need?"

Stroking his chin with his forefinger and thumb, Xavier came closer, looking me over much like he had last night. Something had changed in the way he spoke about me, but the interest he'd shown hadn't left. Maybe seeing Luther holding me had caught him off guard.

Had it meant more than finding me in Luther's bed would have? Probably. From his point of view I was exactly what I'd expected to be. A sex toy they'd both play with.

One didn't cuddle their vibrator.

Not that I was aware of, anyway.

"You could actually hurt him." Xavier stopped in front of me, reaching out to brush a strand of hair away from my cheek. "But I know what he sees in you. I *was* you, Alexander. A very long time ago. Fragile and hopeless. He helped build me up and he wants to do the same for you."

"I just want the job. That's more than enough for me."

"Mhmm, well I doubt that. And it won't be enough for Luther." Xavier glanced over at the other man, his expression softening. "I'll give you a chance to prove yourself, boy. Let Luther show you how the work must be done, but that is all. This cozy little thing you were beginning here? Ends now."

"Xavier—"

"No, Luther. You may be a better judge of character than I am, but these games have caused enough damage already. Even the boy can see it." Xavier gave me a tight smile. "If you're successful in earning my trust, we'll introduce you to the way we play. Until then, consider fraternizing with other employees against the rules."

Striding across the room, Luther grabbed Xavier's shoulder and turned him to face him. "*Employees?* I'm your partner, Xavier. Don't forget that."

"I haven't." Xavier glanced over at Luther's hand on his shoulder and arched a brow until Luther let it fall. "But Alexander will be *my* secretary. I will set the boundaries. If he can't respect them, then he's of no use to me."

"I can." I looked at Luther, who sighed, but inclined his head. "But maybe I should get my own place and—"

"No." Xavier's jaw hardened. "You will be here, where you can be watched. Hopefully Luther can still do *his* job without giving in to temptation."

"Until you have?" Luther shook his head and returned to the table to pour himself another cup of coffee. "I see what you're doing. You felt like you were losing control of the situation and now you're changing the rules to suit you."

Straightening his suit jacket, then his sleeves, Xavier gave Luther a bored look. "The control was always mine, my man. Or have you forgotten?"

"This is nothing but another game."

"True." Xavier's lips curved slightly. "Isn't that the whole point?"

Luther's jaw ticked. He set the coffee aside. "Come here."

Without hesitation, Xavier went to the other man and they kissed, Luther wrapping his arm around Xavier and curving his hand around the back of Xavier's neck. There was something about the kiss that seemed more like a battle for dominance at first, but when Xavier relaxed and leaned into Luther, the dynamics changed, becoming almost tender.

I wasn't sure if I should stay, but I was grateful they'd let me see them like this. Their relationship wasn't public, as far as I knew —I'd never seen them discussed in the gossip magazines I'd fished out of the trash with newspapers during the winter to keep myself warm. Sometimes I'd flipped through the magazines with headlines that caught my interest, escaping from the misery of my own life by imaging what it would be like to be the people between the pages.

People like Xavier and Luther, who seemed to have it all.

There was something complicated about their relationship, something I didn't quite understand, and I still didn't know what kind of role I would play. But they were being honest with one another. And with me.

Turning away from them, I went to the table to collect the dirty dishes and brought them to the sink. Rinsed them off, then loaded the dishwasher, trying to ignore the whispers between the men behind me.

Finally, I heard footsteps leaving the room.

I glanced over my shoulder at Xavier, who simply inclined his head to me before he disappeared into the hall.

At the table, Luther began gathering all the food we hadn't eaten, putting leftovers in the fridge and the rest in the trash. After a long silence, he cleared his throat. "He likes you."

Drying my hands, I kept my head down, trying not to laugh. "He hides it well."

"That he does." Luther smiled and came over to me, placing his hands on my shoulders. "Remember what he said when he offered you the job. He wants you, but he's resisting because I complicated things."

"I figured as much. He doesn't want me to take his place."

"No, he's not worried about that. We wouldn't be playing this way if we weren't secure in our relationship, Alec." Luther rubbed my shoulders. "He doesn't want me to lose control over the situation."

"And he wants to make sure I have none."

Luther chuckled, lowering his hands and taking a step back. "You still don't understand, do you?"

I frowned, not sure what I could've possibly missed. Things seemed pretty clear. "Don't understand what?"

"You have *all* the control here. Whatever games we want to play, you can end it all by simply saying 'No.'" His lips curved as I blinked at him. "That power will be yours until you decide you don't want it anymore. And I'm going to teach you exactly how to use it."

Chapter Four

Later that morning I retreated to my room for a shower, letting the cold water brace me for a day of change. My appearance, my manners…Luther had made it sound a bit like I was going to charm school. With him as my teacher.

Which would've been a lot more fun as some kinky sex game. Luther wearing glasses, slapping a ruler against his palm as he paced behind me, ready to bend me over the desk if I made a single mistake.

Down, dick.

I groaned as I stepped out of the shower, hard as a fucking rock without any time left to give myself some relief. The clothes Luther had left for me wouldn't help either. Xavier might consider himself progressive with his ideas of what gender a secretary could be, but he still liked his eye candy.

Since that would be me, Luther had picked out an outfit that would draw Xavier's attention. Snug, tailored, light grey slacks he'd have fitted later today along with several others, a pale blue shirt, and a grey vest. No tie yet, he had to show me how to tie one. I also had a matching jacket to go with the outfit, but Luther had told me to leave it off. He didn't want me wearing it around the office, so I should 'Get used to being without it.'

And I *would* have to get used to it. Without even looking in the mirror I felt the way the slacks formed tight over my ass, and the vest didn't cover a thing. My cheeks heated as I left my room, heading down to the first floor where Luther had told me his office was, a couple doors down from the kitchen.

I rapped my knuckles on the thick, wood door.

He opened it, revealing a massive library with a large, antique desk in the center. The light was dimmer in here, with a warm glow coming from the partially closed curtains making it just bright enough to work under, without being harsh. The faint rich scent of cigar smoke and old books was almost soothing as Luther ushered me inside.

Grinning, he looked me over, letting the door ease shut. "Oh yes, this will do nicely. How does it feel?"

"Like I'm putting my ass on display." I wrinkled my nose and smoothed my hands down my sides. "Which I assume is your intention?"

"So long as you can get comfortable. If you feel awkward, it will show." Luther folded his arms over his chest and leaned against his bookshelf, jutting his chin toward the large desk. "Walk across the room as you normally would. Let me see what I have to work with."

Simple enough. I walked across the room.

He let out a heavy sigh. "Alec, are you afraid the ceiling will cave in on you?"

I stopped by the desk and glanced back at him. "No...?"

"Then why do you have your shoulders bowed and your head down? Straighten up. Don't take each step as though the ground isn't solid. Sure steps. A confident posture. You're representing Xavier Ashburne."

"Hopefully I'll be wearing a jacket if I'm representing him." I tugged at the vest and pressed my eyes shut. "I'm not trying to get all his clients to fuck me."

Luther spat out a laugh. "No, I suppose you aren't. And you may wear a jacket when you're not at your desk or in his office.

Either way, let's teach you to walk like you know your own worth."

Brow raised, I stared at him.

His smile faded. "Nothing will change if you don't own every bit of progress you make. You convinced me not to turn you into the cops simply by being the honest, loyal—misplaced as it was—man that you are. You convinced Xavier to give you a job. Sure, some of it might have been happenstance, but you were given an opportunity because we thought you deserved it."

"And I appreciate that, but how does that change how I walk?"

"Once you believe you deserve it as much as we do, it'll show." He held out a hand and crooked a finger. "Now walk to me as though you see me as an equal and you have something important to say."

This was ridiculous, but I kinda got what he meant. Walking around Xavier's office all slouching and uncertain wouldn't impress anyone. Least of all, Xavier. If I wanted anyone to take me seriously I had to at least *pretend* to have some confidence.

I crossed the room again. Straighter. Faster.

"All right, that's better. Do that if the building is on fire." Luther's eyes sparkled with mirth. "Let's try that again."

For the next hour I practiced walking, then sitting, then standing, then…drinking. The last was the weirdest, because I'd never imagined someone could drink a glass of water wrong, but apparently it was a thing. I drank like I was dying of thirst and had been given my first liquid in days.

Which had happened, so it made sense.

Everything I did had to be slower. More relaxed. Luther played out scenarios for me. An important investor coming in for a meeting. Going to another department to impart an urgent message. A business lunch with Xavier and someone important.

After the last one, I sat back in my chair, brow furrowed. "None of this is really secretary work. Shouldn't his assistant be doing all this?"

"He doesn't have one. And please don't repeat this, but you *will* essentially be his personal assistant. He uses the term secretary because admitting he needs any kind of help is hard for him." Luther sighed and sat on the edge of his desk. "You will still do some secretarial work, so that'll be important for you to learn. But you'll spend less time typing and answering phones than you will doing tasks that will make his life easier. I'm hoping you'll get to know him well enough to anticipate those without him even having to ask."

"Okay, I can do that." I followed Luther behind the desk, taking a deep breath as he pulled the chair out for me. "I...I haven't typed much since high school. I might be a little rusty."

"Well, Xavier isn't, and he likely won't give you more than a quick email to transcribe." Luther handed me his phone. "I recorded something for you to send as an email. Listen to it, then send it to me. My email address is in the message. Let's see how you do with this so I know what needs improvement."

I nodded, took a deep breath, then pressed play. It was hard to listen to Luther in person without being turned on, but he seemed to have intentionally deepened his voice in the message, drawing out each word just a little, as though to make sure they got the message.

The message could have been exactly how he liked his dick sucked for how turned on I was by the end. My hands shook as I typed as fast as I could, watching my fingers way more than I should. He was talking about different dresses that would be chosen for a magazine shoot and issues the agent was having finding the right model. Not a difficult topic, but I cursed under my breath as I forgot how to spell certain colors.

That was what spell check was for, right? Would he judge me on the mistakes I'd made? Would I have a chance to fix them?

"Good, but you forgot how to sit." Luther squeezed my shoulder when I groaned and dropped my head to the desk. "Relax. You'll always have a chance to go over what you've typed. First you get down the words, then you make sure all the information is there and edit. You addressed this well and even figured out the words I didn't say clearly. We just want Xavier to be able to walk by you and trust you know what you're doing."

"Got it." I tried to sit up straighter, but my dick still hadn't gotten the message that we weren't here to have fun. "This would be a lot more enjoyable as originally planned."

I'd tried to speak too low for Luther to hear as he crossed the room—probably for another assignment—but he looked back with a slow smile. "You're thinking of the rewards I promised you."

My face was probably beet red. I ducked behind the computer. "No. Of course not. I know the rules."

"Yes, but they are open to some interpretation." Luther came around the desk and stood behind the chair, setting his hands on the back of it. Close enough that I could feel his presence without him touching me. "I don't expect Xavier to keep his hands off you for long if he sees you're interested. If he sees you like this." He leaned down and his breath stirred the hair behind my ear. "He's challenging me not to touch you until he does. But there are other things I can do."

Oh fuck. I tugged at my bottom lip with my teeth, my dick throbbing with need as it swelled in the tight confines of my slacks. "I'm pretty sure 'fraternizing' includes everything."

"It may, but we're not at work."

I hissed in a breath as he brought his cheek close to mine. If I turned my head, I could kiss him. Damn it, I wanted to, but...

"I don't want to mess things up here. I need this job."

"Then we'll continue the lesson. Type exactly what I say." Luther remained where he was, his voice dropping an octave as I bought my fingers back to the keyboard. "Every piece of clothing you're wearing was picked out by me. Soft fabric, in colors I knew would suit you. When you move, you can feel it moving over your skin. From the collar against your throat, the smooth cotton against your nipples that are probably tight and hard right now. Even now, you're more aware of them, thinking of what it would be like to have my mouth on them..."

I closed my eyes, heart pounding, more aware of my nipples

than I'd ever been. I hadn't thought a man could get off on just his nipples being toyed with, but if Luther did it now, I'd fucking explode.

"Keep typing, Alec." A hint of amusement laced Luther's tone. He paused, then reached out and braced one hand on the arm of the chair, close to my thigh. "The pants are what really got to you though. Just constrictive enough to feel snug against your ass, to feel pressing down on your dick when you get hard. You know I can see all of you and it makes you nervous and aroused all at once. You don't know when I'll get tired of them and tear them off you. Or what I'll do to you once I have you naked. You want to know, you don't want to wait any longer, but you have no choice."

"Shit." The last few words I typed were jumbled. I shifted to adjust my erection, but the pants were too tight. "Please…"

"Please what?"

"I need…fuck, I'm so turned on it hurts."

"I can't touch you." Luther made a soft shushing sound. "But I won't stop you from touching yourself. Not this time."

The idea of pulling out my dick right here in his office was embarrassing. And bad. And hot. Him watching me wasn't enough, but if it was all I could have, I'd take it.

I lowered my hand, stroking myself through my pants. "This might still break Xavier's rules."

Luther's lips brushed my ear. "It doesn't."

His brief touch broke the rules, but I was too worked up to care. I opened the button of my slacks, then tugged the zipper down and freed my dick from the confines of my new, soft, black cotton boxers. I curved my hand around myself, tipping my head back as I stroked, pleasure spreading from the base of my spine to the head of my cock. Already precum gathered at the tip. I wouldn't last long.

"Look at me, Alec." Luther whispered. I opened my eyes and he brought his mouth close to mine so I was breathing in his every exhale. "Be grateful for the rules, because once you're mine, your pleasure will belong to me as well. It will be my hand on you, taking you to the very edge and deciding whether or not you deserve to go over. I may make you wait." His breathe was sweet, I could almost taste the syrup from breakfast. A hint of coffee and mint. I tried to bring my lips to his, but he stayed just out of reach. "I may make you wait until I have you bent over my desk, desperate for me to fuck you. Begging for it."

Gasping in air, I moved my hand over my dick faster, almost feeling like he was making me wait now. The pressure was building, but my focus was on his words. On how I could have so much more than my hand.

"Luther…please…"

"Come for me, pet. I'm already more tempted than I should be to say fuck the rules, but it won't be long." His lips brushed mine. "For now, give me this."

I came with a shout, warmth spilling over my hand and hitting his desk. My hips jerked and my legs trembled as the surge of pleasure melted through me, stealing the last of my strength. I dropped my head against the back of the chair, panting like I'd run a mile.

Luther remained at my side, still looking like he wanted to touched me, groaning softly before reaching into a drawer and handing me a box of Kleenex. "Clean yourself up and we'll continue."

The lessons continued, first with more typing—of less erotic material—then practice phone calls and an in depth study of Xavier's specific filing system. Lunch was brought in for us by a maid who introduced herself as Julia and let me know she'd put fresh towels in my bathroom and to please inform her if I needed more.

Sitting at the other side of Luther's desk, in a folding chair he'd pulled out from a storage space behind a bookcase, I thanked her for my smoked meat sandwich and fries, stammering 'No, thank you,' when she asked if I wanted a glass for my soda.

When she left, Luther shot me an amused look. "Do women make you nervous?"

"No, they were usually nicer to me on the streets than the

men." I plopped a fry in my mouth and shrugged. "It's just weird having someone serve me."

"She's paid very well for it. I found her working at a local diner and she wasn't intimidated by Xavier, so I hired her on the spot." He grinned at me over the rim of his glass. "She's going to night school to become a paralegal, so we won't have her for long. I'll miss her offhand comments to Xavier about him leaving wet towels on the bed. Nothing I said could break the habit, but she straightened him out her first weekend here."

I laughed and reached for a fry. Mine were all gone.

Luther pushed his plate between us so I could reach his.

"I know this house is huge, but why don't you and Xavier share a room?" I hesitated in reaching for the fries, but Luther gave me a level look, making it clear he wouldn't continue until I helped myself. I grabbed a few. "Thank you. I don't know why I'm still so hungry."

"Because you're getting used to eating regularly again. I'm happy to see it." Luther leaned back in his chair and folded his hand over his stomach. "Our relationship works because we know when to give one another space. When he's designing new lines he stays up late in his room and needs his focus. He comes to my room the rare times he lets himself truly relax."

"Because he doesn't connect your space with work."

"Exactly." Luther used his napkin to wipe his hands, then stood. "Finish up. The tailor will be here any minute."

"Great." I popped one last fry in my mouth, trying to sound enthusiastic, even though the idea of some stranger who was used to dressing up rich, powerful men like Luther and Xavier stripping me down and judging me made my stomach turn.

Coming around the desk, Luther gave me an encouraging smile and held out his arms. "Come here."

"We can't—oof!" I rested my head on his chest as he pulled me close. "This is touching."

"It's a hug. And you need it." He pressed his lips to me hair. "There's a quote I think you need to repeat to yourself at least once a day. No one can make you feel inferior without your consent."

"I've heard it. Eleanor Roosevelt?"

"She's credited with saying it, but…either way, I love that you're well read, despite your circumstances. Feel free to come to my office at any time if you want to grab a book." He tipped my chin up with a finger. "You're smarter and stronger than you think—"

"Now you're quoting Winnie the Pooh."

"—and very difficult to compliment." Luther chuckled as he released me and folded his arms over his chest. "We'll keep working on that confidence. Fake it for now, I won't tolerate anyone looking down on you."

The tailor arrived a few minutes later and the next few hours consisted of me trying on more clothes than I'd owned in my whole life. Kali Brooks, the tailor, worked with Xavier and had been sent shopping for me that morning. While she made sure everything was perfectly fitted, one of Xavier's butlers brought in bags of boxers and socks, jeans, tracksuits, and sneakers.

The butler handed me a note when he was done, his lips curving when I opened it, then stared at him. He left without a word.

Dear Alexander,

I regret that I couldn't join you today, but there were several matters that demanded my attention. I know Luther will have you wearing suits meant to tempt me, but I've asked Ms. Brooks to assure you have a wardrobe that you will be comfortable in. Please feel free to have her return anything that's not to your tastes.

While I enjoy the games I play with Luther, it was not my intention to make you feel used or torn between us. I apologize that my attitude showed otherwise. I believe

you will be an ideal employee, and whatever else I may
desire, that is of the utmost importance.

I look forward to having you join me on Monday.
Warmest regards,
Xavier

I shook my head as Luther came to my side. "I'm so confused."

"Why?"

Holding out the note, I waited as he read it, ducking my head when he laughed. "I thought he didn't like me."

Luther handed the note back to me, his smile warming his dark brown eyes. "You were very wrong."

Chapter Five

My hair had been trimmed, and looked shiny and healthy, but as I struggled to make it behave Monday morning, I wished Luther had let me shave it all off. Gnashing my teeth, I pulled a rubber elastic from the collection I always kept in my pocket—mail carriers dropped them on the street every morning—and tied my hair at the nape of my neck. The harsh hairstyle made my cheekbones stand out even more, I still looked too skinny, but at least it wasn't messy.

The tie was another issue. After practicing with Luther I'd been sure I'd be fine on my own, but no matter how often I tried, it just didn't look right.

I tore it off and threw it across the room, flopping onto my bed and staring at the ceiling.

No matter what Luther said about the opportunities I had, I knew it came down to how much I impressed Xavier today. I wasn't stressed because of my hair or the damn tie. I was terrified I'd screw up and be out on my ass by lunch.

Three days surrounded by warmth and comfort and I wasn't sure I could survive on the streets again. Just yesterday the rain pounding on the windows had reminded me of how many days I'd spent, desperate to find shelter, shivering as every inch of me was soaked, fighting to stay awake because I'd seen too many others like me fall asleep on a cold night in a dark alley and never wake up.

You can do this, Alec. Luther made sure you were ready. I nodded as I gave myself a pep talk, then went over the last two days of instructions. It might be nothing compared to the experience everyone else who worked for Xavier had, but he'd chosen me for a reason. He knew everything about me. He knew I needed the job more than any one of them.

Because of that, I'd work hard to keep up. I wouldn't take anything for granted. I'd put up with his 'moods', as Luther called them, and remember, no matter how much of a jerk he could be, that he was one of the two men who'd saved my life.

Pressing my fist into the mattress, I sat up and stepped off the bed. I did the best I could with my tie, pulled on the shoes I'd spent most of the night polishing, then went to join Luther in the kitchen.

He set down the newspaper he was reading and motioned me over as he stood. "You look good. I like your hair better lose, but whatever you're most comfortable with works." He straightened my tie a little, lips curving as he stepped back and assessed me for a moment. "Perfect."

"Yeah?"

"Yes. And careful with your speech. If Xavier's in his moods, he'll pick at it." Luther reached out and pulled out a chair. "Sit down and have a coffee with me. Today will go well, I promise."

I believed him. Until I got to the office and he left me on the elevator while he went off to do whatever a head of security did. The whole ride up, I repeated his last words to me like a mantra.

You've got this. You've got this. You've got this.

"Are we dressing children? When have I *ever* asked for neon pink? Cerise is not complicated!"

As I stepped off the elevator I almost slammed into a young man in tears who was carrying bundles of bright pink fabric.

A door slammed and we both jumped.

The young man sniffed. "Are you the new guy?"

"Yes…?" Unless there was another new guy? Maybe one who was better suited to dealing with Xavier when he was losing his mind over a color? "My name's Alec."

"Peter." He shook my hand, then balanced the material under one arm and wiped his cheeks with his shirt sleeve. "I wouldn't go in there yet if I were you. He's freaking out."

"Isn't it my job to figure out how to fix that?"

Peter shrugged. "Not sure you can, but either way…good luck?"

Shooting him an uncertain smile, I headed in the direction of the slammed door. All the other offices had glass walls and doors, but at the end of the hall there were light wood double doors with a simple, empty desk beside them.

My desk.

Inhaling slowly, I pulled off my dark blue suit jacket. Laid it over the back of the very comfortable looking office chair. Sitting there and waiting for instructions was tempting, but I had to show some initiative if I was going to prove myself.

I rolled my shoulders, then went to the door. Behind me I was pretty sure every person on this floor was holding their breath.

Bracing myself, I knocked.

"Come in."

The office was cooler than the rest of the building, almost as though Xavier kept the AC on high even though it was late fall. Maybe I should have worn my jacket after all.

Closing the door behind me, I watched Xavier pace, not sure what to say.

He shook his head and sighed, stopping in front of the floor to ceiling window and staring out. "The suit you're wearing, whichever one it is, is my design. For the past two years, I've become more well known for my suits and my magazine. My passion has always been the dresses. The beautiful flow of them, how they are so like moving art, the way whoever wears them can look in the mirror and see themselves how the world does when they truly want to stand out."

I remained silent. I had a feeling he wasn't done.

"My last few designs have drawn a lot of interest, but unless the reveal goes perfectly, I'll be trapped exactly where I am now. I can't afford to invest more in a failed project. Not without putting the core of my company at risk." He rubbed the back of his neck and tipped his head back. "Not only is the fabric all wrong, someone leaked the day of my fashion show too early and a competitor has already scheduled their own for the same day."

"Has that ever happened before?"

"Yes, but I was a phenomenon back then. One of the youngest designers, the first to have his own company producing high-end fashion before twenty-five, with my dresses on every red carpet around the world. All the money I've made can never recreate that feeling of knowing what I was creating was so fresh and new everyone wanted to be part of it." He shook his head. "I knew it wouldn't last, but I can still have some of that glory again, can still share it with the designers who work with me, the models who I brought in to work the runway for the first time because I believe they're different and gorgeous and will have a whole new generation falling in love with fashion."

I wet my bottom lip with my tongue, quietly crossing the room to stand beside Xavier and look out at the city. Dallas looked amazing from up here, with the length of the Trinity River in the distance, the skyscrapers, the suburbs beyond all stretching out with more potential than I'd ever seen when looking up from below. It was hard to feel hopeless when you stood so close to the clouds. There just seemed to be more, just out of reach, waiting for you.

"I know it's not my place—"

"Why wouldn't it be your place? Are you here to help me or to stand there and look pretty?" Xavier glanced over. His jaw ticked. "What have you done to your hair?"

Bringing my hand up to my hair, I frowned at him. "What's wrong with my hair?"

"It's too harsh. You don't look like yourself." He shook his head and motioned for me to turn around. "At least you didn't cut it. May I?"

"Yeah…I mean, yes." I cursed myself internally for the slip, then held my breath as his fingers gently worked the elastic free, then combed through the loose strands until it flowed softly down to my collar.

The tension seemed to seep out of the room as he continued to stroke my hair distractedly, speaking low. "If you want me to stop, please say so. This isn't part of your job."

"I don't mind." I bit back a groan as his hand slid under my hair to the back of my neck. "So long as it's not in front of anyone. I don't want them to think…to think what they probably already know."

"They know nothing. They may be curious about you, but the fact that you were brave enough to come in here when I was that angry will earn their respect. Only Luther ever dares knock on the door."

"I wouldn't have come in unless you'd told me I could."

"I know. But I'm glad you did." He sighed and let his hand fall to his sides. "Come sit and tell me what you think of my set up for the fashion show. I'm trying to appeal to a younger demographic and you're the right age."

"Not sure how much I can help. Fashion isn't a priority when you're starving."

"For some, fashion is *why* they're starving, which is a problem I'm trying to address, but I hear what you are saying. Still, I think you'll have a good eye for this." His lips curved slightly as I started toward one of the two dark red, padded wood chairs in front of the massive executive desk. "Besides, you're too distracting standing there. Luther is determined to make me suffer, isn't he?"

"He did mention you might like this outfit." I ran my thumb under the dark blue suspenders both Ms. Brooks and Luther insisted looked good on me, but I'd felt stupid in until I got a good look at myself in the mirror. Going with a vest had been a simpler choice, but this made a statement.

One I'd been confident with, even though I'd never dressed this nicely before.

"Did he pick out your clothes or simply provide you with a selection and give suggestions?" Xavier rested his hip against his desk, not moving even after I'd taken a seat. "I'd imagine if he'd chosen for you, you'd be wearing a simple suit for your first day. Still snug in all the right places, but nothing to make you stand out too much. That shade of blue shines a bit in the light and brings out your eyes. The suspenders are a naughty kind of cute. He's got good taste, but this is more something Ms. Brooks would have given you as an option."

All right, this man was scary observant. Luther had suggested one of the light grey suits. Which were comfortable, but I figured I'd fade into the background and I wanted Xavier to notice me. For my work and...hell, him finding it difficult to keep his hands off me wouldn't be a hardship.

The feeling would be mutual.

"It was one of the outfits Ms. Brooks brought on her own. She's also making me a few based on color swatches and styles from your magazines that she showed me." I folded my hands on my lap when I noticed him watching me fiddle with the suspenders. The last thing I wanted was to get called out for fidgeting. "I almost refused when I found out how much it all cost, but Luther promised I'd earn it back in a week."

"Did he now?" Xavier chuckled and brought his hand up to frame his jaw. "How much does he think I'm paying you an hour?"

"Fifteen dollars an hour, and double for overtime." I cleared my throat, hoping I hadn't just fucked myself over by telling him, when I'd had a hard time accepting the amount Luther had told me. It seemed excessive for someone with my lack of experience. "It's too much, I know it is, but Luther wasn't willing to talk about it and I'm not trying to start problems."

Xavier nodded slowly. "I'm teasing you, Alexander. That's the starting salary for all my personal assistants. Luther and I agreed on the overtime pay to keep me in check when I forget my employees have lives beyond the job. There's no reason for you to be an exception."

My lips parted.

He arched a brow.

"Your...personal assistant? Luther said—"

"Please stop repeating everything 'Luther said'. It's tiresome." Xavier made a dismissive motion. "I wanted a secretary because I didn't want to waste time training someone new. But you don't irritate me. *Yet*." He reached over and slapped a massive phonebook-sized magazine in front of me. "This is the line we're working on. Tell me your favorites. Then we're going to have the designers present each of your selections and see if it works."

I blinked at him. "No way. You can't let me make decisions that will have such a big impact on your company."

He grinned, pushing off his desk and placing his hand on my shoulder, leaning down and speaking softly. "I have no intention of doing so, boy. I just want to see if you're any good at this, or if I should get you started on the files."

"What about the phone?"

"I have three people who answer my calls. None of them sound as nervous as you, so I believe we'll leave them to it, yes?" He squeezed my shoulder. "Luther gave you a bad impression of how I manage this company. To be fair, he's not allowed on this floor often."

Whoa... All right, these men had to have the strangest relationship. They slept in different sections of the mansion they shared, hardly saw one another in a company they seemed to run together, and then there was...well, *me*.

"Don't look so shocked. We've been together since we were in our early teens. It's lasted because our friendship has always been the priority and we've found a balance that works for us. As a lover, he can't stand the hours I keep. But as a friend, he understands my passion and determination." With a distant look in his eyes, he turned toward the window, not seeming to really see the view. "It's better now, but there are times I miss having a new project to work on together. Like when we took over this building. Or set up a production company in Bali that met international fair-wage standards. Or anything else we've taken on that he was excited about..." He shook his head. "He doesn't share my ambition. He's satisfied with running security and keeping me safe."

I nodded, starting to understand why the two men's lives were so very different. "But you'll never be satisfied."

He looked back at me over his shoulder. "Seen Hamilton, have you?"

"Are you kidding? No way, I'll never be able to afford that. But I've heard all the songs out on the streets. People like blasting them from their cars." I started flipping through the magazine. "And there's this little record store that lets me hang out a bit sometimes and use the employee bathroom to shave and wash up. The guy heard me humming one of the songs one day and put the album on while I helped him move some boxes."

Xavier's brow furrowed. "Please tell me he paid you for that."

"He bought me lunch when he could. He doesn't make enough to have employees. He's owned the place for thirty years. It's not as popular as it used to be."

Tapping his chin, Xavier looked out the window again. "Maybe there's a way I could help him upgrade. Give me the address before we're done for the day."

Biting my bottom lip, I nodded. Jaz was such a cool old guy, he deserved a lucky break more than anyone I knew. If Xavier was willing to do that, I'd definitely point him in the right direction.

"You do know I have less than two hours available on my schedule to see if you'll be any use to me on this project." Xavier kept his eyes on the city skyline, his tone almost bored. "And every minute you spend choosing outfits takes time away from those who have to put them together to present them to me."

Should I have looked at his schedule? Damn it, that *had* to be part of my job, but Luther hadn't mentioned it. Probably because it was fucking obvious.

I quickly flipped through the book, scrambling for a pad and pen and whispering thanks when Xavier appeared at my side with both in hand. He paced behind me as I jotted down my favorite pieces, choosing ten since he hadn't actually given me a number.

He glanced down at the notes and made a soft sound of approval. "Good. Now go let the designers know we'll be ready for them in forty-five minutes." He glanced at his watch. "Someone also should have brought me a coffee by now. Not sure who…"

"I'm on it." I pushed out of the chair, knocking it over, then tripping over it and landing on my ass. "Oh fuck, I'm sorry, I—"

"—need to stop being so terrified that I'd fire you for being human." Xavier stepped up to my side and held out his hand. "I'm demanding, but not unreasonable. There are two interns who make coffee runs every few hours. Go ask Peter to point them out to you. And have him give you directions to the design team. They'll know what to do."

"Okay. That I can do." I could breathe again. This was good. I let him help me to my feet. "Thank you."

"Of course." He waited a beat, then looked at his watch again. "Please do learn to do it faster, if you will?"

"On it!" I ran to the door, slamming it into my shoulder as I bolted through it, wincing as I carefully closed it behind me. "Ah…" I looked around, spotting a young woman who didn't look too busy. I didn't want to bother anyone, but I needed to prove to Xavier I could accomplish this task without wasting any more time. "Do you know where Peter is?"

<hr>

The day passed in a blur, and most of the employees had clocked out by the time Xavier said we were done for the night, but things had gone well. He'd been impressed with all my selections and the design team had done their part to make me look like a damn genius.

Not that it was hard, Xavier couldn't seem to design anything that wasn't a freaking masterpiece. Three of the designs had been for plus-sized models and the women who strutted across Xavier's office in the dresses I'd chosen were pure goddesses. I doubted I'd ever have their confidence, and I still couldn't believe they were new to this. They owned that stretch of black carpeted floor like it was the very runway they'd be on to showcase the outfits. Another three designs had been modeled by drag queens who had massive platforms on Instagram and would bring attention to Xavier's new designs by showing off to their audiences before they even hit the stage.

One of the men had playfully flirted with me after his performance and Xavier practically growled at him, hissing that he could be replaced. The man laughed and patted my cheek, winking at me before walking out.

I'd been kept too busy to talk to Xavier about that earlier, but I made a point to bring it up before we left for the night.

Which was now.

Should you really be testing Xavier already? It's been a long day. Let it go.

But I couldn't. Sure, the drag queen had millions of followers, but this was a huge opportunity. Not just for him, but for Xavier. I refused to be the reason it was ruined.

"Lady Cat's Slits was amazing. And I've been looking at his stats—"

"When did I say that was part of your job?"

"When did you say *anything* was part of my job? You seem to want me to anticipate what you need. Which I've been doing."

Xavier placed his briefcase on the desk and shot me a hard look. "Very well. Go on."

"He's represented some huge brands. And his fans buy things he promotes. If he's on that runway, and talks about it after, they'll jump on your more mainstream designs. You have lines out there that are for teens and they'll ask their parents to buy shirts and pants and dresses for them just because he mentioned your name."

Brow furrowed, Xavier came over to look at the laptop he'd given me, which I'd had open at the end of his desk where I'd been working more of the day. He rested his forearm on my shoulder and leaned over.

"You've been looking up my junior designs. Those haven't done well. I don't see the point of expending more time or energy on them."

"But they're amazing! You just haven't marketed them properly. Judy was talking to me in the line at lunch and she was so excited for the boost in sales just from a snapchat Lady Cat's Slit had done. She didn't think you'd care, but I asked her to show me. She said she wasn't supposed to talk about it, but since she'd probably be out of a job in a month..." I tapped on another tab and opened the email I'd asked Judy, who ran sales in the junior department, to send me. "He got almost three million views when he reposted his snapchat video on YouTube. That's a lot of exposure and it didn't cost you a thing."

"Having him model for me will not be free." Xavier shook his head. "And I never tolerate the attitude he showed. If I do so now, it will never end."

"That wasn't attitude. He was being a little flirty." I gave him a sideways look. "If it helps, he said you were too young and hot to be so serious. And he kept looking at your ass."

"But you weren't, because you were doing your damn job. Which I appreciate." Xavier looked away, his cheeks stained with red. "I'm supposed to tolerate unprofessional behavior to sell a line that's been hopeless from the start?"

"He didn't say anything unprofessional to you. He was joking with me." I snapped the laptop shut. "I'm sorry I mentioned it. I just didn't want you upset because he noticed me. A lot of people did. If you didn't want that, maybe you should have let me stay at my desk."

Xavier shook his head and grabbed his bag. "No, I shouldn't

have. People like talking to you. They've been doing so all day and you've given me more insight into my own company than anyone has given me in years. I simply wasn't expecting to be—"

"Jealous?" I stayed a step behind him as he led the way to the elevator.

He stopped short. Turned slowly. "Careful, Alexander."

Maybe I'd gotten too comfortable today. Or maybe I was just tired. I hugged the files I needed to take home to go over tonight against my chest and met his glare, refusing to back down. "I don't care if you won't admit it. He's good for the company's image and I won't let you throw this shot we have away because of me."

Xavier stared at me. His lips curved slightly. Then he shook his head and laughed. "Damn it, I shouldn't find it so fucking appealing when you stand up to me. If I hadn't challenged Luther to keep his hands off you until I couldn't resist, I'd either spank you, or fuck you. Maybe both."

I leaned over to press the button to the elevator with my elbow. "You have very *strict* rules against fraternization, sir. That language is highly inappropriate."

"Our entire situation could be considered inappropriate. And work hours are over."

"Maybe, but you and Luther both said I had a choice. I'm choosing to put my job first and what you just said makes me uncomfortable." Talking to him like this made me a little sick to my stomach, but if I was going to have him respect anything I said, I couldn't accept him turning it to sex whenever I stood up to him. "You're making me feel like none of the work I've done matters. I busted my ass today. People like and respect me. All I ask is that you do too."

His jaw hardened and he glared at the mirrored wall of the elevator, not speaking again until we reached the parking garage where Luther was waiting with the town car.

He met Luther's questioning gaze and sighed. "Please take Alexander's files and put them in the car. I need to speak to him for a moment."

Luther's brow furrowed. He watched Xavier walk to the far end of the parking lot as he gathered all my files. "What happened?"

I swallowed hard, my eyes stinging as I fought not to cry. I was an idiot. Who did I think I was, talking to Xavier like that? A punk he'd taken off the streets and given the opportunity of a lifetime, and suddenly I could mouth off?

When did you ever back down from your brothers when you knew what they were doing was wrong?

The day I got caught stealing Xavier's car.

He wasn't my brothers. He knew what he was doing.

If he fired me? I deserved it.

Blinking fast, I met Luther's concerned gaze and forced a smile. "I'm not sure how this will go, but whatever happens…thank you."

"Alec—"

"No." I held up one hand and gave Luther a level look. "This is on me."

Making my way across the parking lot, I went over all the things I could say to fix this in my head, but nothing felt right. Whatever decision Xavier made I'd have to accept.

He glanced over as I stepped up to his side at the bottom of the ramp leading up to the streets. With a heavy exhale, he turned to face me. "I have been doing my best to regain control of this situation, but you aren't who I expected you to be. Which concerns me, because I thought I knew that first night. Then I adjusted my opinion when I saw you with Luther that morning. I knew you were dangerous. I'd put up walls to make sure you couldn't get too close, but Luther had already become your savior. So I figured I'd set boundaries to limit the damage you could do."

Rubbing one hand over his face, he looked across the garage at Luther, who was leaning against the back of the car, watching us.

He tipped his head back and groaned. "I don't blame him for wanting to help you. After knowing you for less than a day, I feel the same. But you're not a project we can share. You're insightful, determined, and intelligent. You're a young man with potential and I want you to keep working for me. And I also want you. I likely made this more difficult for all of us because I came up with so many rules that I had no intention of applying to myself. I figured once I was tempted enough, I'd simply have you. As though you were already mine."

I didn't know what to say. He wasn't wrong. If he'd tried and I thought it would help me keep my job, I'd have given him anything he asked for. But it was more than my job on the line and I couldn't ignore that. In less than ten hours, so many people had started to look at me as the person they could open up to. If I kept working here, I could help them.

But not as the boss's piece of ass.

"You told me to impress you." My voice sounded weak. I lowered my gaze when he looked at me. Forced myself to keep talking. "I tried. And I'm not sure it mattered."

"Damn it, Alexander, don't do that. Don't doubt yourself. Don't let others doubt you. You *did* impress me. I thought it would take you weeks. Even months." He shook his head and smiled, reaching out...then letting his hands fall to his sides. "You did it in a day. And you have every right to tell me you've earned my respect. Because you have. This isn't about the game. Or what I or Luther want from you. Even if you decide you don't want to play, I want you here. I want to know what my employees think, because I have the most talented team in the business, but they're too intimidated to challenge me. You aren't."

"I should be. I'm fucking terrified you're gonna get pissed and kick me out. That having a place to sleep, clothes, food...that I could lose it all."

"And I don't want you to give in to me, or to Luther, because of that fear." Xavier gave me an encouraging smile. "Tomorrow you'll sign a new contract. One specifically about the job. The old one still applies if you decide to get involved with Luther and I, but one does not overrule the other. I don't want you to feel pressured."

That sounded...good? But I was afraid to trust his offer too much. He seemed to change his mind on a whim. He had the second he'd seen me with Luther, doing exactly what he'd seemed to want until that moment. "What about the game?"

"The game is separate from work. If you're trying to distract me, make it very clear if we're at the office, because I don't want you to think if you don't give in, you'll be out on the streets. Your job will not be at risk if you say no."

"And if I say yes? To either of you?"

His brow furrowed slightly. He shook his head. "I won't lie. I still think Luther is too close to you. He stopped me from burning my first designs when I was about to lose my scholarship for getting in a fight because someone called me a fag. I didn't want to explain myself. All I heard was my father saying that same word before kicking me out. I was seventeen, and without the scholarship, without an older man sponsoring me, I'd have been on the streets myself. Luther convinced me to keep trying and I love him for it. But he saved me from the old man. He convinced me working at a coffee shop to pay my rent was better than letting myself be used. And he was right."

"But he's tried to save others." The pieces were starting to come together. I'd never hurt Luther, but Xavier didn't know that. Not yet. "And they hurt him."

"They did. There have been too many to name." Xavier pressed his eyes shut. "I never worry when he brings me girls he thinks need help. He's gay. I'm bisexual. One girl we played with was with us for three years. He was affectionate, but other than some mild play, he was simply fond of her. I was able to let her go when she met the man she ended up marrying."

Everything he was telling me was…a lot. But I got it. He was trying not to get too close, but he appreciated my work. He didn't want Luther to get hurt. He was still unsure of me as far as their relationship went. They weren't in an open relationship, but sometimes they found one person who could fill a role. They were both dominant. They both craved control. And they couldn't fill that need with one another.

They thought I could, but they wanted more from me. And it would take time to see if I could fill all those roles.

The most important one, for *me*, I'd fought for today. And I had to stand my ground to rise above the baser one. Because others had been here. They didn't last.

They had other options.

I couldn't be a toy meant to be discarded. I needed something to fall back on when they were done with me. Working for Xavier would finally be something I could put on a resume.

"I'm not looking for a relationship, Xavier." Saying his name scared me, but we were talking man to man. I couldn't back down now. "And I can't say I'm not tempted. By you or Luther. But I can say neither of you can tempt me to the point that I'll forget how often I thought I would die out there. That I went to my brothers because my stomach hurt so bad even a few sips of water made me sick. I wasn't starving when I met you. They'd given me food for a few days so I'd have the energy to steal your car. I never want to go back there."

"You won't. All I ask is you don't expose me or Luther. Aside from that, if you ever decide to quit, I'll give you a good recommendation. But apart from the job, my rules haven't changed. I need some time. Time where I don't worry that Luther will come in one day to see a model flirting with you and wonder if you're done with him." He placed his hands on a yellow barrier in front of the cement wall and bowed his head. "If you think my jealousy is bad, just wait until you see how protective he can be. If he'd seen you today he would have thought I made you insecure. That Cat's Slit wanted to use you. That you were vulnerable to both of us."

"I'm not."

"Aren't you?" Xavier gave me a level look. "Alexander, you've hesitated every time you've spoken to me today. You've waited for me to look at you, then gotten nervous when I do. You want me, but you keep your distance because you're afraid once I have you, and get bored, you'll lose everything."

I was. And we both knew it. What did he expect me to say? "Shouldn't I be?"

"No. And that's why I'll stick with the rules. Because they give you a choice."

"No, they really don't. I work closely with you, not Luther. Crossing those lines would have a lot more damage."

"I've just told you they wouldn't."

"Which is you asking for more trust than you're giving me." I hiked up my chin, trying to fight back the trembling that wanted to take over my whole body. "You could destroy my life with a word. You're afraid to trust your own partner with something you've shared before. I'm not sure what you expect me to do with that."

"Wait. Wait until I don't wonder if you'll destroy the man I love."

"I think he's stronger than you're giving him credit for."

Xavier nodded. "Maybe. But it's been three days and I can tell he wants to come over here and fight for you. What do you think he'd do if he'd already fucked you? If you submitted to him and he felt responsible for you?"

I looked over at Luther and I couldn't find a single thing to say. Xavier was right. I wouldn't mean to hurt either of them, but I could. They were both giving me control. All I had to do was say no, to say I wasn't ready.

But once I said yes, I'd be between them. I had the power to ruin something so tenacious I didn't think either of them realized it. Only Xavier knew enough to be afraid. He needed Luther. But I wasn't sure Luther realized how much.

"I don't want to hurt either of you. But you're both offering me everything. I keep saying no when I want to say yes." I had to be honest. Otherwise, I'd end up playing both sides and...no. *Hell* no. "You two have to talk. You can't put this on me. It's not fair."

"No. It isn't." Xavier rubbed his fist against his lips. "Let's go home. A home that is yours, no matter what happens. If I was in your place, I couldn't resist him. As for you and I..." He shook his head. "You will have to let me know what you're comfortable with.

You've reminded me how much power I have over you. Power he doesn't. Until you can set that aside and see me as a man who struggles to do what he has every day for almost ten years…please feel free to tell me I've crossed the line. It is yours to set and I will respect it. Always."

"I don't get this game. Not even a little."

"I know you don't. Just know I won't judge you. And that despite what you might think, Luther and I understand one another. I'm pushing him. I know I am. You're a test. One he can't fail."

"That's clear as mud."

"It really is, isn't it?" He groaned and leaned against the barrier. "How's this. If he seduces you, we'll talk. But I hope he won't. I'd rather he wait until we all trust this is real."

"It's already real to me."

"I know." He pushed away from the barrier, speaking softly. "But what do you have to lose if you're wrong?"

I watched him go. Watched Luther pull him into his arms and speak softly to him. What they had didn't include me. And I got that.

But the answer to Xavier's question would never change.

Even if he couldn't hear me.

I roughly dragged my sleeve across my cheek to dry the tears that fell.

"Everything."

Chapter Six

A week, then two, went by and my doubts started to fade. Maybe Xavier had actually been listening. Maybe he believed me when I said I didn't want to hurt Luther. Maybe I did have some power.

I still saw Luther every morning, but he never crossed the lines Xavier had set. We discussed the fashion show. My insecurity when those with more experience came to me for advice because they thought Xavier trusted my opinion. My fear of my tie not being straight enough when I pulled on my jacket and went to meetings with Xavier and important people.

Every day began and ended with Luther trying to help me. But he never got too close. Never looked at me too long. I'd become nothing but an employee. Maybe a friend he kept at arm's length. He praised me for helping Xavier. Told me I was doing better than he'd ever imagined.

But we were little more than neighbors sharing the same space. He didn't touch me. Didn't watch me.

My job was all that mattered.

Exactly what I'd wanted.

Until I missed the attention. The touches. The mark he'd left on my neck which had faded. I spent most nights going over files alone in his office. Xavier never came to speak to me. And neither did Luther.

After the first week of making sure I still wore my suit when walking around the house, I brought the latest stack of files to Luther's office in my pajama pants, finished going over them, then grabbed a book. I needed to feel something, *anything*, so I grabbed the scariest book I could find. One about a killer who'd gone after gay men. It was a true story.

I ignored the tears that spilled when I started picturing my father every time the killer found a man. Got him to confess he was gay, promising he wouldn't judge.

The same lie my father had told me before he'd died. He'd been preparing to rob a bank with my mother. I was eight. In school still, doing well because bad grades meant bringing too much attention to my parents.

One of my teachers was gay and he came out at school. The staff supported him. Most of the students did too. I talked to him and told him I felt like him. My parents always put on such a good show when they went to meetings he said I was lucky. I shouldn't be afraid.

My father got everyone to come to the living room. Told me we were family. There were no secrets between us. When I told him, he didn't react. He looked at my brothers.

"Trust is a weakness."

He didn't have to say anything else. My mother looked at me, whispered a word I couldn't make out.

Maybe she'd told me to run. That would've made sense. Because after they left, my brothers almost killed me.

They left me alone when I said I'd been lying. I was scared of girls, that was all. When were Mommy and Daddy coming home?

They never came home.

My eldest brother, Erik, was twelve years older than me. He made a lot of money selling drugs. Until I was thirteen, I didn't realize the 'packages' I delivered were drugs.

When he went to jail the second oldest, Christian, took care of me. For three years until Erik got out. Those three years weren't bad. He never got violent without Erik around. I just had to steal food for us to eat. I was good at it.

Erik was released shortly after my sixteenth birthday. He'd apparently decided on a new career of car theft and either I could make myself useful or I could get the fuck out.

Setting the book aside, I folded my knees against my chest and wondered if my brothers would try to find me. Would they worry about me turning them in? They probably wouldn't go back to Xavier's building, they weren't stupid enough to risk getting caught. If they hadn't already been arrested.

I hadn't asked Xavier if he'd gotten his car back and he hadn't mentioned it. If my brothers were in prison it was their own damn fault. Maybe Christian would come out a better man. Maybe he'd finally be free of Erik, like I was free of them both.

Was it horrible of me that I couldn't find it in me to care? That thinking about my family hurt too much, so I usually tried not to?

Christian hadn't been as horrible to me, but he'd still left scars. *You're thinking about him an awful lot for someone who doesn't care.*

Groaning, I unfolded my legs and brought the book back to the shelf where I'd found it. The office door opened and I glanced over my shoulder.

Luther came over, looking at the book and making a face. "Not the most pleasant read. I had nightmares for weeks after I finished it."

"That doesn't surprise me. At least the guy was caught."

"He should have been caught sooner."

"True." I wrapped my arms around myself, feeling exposed standing here shirtless in front of Luther. I missed how comfortable I'd been around him before all the rules, but there was no way to get that back. "I'm sorry for bumming around in your office. I just wanted a change of scenery."

His brow furrowed. "Alec, I told you to make yourself at home. Don't apologize for doing so."

"Okay, I just…" I lowered my gaze. "I'm gonna go put a shirt on."

I started for the door.

He put his hand on my shoulder, stopping me. "Don't."

Swallowing hard, I held still as his hand slid over my shoulder. He pressed his lips to the side of my neck.

"Luther, we can't—"

"We won't if you ask me to stop." He grazed his teeth along my flesh and I shivered. "I stayed away from you to make things easier for us both. But I fucking hate it. Xavier can have his win. I don't care."

"Yes, you do." My voice was barely over a whisper. I didn't pull away, I wasn't ready for him to stop touching me, but if I let it go too far, we'd ruin everything. "All Xavier asked was that I tell him before doing anything with you."

Letting out a low laugh, Luther rested his head on my shoulder. "This is a conversation he and I should have."

"Definitely. But I don't want him thinking I feel pressured. Or that I'm doing anything behind his back." I moved away from Luther as he lifted his head. Turning, I chewed at my bottom lip. "This is going to change everything."

"But in a good way." He brushed a strand of hair off my cheek and tucked it behind my ear. "If it helps, I trust you with him. I was more afraid that he'd hurt you, but you're tough."

I wrinkled my nose. "Are you giving me permission to fuck your boyfriend?"

He laughed. "You always had that from me. I'm not the one who made the rules."

Shaking my head, I put some space between us. He was so relaxed, so easy to be around, regaining the comfort I'd had with him at the beginning wouldn't take much effort. But I wouldn't go there. Not without knowing Xavier was okay with it.

"Don't stress too much about it, Alec. Get some sleep. Xavier has his business trip this weekend, and since we don't have your passport yet, you won't be able to join him and you can actually enjoy a whole weekend off." His lips slanted slightly. "I may have plans for you."

"Assuming he agrees?"

"No. As enjoyable as it would be, I won't keep you in my bed the entire time. I want to bring you out. Have some fun." He stepped up to me, curving his hand around the back of my neck and pressing a kiss to my forehead. "He won't object to that. We both know you deserve it."

Damn it, why did he have to be so perfect? I smiled up at him, then left the office, heading to my room for the night.

Hopefully, the last time he'd try to tempt me.

And I'd have to walk away.

Chapter Seven

With Xavier's trip coming up, the office was even more chaotic than usual, and I was right in the middle of it all. No one dared approach the boss when he was stressing about samples, hemlines that looked even a little off, or sketches that weren't perfect examples of his work.

Since the sketches were his and he didn't think any of them were good enough, he stayed in his office all day, cursing his pencils, his sharpeners, and whoever had designed the paper he was using because it was 'awkward'.

I didn't draw, so I had no idea how to help him. When I texted Luther, he just assured me his man always got like this before a trip and it was best just to leave him be.

Which was easy for him to say, since he wouldn't see Xavier until tonight when he drove him to the airport with two security guards they both trusted to go with him. I'd asked why Luther didn't go himself and he let out a bitter laugh.

"He's much more concerned with the company's safety than his own. He wants me here so I can make sure we don't have another break in." He *shrugged as we finished up breakfast and got ready to head to work. "I've learned to pick my battles over the years. This isn't one that would lead anywhere good. At least he's finally accepted that he needs protection."*

And that he needed help. Which was where I came in. Fine, everyone else saw him freaking out as perfectly normal, but it didn't have to be. Why shouldn't he be able to start this trip feeling in control and confident? He wasn't too powerful to need some reassurance.

I pushed away from my desk and knocked on his door.

"The building better be on fire!" The sound of something hitting the door made me hesitate. Xavier let out a rough, irritated sound. "Are you coming in or what?"

Opening the door, I braced myself to duck if he threw anything else. But he was standing by the window, hands shoved in his pockets, glaring out at the city like its very existence pissed him off.

"What do you want, Alexander?"

"To figure out what I can do to get you to chill." I spotted his drawing pad on the floor by his bookshelf and went to pick it up, carefully smoothing the pages before setting it on his desk.

He watched me, eyes narrowed. "That's not your job."

"That's debatable, but either way, I hate seeing you like this. Please let me help."

"I'm not sure you can."

Crossing the room, I went behind his desk and patted the back of his chair. "Come sit. I want to try something."

With an exaggerated sigh, he strode over and sat stiffly in the chair. "I appreciate the effort, Alexander, but there's nothing you can do that will...*Mmmphh.*"

"You were saying, sir?" I grinned as I dug my fingers into the tight muscles of his shoulders. He'd probably be better off with a professional masseuse, but they'd probably get their head bitten off. He was less likely to yell at me.

"Unless you want to kneel for me, don't call me 'sir'."

"Hmm...I might be better on my knees that I am with massages." I rubbed the back of his neck, drawing out another muffled groan. "But that would be inappropriate."

His laugh was strained. "Bringing it up at all is inappropriate."

"You're right. I won't do it again." I went back to rubbing his shoulders, sensing the tension easing out of them. His breathing slowed and I grinned as he tipped his head to the side, exposing his neck. There was only one way I could think of to get him more relaxed. I brought my lips to his throat. Tasted his skin with a flick of my tongue. And whispered, "Sir."

He turned and stood abruptly, pulling me against him and bringing his lips to mine in a bruising, desperate kiss. His hands tangled in my hair as he fucked my mouth with his tongue, moaning as I reached for his belt. He grabbed my wrist, holding it in place as he took his time exploring my mouth, taking control from me as he sucked on my bottom lip, biting with just enough pressure for me to whimper.

My dick swelled as Xavier grazed his teeth along my jaw, then down the side of my neck. Just below my collar, he bit down hard enough leave a mark, pinning me against his desk as I writhed against him, gasping in air as the pain warped to pleasure.

"When Luther sees that, he'll get the message." Xavier kissed his way back up my throat, then claimed my lips again. "You belong to us. There's no backing out now."

I flicked my tongue over his bottom lip. "You don't scare me, Xavier. I'm not going anywhere."

His lips curved into a devilish smile. "You might change your mind when you see how demanding I can be."

"Yeah?" I knew he hated when I didn't use proper English, but I wanted to push him a little bit, just to see how he'd react. "You gonna just talk about it or — "

He pressed his fingers to my lips. "We're not starting things off with your first punishment. Behave."

"Do you want me to get back to work? I'm sure there are some files to take care of. Do you want me to double check if the tulle skirts are packed properly?"

"I want you on your knees, pet." Xavier pressed his thumb into my mouth, his eyes hooded as I sucked on it. "Isn't that what you were offering when you called me 'sir'?"

I circled his thumb with my tongue, releasing it slowly. We both knew where this was going, but I wanted him to take control. Something about surrendering to him was safer than just doing what I wanted.

But I still didn't know how far I could push before earning the punishment he'd mentioned. That I'd agreed to when I'd signed the contract.

There's only one way to find out.

"Was I offering something, *sir*?" I gave him my most innocent look. "I'm only your assistant. I'm here to do whatever you need me to."

"Careful." Xavier grabbed the collar of my shirt, lifting me against him. "This room is pretty soundproof, but if I spank you hard enough, someone's bound to hear."

Oh fuck. No, I definitely didn't want that.

"Get on your knees. Now." His hand moved to my shoulder. A warning that he wanted me to behave.

I lowered to my knees.

"Undo my belt and pull it free. Lay it on my desk. I really hope I won't have to use it, but you do seem to enjoy testing me."

Biting my bottom lip, I followed his instructions silently. There was no way I'd chance earning that punishment now, but I appreciated him setting the boundaries. I didn't have to push any more to find them. They were clear.

"Good boy. Now clasp your hands at the base of your spine. Just like that." He stroked my hair. "Fuck, you're gorgeous. I've been imagining this moment for weeks."

"I wasn't ready before." I tipped my head back and met his eyes. "I am now."

His eyes warmed as he smiled at me. Undoing the button to his pants, then his zipper, he freed his dick. "Open your mouth and cover your teeth with your lips. I need to feel you around me."

Closing my eyes, I held still as his dick eased into my mouth, carefully covering my teeth as he'd asked. The heat of his dick, with its smooth head passing over my tongue, made me groan as I struggled not to move closer. He pulled out, then pressed in again, deeper this time until I had to fight the urge to gag.

He stroked my hair, let out a soft, soothing sound. "Very nice. You'll learn to take more in time. For now, just breathe when I pull out, then swallow when I press in. Let me enjoy you."

I stared up at him, hoping my eyes would tell him what he needed to know. That I wanted this. Not gently or carefully, but in any way he wanted to have me.

He tightened his grip on my hair. Thrust into my mouth, then dragged his dick back along my tongue. I tasted slick saltiness. I flicked my tongue over the head of his cock as he drew out yet again and his precum trailed down from his dick to my lips, wet with my saliva.

"So fucking hot." He hissed through his teeth as I licked his dick again. "I'm trying to be careful, but you're making it hard."

"Don't be. I can take it." I held his steady gaze. "Show me how you like it."

He inclined his head. "Relax your throat. This will be difficult at first."

I relaxed and he guided his dick into my mouth. Deeper than the last few times, not stopping when he reached the back of my tongue. I gagged a little. Swallowed hard. My eyes teared as he hit my throat and kept going.

Then he withdrew. Thrust in again. This time, I was ready for the sensation. I found a rhythm as he fucked my face harder. Faster. Kept watching his face as he lost control, using me exactly as I'd wanted him to. My dick throbbed every time I couldn't breathe and it was fucking amazing. I'd never come without touching myself, but I was close. So fucking close.

Jerking my head back, Xavier came on my lips. On my tongue. Pressed in one last time, holding me against him as he groaned and clung to my hair.

Without warning, he dragged me to my feet, then lifted me onto his desk. He undid my slacks and pulled my dick out. I cried out as his lips covered me. He pushed me down on the desk and covered my mouth with his hand.

"Shh, I don't want anyone coming in. If you're not quiet, I'll tell Luther he can't play with you this weekend. But he can punish you." He licked along the length of my cock. "I don't imagine that would be much fun for either of you."

I shook my head and did my best to keep quiet, biting into my tongue as he languidly circled his around the head of my dick, then took it effortlessly down his throat, swallowing around me. He slid up and down, faster and faster, not stopping until I was shaking and so close to the edge I slammed my head on the desk when he released me.

He gave me a sly smile as he sucked on two fingers, then slid them over my taint, pressing one against me.

"You're nice and tight. Luther will enjoy you." He pressed in, his gaze never leaving my face. "A shame I won't get to watch."

He used his spit to slick me up, easing his finger in as he took my dick back in his mouth. The way he pumped his finger into me, matching it with the pace of his mouth on my dick, made my back bow as pleasure crashed into me. He added a second finger as I came and I pressed my fist to my lips to keep from shouting as the erotic sensation wrapped around me, holding me tighter and tighter, like the smoothest ropes wound tight enough to cut off air and blood and movement, but still exquisite as it bound me.

I came hard and he swallowed every last drop, lingering long enough to keep teasing me when I was too sensitive to take any more.

I whimpered as he curved his fingers against my prostate, my whole body shaking.

He licked his lips and smiled down at me. "If we had more time, I'd keep playing with you until you were hard again. Until you were so used to having me inside you, moments where I'm gone are pure torture. But that day will come."

Tears spilled down my cheeks as he withdrew and pulled a package of wet wipes from his drawer. I needed a minute to catch my breath, but he was done with me now. I eyed the wipes, hating that I wondered why he needed them here.

He used one to gently clean the cum and saliva off my stomach, then tossed it in the trash and pulled me up, leaving me sitting on his desk. "Luther used to spend a lot more time in my office. I know that look, Alexander. If you're ever insecure about something, just tell me."

Dropping my gaze, I shrugged. "I'm sorry, I know it's none of my business."

"Knowing who your lovers are with *is* your business. I want you to submit to me, but you're not a doormat. You deserve the same respect both me and Luther will ask for." He kissed me gently, then dried my tears. "This was your first time and I expected you to be emotional. I'm not as sweet as Luther, but I need to know you're okay. Will you stay in here with me until I have to go?"

"If you want me to?" I hadn't expected to feel so fragile. Wasn't sex supposed to be something a guy just did for fun? I'd enjoyed myself. I should just go on with my day.

But I was…still raw. As though I'd opened the most sensitive part of myself and couldn't shut it down. I wanted to be held. I wanted the bright lights gone. Things to stop being so hazy and unsteady. And why was I so damn cold?

"Come here, pet." Xavier helped me stand. Fixed my clothes. Then pulled me onto his lap as he sat. "Let me hold you for a bit. Then you can kneel by my side if you're still feeling out of sorts. Some don't, but I'd considered you might. You don't do anything halfway and when you submit, it's no different. I appreciate that you trusted me enough to give yourself over so completely. Thank you."

His words were soft as he held me and the world began to feel solid again. I rested my head on his shoulder and stopped questioning myself. He had more experience than I did. If there was something wrong with me, he'd know.

About ten minutes later, his phone rang. He hesitated, but I smiled at him and slid to the floor, my head on his knee as he answered. He stroked my hair as he spoke, and I just stayed there and relaxed. The day was almost over. I didn't have anything else to do and he'd be leaving soon.

I'm gonna miss him.

He hung up the phone. Leaned down to kiss me. "I'll miss you too."

I blushed. I hadn't meant to say that out loud. He was going to start thinking I was needy.

Hanging on to his leg for the past hour probably didn't help. I moved away from him, climbing unsteadily to my feet and bracing my hand on the edge of his desk. "I know what I have to do while you're gone. Thank you for letting me look into the junior line."

"You have some great ideas for it. I'm looking forward to seeing what you'll do with them." He packed up his laptop and folders into his briefcase, then stood. "I don't want to cut your night short, but I'd love it if you'd come with me to the airport."

"Absolutely." I quickly straightened my clothes. "I'm trying not to be too clingy, but...yeah. I'd like that."

His lips twitched, but he didn't lecture me about my speech. Motioning me forward, he followed as we left the office, locking the door behind him.

He handed me the key. "I don't think you'll need it, but in case anything comes up this weekend..."

I stared at him. "I'd ask Luther if I needed anything."

"Now you don't have to."

Not sure what to say, I put the key in my own briefcase and locked it. I knew what this meant. Xavier had given me the one thing he valued more than anything. Something I would never take for granted.

His trust.

Chapter Eight

Things were quiet that night. More than usual, even though Xavier never spent time in this wing of the house. I knew Luther still went to the main house to see him almost every day after work. That the staff served him and cleaned up and he spoke to them when he wasn't busy.

With Xavier gone, it was…different. Most of the staff had the weekend off. There were no guests coming to see him, so they weren't needed. Only one maid and one butler stuck around, both who lived here and would do small tasks before enjoying the nights doing their own thing.

Luther had dinner with me, but we simply talked about my new project and how he hoped Xavier would get enough sleep and eat properly. One of the security guards was supposed to remind him, but Xavier didn't take suggestions well from anyone. They'd be on the plane all night, so Luther didn't expect a report until tomorrow.

We both went to bed early. I figured Luther would be in a better mood once he knew for sure that Xavier was okay.

He woke me before dawn with a huge smile on his lips, kissing me before I even had my eyes open. "Are you ready?"

"Ready?"

"Yes. I thought we'd go for a run." He pulled the blankets off me and tossed me a pair of jogging pants and a T-shirt. "You don't get out enough and some fresh air would be good for you."

I groaned and tried to pull the blankets back up over my head. Then settled for a pillow. "You're too chipper for way-too-fucking-early o'clock. Let me sleep."

"I brought you coffee. And I heard from Xavier."

Peeking out from under the pillow, I met his eyes. "How is he?"

"Almost as grumpy as you are. But he made it there in one piece, his meds helped him sleep, and he's having a bite to eat on the way to the hotel." Luther held out a cup of coffee like a peace offering, handing it to me when I sat up. "He complained about my guard being pushy, but admitted he didn't eat enough yesterday. He also asked me to keep an eye on you."

I almost choked on the coffee. "Why?"

He arched a brow.

"Oh... I should have realized you'd discuss..." I hid my face behind the mug. "This is awkward."

"Why? He said only good things." He sat by my side and kissed my shoulder. "And he's gotten past his 'rules'. He trusts you and he wants us to enjoy ourselves this weekend."

"With a..." I glanced at the clock on the bedside table. "6AM run?"

Luther chuckled and patted my thigh. "No. He'd agree with you that I am insane. But this is something I want to do with you. If you don't enjoy it, I'll never ask again."

Taking a sip of my coffee, I studied Luther's face, noticing an uncertainty in his eyes that he'd hidden in his tone. He might pretend to be fine with Xavier's very independent, living-our-own-lives kind of relationship, but I had a feeling he missed the connection they must have had once.

Filling the role Xavier refused to for Luther made me feel like I was crossing some sort of line, but I loved sitting down with Luther for breakfast and supper every day. When I sat alone in my room to watch a movie, I often wondered what it would be like to cuddle on the couch with him, enjoying it together.

I was sappy and I craved the kind of relationship that meant never feeling alone. Xavier wasn't like that...or maybe he didn't know how to be. Either way, I needed to know where I fit with them. Maybe this was it.

"Will we catch sunrise if I hurry?"

The skin around Luther's eyes crinkled as he smiled. "That's the plan."

"Cool." I gulped down the rest of my coffee and hopped out of bed. "I haven't gotten a chance to get new running shoes, but my old ones should—"

"Be in a landfill somewhere by now. I probably should have mentioned that. I replaced them when I realized Xavier had only gotten you dress shoes and the black Vans for casual wear." He stood and started out of the room. "Get dressed, I'll go get them."

"Wait." My throat tightened. I looked around the room, reality hitting me suddenly. I shook my head. "Fuck, there's nothing left, is there?"

Pausing by the door, Luther braced his hand on the doorframe. Then he turned slowly. "I'm sorry. I should have considered—"

"No, it's not that. Those shoes were falling apart. I appreciate you getting me new ones, I hadn't even thought about it. I just..." I shook my head. This made no sense. I'd had nothing for years. Why would it bother me now when there were two men in my life who'd given me more than I'd ever imagined. "It's stupid. Forget it."

"It's not stupid. And the shoes were just a reminder of how much you've had to give up to be safe. To avoid the life your brothers tried to force you into." Luther crossed the room and pulled me into his arms. "The shoes, the clothes, everything you had before you got on your own. It doesn't matter how, they were *yours*. Xavier and I providing for you is different and I understand that." He pressed his lips to my hair. "But you have your own money now. Money you haven't touched. Maybe it's time you use some of it and get the things you've always wanted. Things that you can look at and know you've earned."

"Maybe...I want to save my money in case..." I pressed my forehead against his chest and groaned. "There's nothing I need."

"There has to be something you want?"

Security. But he knew that. One of the things I loved about Luther is he never tried to convince me I didn't need to worry about having a backup plan. He'd helped me set up a bank account and given me the number to an investment firm he used himself. One more paycheck and I'd have the money to get my own apartment if I wanted to. Fill my own fridge with food. Maybe even rent my own car.

But I didn't have my license, so that would be pointless.

I chewed at my bottom lip. Maybe that was one way I could regain some control over my life. I met his level gaze. "I want to get my license and buy my own car. Without your or Xavier's help. Even if it's secondhand and doesn't look great next to your cars, I need this. I know Xavier probably won't like that, but—"

"He'll understand. And so do I." Luther gave me an encouraging smile. "I'll resist the urge to get you the number and set everything up for you, but if you need someone to practice with, don't hesitate to ask."

Good. This was good. It was just a step toward independence, but one I desperately needed.

I smiled back at him. "I won't." I quickly changed, grinning when he couldn't take his eyes off me. It wouldn't take much to keep him right here, doing all the things that had been forbidden for weeks, but I wanted to share something more with him. "Can you go grab the shoes for me?"

He blinked at me. Then chuckled. "On it."

The cool air hit me as soon as we stepped outside and I shivered, wondering if I should've worn a hoodie. Luther was wearing a snug, dark blue tank top and freakin' shorts, but all those muscles must offer some kind of shield from the cold because he simply stretched, not seeming to notice as the wind pressed against us.

I copied his motions, biting back a wince at the strain in the back of my thighs when I wrapped my hands around my ankles. This was *not* gonna be much fun.

But Luther looked so happy, the pain was worth it.

Or at least I thought it was until we'd run the length of the ridiculously long driveway. Keeping up with him had my lungs burning already. If this was his idea of fun, we probably wouldn't be having much of it. The man was trying to kill me.

Running in place as I stopped and bent over to catch my breath, Luther laughed. "This may have been a bit ambitious to start with. We can walk to the spot with the best view if you'd like?"

With a nod, I straightened. "Fuck, I think I love you. Yes, I'd like that very much."

The tenderness in Luther's eyes made me all weird and warm and fuzzy. He held out his hand and I took it, looking down at the drying grass crushing under my feet as we walked beyond the edge of the property. I hadn't meant for it to come out like that, but I was falling in love with Luther. I'd probably started to after he'd brought me here, giving me the first bit of hope I'd had in such a long time, but I wouldn't confuse gratitude with love.

Moments like this though? Luther made me feel like I was important to him. I loved the way he teased me. The way he encouraged me to speak my mind. The casual touches, the smiles, the way he made me feel stronger and smarter than I'd ever believed I was. He'd gone from being my hero to being a man I wanted to share every day with.

"Here we are." Luther stopped at the edge of a ridge after we'd been walking for about half an hour, some of it on an incline. We'd reached the top of Slipdown Mountain, which was more of a hill than anything, but had a nice view. "I used to travel a lot and I love finding the highest point anywhere I go so I can take in everything.

This is nothing compared to some of the mountains I've climbed, but it's familiar. I run here almost every day."

"Maybe one day I'll be in good enough shape to do it with you." Already sore, I stepped forward, plunking down on the packed dirt and rock ledge, bracing my arms behind me and staring out into the distance as the horizon was painted with a brilliant golden glow, with highlights in a deep pink shade I could imagine Xavier trying to capture for one of his most treasured designs. The fluffy white clouds reflected the colors as the sun rose in the distance, brightening the sky to a rich blue. "Wow. That's beautiful. I wish I'd brought my phone."

"You should have." Luther chuckled, pulling his own from under his shirt. He handed it to me. "The picture won't be as impressive as what you see, but it will capture the moment."

Grinning at him, I opened the camera and snapped a few pictures of him. Then some more of the view. I'd have to print them out later and see if I could match up some swatches for the junior line. Xavier was still uncertain of it, and though he'd given me a lot more control over it than I should have, he still made offhand comments that helped me approach the team for improvements.

He'd made a face last time he saw me going over samples during my lunch break last Tuesday.

Looking up at him, I frowned. "What's wrong? These are your designs."

He shrugged, taking a bite of the sandwich I'd left on his desk even though he'd told me he wasn't hungry. Wiping a bit of mustard off his cheek, he jutted his chin at one dress. "I'm curious about the Pepto Bismol pink, that's all. Is that what the youth of today are into?"

That comment had probably saved me from completely screwing up the project. I spoke to Lori, who managed production, and she assured me there was plenty of time to change it. We put the dress on hold while working on others Xavier had given a grunt of approval.

He acted like he wasn't interested in pursuing the line, but he spent a lot of time looking over my shoulder for someone who didn't care. I had a feeling he wanted me to have something I could take credit for, which I appreciated. Still, the credit would go where it belonged. To the team of women who'd been working on this for almost a year and just needed to convince Xavier he hadn't made a mistake by branching out.

I might have gotten him to listen, but their work had given me something to show him. Something to fight for.

"Would you mind sending these to me so I can print them out?" I flipped through the photos. Luther was right, they weren't as impressive as the view, but the color was there. "I don't know much about design, but I think the junior line team can work with these. And they fit Xavier's current obsession with finding inspiration in nature."

Crouching down beside me, Luther looked at the pictures, brow furrowed slightly as though he was trying to see what I was talking about. And failing. "I know even less than you do. I'm better with the diplomatic side of business. And the numbers. It was never my passion though. I spent some time training to become a cop, but…let's just say it didn't work out. I settled on security because it helps Xavier, and it's still something I enjoy doing. I can be a bit protective."

"I never would've guessed." I shot him a sideways smile. "Xavier says I have an eye for stuff like this. I don't know if he's right, but I'm happy I can be useful. I want to take a course in design though so I don't feel like a noob stepping on toes. Even the interns spent years learning the craft before getting a foot in the door."

"True. And you were given an advantage. But you're aware of that. You spend every day proving you deserve it." Luther put his hand on my shoulder. "And you've earned Xavier's trust. No diploma could teach you how to do that."

"I guess so. I just hope he doesn't mind that I want to be able to contribute more."

"He won't mind. If you've shown him half the passion I've seen, he'll just be happy to have someone to share it with." Luther stared out as the last golden rays of the sunrise faded away. "I support him in everything he does, but I know that isn't enough. We're so different, sometimes I wonder how we've lasted this long. He's ambitious and creative. I'm more about stability, about making sure those I love are safe and happy. I can keep him safe, and his drive makes him happy, but sometimes we get lost in finding the middle ground."

"You don't spend enough time together." I'd kept flipping through photos, speaking without really thinking, but when I sensed Luther going still by my side, I glanced over at him. "I'm sorry, it's not my place to—"

He shook his head. "It is. You're part of this relationship now. I can't tell you all our issues and expect you to sit there quietly. And you're right." He sighed. "I go to him every day when he's home. Ask him how his day was. He asks me the same. We talk and maybe have a drink. If we're in the mood, we fuck. Then we go our own ways. Our relationship has become a pitstop in our separate lives."

"I can't change that for you."

"No, but you've given me an idea of what needs to change. You don't let Xavier shut you out. You find ways to be excited about what he's doing, even if you don't always understand it. Your need to find your place has you putting in the effort neither he or I have in a long time." Luther curved his hand around the back of my neck, rubbing the muscles that were tense after so much time spent in front of a desk. "You take nothing for granted. We need to learn that."

"I think that happens with most people. You know them for a long time and they're just...there." I almost shrugged, but I didn't want him to stop, so I held still. "I've never had that, so the first two people in my life who are really there for me? I'm just hoping they want to stay."

Luther tightened his grip. Reached out to tip my chin up with his other hand. "I do, Alec. I've been thinking about this a lot. Whatever arrangement we have, you can decide you want your freedom. That you want the car, and your own apartment, your independence. That's your choice and I'll fight for you to have it. But I'll also fight to make sure I still have a place in the life you build."

"Your life is with Xavier."

"Not just with him. Not anymore." He leaned close, brushing his lips over mine in a soft kiss. "You're a man I could easily fall in love with. That doesn't make me love Xavier any less. There's room for both of you."

Him using the word I had, without hesitation, made me a little lightheaded. I hadn't considered his thoughts had ever gone there. Ever considered what we had more than a distraction. A way for me to satisfy an urge Xavier couldn't. "I'd never make you choose."

"I know." He flicked his tongue over my bottom lip. "And I won't ever have to."

Inhaling roughly, I leaned closer to him, groaning when he laughed and stood abruptly. My dick throbbed unhappily as he held out his hand and I stood. The outline of my erection was obvious, pressing against my jogging pants, but he simply arched a brow at me and started back down the path.

More energized than I'd been when we'd started, I sprinted ahead of him.

"Hey!" He barked out a laugh, easily catching up, then lengthening his strides enough to force me to push a little harder. "Not sure what the rush is, but this is good. See if you can go a bit longer this time."

The burning with each breath was back, but I kept going, his encouraging shouts keeping me focused on just moving forward. On feeling the wind in my hair and the ground growing level under my feet. Teeth gritted, I quickened my pace. His smile made the pain worth it. I could do this.

From the corner of my eye I spotted a man and all the rush of endorphins left me like he'd slashed through them with a sharp knife. My foot hit a dip in the path and I flew forward, catching myself on my elbow and my knee.

I rolled to my side, clutching my arm as blood spilled between my fingers. The pain didn't hit me as hard as knowing the sense of being free and safe was gone. I should have expected this. I should have known it was all too good to be true. Why hadn't I been ready?

"Shit, hold still." Luther eased his arms under my knees and my shoulders, lifting me carefully. "We're almost home. I should have brought a med kit. Are you okay?"

"Don't worry about me. Luther, I saw him. He found me. He's here for a reason." I'd bitten into my tongue when I fell. Blood filled my mouth. My stomach turned as I swallowed it. A sharp pain lanced through my chest and I pressed my hand against it. "You can't take me home. He'll see."

Luther inclined his head and carried me to a bench. He set me down and called for a car to be sent. He picked me back up and carried me down to the street, where the car was waiting.

"Alec, listen to me. Xavier has enemies and I've had to lose them before. Our home isn't known to the public, I've made sure of that." He tucked me into the back seat of the town car, then straightened, surveying the area. "Our doctor will meet us at the house in fifteen minutes. The driver has been instructed to take a route that will expose anyone trying to follow us. Or lose them. He's good at this. Trust me."

"I do." I choked back a sob, struggling to pull in air as he slid in beside me, shutting the door, then pressing my head against his chest. "I'm sorry."

"This isn't your fault." He rubbed my arm, then reached under the seat and pulled out a blanket to lay over me. "Who was it, Alec? Who did you see?"

"My brother. Erik." I shuddered, still gasping. "When my father wanted to put me in my place, he always turned to my eldest brother. He knew what needed to be done. He showed me how bad I was. I'd be dead if he hadn't gone to jail."

"Alec, listen to me. Don't get pulled back there. Stay here." Luther stroked my hair. "I thought he'd been arrested. I don't know if he got out on bail, but I won't let him near you. You're safe."

"I would have been safer if I never went back. I know he hates me." Tears blinded me. I fought to blink them away. "I don't want to…I didn't want to die." My stomach turned as the car hit a bump in the road. The slashing pain stole my vision. "Why can't he just let me go?"

"Because you have everything he wants. But I won't let him take it from you. Look at me. *Alec!*" Luther's grip tightened on my arm as my vision faded and my head slumped to the side. "We should go to the hospital."

"No!" I was wide awake now. I shook my head. "Christian, my other brother, the middle one…he's been my contact person since I was thirteen. They'll call him."

"Alec, you've lost a lot of blood. You're scaring me." Luther put his hand around my arm. "Let me take care of you. I'll figure this out."

"I'm okay. Please. Just take me home." My vision blurred and I tightened my grip on his hand. "Take me home. I want to be there. It's mine."

"It is. Look at me. I've got you."

I believed him, but I wasn't sure he could keep me safe. Wasn't sure I wanted him to. My brothers had been raised in a life of crime. If I was their next target, nothing would stop them.

Nothing but me getting far away from Luther. From Xavier.

But I had to find the strength to make that happen.

And it was slipping away.

"There we are." A tall man with brown skin and a warm smile leaned over me. "How are we feeling?"

"Better?" I looked around the room. I was in the hospital. I tried to sit up. "I can't be here."

Luther came to my sit, pushing gently on my shoulder. "This is a private clinic and they aren't calling anyone. Relax, Alec."

I shook my head, but tried to relax. He wouldn't listen to me if he thought I was freaking out. "You don't get it. They'll find me."

"Take a deep breath, Alec. We don't want you having another panic attack." The doctor set the chart he was holding aside. "There were rocks and several pieces of glass inside the wounds. I removed them. You also needed stitches in your elbow and your knee, but that didn't concern me as much as the way you completely shut down. Have you been assessed for a possible heart condition?"

"Not that I know of?" This was the first time I was speaking to a doctor since I was a kid, and even then, I hadn't gotten more than a few checkups. "But I'm okay? I can leave?"

The doctor exchanged a look with Luther, then sighed. "There's no reason to keep you, but I'd recommend making an appointment as soon as possible. I won't assume anything, you're young and seem to be in very good health, but your boyfriend couldn't tell me of any pre-existing conditions either and this kind of panic attack can be the result of other issues."

"This has never happened before. I just…I just freaked out."

"Do you know why?"

I looked over at Luther and he gave me a bracing smile. "It's all right. You can discuss as much or as little as you want to. Doctor Baqri has been both mine and Xavier's doctor for years. He'll be able to make a referral if you need to see another specialist."

"Thank you, but…not right now. I'm feeling a lot better." I wanted to get back to the house where things were secure. Luther made sure of it, and now that he knew my brothers were looking for me, he'd make sure we weren't followed. "I'll get a checkup soon. I promise."

"All right, well you should be good to go. Take some ibuprofen if the pain is unbearable. If there's any inflammation you'll need to come back for antibiotics, but I don't think there'll be further issues." He turned to Luther. "Keep the stress to a minimum. And make sure he makes that appointment."

"I will." Luther fixed me with a level gaze that left no room for debate. "Thank you, Doctor Baqri."

We left the clinic shortly after, Luther hovering close as I limped to the car, his jaw hard from the moment I'd refused to let him carry me. I'd hoped seeing me walk would prove to him I was all right, but it just seemed to worry him more.

Back home, I hesitated before climbing out of the car.

He leaned into the passenger side, forehead creased with concern. "Are you okay?"

"Yeah, it's just…" I tugged at my bottom lip with my teeth. "I wouldn't say no if you still wanna help?"

His lips curved. He smoothly slipped his arms under me and lifted me out of the car. "About fucking time. Don't ever do that again. I'm fed up of Xavier shutting me out. Don't you start."

I tucked my head against the side of his neck and laughed softly. "You plan to tell *him* that?"

Luther didn't answer until we were inside and he'd set me down on the sofa in the living room. He pulled a fluffy purple throw over me, fussing with it for a bit before meeting my eyes.

"I do."

Chapter Nine

"This is not how we were supposed to spend this weekend." After pulling the coffee table closer to the sofa, Luther set down the tray of grilled cheese and tomato soup. Wearing nothing but the dark grey pajama pants he'd slept in, in *my* bed, he settled on the sofa beside me and handed me a glass of cherry coke and laughed.

"This is exactly how I wanted to spend it. Minus the injury and your brother deciding to stalk you." Luther rubbed my thigh above the stitches and purple and blue bruise covering my knee. "I wanted you to let your guard down and learn to just be with me, knowing what might happen. And that it changes nothing."

Spoonful of soup halfway to my mouth I stopped. And stared at him. "It doesn't?"

"No. It doesn't." He pushed my hand down, leaning close to kiss me, speaking softly against my lips. "If I'd just wanted to fuck you, I could have. Winning Xavier's challenge wasn't that important to me. It was a way to make you both feel more comfortable with the situation."

"And now that we are?"

"Your relationship is developing in a way that works for you and him." He kissed me again. "And you and I will continue what works for us."

I licked my bottom lip, forgetting about my soup, wanting another taste of him. But I was still confused. "This is starting to feel like a relationship."

He arched a brow. "Only starting to?"

"You're with Xavier."

"So are you. And you're better at it than I am." He curved his hand under my jaw. "But this is about us. I want you completely under my control, but I didn't want you surrendering out of gratitude. I don't want to be your hero. I want to be the man you lean on when you're hurt. Who you trust just as much when you're on your knees as you do when you feel like your life is falling apart."

All right, there was no more 'maybe' about it. I fucking loved this man. Which was scary and awesome all at once. He wanted me to submit to him. But he wanted it to be real.

"I don't think getting on my knees right now would be a good idea, but I would if I could."

His lips slanted. "Would you now."

"Yes."

"Do you think that's the only way to submit to me, Alec?" He hooked his hands under my shirt. "Arms up."

Lifting my arms, I let him pull off my shirt, my skin heating as he slipped from the sofa and knelt in front of me. He eased off my boxers next, leaving me completely exposed, my dick swelling as his gaze traveled over every inch of me.

"Do you feel like you have any control?"

I swallowed and shook my head.

He pressed his thumb against my bottom lip. "Good."

Using the moisture from my mouth, Luther traced his thumb down my neck, then rose up to glide his lips where his thumb had passed. Hips spreading my thighs, the soft material of his pajamas brushing over my straining dick, he kissed his way down my chest.

Groaning, I shifted under him and put my hand on his head,

delving into the thick black curls he kept just long enough on top to comb through with the tips of my fingers. I slid my fingers down the side of his head, enjoying the texture of the close-shaved hair, my hips rising as he moved even lower.

"Hands at your sides, Alec. Hold still or you'll have your first taste of the discipline I promised you." Luther closed his teeth around one hard nipple, biting down with a slight pressure at first, increasing it when my hands rose toward him in response. "Restraining you might hurt your arm, but my command should be enough. Imagine my words holding you as firmly as any binding. You can't pull free of them. You don't want to."

A shiver ran over me as I placed my hands by my sides and kept them there, everything going light and hazy when his lips curved with approval. Closing my eyes, I pictured the restraints. Thick ropes around my wrists, tight enough to mark my flesh. Pretending they were there helped, but I hoped one day he'd tie me down for real. Let the ropes hold me rather than force me to remember I shouldn't move.

Still, that awareness made me so much more sensitive to his every touch. His breath on my skin sent little sparks along my nerve and my nipples ached long after his teeth toyed with each one. He spent a lot of time working them under his tongue. Tugging them with his teeth until I opened my eyes, moaning and whimpering, trembling harder as remaining still became even more difficult.

"Such a good boy. Fuck, I love seeing you like this, so desperate to please me." He licked down my stomach, stopping just above my dick. "I'm going to make it harder, pet. You'll want to come, but as of right now, your pleasure belongs to me. I'll help you contain yourself this time, but you'll learn never to let go until I allow it."

"Oh fuck." I tipped my head back as he took me in his mouth. He grazed me with his teeth in warning and I held my breath, not moving a muscle. "Luther—"

"Shh. Don't speak. Feel and listen." He reached out and pulled something from the end table drawer. "All I want to hear from you is if you're in pain. For that I need words." He uncapped a bottle of lube and poured some into his palm. "For the rest, only the sounds you can't help making. I won't punish you if you scream."

He slicked the lube over my dick, jerking it hard and fast, his gaze on my face, a wicked smile on his lips. The pleasure built up and my lips parted as it gathered at the base of my spine. When he spread the liquid down between my ass cheeks, I held my breath.

"Breathe, pet. And open to me." He pulled my ass off the edge of the sofa, spreading my thighs further, then pressing his finger against me. "Don't tense. Let me in."

The second I relaxed, his finger began to penetrate, the lube making a slow, easy glide of it as he pressed in all the way. The sensation wasn't as rough as when Xavier had used nothing but his spit, and I missed the gritty edge of it, but I knew Luther was preparing me to take more.

Much more.

Taking his time with me, Luther added lube, curving his finger to brush my prostate with each pass, bending down to suck my dick until I was panting with the struggle it took not to rise up into his mouth. He released me with a hooded look, pulling out a condom and ripping open the package with his teeth as I watched.

He sheathed himself, then curved his arm under my undamaged knee, lifting me to him as he positioned his dick. The slow press made the sensation of him stretching me so intense I couldn't stop the low moan that hitched with my breath as he began rocking his hips, going a little deeper every time. His dick was thick and long and once he pushed further past that first ring of muscle, the stretch became a burn.

I winced and he withdrew, adding more lube to cover his dick and make me so slippery the next time he pressed in, he filled me with one effortless thrust.

"Oh…Oh fuck…" Holding still was almost impossible now.

The fullness had me desperate to move against him. As he pressed harder against my ass, forcing himself even deeper, I ground out a pleading sound.

He ran his hand down my thigh soothingly. "You're doing well, pet. I've got you."

Lifting my thigh even more, he made it impossible for me to move as he rocked his hips. His free hand wrapped around my dick and he began to stroke me in time to his steady thrusts, fucking harder, faster, twisting me between all the things he was doing to me until all I could do was take it all in. The musky scent of sex and grilled cheese and Luther's faint, woodsy cologne. The slap of his flesh hitting mine over and over. The sweat glistening on both our bodies as all my muscles tensed against the temptation to reach out to him, hang on to his hard, muscular body as he pounded into me.

"God, you feel good, Alec." He released my dick and braced his hand on the back of the sofa, bending me almost in half and he leaned into me. "Imagine when Xavier is with us. All the things we'll do to you. The way I'll train you to please us, train this fucking beautiful ass to take more and more until the day we can both take you. Together."

Pre-cum dripped over the tip of my dick, smearing on my stomach. I gasped through parted lips, trying to imagine the scene he was setting for me, but my mind couldn't quite grasp it. I'd known they'd continue sharing me, but what he suggested didn't seem possible.

He gave me a sly smile, slamming into me hard as though the thought turned him on. "We've done it before, pet. Only never with someone we'd trained ourselves. He was a good slut." He leaned down to suck on my bottom lip. "But you'll be ours."

"Luther…I need to…"

"Hold it back for me. I want to see how good you can be." Luther reached down and clasped his fingers around the base of my cock, slowing his pace to a deep grind. "There you go."

A low hum of pleasure stole through my veins, spreading to every part of me until I was drowning in endorphins. He kept me on the edge, hitting my prostate over and over as he pistoned in and out, slowing, then speeding up right at the moment when I thought I couldn't take anymore.

Panting, he finally released my dick. "Now, Alec. Come with me."

He slammed in one last time and the violent burst of ecstasy took me with the strength of a riptide, too powerful to resist as my core clenched down and the hot spill of him filled me. I cried out, my body jerking, my harsh scream leaving my throat as raw and tender as the rest of me.

Bending down to kiss my shoulder, Luther chuckled as I shuddered, the movement showing me how sensitive I was. "Fuck, you're fun. Brace yourself."

I was about to ask why when he withdrew and all the tender nerves in my ass jolted at the stretch around the head of his dick. Slumping on the sofa, I watched him through half-closed lids as he straightened and removed the condom.

He went still, looking at something in the doorway. Then he smiled. "You're home early."

"Yes, but I didn't want to interrupt. You're so fucking hot together, I almost came just watching." Steady footsteps brought Xavier to the sofa. His brow lifted as he glanced down at me. "And here I was thinking you'd be gentle. What did you do to him?"

When his gaze settled on my knee I shook my head. "That wasn't Luther."

"I know, he called me last night to let me know what happened." Crouching down, Xavier combed his fingers into my hair. "I'm sorry, Alexander."

Carefully pushing myself into a sitting position, I leaned up to kiss him, then shook my head. "It's not your fault."

"Actually, it is." He folded his arms over my chest, then glanced over at Luther. "Could you sit down for a moment? We need to talk."

Luther's expression darkened. He moved closer, but didn't sit.

Facing Xavier, he spoke softly, his tone sharp with barely controlled rage.

"What have you done?"

Chapter Ten

The tension in the room stole away the lingering pleasure and a chill slithered over my skin as I watched the two men I'd given myself to in every way stare at one another. I couldn't sit here naked, not when it seemed like my world was about to be torn in two.

Xavier lowered his gaze as I grabbed my boxers off the floor and pulled them on. He didn't speak until I was fully dressed. "I expected Alexander's brothers might look into what happened to him. That they wouldn't trust him not to turn them in. So I had a private investigator find them."

"I thought you were going to let the police handle this." Luther ran his hand over his hair, an incredulous look in his eyes. "Damn it, Xavier, tell me you didn't go see them."

Pressing his eyes shut, Xavier didn't answer for what seemed like a long time. Finally, he opened his eyes, his focus on me. "The police would have charged you as well. I couldn't let that happen."

"They could've hurt you, Xavier. I'd rather be in jail than have anything happen to you." I knew Luther was mad, but I was just fucking scared. Xavier had no clue how dangerous my brothers were. "This was my mistake to fix, not yours."

"Did it occur to you that Luther's not the only one who wants to protect you? I might not be as good at showing it, but I care about you." He shook his head and slumped onto the sofa beside me, his typically perfectly styled hair mussed up, his suit looking like he'd pulled it on in a rush, not giving a damn how rumpled it was. "I thought I could end it. But I only made it worse."

Seeing this man, always so refined, so contained, come completely undone because of me brought a tight ache to my chest. I put my arm around his shoulders.

"Tell us everything."

He let out a bitter laugh. "I gave them the fucking car. Told them I'd never report them, so long as they left you alone. I had my lawyer draw up all the paperwork. Maybe we can throw it at them next time they decide to come after you. I'm sure that will help."

"Jesus Christ, Xavier." Luther groaned, lacing his fingers behind his neck. "They want more now, don't they?"

"Yes. And I gave it to them right after you called me."

"Which will satisfy them for what, a month? A week?" Luther strode across the room and crouched down in front of Xavier, his hands on the other man's shoulders. "We deal with things like this together. You should have come to me first. We could have figured out a way to protect Alec together."

Xavier nodded slowly. "I know, but you were happy, Luther. I haven't seen you this happy in a long time. I refused to let anything ruin it."

Luther sighed and wrapped his arms around Xavier, holding him close as he let out a soft laugh. "You know, telling him you love him would have been much easier."

"This is true." Xavier eased away from Luther and turned to me. "I'm sorry I kept this from you, but I do stupid things when I love someone. Giving in to blackmail was much easier than telling you how much you mean to me. But now I've put you in danger."

My throat tightened. I pushed off the sofa, hating that he blamed himself for what my brothers had forced him to do. "Maybe I should leave. If they don't think I'm important to you—"

"That's *not* an option." Luther grabbed my wrist, pulling me onto his lap as he dropped onto the sofa, one arm around Xavier, the other around me, as though to make sure neither of us could go anywhere. "From this point on, you let me handle those assholes. It is *my* job."

"But I—"

"No." Luther cut Xavier off, his tone firm. "This conversation is over. Tell me how the trip went before I decide to prove Alec isn't the only one I can control when I want to."

A dark red blush spread across Xavier's cheeks and his eyes narrowed. He inhaled slowly, and at first I thought he'd argue, but he simply nodded. After a long silence, he leaned over, resting his head on Luther's shoulder. "The trip went better than expected. I have buyers for all my new dress designs and several requests for exclusive designs." He caught my eyes. "As well as interest in the junior line. Enough for me to give you the money and resources you need to expand it."

"Really?" I bit back a smile, not sure this was a good time for it, but I was excited. The team wouldn't have to be afraid to lose their jobs anymore. "Fuck, I can't wait to tell Judy. You have to put her in charge, Xavier. I don't mind consulting on your behalf, but this is her baby."

"Agreed. We'll speak to her and the team tomorrow. They deserve the credit for pulling this all together, though that doesn't diminish your part in this. As I told you from the beginning, you have a good eye for fashion." His lips curved as he reached out to cup my cheek. "And a way of managing me when I'm being difficult."

"It's not that hard, really. You're not as scary as you think you are."

"You say that now." Luther brushed his lips against my ear. "But you've never really pissed him off. Just wait until you do and he takes off his belt."

"He did." I ducked my head when Luther arched his brow. "I behaved."

"Smart boy."

For a long time we simply sat there together, Xavier telling us a bit more about his trip, sounding more excited about his project, and mine, as he got into the details of the new deal. He'd never been in this part of the house this long since I'd been here, and I hoped he'd stay, but as it grew late he started checking his watch.

And began pulling away. "I should get some sleep. It's been a long few days and—"

"Stay." Luther eased me off his lap, onto the sofa, and stood. "Alec's managed to get closer to you because he doesn't let you push him away. Which I've been letting you do for too long. We both need control, and I won't try to dominate you, but I want you near me. Come to my bed. It's big enough for all three of us."

Xavier blinked at him, lips parted. Then he took a deep breath. "Fine. I'll give you one night to see how it goes."

"No, Xavier. You'll give me them all." Luther pulled Xavier against him, claiming his lips in a bruising kiss, clasping his hand around the back of Xavier's neck when he looked ready to pull away and object. "I've seen what happens when you're left to your own devices. It'll be a long time before I let you out of my sight."

Letting out a huff as he stepped back and tugged on his sleeves, Xavier shook his head. "That's not how things work between us, Luther."

Luther simply smiled. "It is now. We're going to have some new rules."

Perfectly still, Xavier stared at him. "What rules?"

"Mine."

Chapter Eleven

*O*ne month later

Running through the hall I cursed myself under my breath as the files slipped from my arms and scattered across the floor. I was already late. Skidding to a stop, I knelt down, picking the papers up as fast as I could without creasing them.

Two sets of shiny black shoes stopped in front of me.

I swallowed hard.

"You were supposed to be finished an hour ago, Alexander." Xavier clucked his tongue as he crouched down to help me. "Do you know how much trouble you're in?"

A cold rush of fear and excitement spilled down my spine. "I promised Judy I'd get these to you by the end of the day, but I had to finish my assignment for school and—"

"And we promised one another we wouldn't work so hard. We had plans, Alec." Luther folded his arms over his chest as I rose to my feet. "Xavier's made the attempt. You've only taken on more. Your priority should be your night classes. I told you to hire someone else to help Judy."

Shaking my head, I went to Xavier's office, feeling their eyes on me as I set the files on his desk. "I'm trying, Luther. But this job is important to me. You guys can take time off, you've been doing this for years. I still have so much to learn."

"Mhmm. You really do." Steady footsteps crossed the office. Luther placed a heavy hand on my shoulder. "Lock the door, Xavier."

Oh shit.

The lock clicked. Something hit the floor beside me. My eyes widened as I realized it was Luther's leather toy bag.

"You knew I'd be late." I shook my head and stared at him over my shoulder. "Luther, we can't do this here."

"Why not?" Xavier went around his desk and dropped into his chair, lips slanted as I turned my attention to him. "What's the point of owning all this if I can't enjoy it from time to time?"

All right, he was making me very nervous, but I couldn't deny I loved how much he'd changed over the last month. He was more relaxed. Easier to talk to. And he let Luther come here every single day.

They'd grown closer and it made me happy to see their relationship was stronger than ever.

Even though they were kinda scary when they teamed up on me.

Like tonight.

I cleared my throat. "The private investigator stopped by earlier. He wanted to discuss with you all the evidence he's found against my brothers. He also said they've left the state, so we shouldn't have to worry about them anymore."

"Which you are telling me now because…?" Xavier arched a brow. "Luther asked you not to worry about that."

"I also asked the PI to come to me. Why is he reporting to you?"

"I'm the one paying him." Xavier leaned forward in his chair. "And we're not discussing my transgressions now. I'm not the one in trouble."

Luther let out a dark laugh. "It's amusing that you think so. You signed the same contract he did, my man. And you've broken several rules."

"You can't punish us both."

"Can't I?" Luther picked up his toy bag, sweeping out his arm to clear the desk, ignoring Xavier's shocked exclamation as all his files and supplies hit the floor. He glanced over at me. "Kneel."

I lowered to my knees without a sound. Both men were my masters in their own ways, but the dynamics had shifted between them, with Luther taking control more often than not. His rules kept Xavier from shutting either of us out and obsessing over his work. For me, they were exactly what we all needed.

Xavier was still getting used to giving up that much power.

The sound of Luther unzipping his bag made me shudder and I wet my lips with my tongue as he pulled out a pair of handcuffs and a length of black rope. He palmed the handcuffs and strode around the desk.

"No." Xavier stared at the handcuffs. "*Hell* no."

Luther simply waited.

"You want me to sit here and watch while you enjoy him?" Xavier's lips thinned. "*Again?*"

"You say that as though you don't fucking love it." Luther's lips slanted. "You have him all day at work. Don't pretend that you don't use him as often as you like. One of my rules is he give me every detail when he comes home."

Xavier smirked a little at that. "I had a feeling there was a reason you never pressed too much about me eating every meal with you."

Heat wrapped around the back of my neck. I loved the peace of kneeling for Luther like this, knowing he trusted me to stay where he put me and ease into my submission, but his words made me think about the other day when he'd told me not to clean up after Xavier fucked me. He made me give him a play by play as he recreated every moment, using nothing but was left of the lube and Xavier's cum to fuck me raw.

Having all our blood tests done together had made being spontaneous a lot easier.

"You're thinking about it now, aren't you, Alec?" Luther had turned his focus back to me while I'd been distracted with the memory. "How fast and hard I took you. How messy you were when I was done. Should we let Xavier know what it feels like to have you when you're so relaxed and wet and tender every thrust makes you scream?"

My heart was pounding and my lips parted so I could pull in enough air. I swallowed hard. "Only if he follows the rules."

Luther's eyes warmed with approval. He looked back at Xavier. "It's your call. I won't force you, but we both know he's worth you suffering a little."

"More than a little." Xavier grumbled, holding out one wrist. "You're evil, you know that?"

"And you fucking love it."

After clipping the cuff around Xavier's wrist, Luther pulled both his arms behind the chair to restrain him there. Satisfied, he returned to me, motioning for me to stand.

"To make this more fun, we'll use the belt. Maybe that will teach Xavier that when he breaks my rules, he misses out on all the fun."

I bit my lip as Luther removed his belt. I didn't find the belt much fun, but it was Xavier's favorite tool for punishments. By his expression this was much worse than the handcuffs.

The rare times Xavier punished me strengthened the bond between us. He had a hard time expressing his feelings, but when I pushed him too far, it was a way to bring us back to a level where he could express his disappointment without raising his voice, which he refused to do anymore, even at work where people had grown accustomed to his temper.

He didn't argue, didn't like anyone to see him mad.

There were few things he cared enough to get angry about. But I'd reached that point a few times. Usually by falling into the same habit he had. Working for so long I forgot to eat. Cutting my sleep short because I couldn't always balance how much I wanted to do here, and how much I needed to do for school.

Using the belt was his way of reminding me that he loved me. To pull me away from the edge when I went too far. We'd come to a silent agreement that I'd somehow let him know when I needed it. Which was usually better. A corrective punishment was much better than one he felt forced to give me because I'd upset him by neglecting myself.

"Red." I swallowed at Luther's sharp look. I'd never had a reason to use the safeword we'd agreed on before. But I needed to now. "I'll accept the punishment. And Xavier won't like having to watch me take it, without being involved. But not with the belt. I need the belt to be his thing. You're more comfortable being creative with punishments than he is."

Luther nodded slowly, his expression relaxing. "I understand. I'd use the cane, but I didn't think to bring it with me." He cocked his head, considering me for a moment. "You find spankings humiliating, but perhaps that will be a good incentive not to do this again. I don't enjoy punishing you for wearing yourself out any more than he does."

"I know." My heart sank and my eyes stung as it really hit me exactly what I'd done wrong. I might love having them both set limits on me, but I showed them no respect when I didn't even try to stick to them. "I'm sorry."

"You say you are, but after this, there will be no more punishments for it. If you can't manage school and working *part-time* here, you'll be fired." He held up his hand when I gasped. "I know how important this job is to you. But your health and our relationship is even more important. I stood back and let distance grow between Xavier and I because I didn't know how to fight for us. You taught me how. Don't expect me to do any less for you."

Nodding, I stepped up to him, ready to do whatever it took to prove I understood. "I love you and I love Xavier. I can't promise I'll be perfect, but I haven't been trying hard enough. I will now."

"Good." He kissed my forehead. "Now brace your hands against the desk."

Without hesitation, I faced the desk and bent over, widening my stance even as he reached around me to undo my pants and lower them to my thighs. He stroked my ass, the only warning he'd give me before he started.

SMACK!

The pain exploded over my skin as his rough hand connected with my ass. The next strike was harder, and he continued without pause, not giving me a number because he wouldn't stop until he was satisfied I'd learned my lesson.

I had, but I remained quiet, my eyes tearing with shame and humiliation. The pain was nothing compared to knowing every time his hand it my ass, it meant he still hadn't forgiven me.

SMACK! SMACK! SMACK!

The last slap seemed to echo around us. I lifted my head when another didn't come, tears spilling down my cheeks.

Xavier held my gaze, mouthing the words. "I love you. It's okay. You did well."

Luther stepped up to my side curving his hand under my jaw and claiming my lips in a bruising kiss. He spoke even as he kissed me. "You're so good, Alec. So fucking good. I'm proud of you."

His words soothed the pain, and it spread over me, mixing with the warmth deep within, settling me into a space where everything was right again. I smiled at him and he smiled back as he picked up the rope and unwound it.

"You're going to find it difficult to hold yourself up, but don't worry, I won't let you fall."

I wasn't sure what he meant until he'd wrapped the rope around my wrist, then pulled it down, pushing my feet together and wrapping the length of the rope around my knees. Only holding tight to the edge of the desk kept me from losing my balance. I couldn't straighten. The pressure of the rope had me pushing out my ass to keep myself from slipping.

Cool lube spilled between my ass cheeks. The head of Luther's dick slipped in it as he positioned himself. He filled me with one smooth thrust.

A shocked cry escaped my lips. I groaned as Luther dug his fingers into my abused skin, his hands moving to my hips as he pulled me up to meet the steady pounding of his dick. Already the rough treatment blurred the lines between pain and pleasure. Precum moistened the tip of my dick. But I wouldn't come.

Not until he let me. And I had a feeling he wouldn't let me come while he used me.

This was part of Xavier's punishment as well.

And his reward.

"We've spoiled you so much, being gentle, letting you spend so much time away from us. I think that needs to change." Luther's voice was husky as he quickened his pace, letting his pelvis hit my tender ass with each thrust. "There are so many things I want to do to you. That I want to watch Xavier do to you. Look at him. Look at how bad he wants you."

Looking at Xavier I could see how much it took for him not to fight the restraints. Eyes wide, pupils dilated, he spread his thighs as though any pressure on his dick was painful.

"Who do you belong to, Alec? Who does this body belong to?" Luther fucked me as though he hadn't had me in too long, even though barely a day went by when I wasn't beneath him. When he assured me he'd never had enough. "Tell me."

"You." I rasped out, the moans and cries drawn out every time he slammed into me making my voice useless. "Both of you."

"Fuck...yes!" Luther came hard, driving into me as he let out a final shout. He leaned over me, grabbing my chin and kissing me, slow and wet and hard. "You'll feel this for days. Maybe I won't be too rough with you." He smiled against my lips. "So long as Xavier is."

Pulling away, he left me there, clinging to the desk, my ass still hot and slippery from him. He pulled out a key and undid Xavier's handcuffs.

Xavier came to me as though he couldn't contain himself any

longer, pants already undone, his dick swollen and red. He raked his hands into my head, jerking my head back as he drove into me.

He wrapped an arm around my waist, pinning me to him, chest to my back, his lips on my throat. "Oh God, I didn't realize how much I'd enjoy you fucking messy for me. His cum is still hot inside you. The way you're clenching around me...how badly do you need to come, Alexander?"

"Please." Was all I could manage. Him holding still was driving me insane. "Please. Please. Please."

"Yes. Beg for me." He drew out, then pressed in, teasing the ring of muscle until I was straining back to take more of him. "My beautiful slut. I love Luther's plan, don't you? What if we kept you like this for days? Do you think that would help you relax?"

"Mmm. Fuck yes." I hissed in a breath as he bit into my shoulder, right through the fabric of my shirt. "Agh!"

"Louder." He began working his dick in and out of me, teasing my opening still, but going deeper each time. "Scream for me, my little toy. I want to see how much noise you can make."

Desperate for him to fill me, I screamed out his name, shouting with relief when he began driving into me mercilessly, hitting my prostate, biting me again, almost hard enough to break the skin. He kept me on the precipice with erotic pain and pleasure, balancing it in a way that quieted my mind and let me escape into the sensations.

Just when I thought I'd be there forever, Luther whispered in my ear. "You may come with him. I want to hear you both."

I cried out, clenching down on Xavier, which had him shouting and fucking me so fast and hard my hands slipped.

Luther caught me, holding me in place as I came and the last of my strength evaporated. He braced me against the desk as Xavier pulled out, letting the last of his cum hit my ass. If I'd been messy before, now I was completely ruined. But it was the kind of hot and dirty I fucking loved.

None of us moved for the longest time. Xavier didn't seem capable as he leaned against me, kissing my shoulder and whispering words I couldn't make out. Luther unbound my wrists, then my knees, shifting me just enough so I was supported between them.

Finally, he lifted me up and carried me over to Xavier's chair, sitting with me in his lap. He wrapped one arm around Xavier's waist when the other man came to stand beside us.

"Next time, we do this at home." Luther kissed my hair and let out a tired laugh. "You both need to fix your schedules so we have more time together there. Otherwise, I'm going to start sleeping on Xavier's desk."

"Oh, did I forget to tell you?" Xavier moved away from Luther, a sly smile on his lips as he braced his hip against the desk and faced us both. "I've decided to give everyone a long weekend. After Alexander finishes school tomorrow, we can have all the time we want."

"Shit, I almost forgot about school." I let my head drop back against Luther's shoulder. "After this, you need to give me some time to recover. I'm not sure I can walk."

Xavier let out a soft, dark laugh. "You won't need to. In all our time together, you still haven't seen my room. That will change. I've even made some…modifications. Just for you."

That sounded a little scary. Luther's room had plenty of toys. Several we'd played with already. He enjoyed his impact play and restraints. I loved it too, but Xavier was a bit more twisted. And I'd only gotten a small taste of what he liked.

"I know I said you don't scare me." I tipped my head back and shivered a little at the look in his eyes. "But you are now."

"Good." He bent down to kiss me, a wicked slant to his smile. "Because we're just getting started."

Gilded

Chapter One

Every cut of the fabric, every color, every fit...absolutely perfect. Nothing left to chance, from design to presentation, every name on the guest list carefully selected to either spread the word or invest a fortune. My reputation had drawn them to the fashion show with coveted personal invites, but many faces in the crowd belonged to those who'd love to see me fail.

A shame I'd have to disappoint them. Despite the risk involved, this new venture was already a success. The clothing line I'd almost eliminated now the potential crown jewel, set to make my company stand out in the fashion industry.

But it, like too many things lately, was out of my control.

Which left me standing on the sidelines as the arrogant vultures swarmed vulnerable prey. Not that I'd remain here if there was a hint that they'd cause real damage, but I'd do a fair bit myself if I hovered.

"He'll be fine." Luther leaned close as he handed me another glass of champagne, his tone the low, soothing one that tempted me to surrender the power I'd always craved. His lips brushed my ear as he whispered, "I believe he's earned a reward for a job well done."

Sipping the *Nicolas Feuillatte* champagne I'd been gifted and opened for this special occasion, I kept my expression carefully neutral as Alexander Tremaine, the assistant director for the junior line of Ashburne Style and Media Company, made his way through the crowd filling the ostentatiously glitzed up hotel ballroom. The young man had just turned twenty, and really had no business with the position he held, but being the owner gave me the advantage of not giving a fuck what anyone thought.

Alexander had proven himself invaluable in how well he related to the members of my staff. Yes, he was learning much about the fashion business—between school and simple hands-on experience—but it would take years before he developed the skills required. However, his fearlessness when he strode into my office and shared the ideas of my employees was why I'd ignored the typical hierarchy of management and placed him where I needed him most.

The place I *wanted* him was on his knees, but that could wait until we got home.

"He's earned much, but if you don't stop looking at him like you want to bend him over the closest table and fuck him, our peers may question exactly *how* he earned it." I smirked against the lip of my glass as Luther tore his gaze from Alexander and frowned at me. "His only rule, Luther. We don't make it obvious he belongs to us while he's working. Wasn't it you who reminded me to respect that?"

Luther Cross, my long-time partner in both business and in life, was the only person I was comfortable relaxing with and teasing—for the longest time the only one I was personal with at all. He'd been my friend since our teens, a constant presence, and I wouldn't have survived without him.

He'd become my head of security, preferring to protect me and the company rather than spend his days surrounded by sequins and shimmering fabric. Which was for the best since his fashion sense didn't extend beyond his ties not clashing with his suits.

Tall and muscular, with dark brown skin, deep brown eyes, and black hair that he kept closely trimmed at the sides, but thick enough at the top to enjoy the soft texture of the tight curls, Luther had a presence that drew me to him the second he stepped into a room. Giving in would be so easy, but I'd fought to keep my distance for the longest time, unwilling to let his strength over-power my own. Away from work, I'd indulged from time to time, but until Alexander joined us, we'd had an understanding that suited us both.

A relationship that didn't interfere with my ambitions. That didn't require either Luther or me to sacrifice anything. When either of us craved tenderness, we'd find a submissive young man or woman to play with, setting careful boundaries so the toy wouldn't upset the tenuous balance we'd achieved.

Without even trying, Alexander had tipped the scale, forcing us —forcing *me*—to see how fragile our relationship had become. Luther didn't want a toy to play with, he wanted a man to love. One who would love him in return.

That a boy he'd plucked off the streets—literally, though Alexander had been stealing my car at the time—satisfied my man in a way I'd failed to unsettle me at first. The young thief had seemed like a threat. Instead, he'd managed to bring Luther and I closer together. Proved there was no limit to what we could give. To one another. To him.

Watching him from across the room was difficult, but giving him space was the only way to let him bask in the spotlight. As always, he made sure Judy Stockette, head of the junior line, got full credit for leading the project, but standing at her side he prac-tically glowed with pride. In a dark purple suit, with a bright blue tie, he caught the attention of every influencer in the room. He'd quickly become a fashion icon in an industry where many strug-gled their whole lives to simply be noticed. But to me, he was so much more.

That boyish smile, the fervor in eyes a blue I'd kill to match in a masterpiece of fabric, but selfishly wanted to keep to myself. Light golden blond hair spilled in a stylish mess, long enough to grip in passion or stroke with tender affection. He was spirited, eager to learn and to be something to everyone, so full of hope and excitement I'd never get enough of having him close, of soaking in that pure warmth I'd considered out of reach.

I had a hard time trusting love, but I couldn't deny how I felt about him.

"You're looking at him like he's your whole world." Luther placed his hand on the base of my spine, his lips brushing the sensitive spot behind my ear and making me shiver. "I love that he's helped draw out this side of you. I missed it."

Considering my own warning to Luther, I pulled my gaze away from our submissive and observed the attendees who'd be taking their seats shortly around the runway as Judy and Alexander presented the latest in the rejuvenated line dedicated to teens. Before the guests had arrived, I'd gone to the dressing room on Alexander's insistence, giving my final stamp of approval for every piece that would be showcased tonight.

As expected, there was not a single outfit I wasn't proud to have my name on.

Alexander's official debut in the fashion world would be a success. Still, I was eager to get him home. Luther was right. He deserved to be rewarded for his hard work.

I shot Luther a slanted smile. "You have no problem demanding that 'side of me' now."

"Mmhmm." Luther let out a soft chuckle, his hand moving down to the curve of my ass. "You like me demanding."

"But not so much *distracting*." Shifting away from him, I glanced around to make sure no one had noticed him being too familiar in public. We'd kept our relationship discrete over the years to avoid becoming the focus of lewd tabloids. Giving the bottom-feeding journalists *anything* tonight that would take the focus off Judy and Alexander was unacceptable.

Luther straightened, letting his hand fall to his side with a slight nod. "Shall we take our seats and enjoy the show? This is my last night with you for the next few weeks, and I didn't want to spend it here, but I know how important this is to you both."

"It is. And I'm glad you came." I moved with him, taking my reserved seat next to the raised runway, the glasslike surface under-lit with lights that would shift from pure white to rainbow hues. From this position, Alexander could see me at a glance from behind the curtains if he needed moral support. He'd been content to remain in the background, letting the designers and Judy steal the show—along with the outfits, of course—but none of this would be happening if not for him. Which was why I'd had a new logo created for the line.

The stylized A to represent him, along with my signature to show I stood behind him, win or lose.

With how well he connected with people, I wasn't surprised that he'd excelled at schmoozing with all the most important buyers, but once the lights in the room dimmed and the spotlight hit the stage, my pulse sped up and I couldn't watch the models. I kept my eyes on the heavy black curtains. Willed him to look out. To catch my eye so I could reinforce all I'd said to him before.

"You've got this, Alexander." I curved my hand around the back of his neck, drawing him close and brushing his hands away from where he fidgeted with his tie. "Don't be nervous. Look at me. Now and when you're up there. One look and you'll see how much faith I have in you. You know I wouldn't take a risk with the company just because I love you. You believe in the team I've given you. And you made me believe in them too."

"That's the problem." Alexander pressed his eyes shut and drew in a shaky breath. "If I was wrong, I lose nothing. And they lose everything."

"That's not a problem." I kissed his forehead. "It's motivation."

Relaxing back into my seat, my lips curved as the last model came out, wearing the piece that had frightened Alexander the most. Soft murmurs rose from the crowd, a hint of the excitement and admiration I'd expected.

The design was bold. Extravagant. Art in motion.

Alexander didn't have the experience to predict whether the dress would be a hit or a flop, but I'd done my best to reassure him. Perhaps laughing at him hadn't helped, but he'd accused me of 'Just being nice.'

Nice, was not a word used to describe me. It was cute that he tried to see me that way—maybe I should try harder to leave him with his illusions.

A small part in the side stage curtain drew my attention, too dark beyond to make out his face, but I could sense him there. From having been there myself, I knew he could see me. Pressing my hand to my chest, I inclined my head slightly as the pièce de résistance reached the end of the catwalk. The off-shoulder gown in black silk and torn rainbow tulle wasn't an everyday look, but it would be perfect for high school proms and fancy events. Just this morning I'd received calls from two starlets attending award ceremonies who'd gotten a sneak peek and commissioned custom versions of the gowns to wear.

Alexander still didn't fully understand that what walked across the catwalk represented artwork that would be imitated and reflected on in ways that would make the company millions. What we did here decided what would be trendy tomorrow. What would be created from the most exclusive brands, down to the cheapest knockoffs.

From the whispers around me I'd no doubt he'd hit a homerun, simply by listening better than I could. By passing the message in a way I was willing to hear. He was my ambassador. My eyes and ears within a company I'd founded which had become so overwhelmingly immense I had to filter out the noise. Delegate to people I trusted.

People like him.

Thundering applause followed the presentation of the last piece. Judy took the stage and thanked everyone for coming, then invited Alexander to join her.

He strode up to her side with so much confidence, I had to

fight to sit still and not cheer for him simply taking those few steps into the public eye.

My pulse pounded when Judy handed him the mic.

This wasn't the plan. He should have been able to smile at a brief mention, give a little bow, then walk away while Judy welcomed everyone to come to her with inquiries.

I fisted my hand on my thigh as Alexander stared out at the crowd.

Luther put his hand over mine and squeezed.

"Uh…I…" Alexander cleared his throat. Red blotches formed on his cheeks. "Thank you, Judy. And thank you all for coming. I know I'm new at this, but I'd have to be bli—" He cut himself off, as though realizing his next words could be a PR nightmare. He cleared his throat again and I winced. "The talent in these designs is obvious. I'm grateful to be part of this."

He handed the mic back to Judy, spun around, and dashed behind the curtain.

I moved to stand, but Luther tightened his grip on my knee and leaned close. "Judy will distract them, but if you get up now, it will draw more attention to how awkward he was. Wait until everyone is spread out, enjoying refreshments. Then we can both go see him."

Grinding my teeth, I inclined my head. Luther was right, but I couldn't help glare at Judy as she glided around the room in her peach silk gown, composed and at ease with the focus from the buyers. Exactly what I expected from her, but Alexander should be there as well. This was *his* moment.

He'd disagree.

True. Judy had worked on this line before Alexander joined the company. But I'd been ready to let her go because she'd never convinced me the junior line was worth my time. She was young, an amazing designer, but far too timid.

Maybe I'd done something to make her afraid to approach me, but I doubted it. Her gender certainly wasn't an issue, the majority of the management here was made up of women. None of them hesitated to present their ideas, though Alexander had bridged the gap between me and some talented young designers and interns who wouldn't dare meet my eyes on an elevator.

Because of Alexander, the company benefited from innovation that had been lacking before. I'd accept the blame for being so out of touch with my employees, but how could any of them be grateful for his intervention, yet still put him in a position he wasn't ready for?

As I made my way out of the rows of seats with Luther, I spotted Judy with a fashion editor from a prestigious magazine. As she spoke she turned toward me, then motioned for me to join them.

My jaw ticked at the delay, but I still had a job to do.

"Mr. Ashburne, I was hoping I'd get to speak to you tonight." The skinny blonde—who'd likely tried to be a model before exploring editorials—offered her hand. "My name is Mindy MacKinnon. I'd love to know your thoughts on this newest line."

"A pleasure to meet you, Mindy." I shook her hand, then gave her my most professional smile. "I'm proud of every line under the Ashburne name, but Judy is the artist and the master behind everything you've seen tonight. You're already speaking to the right person."

"But what about Alexander Tremaine? Why is he suddenly so important?"

I stared at her. Then glanced over at Judy whose lightly tanned skin paled. The truth would ruin the night for her and she was Alexander's friend. That I didn't like her much right now didn't matter. "He's an important part of the team, but the models owned the stage. Once you're finished interviewing Judy, please feel free to speak to a few of them. They're very excited to represent the junior line."

"They really are!" Judy patted her sleek brown hair in its intricate up-do, shot me an uncertain look, then drew the editor away, still gushing. "I was honored to work with such a diverse cast. You've never seen anything like this."

Heading backstage, I carefully checked my irritation with Judy against my protectiveness of Alexander. She hadn't overstepped. If he'd been anyone else with his title, expecting him to say a few words would be nothing.

But Alexander had been off the streets for less than six months. He hadn't developed the 'thick skin' expected in this industry. No one besides me and Luther knew where he came from. The trauma of his past. He wanted everyone working for me to treat him as an equal. And Judy had.

The fear he'd shown on that stage wasn't on her. Wasn't on any of us. But as a man who loved him, I'd hide him away until he was ready to face the spotlight again. Remind him how strong he was. Comfort him. Not something I was good at, but I wouldn't be alone. Luther would be with me.

Until tomorrow, at least.

As I made my way backstage the cheerful chatter faded away, then died with each intern, assistant, and model who glanced my way. My spine stiffened with the attempt to ignore the building tension. I wasn't some kind of monster, why were they all so damn careful around me? Yes, I lost my temper now and then when faced with incompetence, but always in my office with the door closed.

If I shouted when every person under my employ seemed to have slowed to a crawl it was simply to ensure they still had jobs the next day. And for years to come. I hadn't built a successful empire by being passive. My company employed the best in the industry on every level and applications poured in daily to fill coveted spots as we expanded, but upper management almost always rose from within. The one exception over the last eight years being Alexander.

The company had the best benefits compared to any other in the city and I'd made damn sure long ago that those who worked for me would be secure and happy here. The one thing I couldn't give them was more of myself, but that was to be expected. Fine, the trepidation might stem from knowing nothing of me save the sound of my voice carrying when someone fucked up, but the generous paychecks should make the occasional amped up pressure negligible.

"Little minnows, the lot of them." I muttered under my breath. "I'm surprised someone hasn't started playing the Jaws soundtrack."

"That can be arranged," Luther spoke quietly, but the amusement in his tone was loud and clear. "You'd frighten them less if you stopped scowling, you know." Luther's lips twitched as I turned my scowl on him. "Don't give me that look. You intimidate people. You're not interested in socializing, and I understand that. But if you don't want a room to go silent when you walk in, it wouldn't kill you to smile."

"What reason do I have to smile? Alexander is upset. I'm worried about him."

"Fair enough, but everyone here worked hard, and they need to know you're pleased."

"Then they'll receive bonuses for a job well done."

Luther sighed, shaking his head before continuing to the storage area at the back of the venue where all the showcase pieces were being carefully packed away, along with boxes of accessories, shoes, and props. Alexander spent his time here during setup, claiming he'd 'freak' if anything was damaged, but I suspected he felt more comfortable around the men and women who unloaded, then loaded up the company vans.

Across the room Alexander was opening a roll of tape with his teeth, laughing at whatever the man next to him said before playfully smacking the taller man's arm. He spat out a piece of plastic, glancing to his left when a young woman asked him something, grinning when the rest of the crew chimed in.

Looked like he was doing just fine on his own.

I started to turn.

Luther placed his hand on the base of my spine, forcing me to keep moving forward. "Hey, Alec. Thought we'd find you here."

Alexander's expression lit up for a split second before he

schooled his features, but his eyes still shone as he looked from Luther to me. He stood, passing the tape to the girl next to him before crossing the storage area, sidestepping boxes and racks.

The smile on his lips stole the urge to make a discreet exit. As detached as I tried to be, there was no way to steel myself against the warmth he shared so effortlessly.

Tie undone, jacket abandoned, Alexander was a complete mess, but at least he'd shaken off the embarrassment from being put on the spot. He stopped a few feet in front of us and hooked his thumbs to his pockets, rocking on his scuffed black dress shoes as though too full of energy to stand still.

"Everything's pretty much done, but I wanted to double check." Alexander licked his bottom lip, rocking again. "A few of us are going to a club to have drinks and celebrate. Did you guys wanna come?"

"Wouldn't you prefer to celebrate at home?" I used my most diplomatic tone, but an edge crept in at the mere thought of going to a crowded club. Surrounded by people shouting and shoving and stealing all the air from a too bright and too humid room… Never mind the incessant pulse of horrible music. He'd have been better off suggesting waterboarding for entertainment. "I bought that terrible movie you've been looking forward to."

Luther muttered a prayer even as Alexander spat out a laugh.

"The movie will be there tomorrow." Luther gave me a hard look the second I opened my mouth. He reached out and patted Alexander's shoulder. "Go have fun. I'm happy you're starting to make some friends—just give me a shout if you need me to pick you up."

"You sure?" Alexander chewed on his bottom lip in a way that was *not* conducive to me letting him go anywhere. He met my eyes, his own filled with uncertainty. "If you'd rather I come home, I will."

"I would." I could feel Luther glaring at me. Decided to throw him off by doing something completely out of character. "But I'll have you to myself for the next week. Enjoy your last night of freedom."

Somehow, Alexander managed to pale and blush at the same time. Absolutely adorable.

I looked forward to making him do that often when I had him back under my control.

"You almost had me there." Luther shook his head, lips curved. "You managed to be unselfish and overbearing all at once."

"He's scary even when he's sweet," Alexander spoke in a stage whisper, his golden blond hair spilling over one eye as he gave a mischievous smile. "Don't tell him I'm looking forward to *whatever* he plans to do to me."

"You're going to wish you hadn't said that." Luther glanced over at the packing people, taking Alexander's hand and drawing him closer when he saw they were all distracted. "I'm damn proud of you. The show you put on tonight—"

"Was *much* bigger than me." As always, Alexander refused to take any credit, but he looked down at his hand in Luther's and drew in a rough breath. "Maybe I shouldn't go. Xavier is right, this is your last night here. I'm gonna fucking miss you."

"Watch your language, boy. I'll miss you too, but I'll only be gone for a week. And you know I hate goodbyes." Luther squeezed Alexander's fingers. "Last night was ours. Tonight will be for me and Xavier. I'll wake you up in the morning for a quick kiss, while you're too tired to make me change my mind about leaving."

Nodding slowly, Alexander lowered his gaze. He was trying hard to be strong for Luther, but this was the first time in months he'd be without our man for more than a few hours. Even with work and school, Alexander still found time to be with Luther, cuddling while watching a movie, going to restaurants, or simply exploring the city. They went jogging together almost every morning.

A week without that, with only *me* to comfort him, would be difficult. Our relationship was strong, we worked well together, but I wasn't good at spending quiet moments with anyone. 'Date nights' were usually the three of us doing something on Luther's insistence. I'd cut down my schedule as much as possible to have meals with both my men at least a few times a week — still, it was rare I spent the night with either of them.

Strengthening our relationship was important, a priority…and yet, I was well aware that my efforts weren't nearly enough. Luther leaving would be my chance to up my game as a partner and a lover. He wasn't responsible for filling my role in Alexander's life, but I'd let him far too often. Just as I'd let Alexander give Luther what was missing from me.

The only way to change that would be to give our relationships the same relentless focus I gave my company all these years. And I'd considered a few ways to do that.

Until my plans were put into action, if Luther believed Alexander being with his new…*friends* would be good for him, I'd at least encourage that.

If they're using him, in any *way, I'll simply get creative about making them suffer.*

Smiling at the thought, I patted Alexander's arm. "Go on. You've earned this night. And I promise, the time will pass quickly. I've taken your advice and started training Tricia as my assistant. Over the next week, I'll let her take on more of my duties, which will free up time for us to spend together." The idea hadn't appealed at first, but seeing the shock on both Alexander and Luther's faces now spurred me on. "If all goes well, I may consider a vacation."

Luther blinked at me, lifting his hand to scratch his jaw, as though I'd given him a puzzle to solve. "You've never taken a vacation. I trust you'd tell me if you were sick?"

I arched a brow at him, refusing to dignify the question with an answer.

Alexander's eyes were troubled. "I mentioned Tricia was hoping for a promotion and she's really good with upper management, but I didn't know you needed more help. Aren't I still your PA?"

We'd discussed Alexander remaining on as my personal assistant, but with how well he'd done with the junior line I'd assumed he'd stay on, establishing himself in the more important role. Having him close at hand to indulge in sexual play during office hours had been enjoyable. I'd miss the time we spent together in my office.

However, part of improving our relationship meant not limiting our interactions to the bit of time I could spare between phone calls and paperwork. And it wasn't like he wouldn't be close enough to call in for impromptu...*meetings* if we both had the urge.

"We'll discuss your position at a later date, Alexander. I'd hoped the idea of a trip to some exotic location would be more appealing than sorting through my files, but if not—"

"No! I'd fucking love to take a trip." Alexander bit his bottom lip as Luther held up a finger.

One.

My lips slanted. If Luther was starting to count the rules being broken, maybe Alexander wouldn't be leaving with these new people after all. Swearing was a recent addition to the list, and only applied at work. Not a rule I would have considered, but Luther was the one who'd taken on Alexander's training.

Our submissive never made it to two and found security in the discipline. My punishments tended to be more immediate, my rules less involved, but the balance between Luther's tender micromanaging and my attention to structure worked out well. At least the power exchange was something we'd laid a solid foundation for.

"Alec, you coming?" The girl who'd been speaking to Alexander earlier called out, glancing uncertainly at Luther, then me. "Everything all right?"

"One sec!" Alexander called back. He stared up at Luther, swallowing hard. "Is me not going my punishment?"

Luther shook his head and squeezed Alexander's shoulder. "You want me to make you stay, but I won't do that, Alec. This will be good for you."

"Then what—"

"Wash my car while I'm gone. Naked." Luther chuckled as Alexander's lips parted. "Swearing equals chores. Was that not clear?"

"But you won't be there to enjoy the show."

"Which is what makes it a punishment. Because you'd have liked that very much." Luther gave Alexander a little nudge. "Now don't make me repeat myself. I may start to think you don't care to please me."

Chewing at his bottom lip, Alexander paused for a moment. "I'll go..." He cocked his head. "But I'm recording that shi—that. Me washing your car. See you in the morning!" He grinned and took off.

Shaking my head, I watched him go. "You had to put him in brat mode right before leaving, didn't you."

"You'll enjoy every minute." Luther turned with me, heading for the exit that led into the underground parking. "I want to know you're both having fun while I'm gone."

"I don't *do* fun." My lips thinned at his level look. "The things you and Alexander enjoy don't amuse me. I'll make an effort, but the idea of noisy movies and greasy food isn't the least bit appealing."

Inclining his head as we reached the town car parked at the far end of the lot, Luther stilled for a moment, a thoughtful expression on his face. "You have trouble with anything you don't find productive, but there are things you enjoy doing. Things I wish I'd convinced you to do more often."

"I wasn't open to suggestions for a very long time, Luther."

"But you are now." There was a wicked glint in his eye. One that immediately sent blood pulsing down low. His deep, gravelly tone was like a firm grip on my swelling erection, full of lust and power. "We'll discuss what I'll allow you to do with our pet. Once I've finished what I want to do to you."

Part of me wanted to resist. To put up a wall of arrogance and deny the need he stirred in me. I slammed the steel door I'd once used to shut Luther out on the urge and smirked. "My submission isn't as easy to claim as Alexander's."

Luther folded his forearms on the hood of the car, brow arched. "Is that a challenge?"

I opened the passenger side door. "Always."

Chapter Two

The echo of footsteps filled the hall as I made my way to the kitchen, anticipation sending sharp sparks along my nerves, as though every inch of my skin lit up just knowing Luther was near. Since I'd given the staff the night off, everyone had either gone home or retired to their wing of the house. The convenience of a butler and maids simplified life, but doors being open and tea waiting wasn't worth losing the bit of time I had left alone with my man.

Most of the lights were off, casting the halls in shadow, but the dim glow from the kitchen was more than enough. I passed the expensive paintings lining the walls, the thick, burgundy curtains drawn shut over long windows, ornate tables with pricey knick-knacks, all things I'd bought to make the mansion more like the place I'd grown up. As always, the display of wealth left me with a hollow feeling in my gut.

And still, I'd embraced this life, made it a showcase for the rich and famous who came here hoping to do business, to impress me, to make themselves feel important. I hated them almost as much as I needed them. Being shut away from all those I'd admired as a child had been a painful reminder of how far I'd fallen when my father disowned me.

Aside from Luther, no one knew how little the money actually meant to me. Of course I bought all the material things that would display my position, but more often than not my butler, Mr. Mathews, or Luther, made the purchases. I didn't enjoy having...*things*. What they stood for was much more important.

My father had tried to shame me. Had figured without him I would be nothing. He'd taken everything I'd ever known, isolated me, and likely hoped I'd disappear from his world.

The riches, every damn overpriced vase, every painting bought on auction for millions, every car, every piece of jewelry was to show him he'd failed. If my name wasn't in the papers for my accomplishments, it was there because I'd acquired something coveted by members of the 'one percent'.

Reaching the kitchen, I strode across the room, filled the kettle, and put it on. Every movement was stiff. My throat tightened as I struggled to shove away the memories that came every time I walked down that hall. I usually avoided going further than the stairway leading up to my room, or my office located on the other side of the entrance, but when Luther came to this section of the house I forced myself to move around my home as though it was completely natural.

If he suspected what being here did to me, he'd worry. Which was unacceptable.

As the kettle heated, Luther took a seat on a stool at the kitchen island, picking up a woman's magazine likely left there by the cook. She lived in the west wing of the house with a few of the maids even though I didn't eat enough to need her fulltime — having Alexander around finally gave her more to do. Her presence was comforting and she'd been with me longer than the rest of my staff. Left an abusive relationship after fifteen years the day I'd hired her.

Her youngest daughter had come with her, still too young to be out on her own. Eight years later and the young woman was going to Stanford University, a gift to her from me for letting her mother take the place of the one who'd abandoned me.

"Ms. Lacey was waiting for you." Luther set down the magazine. "Which means you skipped lunch. Likely breakfast as well."

The man was much too observant. I folded my arms over my chest and leaned back against the counter. "Perhaps she simply decided to spend time in the kitchen with the staff. Enjoy her day off."

"Even on her days off she makes sure you eat."

"You took Alexander out for breakfast and made him lunch. She likely assumed I ate with you or went out myself."

"But you didn't. You can't stand restaurants and only go to them for business meetings." Luther sighed and shook his head. "Xavier, I know you were worried about Alec, but you need to take better care of yourself."

The soft reprimand made me smile. As much as I didn't want Luther to worry, I loved that he cared. I always wondered if others, like my staff, cared only because I paid them well. Maybe not Abigail Lacey, I knew she was genuine, but I tried to shield her from my more self-destructive tendencies.

I couldn't hide anything from Luther.

"I had an energy bar this morning. Disgusting thing, but I promised you I'd have at least that if I couldn't stomach a full meal." I turned and opened the cupboard, pulling out two mugs. "I keep my promises."

"I know you do." Luther watched me fix the tea, his lips curving slightly. "You've gotten better at that. Do you remember when Ms. Lacey was making Thanksgiving dinner for your new business partners, rushing around because you'd forgotten to tell her Ted Brosner was allergic to nuts? You kept apologizing while trying to make yourself a tea and spilled the milk all over yourself. Almost knocked over the cup of boiling water before she took over."

My cheeks heated as I set down the kettle after filling both cups. I'd been all of twenty-one, with more money then I knew what to do with after several of my designs were bought by fashion moguls. I hadn't acquired the mansion yet, but I had a large house

I shared with Luther, the butler who'd left my father's employ to work for me, and several maids we'd had to hire to take care of the house.

An older entrepreneur had taken me aside at a big event and told me I should be producing my own designs, rather than selling them. Her name was Ashlee Madison, a transgender woman who worked on technological advances for several companies and had started her own business days before her fiftieth birthday, having established herself enough that even the most conservative were willing to work with her, even if in secret.

She came to my house with Ted Brosner, her long-time lover, both invested in my success for some reason I still couldn't fathom. They'd built the kind of life I wanted to have, so I'd invited them over. I'd been nervous. A complete mess. And Luther hadn't known how to calm me down.

But Ms. Lacey had. She'd worked for the elite before and considered me one of them, though I hadn't seen myself that way. She sent me away to change my suit, then sat me down at the table while the turkey was cooking.

"Xavier, baby, you're doing just fine. I wish you'd see that." She set a cup *of tea in front of me, just the way I liked it, even though she'd been there less than a day. She was a small woman, a mix of Chinese and Haitian, and one of the strongest people I'd ever met. "I hope you don't mind me being informal for a moment, but you remind me of my son. You're so young and you're trying to do so much. Someone needs to tell you they're proud of you. Will you let it be me?"*

That was the last time I remembered crying. I'd gone almost four years after being kicked out of my home and never shed a tear. I'd been too obsessed with proving I didn't need my father. Didn't need his money. Didn't care if he tried to cut me off from the only world I'd ever known. Didn't need the pathetic excuse for a family...

"I'm not paying you to coddle me." I lowered my gaze as the tears fell, *powerless to stop them. "But...thank you. And please don't tell Luther I...I*

*let this get to me. He's afraid that I'm not ready, but I am." I lifted my head
as she put her hand on my arm, the gesture making it so I stopped trying to
hide my tears. "I am."*

*She cupped my face in her hand. "I know you are, honey. But that man
of yours loves you. Don't be afraid to lean on him. He needs to know how
much you need him."*

*"And I need him to be here because he wants to be, not because he thinks
I can't do this on my own."*

*"Xavier, he doesn't think that. He believes in you. I hope one day you'll
realize letting people care for you isn't a weakness." She smiled and patted
my cheek. "Not that I'll give you a choice."*

If Ms. Lacey had been working for my fledgling company not
long after, I'd probably have fired her for that. But she was part of
the home I was trying to build, and she found a way to fill a role in
my life that no one else could. I'd still learned to close off part of
myself to her over the years, but no more than she allowed. She'd
helped me become the man I was today by refusing to back off,
while still letting me grow.

Even if she didn't always approve.

Her disapproval was a sign that I still had a long way to go.

She'd been expressing that disapproval more lately. Ever since
Alexander had come here. He'd been taken under her wing as
expected. If I hurt him in any way, she'd never forgive me.

For the next week, I'd have to make sure she was never too far.
Because I didn't trust myself not to fuck up. Alexander wasn't me.
He'd managed to survive losing his family without becoming hard
and cold and I wanted to keep it that way. But I was the last
person to show him how.

"What's bothering you, Xavier?" Luther stepped around the
island, taking the mug I handed him and studying my face. "You're
thinking hard."

Bringing my own mug to my lips, I inhaled the steam, letting
the warmth and the first sip center me. The brew was strong, with
no more than a splash of milk and half a teaspoon of sugar to bring

out the flavor. I set the mug on the gleaming granite countertop, rolling my shoulders and trying to sort through my thoughts.

"Any uncertainty may come across as a reason for you to stay and I won't allow that." I stroked my thumb up the side of the mug, my hand still curved around it. "You've been eager to see your brother after being apart for so long."

"I am cautiously optimistic, yes." The edge of his lips tightened slightly as he looked past me, his expression troubled. "He couldn't live with my 'lifestyle' before. Speaking to him over this past month has me believing he's changed his views, but we're strangers to one another now."

"That could change."

"And it might not." He sighed and shook his head. "I'm not certain I want it too. He's not the little boy who looked up to me, always wanting me to teach him things and tag along when I went out with my friends. He's the man who looked at me with disgust before cutting me out of his life. That fucking hurt."

I nodded slowly. We'd discussed this before, but Luther's words hadn't been so raw then. He'd been trying to talk himself into visiting his brother while giving me all the reasons he should. Had simply showing support been the right move? Telling him I'd be fine, that I'd spend time with Alexander, that I'd listen to Luther's second-in-command and be safe...had any of that been enough?

Grinding my teeth, I went to him, putting my hand over his on the cold slab of granite of the kitchen island. "I...am horrible at giving advice. I tried, but nodding and saying the right words clearly didn't work. Do you want to know what I really think?"

Cocking his head, Luther met my eyes. "It worries me that you have to ask."

"You owe the man nothing, Luther. And that's not what you wanted to hear, so I didn't say it. You don't have to forgive him." My tone sharpened as the anger I'd been holding back flowed freely. "You missed your mother's funeral because he refused to call you. He didn't call your father either. He's a selfish asshole and I don't want him given a chance to hurt you again."

Wincing, Luther lowered his gaze. "My father forgave him."

I let out a bitter laugh. "His choice. One he had every right to make, but pulling away from you because you didn't make the same one was fucked up."

When Luther went still, not looking at me, not replying for the longest time, I cursed myself for opening my fool mouth. I had no right to judge his family. My parents were both alive and liked pretending I was dead. Changing my last name had helped them. Those who hadn't known me before I'd been disowned didn't connect me to them now. If not for the infrequent articles mentioning my past as the heir to the Redstone oil company, a multi-billion dollar legacy I'd lost by choice, I'd be completely erased.

"You're right." Luther let out a soft laugh and cupped my cheek in his hand, a tender gesture it was hard not to pull away from. I would have once. Instead, I met my man's calm gaze as he continued. "Everything you've just said occurred to me, but forgiveness is always expected. The pain someone causes you is always less important than your willingness to accept an apology. As if words heal a damn thing. As if easing guilt is now your responsibility."

I inclined my head. "If I'd told you not to go—"

"I'd have been angry with you. Stop wondering if you're behaving human enough, Xavier." Luther pulled me against him. "The man you are hasn't been with us long. And yet, I love him as much as I loved the man you'd tried so hard to be."

That made me laugh. "I am the same person, Luther. A new name didn't change that."

"I disagree. Edmund Redstone The Third was a talented young man, but his family was killing him. Smothering him with expectations." Luther fisted his hand around my tie, his deep brown eyes darkening as he held my gaze. "Xavier Ashburne is a survivor. And he shut away—*you* shut away—the fragile side of yourself. And I understand why you did. But you're slowly letting it back in. Edmund is gone. But who you are is who he'd have wanted to be."

Shaking my head, I grinned up at Luther. "You're a sentimental fool. And I love that about you."

"Which is why you won't stop me from leaving in the morning."

"Yes." I groaned as the point of the conversation hit me. Luther didn't need me to help him sort out his misgivings, he'd already come to peace with them. He appreciated my honesty, but this was one of his lessons. "Loving you doesn't mean shielding you from pain. It means being there as you heal, someone you can count on not to hurt you."

"You always try not to, Xavier. None of us are perfect. You've hurt me when you've shut me out. You were afraid to love me. Just like you're afraid to love Alexander." He smoothed my tie and stepped back, as though to avoid his touch distracting from his words. "He sees you're trying. And when he's hurting, he'll come to you. Let him fail. Let him be the one to tell you if you're not giving him what he needs. Let what you share be imperfect."

"Unless what we're sharing is him tied up and opened wide for my pleasure." My lips slanted. "Then mistakes aren't an option."

"True. Don't break him."

"Even a little?"

"You scare me when you're trying to be cute." Luther smirked. "Or is this an invitation?"

"I have no idea what you're talking about." I leaned back against the island, smiling at him, eyes hooded. "And I'm never *cute*."

With a low laugh, Luther nodded toward my tie. "Take it off if you don't want it ruined. I know how fussy you are about your silks."

His words were both arousing and irritating. Letting Luther take control was a high, but there was always a moment before I gave in that I couldn't help resisting. To put me in the submissive mindset, he'd say things like this. Call me adorable, which I wasn't. Tease me about being uptight until I needed to prove him wrong.

Jerking at my tie, I pulled it free, then let it fall to the floor. My stomach twisted as I considered the work that had gone into crafting the fine piece of fabric, acquired from an ethical company I'd supported at its founding. The intricate pattern in the fine silk was hand woven over months. I'd traveled to India to make sure the labor standards were up to par and was impressed with what the company was doing for the community. Only a piece of material, but I wasn't able to detach myself from it as I did so easily with people.

Luther bent down and picked up the tie. "Don't ever do that again. I was teasing you, Xavier. I know how much everything you wear means to you."

"They're just clothes." Still, I watched him set the tie on the counter, fisting my hand by my side so I wouldn't be tempted to reach out and neatly fold it. "I enjoy your passion."

"You enjoy my restraint more. Over you and myself." Luther stepped up to me and reached for the top button of my shirt. "Today wasn't a day for you to dress in what you'd consider 'casual wear'." He slipped one button free of the fine, ivory-white cotton. "Taking this off you is like removing armor, a piece at a time, and I know *exactly* what it does to you."

I pressed my eyes shut as he undid another button. Carefully. Too careful for some. Torn fabric and buttons flying, was always portrayed as so much sexier, but the way he slipped every smooth mother-of-pearl button through the hole stole the urge to take over. It was as though the buttons remaining attached, the material undamaged, grounded me. Brought me to where I'd be able to surrender without a fight.

Not that I didn't enjoy the fight at times. When Luther came to my room in the middle of the night, while I was lounging in my bed in nothing but boxers, I enjoyed giving him a bit of a challenge. My physical activity was always so tame. Running on a treadmill. Lifting weights and doing cardio according to my trainer's strict regime. When Luther had begun exploring his control over me I'd realized I enjoyed a bit of wrestling. Being held down. Being taken.

What he was doing now was something else.

"There we go." Luther finished with the last button, then eased the shirt off my shoulders, freeing each arm in a smooth motion. He laid the shirt next to the tie. "When you're with Alec, put on a pair of jeans. Take yourself out of your comfort zone." His hard look killed any protest. "Take the next step, Xavier. Don't wear the armor with him, he doesn't know how to get past it. Give him you. Completely raw. He needs to be able to trust you, but that trust has to be given as well."

Inhaling slowly through my nose, I nodded once. "I will."

"Good." Luther undid my belt, set it aside, then slipped the button of my pants free, holding my gaze. "Do you have any idea how precious your surrender is to me? I know what it costs you. I know you see being vulnerable as a weakness. But you're strong. So much stronger than you know. And that's where I failed. Because I never made sure you did."

As he bent down to lower my pants, waiting as I stepped out of one leg, then the other, I wondered how he could maintain his dominance while tending to me like this. My butler helped me dress at times, when I was in a hurry, listening to details about a new business partner while my assistant transcribed my responses to emails and messages. He'd quickly button my shirt and fix my tie while my mind was caught between a dozen different tasks.

A detached routine I'd become accustomed to. This with Luther was new. And once I was standing there, facing him in nothing but my boxers, while he remained fully dressed, there was no way I was giving out orders.

Hands still fisted by my sides, I watched him warily as he stepped away and went to the cupboard, pulling out a small tub. My brow furrowed when I realized it was coconut oil.

Are we baking?

His lips slanted. "We've improvised before, Xavier. Remember the conditioner in my college dorm?"

"There were no alternatives." I wet my bottom lip with my tongue as he opened the tub of oil, white and solid, with a slightly sweet scent that reminded me of piña coladas. "There are plenty in my room."

"But we're not *in* your room." Luther scooped out a bit of oil on his finger, bringing it to my chest and letting it melt on my skin. "I love the scent and I want it all over you. I want to slide against you, inside you, and know that you're covered in nothing but what I've put there."

His finger slipped over my nipple and I hissed in a sharp breath. I didn't know how to react to Luther slowly attending to every inch of my skin, heating it with his touch, softening it with the oil. The sensation was luxurious, the glide of his fingers mesmerizing as he spread the oil over my chest, up over my shoulders, down to my pecs, my ribs, my stomach. I jerked when he reached my hips, leaning against the counter as he knelt and hooked his slick fingers to the edge of my boxers. He eased them over my swollen erection, letting them fall as he turned his attention to my thighs.

Fully exposed, my dick strained forward, aching for his touch, but he ignored it. He set the tub of oil on the floor by his knee, continuing to massage it over my skin, covering my thighs, my knees, his lips close to my cock as he reached down and slicked the oil over my shins and feet.

On his way back up he smoothed the heated liquid over my calves. Then the back of my knees, which had my legs shaking. I put my hands behind me, bracing myself on the counter as his hands stroked over the back of my thighs. My ass clenched, but he didn't touch it.

Instead, he rose and cupped my cheek again, smiling at me. "Don't try to anticipate what I'll do next, Xavier. I like keeping you off guard."

"And torturing me, it seems." I swallowed as he massaged my shoulders with his slick hands. "Why are you doing this?"

Luther kissed me, a soft press of his lips, gliding his hands down my arms, then wrapping his hands around my wrists. "I was remembering our first time. You were so full of self-hatred before that, you wouldn't even touch me anymore. You'd defied your father after a few kisses. Told him you loved me. Then struggled to make it on your own. Found someone willing to support you and suddenly love didn't matter anymore. If I'd known that night what would happen after, I'd never have let you go."

"Neither of us would be where we are today if I hadn't made that sacrifice."

"No, but we'd be together. And you wouldn't still be tearing down all those walls you put up."

"I don't know who I'd be, Luther. My father tried to destroy me. He failed. That was all that mattered."

Curving his hand around the back of my neck, Luther pressed his forehead to mine as he tightened his grip. His eyes had gone dark. Hard. "I would have protected you."

I pressed my eyes shut. "But I wasn't ready to let you."

My man still didn't know how far I'd fallen before I'd been ready for him to pull me out of the pit I dove into, head first. But not a day passed when I didn't remember.

For two years I'd been cut off from the world I'd grown up in. My only ties from the past were Luther— who I'd met in high school and fallen in love with —and my father's ex-business partner. Joel Bradley was old money, established enough that being shunned by my father didn't diminish his prospects, but when he heard I'd been disowned, he encouraged me to file for emancipation. Then provided the funds for me to find my own place.

For a price, but one I didn't anticipate. In his fifties, Joel reminded me of my father. A kinder, more attentive version. He reached out to me while I was crashing on the sofa at Luther's parent's house. Offered to provide a place to live, the means to finish my schooling at the private school both Luther and I attended. He said he was lonely and would appreciate if I visited now and then.

For almost two years he'd asked for nothing else. At times I was uncomfortable in his presence. The way he watched me was too intense. His questions too personal. Aside from Luther, his parents and mine, he was the only one who knew I was bisexual.

A few days after my eighteenth birthday he finally told me what he expected for all he'd given me. I'd gotten a scholarship to an elite art program I'd applied to. He told me he could take that away. And I believed him.

The career I hoped to build with the one skill I had was my only way to prove my father wrong. I wasn't pathetic. Or worthless. I had so many dreams.

But to reach them, I'd have to let Luther go.

I didn't want to.

Joel laughed when I told him I was in love. He knew Luther's name. He said he would ruin him too.

I had twenty-four hours to give him an answer.

Not enough, but I went to Luther, knowing this would be our last time together. I couldn't tell him why because he'd stop me. And I loved him too much to let him face the consequences of my decision.

The second Luther opened the door, I threw myself at him. He laughed and held me close, kissing my neck, helping me pull off my cheap T-shirt. The kind of clothes Joel told me would destroy any chance I had at a future. He'd provide better. Did what it would cost me really matter?

Luther tugged me to the shower, whispering that he'd hoped I wanted him as much as he wanted me, but thought I'd changed my mind.

"Don't stop." He groaned as I sucked along the side of his neck. "Fuck, Edmund, you—"

"Xavier. I'm Xavier now."

"Xavier, you don't like to get messy. I just finished working out and I'm all gross. Come with me to clean up. There's nothing wrong with this. With us. Please just…" Luther stumbled into the bathroom, holding me against him as he slammed into the side of the sink. "Tell me you want this."

"I want you." My throat tightened because I did. I wanted him now. And forever. But we couldn't have that. "Don't make me think. Tell me what to do."

Tugging off my shirt, Luther lifted me up into his strong arms, kissing me again, trying to get us both naked as he moved closer to the shower. "Don't regret me, Xavier. Don't hate what we have. I'm sorry you lost every-thing. But we can get it back. Together."

"You are what I have." I slid down Luther's body, shoving his boxers off

*his hips, then dropping to my knees as he reached over to turn on the shower.
"You're everything."*

*Lips sliding over his dick, I let out a soft moan as he cupped the back of
my head and thrust in deeper. We'd fooled around before, kissing and grinding, even jerking one another off once or twice. But not this. This had been
how my father pictured me. A man's whore. On my knees with a dick in my
mouth.*

*The rough pressure almost got me off, but before I could come, Luther
pulled me up and into the shower, he lifted me, bracing my back against the
wall.*

"I want to feel you. No one else. I can't imagine wanting anyone else."
*Luther fumbled the conditioner, opening it behind my bowed back and
dumping some in his palm. "Tell me you want me too."*

*As Luther's slick fingers filled me, I forced myself to remember it was
him. To shut away Joel whispering what he would do to me. What I'd told
him he could have. He wasn't here.*

Luther was.

Only Luther.

*And I'd remember this when I was finally free. When I could come back
to him.*

*His fingers left me and he let me set one foot on the floor, lifting the other
and pressing me against the wall as he positioned his dick. He rocked
forward, the head of his dick easing in, then slipping away. He kissed me as
he tried again, driving his fingers in deep before guiding his dick to my slick
hole.*

*"This isn't working." Luther tried to lift me, still kissing me. "You're so
fucking tight."*

*I pressed my hands on his shoulders, nudging him away, then turning,
my hands braced on the tiled wall. "This will be easier."*

*"But I want to see you, Xavier. I don't want you to shut down. I want to
know I'm not hurting you."*

"You won't. I trust you."

*Groaning, Luther stepped behind me, kissing my shoulder as he used
more conditioner to slick his fingers. "Relax. Show me what you can take."*

His fingers filled me, faster than I'd expected, but when he worked two in deep and began thrusting, I pressed back, needing more. And he gave it to me. His fingers slipped away and his dick slid, over and over, pressing, then easing back. He slapped his hand against the wall as the head of his dick stretched me.

Gasping in air, I fought not to pull away from the intense burn.

"Shh, let's wait. Try to relax."

I laughed at Luther's calm tone. "I think your fist would feel better in my ass."

"Do you want me to try that first?"

"I don't know. Is your dick bigger than your fist?"

Luther chuckled and kissed my shoulder. "No. But I've done this with dildos. It will feel good. Just press back and stop clenching. Like you did with my fingers."

We both moaned as I followed his instructions and the head of his dick breeched my ass. I was completely open. Vulnerable. And it scared me, but this was Luther. Feeling him, even with the burn, was the purest thing I'd ever felt.

Shoving back, I let out a rough sound as another inch filled me.

"Oh fuck." Luther, slid back, then forward again. "Xavier, I wish you could see this. Your ass is stretching around me. Holding me so tight. Pulsing around me." He pressed a finger against the rim holding him, "So fucking tight, but you're taking it all." More pressure and I jerked forward, then back. "I want to open you up more. Hold still."

His dick inside me, only a few inches, was almost overwhelming, but also…perfect. The way he touched me was perfect. My vision blurred as he squirted more conditioner over where we were connected. He eased out, then in, his finger tracing where I was stretched around his cock.

"What are you doing, Luther?" I panted, but rocked back against him, feeling his eyes on me. "You should be fucking me."

"I should, but you relaxed more when I did this. Like I overwhelmed whatever's in your head, holding you back." He curved one hand around my hip, holding me still as he slid his dick in deeper. His pelvis hit my ass. His finger had gone and I tried moving again. He tightened his grip and his finger returned as his dick slid out. "You're prepared for my dick, but not the extra sensation of my finger."

"Your dick is enough."

"Is it?" Luther drew out all the way. Latched onto my hips with both hands and thrust back in. I braced myself, wanting to show him I could handle anything he threw at me. "What if I want to give you more?"

"Take it. Take everything." The burning had eased as my body adjusted to Luther's girth. But then he withdrew, curving his finger inside me instead, exploring my body, my reactions. It shifted my attention. Made it harder to predict what he'd do next. "More."

His fingers filled me. Three. Then four. I moaned, begging for his dick again. He gave it to me. Stretching me with it. Moving slow. Opening me more and more. Leaving me and using his fingers again, curving, stroking, and I cried out. Jutted back until almost his whole hand was inside me. I wanted it. His fingers, his dick. My hands slipped on the tiled wall and I whimpered when he turned the shower off.

"I need you in my bed."

My legs didn't work properly as he guided me, half carrying me, to his bed. He laid me on it, the bottle of conditioner in his hand.

Then he went still. "Xavier, I should be using a condom."

"Have you been with anyone else?"

"No. Have you?"

I shook my head. "No. Please don't stop. I love this. You're driving me crazy and I love it."

Eyes darkening with pleasure, he knelt between my thighs, pushing them apart and tipping the bottle of conditioner until the cool liquid dripped over my balls and down to my over-sensitized hole. His dick was hard and glistening, jutting up against his stomach, but he seemed too fascinated with toying with my body to take his own pleasure.

"I don't think this virgin ass is ready for my fist, but one day…" Luther's lips curved as he sank two fingers in deep. "Fuck…the things I want to do to you."

With a breathless laugh, I writhed impatiently on the bed, lifting my hips to make him move faster. "If you could get back to fucking me, that would be awesome."

He shook his head, tapping the tips of his fingers against my prostate, smirking when I jerked and slammed my head back into the pillow. "Not yet.

It'll be over too fast. You stayed away from me for too long, Xavier. I want you begging. I want you to need me so much you'll never even think of leaving me again."

How I hadn't figured out that night how much Luther craved control, how good he was at wielding it, was beyond me. He'd drawn our first time out for hours. Took me fast our second time. Then shocked me by proving I could be aroused without getting hard for the longest time, a mess of need, simply drowning in sensations.

That night he'd done everything in his power to prove I belonged to him. Only him.

And he'd woken up the next morning alone.

Luther's grip on my neck tightened, bringing me back to the present. The look in his eyes was more intense than it had been that night, harder and lacking the raw eagerness he'd had to own me in every way. We'd spent years healing from my betrayal, but it had left many scars. We'd built an incredible life together, and yet we still had a long way to go to reach the level of trust he'd once given me.

The trust I'd always had in him remained, he'd earned it over and over again, but knowing it was there and showing it were two different things.

I forced myself to relax. To let Luther take his time, turning to face the counter so he could massage the oil over my back. His fingers dug into muscles that were still tight even though I'd lost most of the tension that usually settled in from the moment I woke in the morning. Luther focused on them, letting out a soft laugh when I hissed at the deep ache.

"I'm waiting for you to tell me it's too much, Xavier. You're not a fan of pain." Luther pressed his lips to my shoulder as he massaged a knot by the curve of my spine. "Though your excuse is usually that you don't have time to be pampered."

"I don't, but you're right." I pressed my eyes shut as he continued the torture/massage. "I gave the gift certificate you bought me for the spa to my new assistant."

Letting out a heavy sigh, Luther went to work on my lower back. "Your doctor said a massage would be good for you."

"And you're giving me one." I grunted at another deep, painful rub. "Thank you."

"I'm hardly a professional. And giving away my gift was a dick move." Luther's tone hardened, but his touch remained the perfect balance between effective and soothing, despite my complaints. He might not be a professional, but even with the pain of his fingers digging into my muscles, he'd gotten me to relax more than any stranger laying me out on a padded table could have. "But I can't say I'm surprised."

His hands moved to my ass and I bowed my head between my arms, resisting the urge to tilt my hips and tempt him to change the game. He wanted to take his time and I wouldn't rush him.

The way his fingers, slick with more oil, slid over me, I didn't need to. His hands left me for a moment, followed by the sharp sound of his zipper. Kicking my thighs apart, he pressed into me, hot and hard, easing past the slight resistance of my body and driving in deep. He crossed his arms over my chest, his pelvis flush against my ass, and kissed the side of my neck.

Inhaling slowly, I braced myself as the burn faded away, leaving only the familiar fullness of my man, his firm grip on me, his breath as he whispered in my ear. "Maybe I shouldn't have given you a choice."

Before I could respond, Luther shifted back, drawing away from me, then thrusting in. A rough sound escaped my lips as my fingers slipped on the counter and a surge of pleasure sank into my core, spreading out as Luther angled his hips so each stroke within hit my prostate. I bit into my cheek as he reached around me to fist his slick hand around my dick, stroking in time with every slap of flesh.

He was good at keeping me off balance when he wanted to. Already I'd reached the edge of my restraint, ready to find my release, but playing with him this way, even if only for a few months, forced me to hold back. Accepting pleasure had always been difficult for me, but once he took full control of it, I'd stopped caring how vulnerable that moment when I let go made me feel.

Unless I was completely out of my head, he'd keep me like this. Driving me closer and closer to ecstasy, then holding it just out of reach.

"Fuck, Luther." I gasped in air as he slowed his pace, pulling out completely, then sliding back in so every nerve lit up, keyed to the sensation. "I can't hold back much longer."

"I didn't ask you to."

"But you will."

He let out a soft laugh. "Yes. You aren't begging yet."

This was the game, with rules I still didn't fully understand. With Alexander, Luther was careful. Established structure, taught our sub what was expected. Which Alexander needed because his desire to please, to have his efforts rewarded, was part of rebuilding his confidence. Of earning his trust.

With me, Luther steered away from the expected, from the careful order of the life I'd built. While he showed amazing restraint, he didn't need to be gentle. Gentle would lead to me shutting down. Refusing to give in fully.

As he pistoned in and out, over and over, my whole body tensed. Precum beaded on the tip of my dick and he spread it with his thumb, letting out a soft moan as his hand tightened at the base of my cock. He didn't stop moving, but added a deep thrust every time he filled me.

The urge to come became an ache, settling at the small of my back and billowing outward, throbbing in my balls, tight and lifted and sending sharp pangs of pleasure up the length of my dick. Every stroke once he released me was a tease, because he read me well. The second I jerked, tipping my head back, fighting not to let go too soon, the grip of his hand helped me.

This could continue all night. And part of me wanted it to. The part of me that knew I was never as honest with him, as connected to him, as I was when he had me this desperate. So fucking close to surrendering to all my chaotic emotions that begging didn't seem that bad. Being vulnerable was safe because he was with me. Because it was exactly what he wanted.

At first, the words escaped me. I released a gritty noise, nothing intelligible, because the feel of him slamming into me over and over stole my ability to speak. But when he slowed again, I clenched down and rasped in enough air to say what he needed to hear.

"Damn it, Luther! Please...please just let me..." Sweat slicked my face, my chest, the hands I had braced on the counter. "I'll do better. I'm trying. I'm fucking trying. I don't ever want you to stop, but I can't keep going. You're driving me insane."

Luther slowed his pace, kissing my throat, then bringing his lips to my ear. "We don't have to stop, Xavier. You're mine tonight. Sleep in tomorrow. Wait for Alec to come to you and be careful with him. Promise me that and I'll let you come."

"I will. Fuck! Luther..." My whole body shook as he tightened his grip on my cock. "I would have anyway. I won't hurt him any more than I'd hurt you."

Hand moving up and down my length, hard and fast, Luther nodded with his head on my shoulder. "Good. Then come for me. And know you'll be doing it again soon. Because I'm not done with you."

Pleasure tore through me with the strength of every muscle within, fighting to absorb the undulating pressure. I shouted as Luther used his palm to stop my cum from hitting the counter, his calloused skin making already sensitive flesh spark as though every nerve lit up with the flick of an erotic flame. He stroked me slowly as the last few spurts spilled over his hand, his dick still hard inside me.

As my knees buckled, he withdrew, holding me up, smearing my own cum on my skin as he pulled me against him.

Leaning on him, I huffed in as much air as I could manage, brow furrowing as I tipped my head back. "You didn't—"

"No. I told you I wasn't done with you." His lips slanted as he brought them down to mine. "I want you in my bed. And I want you to stay."

That he planned to use me all night didn't bother me. His endurance could be overwhelming, but in a way I'd never get enough of. When he was in this mood, I could expect to feel him for days. And I'd need that while he was gone.

But he wanted me worn out so I'd sleep with him. *Actually* sleep, too worn out to slip away in the middle of the night because I couldn't handle waking in the morning relaxed in his arms. I preferred my bed cold. My mornings steeling me for a day where I had to be strong. Detached.

He enjoyed cuddling. Enjoyed soft mornings with lazy smiles over coffee and sweet kisses that didn't lead to more. All things Alexander could give him. Things he wouldn't get from the young man for a week. Things Alexander needed as well.

Which I'd be expected to give him, but hadn't the first idea how.

"I think it would have been easier if I'd asked you for a kidney." Luther pressed his lips to my hair and laughed. "You're not working tomorrow, Xavier. You're taking time off to be with Alec."

"I am…" It had seemed a good idea at the time, but now I wasn't so sure. "But I still have responsibilities that—"

"That you can manage while being human."

"I'm always human, Luther. Don't be ridiculous." Standing there, naked, made being indignant rather difficult, but I did my best as I gathered my clothes. "Being professional isn't a bad thing."

"It is when being held until you're fully awake makes you feel weak. That's not professionalism. That's fear." Luther grabbed my shoulder before I could step away and pull my clothes back on. "Leave them off. Show me you can do this."

This being everything I'd avoided because Luther was right. I couldn't imagine starting the day feeling as exposed as he had me now. As I was whenever I let my guard down and woke by his side, wishing I didn't have to leave. But a few hours in my own bed and I was able to close myself off from any foolish urges. From the idea that everything I'd built could be taken if I wasn't the man everyone saw me as.

Cold. Ambitious. And unfeeling.

I wasn't that man to Luther.

Or to Alexander.

And it was past time I prove it.

"I'm not sure I can." If nothing else, I'd give Luther honesty. "But I will try."

Luther smiled and brought his lips to mine. "Which is all I've ever wanted from you. But don't worry. I'll make it easy."

"How so?"

"When I'm finished, you won't want to move." His lips slanted into an evil smile. "The staff doesn't come to my room, so you'll be left with two options."

Walking naked down the hall, I rubbed my arms, eager to climb into his bed and soak in the heat of his body, while fully aware I'd regret it in the morning. "Which are?"

Luther pulled off his shirt, tossing it in the half-full wicker hamper behind his door, his pants and boxers joining it second later. He slid under the dark blue comforter on his bed, not speaking again until I lay at his side.

He traced a calloused fingertip along my bare arm, clearly in no rush to find his own release. "You walk to your section of the house either completely naked or wearing my clothes, which are much too big for you."

An option I wouldn't even consider and he damn well knew it. This game of his was becoming less appealing by the minute. I frowned, waiting for him to tell me the second option.

"Or…" Raking his fingers into my hair, he tipped my head back and brought his lips to mine. "Alec will come to my room, all sleepy and affectionate and eager to please. You'll be too worn out to fuck him, so you'll relax and let him bring you coffee. And something to lounge around in once you're ready to leave my bed."

"You've got this all planned out, do you?" Brow lifted, I held his gaze, torn between wanting to challenge the way he'd assumed control of my entire day, or simply enjoy what sounded like a rather pleasant way to spend it. "What if I decide to keep Alexander here and make him pay for you being so goddamn manipulative?"

Kissing me again, Luther laughed. "I'm sure he'd enjoy that very much."

Chapter Three

The rich aroma of coffee was damn tempting as it eased me awake, but I kept my eyes shut, giving myself a moment to remember how to be a civil human being. Alexander had done exactly what Luther predicted because he was sweet and thoughtful, but I never knew how to function the mornings I wasn't on autopilot. When my butler brought me coffee I simply gulped it down while he went over updates to my schedule and waited for any orders concerning the household.

I wasn't rude to my butler, but neither of us wasted time on pleasantries. We both did what needed to be done.

Since I'd taken the day off, there was nothing that required even getting out of bed.

Which wasn't as appealing as it should have been. Not when Luther had left me sated and sore and completely worn out. What could I possibly do to make sure Alexander had a good morning with me? A young man with as much energy as he had would be bored with anything I found remotely entertaining.

Letting out a heavy sigh that matched the one I'd stifled, Alexander sat on the edge of my bed.

I frowned, turning my head to look at him. "What's wrong?"

"Nothing." Alexander rested his hands on his thighs, forcing a smile. "I brought you coffee."

"I can see that." I pushed up to sit against the headboard, studying the young man, hair neatly styled and dressed as though ready to head to the office. Considering we were spending the day at home, I'd expected him to be shirtless, in the pajama pants he usually lounged around in on the weekend, adorably rumpled and sleepy.

Instead, he was as stiff as he was at work when everything was going wrong and he'd decided it was his fault. On those days I usually wasn't in a great mood myself, but if it really *wasn't* his fault, I did my best to let him know.

Much easier to do when I knew what the problem was.

I guess this is where the talking *comes in.* Reaching over, I grabbed the mug of coffee I assumed he'd prepared for me, though both were black. Strange, since he took his with cream and sugar. Neither were on the tray.

"Did something happen that I should know about?" I took a sip of coffee, brow furrowing when he simply shrugged. "Alexander, talk to me."

"I…" Alexander looked down at his hands. "I'm not sure what I'm supposed to be doing. Luther usually brings me coffee and kinda bugs me until I get up to go for a run. He teases me about being grumpy until I'm…not."

*Ah…*I hid a smile behind my mug. "I take it you're not much of a morning person?"

He wrinkled his nose. "No. But you're…not usually around to see it."

All right, that stung. It was true, but I'd done my best to spend a reasonable amount of time with him. Mornings were nearly impossible—that was when the most demanding parts of my business were prepared for, then executed. Meetings tended to be scheduled fairly early to give me an advantage because I tended to be more alert than my peers. An underhanded strategy, but I hadn't gotten where I was today by being a saint.

Not one that would work with Alexander, though.

What would Luther do?

Alexander just *told you.*

Yes, but there was no way I was dragging him out for a run *neither* of us wanted to go on. The plan had been to stay in bed all morning and relax.

I eyed him for a moment, then jutted my chin at his crisp, light blue shirt and dark blue slacks. "Take those off."

Eyes wide, Alexander immediately began unbuttoning his shirt. "Shit, I'm sorry. I didn't mean to piss you off. I — "

"I'm not pissed." My brow furrowed at the uncertainty in his eyes. I shook my head and shoved off the blankets. "Get in the bed. I'll be right back."

The second I was in the hall, I realized I was naked. I retreated back into the room and cursed under my breath. Why had I let Luther talk me into such an impractical arrangement? What if the house had caught on fire?

"Xavier?" Alexander's tone was hesitant, but I caught an undertone of laughter. "Luther's robe is right there." He pointed at the back of the door where Luther's heavy black robe with purple lapels hung. "The staff doesn't come to this side of the house much, but just in case…"

Groaning, I grabbed the robe. "Go ahead and laugh. I feel ridiculous."

"You look fucking hot though."

Heat crawled up the back of my neck and I shot him a sideways glance as I tied the robe snug around my waist. The way it dragged on the floor and covered my hands couldn't be helped. "I look like a fool."

"I meant before you put on the robe." His lips slanted. "Now you look kinda cute."

He was pushing the limits and he knew it. At least he didn't seem moody anymore, so I'd let his cheekiness slide. Slipping into the hall, I glanced around, then crossed the short distance to the kitchen. I heard a door open at the far end of the left wing, where this part of the house was connected to the main. Ms. Lacey, probably, worrying that I'd starve to death if she didn't check on me. She knew I hadn't gone to work.

After grabbing the cream out of the fridge, I half skidded across the floor in my haste to snatch the sugar dish from the counter, cursing as the top popped off and a spray of white flew out onto the floor. Not much, but enough to notice.

Spilled sugar wouldn't be as embarrassing as Ms. Lacey seeing me like this, though, so I cut across the hall, ducking in Luther's room just as I heard the cook's footsteps. I pressed my forehead against the door, calming my breath, wishing I'd considered how badly things could go when Luther asked me to spend the night.

Rather than being prepared to come across members of my staff, dressed like myself and behaving as though being here was perfectly normal, I was rushing around, avoiding them in my own home. I shouldn't have to, but the only way I managed this household was with a staff who expected nothing more from me than a good paycheck, seasonal bonuses, paid vacations, and insurance. I tried to be an exemplary employer, but I *was* their employer. There was nothing personal between us.

I couldn't live my life with so many around me and let it be personal. Sometimes Ms. Lacey came close, but even she respected my boundaries. Many of which I'd developed over the years to maintain both my sanity and this lifestyle.

If she saw me like this it would be an invitation to approach me. To ask questions.

Opening up to Luther and Alexander was hard enough. I refused to let anyone else that close.

"Xavier?" Alexander sat up as I turned, hesitating before pushing off the bed and coming to me. "Shit, that really stressed you out. Why didn't you let me go get the cream and sugar if you wanted some?"

Inhaling slowly, I schooled my features. "They're for you."

"Oh…" A small smile curved his lips. "Thank you."

"You're welcome." I handed him the cream and sugar, making

my way to the bed at a more reasonable pace. I didn't bother taking off the robe. Uncomfortable as it was to parade around the house in, the warmth, the faint scent of Luther clinging to the soft, lush fabric, was soothing.

My coffee had cooled slightly, but not enough to be unpleasant. I took a sip as Alexander fixed up his own.

He sat crossed legged on the bed facing me and took a few sips, his expression pensive. "I never realized you're the same way with the staff here as you are with people at work. When do you get to relax if you're...*on* all the time?"

I chuckled at that. "I relax just fine when I'm by myself. Or with you and Luther."

"Only when Luther calls you on it."

"You're overstepping, Alexander. If you have a question pertaining to *our* relationship, just ask it. But please refrain from analyzing what I have with our man."

Alexander stilled, his eyes narrowing slightly. "If you're going to talk to me like an employee, can I put my clothes back on?"

Taking another sip of coffee, I went over what I'd said, not sure what had irritated him. "I'm not speaking to you li—"

"Yes. You are." He huffed out an agitated breath. "You're all stiff and formal and I'm not dealing with that shit first thing in the morning. I love you, but I don't know enough about you. You won't let me in and it fucking sucks."

Damn, that was...the most brutally honest Alexander had ever been with me. If I didn't want to deal with this side of him, I'd probably have to avoid him during his raw and unfiltered morning stage. He seemed incapable of holding back.

But I didn't want him to. Even if it would be easier, I loved him too. I loved how he'd disrupted my life and made me feel more than I'd allowed myself before. How being near him made a room lighter. How addictive his passion was.

After six months we were still slowly getting to know one another and he was right to be fed up. The pace was my doing and it wasn't fair.

Finishing my coffee, I set the mug aside and inclined my head. "You're right. My defensiveness was uncalled for and I'm sorry." I ran my hand over my hair. "The staff is necessary to maintain the mansion, but I'm uncomfortable around too many people when I'm not in control. Being 'stiff and formal' is one way I set boundaries, but I don't need them with you."

The edge of Alexander's lips curved and his eyes warmed. "Thank you. I like hearing that."

"Good. I'll make a point of telling you more often."

"Are you going to make note of it in your planner?" His tone was teasing, but I didn't miss the point he was trying to make. This thing between us should be natural—and could be if I let it.

"No notes, but we should talk more. Tell me something about you that I don't know."

Cocking his head, Alexander set his mug on the nightstand. "What's there to know? I grew up poor even though my parents were pretty successful thieves. Money was gambled away almost as fast as they got their hands on it." He tapped his chin thoughtfully. "My brothers used me as a punching bag and I was safer starving on the streets than anywhere near them. But then I got desperate, tried to steal your car, and got fucking lucky. The end."

"Not 'The end'." I put my hand on his knee with a light squeeze. "And things I *don't* know, Alexander."

"I hate being called 'Alexander', how about that?" His eyes widened and he swallowed hard, as though shocked by his own words. "I'm sorry, I didn't—"

"You meant exactly what you said." I rubbed his thigh soothingly, holding his gaze. "Would you rather I call you 'Alec', like Luther does?"

"Unless I'm in trouble?" He licked his lips, then nodded. "My parents used to call me 'Alexander' when I pissed them off. Started doing it more and more as I got older until they rarely called me anything else." He lowered his gaze. "I never said anything because you don't use the same tone they did. Like you're annoyed or disgusted."

But I'd still been using a name he couldn't stand for six months without the slightest idea how much it bothered him. He likely hadn't told Luther either, because our man wouldn't have hesitated to set me straight.

Names were important to me. Choosing my own had given me a sense of control. A sense of worth I'd lacked before. Pride that the man I was, I'd fought to become on my own.

Still, I couldn't let my feelings influence how I responded to Alexand—to Alec's. I reached out and took his hand. "Why do you still want me to call you that if you're in trouble?"

He ducked his head. "Being in trouble with you isn't cold and ugly. I love the limits you set. When you enforce them it feels like you actually give a fuck. We're closer once we work things out. I'd be cool connecting the name with that."

"Fair enough."

"Now it's your turn." Alec wet his bottom lip with his tongue. "Tell me one thing about you I don't know."

My pulse stuttered and I reached for my mug, knowing it was empty, but needing something to do with my hands. I stared at the dark blue of the comforter in the space between us, hesitating as though he'd asked me to open a vein, rather than simply open up to him.

Because that's what it felt like. What he knew of me was more than most, but still limited. Controlled. He wouldn't recognize the man I'd been at his age.

"Hey, only what you're comfortable with." This time it was Alec who took my hand. His skin was more tanned than mine, enough that I wondered if I should get more sun. And there were callouses on his fingers where I had none. Strength where mine was lacking. But he tightened his grip like he was trying to share it. "We're alone, Xavier. And I love you. I'm happy with whatever you give me."

Nothing I could give him would be pleasant. I let out a soft laugh and shook my head. "I hate this house. I hate what it represents."

Alec's brow furrowed. He waited for me to continue, nodding slowly when I didn't. "Does it have something to do with how you grew up? All the articles say you're self-made, so I assumed you grew up poor. Like me."

Damn it, how the hell could I have let him believe that? After what he'd gone through, my stupid hang-ups were pathetic.

I shook my head. "I wasn't poor. I had more than I needed. I never went hungry—far from it. I was lucky."

"Xavier—"

"I think Ms. Lucy is making us breakfast. Would you mind going to my room and getting me some clothes?"

Alec held my gaze for a moment. Then inclined his head. "Sure. No problem." He shoved off the bed and quickly pulled the clothes he'd been wearing back on. His stiff posture and closed off expression made it seem like he'd pulled on armor. But he forced a smile. "I'll be right back."

Once he was out of the room I slumped back on the pillows, groaning and covering my face with my hands. I'd been given the very opportunity Luther had been hoping for. A moment to connect with Alec. To bring our relationship to another level.

Instead, I'd pushed him away.

Chapter Four

Over breakfast I did my best to ease Alec back into the relaxed mood he'd found so briefly in Luther's room, but his tight laughter and shallow small talk put me on edge. I was relieved when he got a call from Judy asking him to meet her at the office because something had come up with their line. We could both go to work. Be distracted. Get back to normal.

And I'd have time to fix the mess I'd made. Figure out how to prove I was ready to let Alec in fully.

Even though this wasn't how Luther wanted things to be, there was no rush. I'd see Alec after work. Decide what I was ready to share. Make sure it was enough.

In the cool solitude of my office I lost myself to the mindless rhythm of paperwork, setting aside drafts for designs I'd consider, and filing away those which would need a carefully worded rejection. The designers who worked here were some of the best in the industry, I respected their talent. But I didn't produce anything that didn't blow me away. A few of the dresses created for the summer line came close, but I couldn't find any enthusiasm in seeing a single one fully realized.

Maybe I was too distracted to do this now. Missing out on a potential show stopper because I couldn't stop picturing the closed off look in Alec's eyes. Couldn't stop thinking that I should be at home with him, enjoying his company, his easy laughter, the way he felt when he lay his head on my chest and made me wonder why I'd decided cuddling 'wasn't my thing.'

Bracing my elbows on my desk, I lowered my head to my hands and rubbed my temples. Tonight I would do better. We had the rest of our lives together—not a thought I had often, but exactly what I wanted. A future with both Alec and Luther. One that didn't revolve around the company and my insane work schedule. The time would come when I didn't have to give the business all my energy.

You didn't put a fucking wall up because of business, you coward.

No. I'd done that out of habit. Maybe telling Alec a bit about my family would've made things seem more level, but they weren't. Alec had been through so much worse. His pity would be unbearable. *He* was the one who needed to be protected. Supported. Given everything and anything I could offer.

Except you. Who you really *are.*

But I *wasn't* that pathetic child anymore. I was almost thirty and that part of my life was best left behind. Forgotten.

The door clicked open, drawing me away from my tangled thoughts. I frowned as Denise Croft, editor-in-chief of the magazine I owned, *Espoir*, strode into the room. We'd known each other for a long time, and I'd tempted her away from another magazine because she was one of the best in the business, but I wouldn't consider her a friend. Nor would she consider me one.

More to avoid reminders of our shared...past than anything.

Her skin was a rich, smooth, light brown shade, black hair cut short so it framed her angular face and wide green eyes. She had a poise and classic beauty that had people assuming she came from wealth and they'd be right. To a point.

Like me, she'd fallen from grace when she'd opened up about her sexuality. She'd also driven the final nail in, as I had, by refusing to follow the path laid out for her by her family. They'd expected her to be a socialite, marry into the right family and broaden their prospects by solidifying their place in the world of the elite. Her 'phase' of dating other women could fade into the background in time.

Instead, she'd married her high school sweetheart, a young woman who'd been known only for the graffiti she'd painted around their small town in Wisconsin. Gretchen was still painting street art, but on canvases that fetched the highest prices at auctions full of rich people who considered themselves edgy.

She made more than Denise did and I paid my editor-in-chief *damn* well.

But she'd only come under my radar because she'd been black-mailed by Joel as well. She'd broken up with Gretchen while they were still dating. We'd met just as I'd started losing his interest. When I'd finally had hope he would set me free.

Then he did. And turned all his attention to her.

I still remembered holding her as she broke down, whispering to her that it would end. That he would find someone else to play with. That I wished I could help her protect Gretchen, but…but Joel had found a way to threaten Gretchen's scholarship in a prestigious art school. Even though her juvenile record was sealed, he'd dug up enough dirt to ruin her.

And Denise would do *anything* to prevent that.

And had.

Being free, we'd seen one another as the final reminder of what we'd gone through. While we were still civil, we tended to avoid one another. She was the best at what she did, so of course I'd offered her the job. I was the best at what I did, so naturally, she accepted. But that was the end of our interactions. Without saying so, we agreed to stay out of each other's way. It was less painful.

Seeing her in my office brought it all back. My throat tightened as I met her wide eyes. I closed the file I'd been working on and stared at her.

She smoothed her hands over her crisp, emerald-green skirt suit and stared back. "He's here."

My stomach dropped. My mind immediately went over all she

could mean that wouldn't be the absolute worst. "The reviewer who bashes every issue? Denise, you've handled him be—"

"Don't be obtuse, Xavier. You know *exactly* who I mean. I wouldn't be here otherwise." She raked her fingers through her hair, visibly shaken. "Please tell me you told Alec about him. I told Gretchen, so I don't think he'll go after her. But when I saw him talking to Alec…"

"No." Acid burned my throat as I stood. "He can't—"

"Xavier…" Denise's eyes went wide. "He can and he *will*. I've heard whispers about Alec. How no one knows much about his past. People guess, but he's so well-liked no one really cares." Her eyes narrowed as my jaw ticked. "There's something Joel can use against him, isn't there? And you're such a closed off fucker, your boy doesn't have a clue. He just sees you as the man he loves, who gave him this perfect goddamn life."

"Not so perfect, obviously." I pressed my eyes shut and leaned back in my chair. I didn't usually let anyone see me as less than composed and in control, but this was Denise. She'd seen me at my lowest. "I didn't think he needed to know."

"Tell him now. Xavier, you can't—"

A soft knock at the door silenced her. She stiffened as the knob turned, and our eyes met. No one came in without my invite. Even Alec would wait for a response.

But Joel wouldn't.

A chill ran down my spine as he stepped into my office. Even in his late fifties, he was still an imposing man. Handsome in a way that made the media salivate for any excuse to put his picture on a magazine or newspaper, or show a clip of him in a news brief. His hair was still perfectly blonde, likely dyed, but his hairstylist made it look natural. He was tanned, as though he spent a lot of time in the sun, but he was as much of a workaholic as both Denise and I were, so the color had a price tag.

He had a wiry strength to him, was an inch or so taller than I, but somehow seemed much larger as he closed the door behind him, trapping us in my office with him. This space where I always felt calm, separated from everything, safe in my own power, was suddenly too small. He was too close as he approached the desk.

I stood, glancing over at Denise as she visibly struggled not to take a step back.

"Xavier, it's a pleasure to see you after all this time. You're looking well." He smiled at Denise. "As do you. Though…if you don't mind, I'd like a moment alone with my dear friend. We have much to discuss."

Denise hesitated, which made me wish we could have reconnected, despite the scars this very man had left behind. She held my gaze, inhaling slowly when I nodded. Then she turned and slipped out of my office, closing the door quietly behind her.

"A shame Gretchen heard I was in town before Denise did. It would've been fun to play with her again. But Gretchen already did an interview that's releasing tomorrow revealing her entire, sordid past. Which will only add to her appeal. She's a smart woman. And has the money for the PR to handle any backlash." He let out a heavy sigh. "I hope you won't make things so difficult."

"What 'things'?" I pushed away from my chair, standing stiff, grateful that my legs didn't shake, though I had to fist my hands by my sides to keep them steady. "Why are you here?"

"I was bored." The edge of Joel's lips quirked. "I saw a picture of your boy online when your new line went viral. He's too precious. I want him."

"No."

"No?" He let out a sharp laugh. "Think of the opportunities I could offer him. Rather than standing in your shadow, he could be running his own company. After speaking to his friend, the designer… Judy is it? She thinks the junior line could go far. Much further than you'll allow it to. Alec is charming and he'd be perfect as the face of a new brand."

"He's happy *here*." Of that I was sure, but Joel bringing up Judy gave me some doubts. Alec's ambitions revolved around what he could do for others. He cared for Judy, and if she felt limited here, he'd be tempted to help her.

And Joel was a master of temptation.

His lips quirked. "You're not as certain as you sound, are you?"

"I'm certain you'll hurt him if I let you anywhere near him."

"Now, Xavier, let's not be dramatic. Why on earth would I hurt that sweet boy?" Joel took a seat in front of my desk, watching me expectantly until I returned to my own. "He's been through so much already. Why, when Luther hired the private investigator I sent his way, I knew there must be something interesting going on in your life, but I never dreamed you'd become so charitable." Joel let out a light laugh. "Taking in a homeless thief. Well done. He'll be indebted to you for life."

"That's not why he's with me." My response came automatically, but I couldn't get past Joel's words. He knew about the PI — he'd arranged for an investigator on his payroll to respond to Luther's queries. Damn it, why hadn't I asked Luther how he'd found the man? Joel was embedded in the dark underbelly of the elite, nothing happened that didn't make its way back to him. That I'd done my best to erase him from my life didn't mean I was out of his reach.

Jaw clenched, I forced myself to meet dark blue eyes that didn't match the lightness of his tone. They were cold. Calculating. Had intimidated me once, but not anymore. "Our relationship is none of your concern. Leave my office now or I'm calling security."

Joel's brow shot up. "Now that would be a neat trick. Go ahead. Call them. Then explain to all your employees why I'm such a threat. Why you're rejecting my offer to invest millions into your junior line. I'm sure they'll be very sympathetic."

The idea of having *anyone* know the raw details of my past, of them believing I couldn't deal with Joel on my own, made my stomach turn. He was right, I wouldn't call security.

Which left him here, playing his same old games.

Only, this time, he wanted to play them with someone I loved. I couldn't let that happen.

My eyes narrowed as his shone with amusement. "What do you want? If you think you can blackmail Alec, you—"

"Blackmail? With what, exactly? You gave his brothers the car, so he can't be charged with attempting to steal it. They wanted more of the money they could leech out of you in your pathetic attempt to keep him safe, but I have them distracted. For now." He leaned forward, bracing his hands on his knees. "I could rid you of them permanently, Xavier. All you have to do is ask."

"I don't want Alec's brothers dead."

"Don't you? They'll likely kill him if they get their hands on him."

"They won't."

"I agree. Because we'll both make sure of it." Joel slapped his hands on his thighs and stood, stepping up to my desk and smiling down at me. "Now that the unpleasantness is out of the way, let me explain to you how this game shall be played. You claim to love this man and believe he loves you in return?"

I shoved my chair back as I rose to face him. "There will be no games, Joel. Find someone else."

His eyes narrowed, his tone sharpening as he fisted his hands by his sides. "Don't test me, Xavier. I'm willing to play fair and forgo needless threats, but you know very well I won't hesitate to use any means necessary to get what I want. The game means rules. You don't want to play with me without them."

My throat tightened as I considered what he was implying. Joel knew where Alec's brothers were. He could bring them back. Put Alec in danger. I'd do whatever I could to protect him, but I needed time to figure out how.

Until then, the safest thing would be to let Joel believe I'd play along with his twisted game. He *would* stick to his rules. He always did.

"I see you understand. Good." He jutted his chin at my chair. "Sit and listen."

Lowering back onto my chair, I watched him as he began to pace in front of me.

"You aren't to tell Alec any stories about me. Let him make his own decisions. I will met with him, as I would any other prospective business partner. I will offer him everything he could possibly want." He stopped pacing, glancing back at me over his shoulder. "And if he loves you as much as you believe he does, he'll turn me down. I will accept my loss gracefully and leave you to go on with your happy lives."

The fact that any of this sounded reasonable only proved how much my time with Joel had fucked with my head. I'd been trapped in his world for three years and knew exactly how depraved rich men with too much time on their hands could be. They bought and sold people like playthings, dropped millions on every vice imaginable, and it was never enough. At every chance, they'd continue to push the limits because money gave them a free pass.

Compared to what I'd seen, Joel's suggestion was nothing.

I nodded slowly. "So long as you don't force Alex to do anything he doesn't want to."

"You have my word."

Holding back a sharp laugh was hard, but I managed. Inclined my head. "And what of any business arrangements made? Will you withdraw them if Alec rejects your offer?"

"So mercenary. I'm impressed, my boy. The creative dreamer fits into this life after all." Joel chuckled. "Any investments I make in the line will stand, no matter how this ends."

"Very well, then I accept your challenge. I won't stand in your way." Not wanting things to seem *too* easy, I smirked. "But don't be surprised when Alec shows no interest. As I said, he's happy where he is."

Joel's brow lifted. "Is he? He didn't seem very happy when he came in, but I appreciate the warning. It would be refreshing to actually have someone resist me." He held my gaze for a moment and cold slithered down my spine at his predatory look. "None have so far."

For a few moments he stood there, unnerving me with his

silence, as though waiting for some kind of reaction. I gave him nothing, simply giving him a dismissive glance before returning to my paperwork. My skin crawled at his presence, but I couldn't show him how much he still affected me. Let him think he'd already won.

He didn't know Alec.

Once Joel left my office, I lowered my head to my hands, fighting back the urge to throw up the little I'd eaten that morning. Joel might not know Alec, but he was a manipulative son-of-a-bitch and because of me, Alec was vulnerable. If Luther was around, I'd no doubt Alec wouldn't even give Joel the time of day, but with only me to come home to?

What if Alec started questioning the kind of life I could give him? Not the money, but time and affection. Someone he could feel close to. Who could blame him for being lonely when I couldn't manage one goddamn conversation before jumping on the first opportunity to distract myself with work? Joel was good at making people feel wanted. Appreciated.

I…wasn't.

Pulling my phone out of my pocket, I set it on my desk and stared at it. One phone call and this would end. Luther would tell me I was an idiot and he'd come home. Figure things out.

But no matter what he'd said, he craved some kind of connection with his brother. How the hell could I cut short the one opportunity he had after so long? And why, because I couldn't say for sure that Alec would choose me over that fucking snake who'd slithered into our lives?

The game was nothing but a delay tactic on my part. I would find a way to remove *any* threat to the man I loved.

And until then…

I'd do what I should have in the first place. Make sure Alec was happy exactly where he was.

Even though I didn't have the slightest idea how.

Chapter Five

The day dragged longer than any workday in my life. Even those stretching close to twenty-four hours, with nothing but a short pit stop at home to shower and grab the least amount of sleep I could get away with. I'd never been this desperate to get back home. Both Luther and Alec were usually here. Close to me. All I had to do was reach out...

That wasn't an option now.

To keep myself busy, I read all the files Judy and Alec had put together about the junior line, familiarizing myself with it in a way I'd put off before since all the important tasks had been delegated. I'd had no real interest other than knowing the designs would bring in a profit.

Since agreeing to continue the line, I'd allocated enough resources to make it a success, but for it to truly thrive the team assigned to the project would need more than the basics. Judy was a talented designer, but too young to have the weight behind her name to draw massive interest. There were three designers I'd been considering for my new summer lines, one a Korean woman in her late sixties, Eun-Kyung, who was in high demand, had been in the industry for forty years. Judy could learn a lot from her and she'd amassed a huge following with her quirky way of engaging viewers while admitting she struggled to adapt to modern technology.

Eun-Kyung was not only an established talent, but her loyal following could potentially bring the junior line some much-needed exposure. Hiring her for that line, instead of the more popular ones, would be a risk. A calculated risk, but one I never would have taken before.

And I knew damn well that was part of the reason the junior line had almost become obsolete. Eun-Kyung could eliminate the possibility of that happening again.

She didn't like speaking on the phone, so I wrote her a long, personalized email, offering her a position with the company. Temporary consultant to start, with full benefits and a long term contract if she desired. She tended to keep her options open, and didn't like feeling tied down, so I had to make it clear from the start that I didn't expect her to be.

Leaving my office to explore the logistics of my next plan was much more difficult, but I ignored the unsettling sensation of having so many eyes on me. The silence surrounding me the second I stepped into any office made my blood pressure rise, yet I maintained the detached demeanor expected of me as I gathered the information I needed. Thanks to Alec, I'd heard rumors about how the interns with the magazine were treated and, after speaking with a few he'd mentioned, had an idea to improve the situation.

I called in the building manager to explore the option of allocating the entire 20th and 21st floors to the junior line. Right now they had a few offices on the 40th floor and one below, close to me because that's where I preferred Alec to be. But to have the space to expand, I had to let go a little.

And hope the space wouldn't play into Joel's hands.

The manager, Freddy Prado, came into my office with a confused look on his face, blinking at me for a moment before he finally spoke. "The magazine has the 20th to the 35th floor."

"I am aware. I've also been to the lower offices and know they're pushing writers they feel are less important into areas they haven't bothered to maintain." *Denise will understand. There's no way she knew about the toxic hierarchy taking place in her department. And if she did, we're damn well going to have a little chat.* "They'll be forced to restructure and get some fresh ideas when they can't ignore their 'underlings'. Let me handle that. All I need from you is to know what steps must be taken to renovate the floors for the line's design team and management."

"Mr. Ashburne, that's...not really my area of expertise. But I can relay your request to the right people." He smoothed his hands over his suit self-consciously. It was cheap, but well maintained. Not something I would have paid much attention to without his fussing—he wasn't one of my models—but I could tell he felt out of place.

This was the longest conversation we'd ever had. I'd typically have my assistant handle any restructuring, but doing it myself mattered. Alec might never know how much time I'd put into the project he loved, and yet...I needed to be part of the process.

And not make a huge deal out of it, because that wasn't my style.

I cleared my throat. "You'll be paid extra for your time. I appreciate you handling this for me."

"Of course, sir. Thank you." Freddy smiled and let his hands fall to his sides. "My brother does renovations and has been looking for new contracts. I'd wave my fees if you'd consider him for the job."

I arched a brow. "Mr. Prado, you've been running buildings for longer than this one even existed. I trust your judgment. You'll take your fees and hire anyone you feel can do the job. Please consult with Judy for the specifics." I hesitated at his broad grin, not sure what else I should say. I tended to nod at people and they went away, but he didn't move when I inclined my head. "Was there anything else?"

He blinked, his cheeks reddening. "No, sir. I just wanted to say I'm happy with the changes being made lately. There was talk that things weren't going well. That you may close down or move the company. I…I'm happy you've decided to stay."

My brow furrowed as I considered the 'talk' he'd heard that I'd apparently missed. Granted, I had considered drawing back from several projects, uncertain if they'd be good investments, but putting more trust in my department heads had been the best move I could've made. Both financially and personally.

There were whispers that I'd made those moves because of the influence of an inexperienced young man I'd fallen for, but that was only half true. Alec had simply opened my eyes to what I should have known all along. And he wasn't always right. I'd fired one man he'd thought I should promote. An executive who'd been charged with insider trading a month after I'd had security escort him out. He'd been charming and good at his job, but something about him always rubbed me the wrong way. My accountant approached me with several concerns once she saw I'd decided to get more involved with the inner workings of my company.

Alec always saw the best in people.

Which was both his greatest strength and, possibly, his most devastating weakness.

Speaking of which…it was time to get him out of Joel's reach.

This game might be unavoidable, but I could limit its impact.

I stood, smiling at Freddy when his brow creased. "I apologize. I didn't realize there were so many rumors, but I assure you, you have no reason to be concerned. There are several new investors, and many new projects, so I'll be making a lot of changes here. I appreciate any assistance you can give in that regard, including recommendations."

"That's good to hear, sir. Thank you." Freddy grinned, giving me an awkward half-bow before backing out of the room.

I'd have to stop him from doing that.

Starting tomorrow.

Tonight, I needed to get home. With Alec.

Jaw clenched, I shut down my laptop and slipped it into my briefcase. Knowing Joel, he'd still be hanging around the junior department. Likely with Judy, giving Alec the barest attention if his tactics hadn't changed. Judy was Alec's focus, the person he'd put at the center of this whole project. With good reason, but he'd made her his weak spot. By focusing on her, Joel would appeal to Alec that much more.

Coming between them without making it obvious would be difficult, but I had the advantage. Alec still wanted to be useful to me. And I'd had a *very* long day.

Pressing the first in the pre-set buttons on my phone, I waited for Tricia to answer.

"Ms. Glades, can you please have Mr. Tremaine to come to my office as soon as he's available?"

There was a brief pause. Then Tricia's calm, soothing voice. "Of course, Mr. Ashburne. Right away."

I waited for her to ask if there was anything *she* could do, but there was only silence. One of the many things I liked about Tricia, which made her the perfect assistant for me. As much as I'd appreciated Alec anticipating my needs and pushing beyond what I'd ask, that had more to do with our relationship than what I expected from anyone in the office.

He or Luther always seeing beyond the surface was one thing, but I couldn't function in my position without some distance between myself and my employees. My assistant needed to be able to follow instructions first and foremost. And Tricia was good at that. She anticipated the necessary tasks in a way that didn't feel intrusive.

Not that Alec had ever been intrusive, but I'd accepted any excuse to have him near.

After my call to Tricia, it took exactly twenty-five minutes and thirty-three seconds for Alec to finally show up. Not that I was counting. Or staring at my pocket watch which needed tuning because the second hand *must* be slow. Or clenching my jaw with. Each. Passing. Minute.

His broad grin when he slipped into my office only made my jaw clench harder, but he didn't seem to notice. "Sorry it took me a bit, Judy and Joel—he's a new investor she's working with for the line—were brainstorming some ideas for the casual designs we're introducing for this summer. Going from dresses and formalwear to T-shirts didn't seem practical, but it won't be that hard once the brand is well-known with younger consumers."

Finally, he took a breath. And I managed what I hoped was an encouraging smile, holding my hand up before he could continue. "I'm pleased to hear that. This...*investor* sounds very hands on." I stood, heading to the closet to grab my dark grey, wool jacket, pulling it on and pretending not to notice the question in his eyes. "We have casualwear with some of the adult lines. Perhaps you'll be able to pass on useful information that may crossover well."

"Yeah, I can do that..." His brow furrowed as I stepped up to his side. "Are you leaving already? It's only 5:30."

"Later than we should have stayed, considering we both had the day off."

"Sure, but—" He cut himself off and shook his head with a laugh. "You know what, doesn't matter. It's Friday. I'll go tell Judy I'm heading out and meet you downstairs."

Oh hell no. I stepped in front of him, blocking his path, not sure what reasonable excuse I could come up with to get him to leave with me now. If he went back to Judy's office, Joel would come up with a reason for him to stay. And Alec was easily distracted when he got pulled into his work.

Calling for him again would make it obvious to Joel that I was doing my best to cut their time together short. Which he'd consider 'breaking the rules'.

"Just come with me, Alec." I silently cursed myself for how desperate I sounded, but I needed this weekend alone with my man. Needed a few days to make sure he'd be so disinterested in Joel the game would be over before it had even begun. "We'll do something...fun."

Alec's lips quirked at that. "'Fun'? Why do you make it sound painful? We don't have to watch that movie if you don't want to."

"I do want to. I believe I may develop a taste for action movies.

And maybe video games. You like those, don't you?" I smiled as his eyes widened. "Why do you look so surprised? I was young, once."

"You're still not that old." He gave me a level look. "And I doubt you were into video games, even as a kid."

All right, he had me there. My father likely wished I'd spent more time shooting fictional characters than drawing them, but that was irrelevant. I'd learn to like it. And anything else Alec enjoyed doing. "Are you saying you won't teach me?"

"I'm saying I'm not sure I can. I read a lot when I was a kid, but my brothers hogged the PlayStation and were assholes the rare times they let me play, so I never got into it."

"Oh…" Yet again, a conversation that would go much smoother if Luther was here. He'd know how to comfort Alec. How to distract him.

My efforts were sorely lacking.

"Hey, are you okay? You're acting weird." Alec went to my closet, where he'd left his own jacket. The wool was thicker than mine—he never seemed warm enough outside—and a dark blue-black, reaching down to his knees. The style suited him, both professional, yet edgy enough to give the whole outfit a youthful appeal.

An appeal that made me feel like I'd aged much too fast in comparison. Had I ever had that warmth in my eyes? That *hope*? In ten years, would he be this cold and jaded?

Not if I can help it.

I took a deep breath and gave him enough of the truth to ease his mind. "I'm fine, but I have some concerns about boring you. Luther can make anything entertaining. I don't share his skills."

The edge of Alec's lips curved slightly. "You share some of them. And hey, if you want to try some video games and really bad action movies, I'm good with that. Or you can teach me to play chess."

My brow furrowed. "What makes you think that I play chess?"

"It's a strategy game. Something you're probably awesome at." He bumped his shoulder into mine. "And as your assistant I got to see your schedule. Which includes a weekly game of chess with two board members."

"True, but I do whatever's necessary to keep them happy."

"Not that, Xavier. And hey, I think chess is cool. I'd love to learn." He held my gaze for a moment. "Stop worrying about what I wanna do. I *want* to spend time with you. Do things you enjoy. Get to know you better."

"You *do* know me, Alec."

There was a sadness in his eyes as he shook his head. "No, I really don't. You always turn the focus to me when we talk. Whenever something about your past comes up, you change the subject. How about we do things different this weekend? We don't have to discuss anything you're not comfortable with, but give me *something*."

That sounded like a *terrible* idea. But the second I let out a light laugh and shook my head, I knew I'd already fucked up. But I couldn't stop. "The point is for you *not* to be bored."

"Wrong answer." He shook his head again and crossed my office in three long strides. "I'm going to tell Judy I'm leaving. I shouldn't be long, but just in case, head home without me. I'll catch a cab."

"At least let me send a car—"

"No." He stopped at the door, grip tight on the doorknob and spine stiff. "I'm not a little kid who needs to be entertained and taken care of."

"I know that, Alec."

"Do you?" He shot me one last cold look over his shoulder. "Could've fooled me."

When the door clicked shut behind him I leaned back against my desk, staring at the ceiling, grinding my teeth as my mind raced. I couldn't have handled that worse if I'd tried. Alec had been willing to forgive me shutting him out this morning, so long as I made the effort not to continue doing so.

But I couldn't. Joel's impact on my life was woven into every part of the man I was today. And I couldn't tell Alec about Joel. I trusted Alec to keep my secrets, but if he knew the truth it would show in his eyes every time he looked at the other man. He'd be angry. Disgusted.

Joel would retaliate.

Which left me with two options.

Either I let Alec know everything and hope his brothers couldn't get to him before Luther returned and put the necessary security in place.

Or I let Alec be angry while I saw to his safety myself. Delay Joel as much as possible and use the resources Luther had already put in place.

With that in mind, I called Tricia into my office.

"How soon would I be able to arrange a meeting with Luther's second-in-command?"

Her brow lifted. "I can send him up now if you'd like, sir. He's seeing to the loading of several pieces for the show in New York, but I'm sure someone else can handle that."

The event included pieces that cost well over a million dollars, and Luther had spent months making sure the delivery would be secure, but I knew he'd agree Alec's safety was more important. And while his second-in-command was his most trusted man, every single person he'd hired was more than capable of handling the shipment.

I inclined my head. "Please do."

Before I'd taken my jacket off and settled back behind my desk, a huge, muscular man was in my office. Light brown skin, deep scars on his face and a menacing expression. For a moment I wondered if he'd been sent here to kill me.

I'd met several members of Luther's team, but not this guy.

He stepped up to my desk and thrust his massive hand across to me. "Mr. Ashburne, I'm Brendon Hyles. It's a pleasure to meet you."

Rising, I quickly shook his hand, careful to hide my wince when he squeezed harder than likely intended. "Thank you for coming, Mr. Hyles. I won't keep you long, but as you might know, Luther hired a private investigator a few months ago and—"

"He's a fucking snake. You should fire him."

"Excuse me?"

"The PI. Not Luther. Luther's a good man, but he doesn't have the connections I do. He hired me for them and I've been looking into every member of your staff." Brendon's eyes narrowed. "That new investor, Joel? You can't trust him either."

"Believe me, I know." I cocked my head, studying the man Luther apparently trusted enough to promote over people he'd known for years. "If I asked you to protect Alec, above any other, would you do so? No matter what it took?"

Brendon chuckled. "Mr. Ashburne, I am here to protect you and Alec, first and foremost. There are no limits. That's why Luther hired me."

"But I'm not the one in danger."

"You receive a dozen threats a day. Which your assistant, Tricia, forwards to me the moment she receives them."

All right, *that* I hadn't known. But this wasn't about me. "The threat I'm referencing is more immediate."

"And I've heard nothing besides the constant threat of his brothers, who are in Ohio at the moment." The guard's eyes narrowed. "If they've been in contact with you, you need to tell me how. I've been closely monitoring any access they might have to either you or Alec, on Luther's instructions, but so far there's been nothing."

"With good reason. They're being paid well to stay away."

"By who?" Brendon's tone took on a rough edge as he flattened his hands on the desk. "I don't give a fuck about your past, or what you had to do to get where you are. Luther warned me that you're very private about all that shit. Fine. But if you want me to keep you alive…" He paused, giving a short nod as though seeing something in my eyes I couldn't hide. "If you want me to keep *Alec* alive, you will keep *nothing* from me."

"Luther hired the PI you distrust. Why should I believe his hiring of you wasn't a mistake as well?"

"Because I trained Luther while you were off trying to reconnect with all the rich fuckers who'd cut you out. I kept that boy alive when he was so distracted over losing you, so determined to numb himself to the pain, he almost drank himself to death." The ice in Brendon's tone sliced right through me. "I almost didn't let him go back to you. I thought you'd destroy all I'd rebuilt in him. But the damn boy loves you. And after seeing how you've built your company, the integrity you hide behind that stiff ass attitude, I believe he has a reason to."

I lowered my gaze, thinking back on everything Luther had admitted when I was free of Joel and begged for another chance. He didn't drink often and never had a problem with knowing his limits. But after I'd disappeared from his life, he'd stopped caring. He'd gotten the training to become a security guard, and excelled on every level, but thinking of me made coming back to an empty house too hard. He'd gone months completely sober, but after a hard day he'd finished off a bottle of whiskey. And went into work still drunk.

He got shot. Spent weeks in the hospital.

And for months only had a beer now and then, careful not to go too far. Until I called him. In a moment of weakness, I'd needed to hear his voice. It was all that kept me going.

But reminding him of what he'd lost had sent him over the edge. That must be what Brendon was talking about. Luther told me he'd finished off every bottle in his liquor cabinet. He couldn't deal with the fact that I wouldn't come to him. Wouldn't accept his help when I so clearly needed it.

The man who'd shown up and nursed Luther back to health when he refused to go to the hospital must have been Brendon.

I hadn't told Luther much of what happened with Joel, afraid he'd hunt the bastard down. That I'd lose the man I'd fought so hard to come back to.

I hadn't told Alec about Joel because, by the time I'd even considered doing so, it was too late.

Looking at Brendon, I didn't want to tell him. I didn't want to be that vulnerable. Didn't want to seem so fucking weak. But there was no other way. No matter how hard I tried, I couldn't protect Alec on my own. Even if I wanted to pay his brothers off again, I didn't have the first clue how to find them. Their number had been disconnected for months.

Folding my hands on my desk, I took a slow, even breath. Then met Brendon's eyes. "There's something you need to know about Joel. About why he's really here."

Chapter Six

Footsteps echoing down the long, overly bright hallway, I made my way to my room, all the ways I'd fucked up weigh on my shoulders like a bag of bricks. The discussion with Brendon had taken well over an hour, in which time he'd sent one of his men to find Alec and bring him home. Letting Alec find his own way wasn't an option—Brendon's words, not mine, though I agreed. He'd reported back later that Alec hadn't put up a fuss once he'd heard the security detail was under strict instruction from Luther not to let either of us leave the building unaccompanied.

Security would be heightened here as well, but Brendon conceded that we shouldn't arouse Joel's suspicions until every possible threat he posed was neutralized. Which meant keeping Alec in the dark, at least a bit longer. Brendon hoped he'd be able to locate Alec's brothers over the weekend, but if he didn't Alec couldn't behave any differently toward Joel come Monday.

Dropping my jacket on the ornate, blue velvet chair by my dresser, I took a moment to stare into my massive, perfectly clean room with my huge, neatly made bed. Gleaming, dark wood furniture gave the room a classic elegance, but there wasn't one personal item on any surface. Like every other room in my part of the house, this one could be a display in a museum, showing the life of someone long dead.

The space was tolerable when Alec or Luther were in it. When they rumpled the covers and threw the pillows on the floor. When their laughter broke the silence or their moans filled the vast space. I'd installed restraints on the bedposts and enjoyed several passionate nights in here with Alec, toying with him until he was begging and the scent of him lingered for days. We'd woken early each morning, heading to the office exchanging secret smiles, lingering in one another's presence whenever possible. Not something that happened often enough once the 'honeymoon period' of the relationship faded away and we'd both gotten wrapped up in our careers, but memories of him covered every inch of the room when I looked past the muted colors.

What would the room be like if it belonged to him too? What would it be like to wake up next to him every morning? Would Luther be tempted to stay as well? He wasn't fond of this space, but I would change it for him. For both of them.

"You look fucking miserable."

Alec's soft words startled me, but I remained where I stood as he slipped into the room and came to my side. So far everything I'd said had upset him, because I couldn't give him the answers he wanted. Didn't know how to let him in the way he needed me to.

So I kept my mouth shut.

"I think I might've been pushing too hard." Letting out a heavy sigh, Alec walked up to the bed, and dropped down on the edge, glancing up at me as he leaned back. "I was looking forward to this time together. I thought things would be... I don't know, different I guess. But spending all my time pissed off isn't cool. I'm sorry."

"Don't be. You have every right to expect more from me."

"Not more than you're willing to give."

I lowered my gaze, not sure how to explain without giving away too much. There had to be some middle ground. "I want to give you everything, Alec. And I *will*. If you can be patient with me, there's a lot I need to tell you."

He nodded slowly, reaching back to grab a pillow and stuff it behind him. A few cushions fell off the bed and he glanced over, looking like he was going to pick them up.

With one swift step I grabbed his shoulder, firmly pushing him back on the bed. "Leave them. I was just thinking how much I enjoy having you in here."

"Making a mess?" He laughed at his own words, then gave me a hooded look. "Actually, yeah. I can see that. You're probably too busy though. Do you want me to go?"

Fuck, he was hot when he got in the bratty, teasing mode. Trapping his wrists in one hand, I pinned him down with my body. The way he tugged at his wrists sent blood pulsing to my dick as I held his gaze, pale blue eyes darkening with lust.

"I have no intention of letting you go anywhere." I scraped my teeth along his jaw. Whispered in his ear. "But stop distracting me." I loosened my grip. "You wanted me to be more open with you. And I'm telling you I want you here. I want your clothes on my floor every day. I want to wake up and feel you beside me. I fucking hate this goddamn room when you're not in it."

Jerking one wrist free, Alec brought a hand to my cheek, forcing me to meet his eyes. "I usually sleep with Luther... I thought you preferred sleeping alone."

"I don't."

"But if you hate this room, why not stay in mine? Or Luther's? We could all fit—"

"Because I have control here." Irritated at myself for ruining the mood, I began to rise, but Alec pulled me back and wrapped his legs around my waist. Flattening my hand on the bed by his head, I stared at him. "Careful, pet."

He leaned up and nipped my bottom lip. "Don't fucking 'careful' me. I'm not submitting to you until you explain. You can have me here whenever you want. All you have to do is ask."

Letting out a heavy sigh, I rested my forehead on his. "And explain why it has to be *here*."

A wry grin on his lips, Alec broke the tension of our little talk, his tone soft and encouraging. "That too." He held my gaze. "This room is…it's not exactly welcoming. I thought it was the way you liked things, all rich-looking and dark, but it's like you're on a damn stage all the time. Like it's so fucking hard to step out of the spotlight, you just don't bother."

My spine stiffened, and the urge to protest was on my lips, but…he was right. I inclined my head. "One of the many things I love about you. You see right through my shit." I lifted him, sliding him up the bed so I could lay over him with the mattress supporting some of my weight. Braced on one elbow, I brought my other hand to his hair, sliding my fingers through the soft, golden strands. "What you see around you is a reminder to myself that I am worth something. But it's also a reminder of when I wasn't. You and Luther both change how every room in this house feels. You make it feel like a real home."

"Then why don't you stay with us more often? We can make this into a home, Xavier. The whole damn mansion if you wanted. But you have to be ready, and I'm not sure you are. You still come here to hide." He curved his hand around the back of my neck. "I was so pissed when I saw your car pull up and you didn't come to me. You should have. I get that I was pushing, and maybe I went too far, but I was hurt. I need to know you care when I am. That I won't always be chasing you to make things better."

"You won't, Alec. And you're right, I should have gone to you. I was afraid to make things worse." I smoothed my hand over his hair, leaning down to kiss him. "Thank you for being willing to chase me, though."

"Mmm, if you're gonna be this sweet, maybe I should do it more often." His hands slid down my back and he tugged at my shirt. "I need to feel you, Xavier. Like this. No games, no restraints, no control. Just. You."

Rising up, I unbuttoned my shirt, letting him shove it off my arms as I claimed his lips. Getting emotions tangled up with sex was difficult—only Luther knew what buttons to push to force me to let down my walls—but right now, there was nothing holding me back. I needed this connection with Alec. Needed the warmth in his eyes. The deep, hot pressure of his lips, a hint of sweetness lingering from the heaping teaspoons of sugar he put in his coffee. Needed the way he moved against me, barely holding still as I freed the first few buttons of his shirt, then gave up and swiftly pulled it up over his head.

The button on his pants broke loose when I tugged at it, but I barely noticed as I shoved them off his hips and down his thighs. His restless movements had my dick straining against my own pants and I ripped the seam along my zipper undoing it. Dick hot against his thigh, I raked my fingers into his hair, slanting my mouth over his and tasting him, drinking in his soft pleas. Sucking on his bottom lip, I finally wrapped my hand around his cock and began stroking him, using the weight of my body to hold him still.

Pressing his thighs apart with my knees I rose up, sliding my hand over him until I reached the smooth flesh of his taint. A bit further and I penetrated the tightness of him with a single finger, watching his face as he struggled not to resist the gritty pressure. Bending down, I flicked my tongue over the head of his cock, laving it over his balls, getting him wet enough that my finger began to slide in deeper without much effort.

"Fuck, Xavier. Don't tease me." He lifted his hips, taking me in deeper. "Don't hold back—not tonight. I need to know you can't. That you don't want to."

Holding close to him, I kissed his throat, then nodded, keeping my finger inside him even as I reached back and fumbled in my top drawer for the lube. Using my teeth to pop the cap open, I poured a generous amount into the hand still half pressed against him, easing my finger in and out as I prepared him.

Guiding my dick to him, I pressed in the second I withdrew my finger. He tensed, then relaxed, the smooth ring of muscle surrounding me as I stretched him with the head of my dick. Easing back, I lifted his hips, driving in with one deep thrust.

Muffling his gasp with my lips over his, I hooked his knees over my forearms and pulled him to me as I slammed in yet again.

The grip of his ass around my dick made it hard not to lose myself in a release that was already so close, but I didn't want this to be a quick fuck.

I'd planned to toy with him over the weekend. To keep him guessing when I'd finally take him. Instead, he'd asked for tonight. For me to take what I wanted without thought. Without a plan. Which I only ever did when I amused myself with him at work.

Those times were quick and explosive, but there was an edge of me using him. Of him wanting to be used. There were times I left him unsatisfied, knowing he'd come home to Luther, desperate and ready for our man's intense form of pleasure. A pleasure that left his lovers completely taken apart, needing to be put back together before they could even *think* of climbing out of his bed.

There would be no sharing for the next week. No relying on Luther to satisfy Alec both physically and emotionally. The way Alec's fingers dug into my shoulders, the way his lips parted and his gaze locked with mine as I angled my hips, was raw and open. This man I loved had left himself vulnerable. The only one to protect him from at this moment was me.

Lifting him further onto the bed, shifting my hands to his shoulders and letting his thighs grip my hips, I spoke against his lips. "While Luther is gone, I need you here. No matter how much I piss you off." The rhythmic slapping of my flesh against his made my balls lift as release taunted me, so close my vision blurred with the effort to delay it. "I need you next to me. I need to know you'll always come back, no matter what happens."

"Always. Fuck, Xavier, you could've had that already if you'd asked." He cupped my cheek, the pressure of his thighs on my hips slowing my steady thrusts. "I'm not leaving you. Even when you push me away because how much you love me scares you, I'll be right fucking here." He brought his hands down to my ass, gripping tight and driving us together. "Don't ever doubt that."

"I don't."

"You're lying." He tipped his head back as I slammed into him, over and over, desperate to push him too close to the edge to continue the conversation. "Ugh, and you're not playing fair."

I pressed my lips against his throat and laughed. "Do I ever?"

"No. But I'm getting better at this game." His blunt nails dug into my ass and he gripped me so hard one deep thrust set off a blast of pleasure like a trigger he'd had his finger on all along.

Letting out a rough, incoherent curse, I fell against him, the earth splintering in a rush of blinding white light. I moved with the last pulse, sucking in a sharp breath, the tightness around me as Alec came taking the pleasure to the razor's edge of pain. My dick was so sensitive it throbbed with a weak effort to harden again, even as I ground my teeth and took a firm grip on Alec's thighs to hold him still.

Being the evil brat he was, if he had *any* energy left, he'd keep clenching around me just to make me suffer. Struggling to catch my breath, I braced myself for some well-deserved torture.

He laughed like he'd read my thoughts and slumped back on the bed as I drew out, watching me collapse beside him, completely boneless. "I love make-up sex."

Arm over my eyes, I chuckled. "Is that what that was?"

"Mmhmm."Alec pulled my other arm out and rested his head on my shoulder. "If it helps, you're easier to deal with than Luther. He thinks sex is a cop-out. The last time we had an argument that was his fault, he brought me flowers and chocolate and wanted to have a fancy date. I ruined the night by climbing on his lap and grinding on him until he let me ride his dick."

Moving my arm, I glanced over at Alec with a smirk. "That doesn't sound like you ruined the night at all."

"Well…it was a nice restaurant. And he had to pull in favors to get the reservation." Alec's lips thinned. "Some places won't hold a spot unless he uses your name. And he hates doing that."

"He shouldn't have to. He's worth quite a bit in his own right."

"Yeah…I kinda felt bad after." Alec's lips quirked. "So he spanked me and told me I was being ridiculous. The point is, you can both be difficult. And that's okay. My job is to work around that."

I nodded slowly, wondering if I should take Alec's lead when it came to making things right when I had disagreements with Luther. I would have gone out for dinner and considered the issues we had less important than whatever time we had to spend together.

Though...it wasn't often we *had* issues. Not that we discussed, anyway. If Luther was angry I'd give him some space. He did the same for me. When we'd calmed down, we'd continue as though nothing had happened.

What would it be like for Luther to be in the wrong and apologize with something nice? Or to realize I'd fucked up and find a personal way to show him how sorry I was? We'd explored a power exchange and I enjoyed submitting to him, curious what kind of punishments he'd come up with, but that wasn't an option when he was truly upset. When I hurt him or angered him too much for him to crave that kind of control.

Flowers and chocolate weren't something I'd have considered, but I could see Luther appreciating the effort. If he'd done it for Alec, the gesture had to mean something to him.

I pressed my face into Alec's hair and let out a heavy sigh. "No one's ever brought me flowers."

"I don't think anyone knew you'd like them." Alec flattened his hand on my chest, over my heart. "If they did, you'd have them every day. But now that I know, maybe they'll be special."

"Everything you do is special."

Alec pushed up on one hand, looking down at me, his brow furrowed. "Are you okay? You do know Luther will say you're spoiling me if you keep being so sweet."

Laughing, I pulled Alec back down, holding him against me as I tugged the blankets over us both. "Luther wants me to spoil you. And I'm not being sweet, I'm being honest. Which is what you asked for."

Hand back on my chest, Alec inclined his head. "I did. And you were. And I'm fucking happy. I love you and I wonder every day if I deserve you. If I have any right to tell you off when things aren't going great."

Drawing him closer, I leaned over, my lips brushing his cheek. "You deserve the best of me. You have every right to demand it. Don't ever doubt that."

"I'm still not sure I belong here, Xavier. If I'll wake up tomorrow and do the wrong thing and end up back on the streets."

My throat tightened, because I should have paid enough attention to ease his fears, but I hadn't. I always worried if he had enough to eat. Asked for details after he saw the doctor, certain he was still too skinny. I made sure he was warm. That he had nice clothes. Security.

But the security he needed was more than money could buy. It might take years for him to trust he wouldn't lose all he'd gained. That being alone, sleeping on the streets, wouldn't happen again. He'd finally agreed with Luther to see a therapist after waking several nights in a row, screaming in the throes of a nightmare, seeing someone who'd come at him in the weak, temporary shelter he'd found, ready to take the little he had.

No amount of gifts, or money, or promises could erase what he'd been through. But earning his trust might help.

"You belong here, Alec. You do because I love you. And more importantly, because you've found your own place. You don't rely on Luther and I. If you decided to leave tomorrow, you'd be fine. You have your own money. You'll have your own car soon—sooner if you let me—"

"No."

"All right, but I hope you understand what I'm saying. You've built your own life. You don't need anyone to keep you from going back where you were. You've already done that."

"But you're still trying to protect me." Alec frowned when I dropped my gaze. "There's something you're not telling me. Something you don't think I'm strong enough to handle."

"I know how strong you are."

"Then tell me." Alec hesitated, then rested his head back on my chest. "In the morning, because right now, everything is good. I could get mad and go back to my own room, but I want you to hold me. I want to wake up next to you. Next to a man who loves me enough to trust me with the truth."

Holding Alec, I considered the distance trying to protect him from Joel could put between us. Would he forgive me once I'd 'fixed' everything and could finally tell him the reasons behind what I'd done? I'd wanted more time, kept telling myself that was all I needed to make things better, but hadn't I told myself the same thing when Joel had me under his control? That with enough time, I'd finally be free?

Yes, with *time*, he'd gotten bored of me. But I was all too aware of the damage he'd done.

In trying to protect Alec, I was exposing him to the very man who'd almost broken me, without giving him the chance to protect himself. Alec's brothers would continue to be a threat, whether Joel was involved or not. Not a threat he had to handle alone, but one that was his to decide *how* to handle.

Joel was counting on me being the man he knew. The one he could manipulate. Who he could play on old fears. And I'd proven him right.

But what if I didn't?

What if I did the last thing he'd ever expect? Take away his power. Refuse to play at all.

It would mean exposing myself in a way I never had. To *anyone*.

Doing so with a man I loved shouldn't scare me so much, but I couldn't help wonder how Alec would look at me once he knew the truth. Once I finally gave him exactly what he'd asked for.

Tonight he was here. In my arms. Trusting that I was ready to be there for him. Not as I wanted to be, but as he needed me.

Tomorrow, I had to decide if I was worthy of that trust.

What kept me awake was not knowing if I was.

Chapter Seven

"Kill him! Xavier, hit the button I showed you! No, aim first!" Alec let out a rough laugh as we both died. "You're not paying attention."

The sad thing was, I had been. Gripping the controller, leaning forward on my bed, I bit into my tongue to keep from letting out every curse I knew as my character in the two-player shooter game died again, leaving my partner, Alec, vulnerable at a pivotal moment.

Why is this my life?

Shaking my head, I started the game over for what had to be the hundredth time, ignoring my phone as it rang in the distance. The same two villains would pop out...*now!* I shot them, careful to aim as Alec had instructed, pumping my fist in the air when they went down.

"Yes!"

"Not yet, you have to—" Alec groaned as yet another villain jumped out from behind a tree and riddled my character with bullets. "Finish this level before you celebrate."

With a short huff, I tossed the controller on my pillows and climbed off the bed, stretching the stiffness from my spine. We'd been playing all morning, stopping only to devour the breakfast

Ms. Lacey brought in, a happy little smile on her lips as though playing a video game was the best thing she'd ever seen me do.

Granted, it was a pleasant distraction. If one considered losing again and again in the bloodiest way possible *fun*. I couldn't see myself becoming a passionate gamer, but I couldn't pretend I didn't enjoy playing with Alec.

Without me holding him back, he'd probably have finished the level an hour ago, but he seemed to have a blast shouting at me as though we were really out there, in the field, soldiers fighting for survival against all odds. The huge grin on his face when I shouted back, racing forward by his side, sharing his excitement as we reached each checkpoint, was worth the humiliation of not having mastered the simplest aspects of the game. Being great at playing wasn't the point.

Alec had never had someone to just relax and have fun with. He'd always been competing with his brothers, struggling to get what little scraps of attention his parents could spare. But that wasn't his life anymore. He was part of my family. And if killing things—or rather, killing *fictional* things—made him happy, then I'd make sure he had every opportunity.

And that he wasn't killing them alone.

So long as he didn't want to keep going longer than I could manage, anyway. I might not be old, but my body didn't appreciate the position I'd been holding for the past three hours and was making damn sure I knew it.

The soft sound of Alec sliding across the bed brought my attention back to him just as he curved his hands around my waist and began digging his thumbs into the stiff muscles along the base of my spine. Painful, but so fucking good. I hissed in a breath when he found a knot and rubbed it until the ache faded away.

"If you lie down I could get the rest." He ran his hands up and down my back. "Not sure if you've got other stuff to do, but I'm starting to like this room."

"Are you?" I looked at him over my shoulder, one brow raised. "Because I had Mr. Mathews install a TV and PlayStation?"

"No. Because hanging out in here with you all morning was nice. Just being lazy, not getting dressed, not having anywhere to go." He picked up my abandoned controller and grinned. "Doing my best to teach you how to stay alive."

I grinned back at him and shook my head. "With how often I died, you're clearly a horrible teacher."

"Or you just suck at following instructions."

Spitting out a laugh and shoving his shoulder, I sat on the bed next to him, deciding I wasn't ready to face the real world yet. There was nothing else I needed to do today, so why not stay right here?

"Speaking of instructions..." Alec lowered his gaze and brought his hands to his thighs, rubbing them over the dark blue, silk pajama pants he'd borrowed. "I haven't forgotten what we discussed last night."

There's your reason.

Nodding slowly, I stared at the wall by my dresser, a rich, matte brown that gave the room an elegant distinction, but also seemed to absorb all the light. The life and joy that had filled the room dimmed, a cold hand gripping my throat as the memories I'd fought so hard to erase returned.

"There's...a lot you don't know about me. About how I avoided living on the streets, like you did. How I finished school, got my art degrees, gained the skills to have my work in such high demand." I placed my hands on my knees and took a measured breath, letting my tone take in some of the cold around me, numbing me to the pain. "My parents weren't thrilled when I told them I was bisexual, but they would have allowed me to stay if I'd agreed to follow their plans for me. Continue training to take my father's place in the oil company, marry the right girl, and satisfy any *urges* I might have because of my 'proclivities' to private affairs. Within days they had it all figured out."

Alec chewed at his bottom lip, putting his hand over mine. "You've kept things private. Is it because of them?"

"No. Once I started getting an excessive amount of attention in the media, I wanted to control the narrative. To keep as much of myself from them as possible and force them to focus on my work." My jaw clenched. "Because it's the work that made my parents give up on me. Decide I'd never be the son they wanted. I had a cousin who fit the role much better. Who didn't draw silly pictures and look at dresses all the time. Who could make my father proud."

Alec's brow furrowed. "Your parents disowned you because you wanted to be an artist?"

I wasn't sure I'd ever used that word around Alec. *Disowned*. I'd implied my parents were alive. No longer part of my life. But put that plainly was somehow easier. Simple and precise, because that's exactly what they'd done.

"Yes and no. It was a combination of things. At the time I'd been ready to come out to everyone. I'd met Luther and I was in love with him, but I wasn't sure he wanted to be out. His family hadn't reacted badly, but they were still...adapting. There was no rush, so I agreed with my parents' initial demands. Figured I'd talk to him before pushing too hard..." I sighed and shook my head. "Then they told me they were sending me to Europe to finish high school. And to attend college—for courses they chose. Leaving would 'fix me'. I'd return as the man they'd always expected me to be."

"So you'd have to leave Luther *and* give up all your dreams."

"Of course. Which I refused to do. So they gave me an ultimatum." I pressed my eyes shut, a stiff smile on my lips. "Either I accept the *amazing* opportunity they were giving me, or I'd be left with nothing. My mother even packed my things and left them in the foyer to prove how serious she was. My father closed all my accounts and took my credit cards. I had hours to decide."

"You left."

"Yes. And went straight to Luther's house. His mother let me sleep on the sofa. Didn't ask too many questions, just told me I was welcome to stay as long as I needed." My throat tightened. "I love Luther. I have for so long...but it wasn't enough then. I had nothing to offer. No plans. No future. I couldn't go to school and even applying for jobs got me nowhere. How could I be the man for Luther when his parents had worked so hard to put him in an expensive school, to give him a great life? Here I was, sleeping on their couch for months, nothing but a pathetic distraction."

Alec's jaw hardened. He squeezed my hand. "There's no way Luther saw it that way."

"He didn't, but I was making him miserable. He missed school some days just to make sure I was okay. Things had to change." My lips parted and...at first I couldn't speak. Couldn't tell him what came next. But then the words began to flow. "I had this idea that I could work for a design company as an intern. My art teachers had always told me how good I was. How hard could it be?" I let out a bitter laugh. "It was humiliating, but I went to every single company I could find in the phone book, carrying around my portfolio as though it proved anything. Most places wouldn't even schedule an interview—no surprise, I was only sixteen. They sent me away again and again. My old friends from school stopped talking to me because they were so embarrassed. Even without an interview, word got around. The 'golden boy' was begging for a job."

"Bet they fucking regret that now." Alec's tone hardened. "Assholes."

"Oh, they do. I invite several to every event. I'm a petty bastard." I smirked at his sharp laugh. Turned my hand in his and stroked his knuckles with my thumb. "My efforts got the attention of one of my father's old friends. When he asked to meet me, I thought all my humiliation had finally paid off. And it did...in a way." This time, when I paused, Alec didn't speak. So I continued, swallowing hard. "Sixteen years old, meeting with a man I'd looked up to most of my life. I was willing to accept any offer he made. Instead of a job, he gave me advice. Guidance. Support. He helped me get back in school. Found me my own place and dealt with the legalities. He called all the money he gave me 'a loan'. I assumed it meant I'd pay him back once I began making money off my designs. That he meant what he said—my work would grace every red carpet, every runway, in just a few short years."

"That's not how he wanted you to repay him."

"For almost two years he made it seem like it was. He was affectionate, made sure I had everything I could ever need. Life was almost as easy as it had been back home." I shook my head. "Not a home really, it was never that, but... That's not the point. I had the lifestyle I was accustomed to. Luther had his own problems, his brother cut him off and his parents were concerned about his 'choices.' Which I assumed meant me. So I started giving him more space. Became obsessed with my art."

"And this man—?"

"When I turned eighteen he told me he'd continue to pay my schooling, my apartment, whatever I might require, but I had to give him anything he asked for—leaving no doubt as to exactly what *that* was. I was disgusted at first. He was more than twice my age. I wasn't attracted to him. I loved Luther and I told him so." My eyes burned and I looked away, not sure I could continue if I saw my own disgust reflected in Alec's eyes. "He wasn't surprised. He'd planned for my response. And told me he'd destroy Luther's life if I didn't cooperate. He had connections—I knew he could do it. At the time Luther wanted to be a lawyer, so he didn't need powerful enemies. So I went to Luther one last time...and left without saying goodbye. I didn't see him again for three years."

Alec squeezed my hand so hard it hurt. He made a rough sound in the back of his throat. Reached out and grabbed my shoulder. "What did he do to you?"

I stared at the wall. "Luther? We didn't—"

"The man. You know I mean the man." Alec hesitated. "You don't have to tell me."

"Yes. I do." My jaw clenched, I kept my focus on the wall, my words coming out completely lifeless. "He fucked me. He had parties and let his friends fuck me. I was his new little toy. Not the first and not the last. I hated it, I wasn't a very good toy, but that was part of the appeal, you see. He'd enjoy pushing me until I was almost fighting to get away, then he'd remind me why I was there. And I'd…give in."

"Jesus fucking Christ, Xavier." Alec moved as though to hug me, his eyes wide, glistening with unshed tears. His voice took on a rough edge. "Can I… Do you need…?"

"Not yet." I couldn't finish if I hugged him. It would feel good. Be a reminder that the worst had passed. But letting the words come out was the only way I could get through this. And he needed to hear it all. "The threats didn't come for the first two years of him supporting me. There were moments I felt a little uncomfortable, but I needed him. And he was good to me. I wouldn't have survived without him. That's how he operates. He likely had a toy already groomed to play with while he was working on me. I'm sure he has one now."

"Now?" Alec's brow furrowed. "Xavier, have you seen this man again? Is that why things have been off? You know he can't hurt you anymore, right? You've accomplished so much since you got away. And he can't go after Luther—"

"But he can go after you." Fuck, was he going to hate me for telling him this? Not when I should have, not when Joel had first shown up, but after I'd fallen back into the same pattern?

It doesn't matter.

I had to tell him.

Had to give him the choice. To show I believed in him. That I knew he was strong.

Stronger than I'd ever been.

"The man is Joel. He came to me and told me he wanted you. Offered to play a game. And I agreed."

"*Joel?* But he… I…" Alec's eyes widened. He shook his head. "You *agreed?*"

"He is the one who sent the PI to Luther. He's been paying off your brothers." I winced as Alec shoved off the bed and swept his arm across the nightstand, smashing our mugs against the wall. "I needed time to figure out how to keep you safe. I'll hire a new investigator. I'll pay off your brothers. Whatever you need me to do I'll—"

"Xavier, *stop*." Alec spun around, dropping to his knees in front of me and grabbing my shoulders. He shook me, tears streaming down his cheeks. "Please. Just. Stop. This man fucking hurt you. He *used* you. Then he shows up and you're too fucking scared to tell me? You let him manipulate you again? Try to use me against you?" His jaw hardened. "Yes, I'm fucking pissed that you didn't tell me right away. Yes, it freaks me out that you let anyone believe I'm someone you could put out there like a fucking prize. But he can't touch me. Because you finally decided to tell me the truth."

"It wasn't…my *first* inclination."

"I bet." His lips quirked slightly, but his expression remained hard. "This isn't about me. It's about proving he still has power over you, isn't it?"

I frowned and shook my head. "He's a bored old rich man. It's not that complicated. He saw I had someone he wanted and thought it would be entertaining to prove he could steal you away."

"Then he would've just tried to tempt me and avoided you even knowing he was there until it was too late. And hey, it might have worked. If he'd threatened you or Luther, I might have…" Alec swallowed, paling slightly. "I don't know."

"I wouldn't have let that happen. I've seen how he works. How patient he can be."

"Because you were in the middle of it. But Luther didn't know, because Joel kept you apart. He didn't do the same this time because you're the target, not me." Alec let out a rough groan, pushed to his feet, then climbed onto my lap. Straddling my thighs, he wrapped his arms around the back of my neck. "We have to tell Luther. Take away every opportunity this fucker has to come between us. Then we have to expose him somehow."

"I just want him gone, Alec." I folded my arms around him, tipping my head back and brushing my lips over his. "I want to find out where your brothers are. Make sure they'll never hurt you again."

Alec raked his fingers into my hair, tugging lightly. "And I want to make sure Joel never hurts *you* again. Or anyone else."

"Should we…" All right, I didn't think Alec would like this suggestion, but it was worth considering. "Luther's right-hand man has connections. I could speak to him and…Joel wouldn't be a problem anymore."

With a soft snort, Alec shoved forward, knocking me back with him on top of me. He kissed me, then nipped my bottom lip. "Let's save the homicide for our video games. An asshole like Joel's gotta have secrets. Actually, we can handle my brothers the same way. They're both on parole. If we can prove they've broken it, they'll be back behind bars."

I inclined my head. An obvious solution, but one I hadn't suggested because they were still Alec's brothers. I couldn't be sure he'd *want* them in jail.

But since he'd brought it up, I wasn't about to argue. "Whatever you decide, I'm right behind you."

He stilled, then buried his face against the side of my neck. "I won't have you and Luther afraid for me and doing stupid shit to keep me safe. I always figured I *should* be loyal to them because they're my brothers. But blood doesn't mean a goddamn thing. They're not my family."

"I am. And so is Luther. You don't need them."

"No, I don't." He huffed out a breath. "But I *do* need to wash Luther's car."

Before I had a chance to react, Alec slipped away from me, pulling off the white T-shirt he'd been wearing all morning, then doing a little shimmy as he took off the silk pajama pants. Completely naked, he winked at me before spinning around and heading out into the hall.

Fuck me, he's actually going to do it. I shook my head, hesitating for a moment, looking at my own black silk lounge pants and plain white T-shirt. The staff had *never* seen me out of my room dressed like this.

But with Alec *naked*, they might not even notice. And I wasn't sure I cared if they did.

Rolling my shoulders, I stepped into the hall. Paused as Ms Lacey passed, her cheeks red. She gave me a quick once over, then chuckled.

"I'll keep the staff away from the windows, Mr. Ashburne." She gave my arm a light pat. "You're a lucky man."

My own cheeks heating, I inclined my head and continued out to where Alec was pulling Luther's classic Chevelle onto the driveway curving to the front entrance. The car was nice, but I didn't know much aside from how much Luther loved the thing. His possessions were special to him. Unlike mine, they didn't represent a bitter idea of status. Both he and his father loved classic cars and always talked about getting one, but his father never had the time or urge to make the actual investment.

He'd been excited to come visit and check out Luther's purchase when he got it last year, though. They'd spent hours discussing all the specs over a couple of beers, doing their best to include me, but I had nothing to add. I'd simply sat there, enjoying their excitement, trying not to wonder if I ever would've had the chance to share a moment like that with my own father.

Probably not, and only if I'd given up on Luther for good. Even when I was trapped with Joel, losing Luther was never an option. Yes, I'd been afraid he'd meet someone else, but part of me belonged to him and always would. I'd counted on him knowing that. On him being willing to forgive me.

I was damn lucky he had.

Descending the steps, I watched Alec ease the car into park, much smoother than he had when Luther first started teaching him to drive. He still drove with some hesitation, but he was so damn proud to have his license I loved watching him do it.

If only he'd let me buy him his own damn car. He'd started saving up and wanted to buy an old beat up thing, but Luther took one look at it and insisted Alec *at least* make sure his vehicle would last a few years and be safe. When they started shopping around,

Alec grew more interested in classic cars, which meant increasing his savings.

And, for now, sticking to driving one of my cars.

Which he wouldn't even let me give him as an alternative to buying his own.

Stubborn. But I respected his determination, no matter how much I grumbled about it.

Reaching the bottom step, I leaned against the wide, stone railing as Alec jogged back to the garage for a bucket, some soap, and the long hose to attach to the faucet behind the hedges. He filled the bucket, glancing up at me once with a broad smile, his rumpled hair falling over his eyes.

"You gonna help?"

Snorting, I shook my head. "This is *your* punishment. That wouldn't be right."

He nodded slowly. "Fair enough. But can you grab my phone from the front seat and record me doing it at least? I wasn't joking about making sure Luther can watch."

"*That* I can do." I started across the pavement, wincing as a small piece of gravel dug into the bottom of my foot. Alec and Luther came here barefoot regularly, sometimes running around in the grass to toss a football. I could manage a few steps. Schooling my features at the sharp jab of several more small rocks, I reached the driver's side, opened the door, and grabbed Alec's phone.

He joined me, setting down the sudsy bucket of water, a sheepish grin on his lips as he waited for me to begin recording. Then he took a deep breath. "Hey, Luther. So...I'm about to do my punishment, but I just wanted to say I miss you. And thank you for giving me something special to do for you—which makes it not really a punishment, but whatever. I'll make sure she's gleaming and it's weird being outside like this naked. But Xavier's here, so I feel safe." He licked his lips, then inhaled slowly. "Things have been good. We've spent a lot of time together, so don't worry. I'm taking care of our man. He needs it more than he'll say, but hopefully, whatever he hasn't told you already, he will when you get home." Alec's gaze shifted, locking with mine. "I'm telling you now, we're not letting him sleep alone anymore. I'll keep your spot on the bed warm." He brought his fingers to his lips, kissed them, then held them out. "I love you."

I swallowed hard, lowering the phone as Alec ducked his head and grabbed the bucket. Turning so I could put myself into the shot, while not losing sight of Alec dunking a soft rag into the soapy water, I smiled.

"He's something else, isn't he? I'll do my best to make sure you don't miss a second of this, because he's…" My words trailed off as water from the soaked rag trailed down Alec's thigh before he brought it to the hood of the car. Those taut muscles, under smooth, lightly tanned skin, were mouth-watering. His ass was a few shades lighter than his thighs, almost as though he'd tanned there too, but not as often. "I noticed he said 'like this'. Alec's been naked outside before, hasn't he? With you." I shook my head. "I've missed too much. The two of you, lying out here enjoying the sun together, while I was in my cold office, rejecting yet another invitation to join you."

Glancing up at the house, I eyed every curtain, sure at least one member of the staff would sneak a peek, but there was no one.

"You've made sure you can have privacy out here. That's why… Ms. Lacey told me she'd keep the staff away from the windows. She's done this before." My lips curved slightly. "I wish I'd been with you both, but I'm not upset. You have something special with Alec. You deserve it. And I hope I will too." I rubbed a hand over my face. "In any case, I will repeat what Alec said. I miss you, but things are good here. We've spoken about so many things. Things I need to tell you. Things I should have already, but…" From the corner of my eye I could see Alec moving as though dancing to a song in his head, each sultry movement as he rubbed the cloth over the gleaming black hood making it more and more difficult for my lips to form even the most basic syllables. "Fuck, just look at him. I'm sure you understand, but I'm rather…distracted."

I clicked to stop recording, sending the video to Luther before I started recording again, not sure when he'd watch, but knowing he'd want to see it right away if he was alone now.

My phone rang just as Alec moved to scrubbing the fender.

"I needed to hear your voice." Luther let out a rough laugh. "This is ending up as more of a punishment for *me* than anything else. I just had brunch with my brother and I'm back in my room. Can you record live?"

"Absolutely." I switched to video chat, positioning myself again so Luther could see both me and Alec. Luther's face on the small screen brought a tightness to my chest that I hadn't expected. We'd been together so long, I'd figured a week apart would be no different than being on a tight deadline and only seeing one another in passing, but it was. The security of having Luther within reach was gone.

I'd taken him for granted and I knew it.

"What's that look?" Luther frowned. "Xavier, if you need me to come home—"

"No. We discussed this. I'm fine." I sighed and brought my fingers to brush over the screen. "I just realized I've missed too many opportunities. Like Alec told me earlier today, I could have you in my bed every night. But I was distant and let that be something the two of you had. I never realized how much I want it."

Luther's expression softened. "But you have now."

"Yes."

"Then when I get home, we'll make one of the rooms ours. I don't care which one. We'll each have our own space if needed, but every night it will be the three of us together. No exceptions."

"I'd like that." I gave myself a little shake. "We'll discuss logistics when you get home. Is he fucking hot or what?"

Laughing, Luther arched brow at me. "*He's* being punished for swearing."

"Try it. I dare you." I smirked. "I won't agree to those kinds of rules and you know it. For Alec, I understand why you both found it necessary. He'd slip at the wrong time and didn't want to seem unprofessional at work. I *do not* have that issue."

"All right, force me to be creative then." Luther's gaze fixed on something behind me and his lips quirked. "I see you have your hands full."

He was right. While I'd been distracted, Alec had climbed up on the slippery hood to scrub the roof, getting more soap and water on himself than on the car. Carefully balancing his weight on his knees, he was so close to the windshield that several imprints of his dick were on the glass.

I'd seen the typical video of hot chicks in bikinis washing cars, and enjoyed them *very* much, but this was ten times more erotic. And not only because Alec was naked.

The way he moved. The way the water sluiced over his skin. The fact that I could remember how every inch of him tasted, how his body felt against mine... The lure of him was so fucking intense I couldn't hold still.

But I couldn't get much closer without getting wet.

"Xavier, put the phone on the dashboard so I can keep watching, but don't just fucking stand there or I'll book the next flight home." Luther's tone took on an edge of need that reached straight down to my core. "Damn, convincing him that sunbathing naked on our property is acceptable definitely paid off. He's absolutely shameless."

"He is that." I opened the door on the driver's side, where there was no water spilling over yet, and set the phone on the middle of the dashboard, looking around for a way to prop it up so Luther would get a good view. There wasn't much in the car, so I took off my shirt, bunching it and positioning the phone against the windshield. The sun was almost behind the house, so the light shouldn't be a problem, but it was hard to tell if the angle was right.

Crouching on the hood, wet hair tumbling over his eyes, Alec grinned at me. "I can see him, so this should be good."

"Perfect." I reached across the seats and opened the glove compartment, grabbing the lube from Luther's stash. I closed the door, then dropped the bottle onto the ridge against the windshield before circling the car, my gaze fixed on Alec, who'd slowed his little dance.

A breathy sound left him as I latched onto his calves and brought him to the edge of the hood, angled toward the passenger side of the car so Luther could get a decent look at what I was doing to our boy. Not perfect, but he could use his imagination.

Hooking Alec's calves over my forearms, I lifted him, cupping my hands under his ass, smiling at the rough hiss he released when I brushed my lips along his inner thigh. The scent from his earlier shower lingered on his skin, a fresh hint of citrus with amber undertones, along with a warmth that was all him, making my mouth water. He'd shaved recently, leaving every inch of him completely exposed. Fucking gorgeous.

Elbows braced on the hood of the car, he tipped his head back as I breathed over his taint, spreading him open before flicking my tongue over his tight little hole.

"Fuck, Xavier." He jerked when I licked him again, slamming his head on the hood. "And I thought Luther was the exhibitionist."

"No one is watching." I licked up to his balls, sucking them lightly and tightening my grip on his ass when he tried to lift to my mouth. "Be still. If I have to stop to find something to tie you to the hood, the phone will die and Luther will miss the show."

Glancing over at the phone on the dashboard, Alec groaned. "Oh fuck, I don't think I'll last long."

Following his gaze, I grinned as I saw Luther had pulled out his dick and was stroking himself, letting us get a good look before bringing the phone back up to his face. His lips slanted before he licked his lips, then jutted his chin out as though to say I should continue.

"You'll last at least as long as he does." I brushed my lips over his balls, enjoying the soft give, the slight texture of them, all tight and hot. Moving down, I drew a figure eight over his taint with tongue, shifting closer and closer to his hole with longer strokes. His thighs were trembling, but he was doing well. Keeping still.

I rewarded him with a bit of pressure against his hole, swirling my tongue, then dipping in as his whole body jerked.

"*Fuckfuckfuck!*" Sweat beaded on Alec's skin as he dropped his head back. "Don't stop. That feels so fucking good."

"Mmm." I hummed with my lips against him, testing his entrance with a firmer press, while reaching over for the lube. Saliva could be drying during anal play and I wanted him to enjoy every moment. Luther had taught me how a bit of flavoured lube could turn teasing into full-on, exquisite torture.

Pouring some of the Pina Colada—this was new—flavored lube over Alec's ball and letting it trail down, I used my fingers to spread it, then went back to using my tongue to drive him out of his mind.

"Xavier...oh God, I'm so close. Please, fuck me. I need you to feel good too." Alec's words came out in a breathy rush, hands fisted by his sides as he fought to retain some control. He let out a loud moan when I reached my hand up to stroke his dick, while fucking him languidly with my tongue. "I can't...I can't..."

"Come for me, Alec. I want to see how much you're enjoying..." I pressed my tongue into him. Withdrew and formed a slow letter A over the slick ring of muscle. "This little gift."

His shaking intensified. He swallowed hard. "But you..."

"Are going to come all over this hot, tight body of yours when I'm done with you." I stroked him faster. "You know how much I like you messy."

"Yes...*fuck yes!*"

The second my tongue touched him, he came, groaning and writhing on the hood of the car. I kept stroking until the last bit of cum hit his stomach and smeared on my hand. Then I straightened, pulling my own painfully hard dick out and gripping it tight.

With him spread out in front of me, thighs open, asshole glistening with the lube and my saliva, it didn't take long before pleasure seized the base of my spine and burst out, sending a long stream of cum onto Alec's thighs, on his dick and balls, so intense I had to brace my hand on the hood to keep from dropping to my knees.

Sex with Alec was always amazing, but even without penetration, taking him completely apart like this satisfied me on every level. This man trusted me with every inch of himself and that kind of power was intoxicating.

I kissed the edge of his hip, rising slowly to get the phone, then returning to lean against the car as he sat up, both of us focusing on Luther, who'd collapsed on the bed in his hotel room. Our man looked pleasantly spent.

At another glance, I realized the walls of his room were much too close to the bed. I frowned at him. "That doesn't look like a suite."

"It's not, man I love—who is a complete snob." Luther let out a tired chuckle. "I wasn't spending three thousand dollars a night for a full week when it's just me."

"But who will unpack your clothes, and bring you the paper in the morning, and…did you have to check in at the front desk?" Stupid details, every one of them, but Luther worked hard and deserved the best. I needed him to have the best.

His expression softened. "Xavier, I'm okay. It's a nice hotel, right downtown. If it makes you feel better, I have a driver who's been bringing me to my brother's house. I treated him—my brother, not the driver, though I did offer—to a fancy meal. And I get room service when I'm not in the mood to be around people."

I nodded, still not convinced, but unless I was with him, he'd always go with the bare minimum.

He's right, you really are a snob.

Alec squeezed my shoulder, then smiled at Luther. "So you're having a good time?"

"I really am. My brother's mellowed out a lot. I've told him about you both and he's hoping to come down and meet you one day. He apologized for things that have…happened in the past. I believe he means it." His lips curved. "I also got to meet my nephew. Cutest little thing. He's almost a year old."

And Luther had missed out on all that time. But he didn't seem angry. More hopeful than anything. Maybe this trip would be worth it after all. My man was big on family.

"Have you ever considered…" What was I thinking? I shook my head and laughed. Missing him was making me sentimental. "What about your brother's wife?"

"Uh uh, you are going to finish that question, Xavier." Luther sat up, fixing me with a level gaze. "Have I considered what?"

Unfortunately, I'd chosen this week to start being more open with both my lovers, which meant, by my own rules, I couldn't be evasive.

Though, I was tempted. This wasn't a conversation I'd ever put too much thought into, and I didn't particularly want to start now. But Alec gave me a knowing look before grinning at Luther.

"He saw how you lit up talking about your nephew. He probably wants to know if you want kids."

Luther's eyes widened. "Whoa…I never thought… Is that it, Xavier?"

"Yes, but I was simply curious. Obviously none of us have time for children." I cleared my throat, reaching to loosen the tie I wasn't wearing. Right. I was shirtless. What in the world was so tight around my neck? "But if it was ever the kind of life you wanted… I mean, I'd make a horrible father, but you…" The tightness eased. I met his eyes and couldn't help picture him holding a small child, protecting them from the world and teaching them so much. "You would be amazing."

Drawing in a deep breath, Luther gave me a look that brought a deep warmth to my chest. One that would have me giving him anything he'd ever ask for. His voice was soft when he spoke. "I think you'd be better than you realize. You care, my man. More than you know how to say. But you show it. And you have a lot of love to give." He nodded, a tender smile on his lips. "Yeah, one day

I'd like to adopt. Bring a couple of kids into that big house and make it a real home."

"We'll make it a real home first. And then…" I glanced over at Alec. "Then the three of us can talk about our future. About what we all want."

Shifting closer, Alec rested his head on my shoulder. "That sounds perfect."

With a shake of his head, Luther let out a regretful laugh. "I wish I was with you both, but since I'm here for a reason, I should probably go shower and check out my little side project. I have a meeting with a clothing store that's shown interest in carrying some pieces from the junior line." He pushed off the bed. "Not my usual gig, but I figured I should do my part in expanding the business."

Almost slipping off the car in his excitement, Alec leaned forward. "We've been trying to get through to a few places in New York for months! How did you do it?"

"Connections." Luther winked. "I might just be a glorified bodyguard, but there are some people who remember that Xavier and I built the company together."

"*Everyone* should remember." I didn't mean to sound irritated, but after Alec mentioning how often Luther had to drop my name for something as simple as a reservation, I was bitter. "If you'd just let me, I'd —"

"I prefer being a silent partner, so no." Luther's tone was gentle, but firm. "The two of you getting all the spotlight is fine by me. Now tell me you love me and let our man finish washing my car. I'm happy to see you both look happy and are taking care of one another, but make sure to save some of that energy for me."

"We will!" Alec blew Luther a kiss, then wrapped his arm around my waist. "And things really are good here. Xavier wasn't joking about taking time off. He even left work *early*."

"You're a good influence then. I approve."

I gave Alec a little shove, then grabbed him before he could slide off the car. "I had to *force* him to leave. Good influence my ass."

"That's just because I didn't know..." Alec paused at my hard look. Inclined his head. "Didn't know the work could wait. But it will be taken care of, one way or another."

"Yes. It will."

Luther's eyes narrowed. "Is there something you're not telling me?"

Giving him my most innocent smile—which was unconvincing if his frown was anything to go by—I shook my head. "Of course not. We'll talk to you later. Give your nephew a kiss for me. I love you."

"I love you too!" Alec shouted, planting a kiss on the screen before ending the call. He held the phone for a moment, brow furrowed, then sighed. "He's gonna be so pissed."

I took the phone from him, giving him some space to climb off the car and use a fresh rag to clean himself off. Straightening my pajama pants, I considered my words carefully. It was my fault Alec had to keep anything from Luther.

There was no way I'd let him take the blame.

"He won't be happy about this, but I believe he'll understand. If he knew about Joel, he'd cut what's turned out to be a pleasant visit with his brother short." My jaw clenched as I considered the presence of that bastard, Joel, hurting not only Alec, but Luther as well. I had to find a way to get rid of him so we could all move on with our lives. I'd work things out with Luther after. "I won't let that happen."

"But we *will* tell him."

"Yes. We will." I ran my tongue over my teeth. "Once it's no longer an issue."

Chapter Eight

After speaking to Brendon, I decided to give Luther's second-in-command more time to investigate Joel by calling in sick for two days and forcing Alec to do the same. Avoiding too much concern from my employees was difficult, considering I *never* missed a day, no matter what condition I was in, but hopefully that would keep Joel from being too suspicious. The man he knew wouldn't lie about being sick to avoid him. Wouldn't consider anything short of being completely incapacitated as a reason not to be at the very place I'd sold myself to create.

The man I was for both Luther and Alec found it hard to care that a few meetings got rescheduled if it meant keeping them safe. Not that Joel could hurt Luther's reputation, or harm him physically, but if he somehow revealed my past before I gave Luther the truth myself, it would do serious damage to our relationship.

As for Alec, he was the target, and there were too many ways Joel could try to ruin him. Or worse. There was still no trace of his brothers and I wouldn't put it past Joel to let them get close just to prove he was serious.

But by Wednesday morning Alec was restless and my excuses were wearing thin at the office. Rumors that I was seriously ill had stocks dropping and my phone wouldn't stop ringing. I had to go in to prove I was fine and Alec was desperate to help Judy with the overload of work the junior line was getting with so many new contracts.

At the table in Luther's small kitchen, I stared at the pancakes Alec had made, touched that he'd gone to the effort to keep the domestic atmosphere we'd managed over our extended weekend going for a little longer. The staff had gotten several days paid leave while Alec and I took turns making meals and lazing around. I'd even followed a YouTube video to make him spaghetti—one of his favorite meals. Not the best pasta I'd ever tasted by far, but I was rather proud that it had been edible and he'd taken seconds. We'd also slept together every night.

But as good as the pancakes were, it felt like our time had come to an end. How could I keep this going when the past I'd tried to hide was still a threat? How could I be the man Alec needed, or the one Luther had loved for so long, when the pathetic one I once was had brought someone so destructive into our lives?

"Xavier, it's gonna be okay." Alec reached across the table and put his hand over mine. "We're in this together."

Setting down my fork, my lips thinned as I stared at the table. "Because I fucked up."

"Yeah? Well so did I. Joel would have nothing if I'd found a way to deal with my brothers. But I didn't and he used that to scare you and instead of giving him all the power, you told me everything." Alec tugged at my hand, bringing it closer to him and forcing me to look up. "You did the right thing."

"But I haven't always. And I'm paying for it now."

"You survived. I know what that's like. If I'd been in your place, I'd have done the same."

"No. You would've found another way. You avoided the life-style you were raised in for years. You fought so fucking hard to—"

"To end up doing exactly what I didn't want to. But you gave me a way out. You and Luther. I didn't do it alone." Alec laced his fingers with mine. "And neither will you."

My phone rang before I could tell him how fucking perfect he was, but I smiled at him and nodded before I answered. He was right. With him by my side, I could put Joel in my past. For good.

Denise's number flashing onto the screen killed the brief moment of hope. A chill slithered through my veins. She *never* called.

And thankfully, didn't waste time getting to the point. "Xavier, listen. I overheard Joel's looking for his phone. My assistant saw it in his car."

Brow furrowed, I pulled the phone away from my ear, exchanged a look with Alec, then brought it back. "I'm missing something."

"Your security guy has been carefully asking around about Joel. I know you're trying to find something on him. Now's your chance!" Her tone was sharp and irritated. "His phone will have *something*. Evidence of blackmail at very least. She couldn't figure out a way to get to it, but you have to. I'll find a way to distract him. Go. Get. It."

She ended the call and I sat there, staring at Alec who, by his thoughtful expression, had clearly heard every word.

He started nodding slowly.

I shook my head. "No."

He sighed and finished his last bite of pancake. "We should get going."

"Alec, we *are not* breaking into that man's car."

"Okay." Alec grabbed his plate, then mine, bringing both to the sink. "Do you want some coffee to go? I can fix up one of my travel mugs."

His light tone was not fooling me. I shoved away from the table, crossing the room in two long strides and spinning him around to face me. Trapping him against the counter, I met his wide eyes, my tone firm. "*You* are not breaking into his car."

Jaw hardening, Alec avoided my gaze.

"Goddamn it!" Grinding my teeth, I brought a hand up to rub

over my eyes. This was insane. I shouldn't even be *considering* stealing Joel's phone, and yet…

What if Denise was right?

What if there was something incriminating on it? The tables would be turned. Joel would leave if the alternative meant being exposed. And he'd never come back.

The stubborn look on Alec's face told me one thing. He'd figured this out already and he'd do it, with or without me. But this was my mistake. If anyone was going to risk being caught committing a crime, it would be me.

I let my arms fall to my side and went back to my chair to grab my suit jacket. "Let's go."

"Xavier, I can do this." Alec hurried to catch up with me as I headed out to where the car was waiting. "It's not my first time and—"

"You got caught last time. If you're trying to be convincing, you're failing miserably."

"But we *are* going after the phone?"

"Yes."

"Then…" He lowered his voice as the driver opened the back door of the town car for us. Continued once the car started moving, whispering. "How are you planning on getting into the car? And how will you know which one's his?"

I smiled a little at the last. "Every one of my employees has their own parking space. Some closer to the elevators because of their needs, all regularly checked on because I won't have assholes trying to throw around their weight and take extra space, or someone else's, assuming someone is too timid to complain. I may be distant asshole at times, but I've worked hard to make my company a good place to work."

"I know that." Alec's brow furrowed. "But what does that have to do with where Joel will be parked?"

"Guests to each department have a designated area, unless a special request is made to accommodate them. Joel wouldn't have made that request, he considers himself just as fit as a man half his age." I made a dismissive gesture. "Which he may be, but regardless, the junior line only has three spots open for guests. And unless you've brought in someone else, his car should be the only one there."

"Okay, that works." Alec ran his tongue over his teeth. "And getting into the car?"

"Simple." I pulled out my phone. "YouTube."

That Alec was laughing the entire time I searched for a useful video on my phone wasn't helpful, but it definitely lightened the mood. I watched one video several times, hushing Alec to hear the tips, then scoured the backseat of the town car for the tools I'd need.

Coat hanger? Check. I often kept extra jackets in here for emergencies, such as spontaneous blowjobs being too messy. And with Alec around, that had become a necessity.

Something flat and firm to force some space between the door and the frame of the car? Check. Luther kept his assignments for his security staff on a clipboard that he'd left in the slot behind the front seat. That should do nicely.

If Alec had known how simple breaking into a car could be, our lives would be very different now. He could laugh all he wanted. Not a single one of the videos I'd watched suggested breaking a window. That was for amateurs.

Not that I planned to become an expert, but this was almost as amusing as shooting animated characters on a screen. With better results.

Hopefully, I'd be more successful at this than I'd been at the latter.

The driver dropped us off at our usual spot, then drove away. I handed Alec the clipboard, focused on unwinding the metal coat hanger and curving it like I'd seen in the video. We crossed the underground parking at a brisk pace, reaching the end where there were few cars and no witnesses. The sleek, dark grey BMW was parked between two empty spots. An easy target.

My pulse picked up as I took the clipboard. "All right, this should be fairly simple."

"You said the same thing about the spaghetti."

"And I managed."

"You only ate the sauce."

"The noodles were overcooked."

"They were *fine*."

I huffed at that, not in the mood to be placated. Next time, I wouldn't cook the noodles for so long, but this was hardly the same. Joel didn't even have an alarm on his car. All I had to do was… I cursed under my breath.

"What's wrong?" Alec leaned close, frowning as I continued to try to shove the clipboard into the narrow space between the door and the frame.

This wasn't going to work. "It's too thick."

"What if we just break the—"

"No." I grabbed the coat hanger from his hand and tried to see if I could slip that in on its own, as I'd seen in another video. After some maneuvering, the long piece of metal was in. "There we go. Now I just need to press the—"

"Don't. Move." A hard voice broke my concentration and I cursed again, missing the button I was supposed to press.

Alec put his hand on my arm, then turned, his face white.

I glanced over my shoulder and froze.

There was a police officer. With his gun out. Aimed at me.

I sighed and turned. Slowly. "Officer, locking myself out of my own car is not a crime."

He let out a cold laugh. "Only, this isn't your car. The owner called in a report that he'd seen on surveillance that someone was trying to steal his car. Which is what you're doing." His tone became clipped and detached. "Turn around and place your hands on the car. Both of you. You're under arrest."

The temptation to laugh was strong, but I realized two things, very quickly. Denise hadn't heard about Joel's phone having gone missing by chance. Joel must have known how desperate she'd be to get rid of him. Known that she'd call me.

And I'd played into his hand and proved I had no intention of following his fucked up rules.

The officer jerked my arms behind my back and slapped the handcuffs on, leaving me to do the same to Alec. My jaw clenched when I glanced over and saw Alec slumped against the car, looking so fucking defeated. I'd done this to him. I'd put him in a place he'd fought his whole upbringing to avoid. Sure, I could get him out of it, but he didn't know that. Not now.

"Alec, listen to me. You did nothing wrong."

"You did hear me read you your rights, didn't you?" The officer muscled me to the back of a police car I hadn't noticed, parked only a few spots away. "You have the right to remain silent."

The second officer was far more gentle with Alec, speaking to him softly as she eased him into the back seat of the car. I hardly noticed the officer shoving me in beside him. All I could see was the hopelessness in Alec's expression.

I slid over, as close to him as I could, and nudged his shoulder with my own. "You were right."

Alec blinked. Stared at me. "How was I right? You didn't want to do this in the first place."

"Hush." I jerked my chin at the officers in the front seat. "I have very good lawyers, but let's not make this difficult for them."

"Xavier—"

"No. Alec, you did nothing wrong. *Nothing*. But I need you to trust me. I need you to be very quiet and let me take care of you." The fear in his eyes had a heavy weight settling on my chest, but he finally nodded and leaned against my side. I kissed the top of my head. "You're so good. So fucking good. Don't ever forget that."

Being arrested didn't bother me. I was well aware of the position I was in. Of the power I had. It would be uncomfortable, but all I could think of at that moment was Alec.

No matter how quickly I'd get him out of the situation, he was here now.

Which meant I'd failed him.

Chapter Nine

Turned out my lawyers could not work magic when I was being made an example of. Which was...unfortunate. The bail hearing was postponed for the next day. Meaning Alec and I had to spend the night in a cell.

Complaining that Luther hadn't gotten himself a suite seemed more ridiculous every hour that passed, sleeping on a slab of cement. Not that I slept much. The officers kept Alec and I separated and it killed me that I couldn't comfort him. He had this lifeless look in his eyes, as though he'd resigned himself to some terrible fate.

I'm going to get you out of this, Alec. Trust me.

A meaningless, silent promise—his trust had gotten him nowhere so far—but I had nothing else to offer.

The officers came early the next morning to bring us to the hearing, where my lawyer began the argument by stating we shouldn't have been held at all, that I was a prominent figure in the community and neither Alec or I were a flight risk—only to be cut off the very irate judge. Who agreed and set bail.

Once the paperwork was filled out, I took Alec's hand as we left the courthouse attached to the station, trying to warm his fingers, the most detached expression I could manage on my face.

The stares of the cops around the us were heavy. Judging. And I couldn't blame them.

My reasons didn't matter. I'd broken the law. And their job was to make sure I didn't get away with it—though we all knew they'd likely be unsuccessful. Keeping me as long as they had was all the justice they'd get.

"Perhaps we should look into making a contribution to the police station." The scent of burnt coffee tainted the air. I glanced over at the officer beside me as she opened the door to the reception area. "I could at least donate a better coffee machine."

Alec shot me a horrified look.

Across the reception area, my lawyer, Connor Briere, cleared his throat. "While generous, Mr. Ashburne, that offer could be misconstrued. Could you avoid implicating yourself in another crime before I've cleared you of this one?"

"Yes, I apologize, I didn't…" As we approached, my pulse quickened and my lips parted. I couldn't get a single word out. Standing there, beside Mr. Briere, was Luther.

Arms folded over his chest, expression hard, he stared at me. Shook his head the second time I tried to speak. "Save it for when we get home."

Sticking close to my side, Alec muttered under his breath. "We're fucked."

"Not 'we'. This was my—"

"Mr. Ashburne, with all due respect." Mr. Briere held the door to the police station open, his tone clipped. "Shut. Up."

Clamping my lips together, I inclined my head, heat spreading up the back of my neck. I didn't speak again until we reached the car, angling my body to shield Alec as a few flashes went off in the distance. News hadn't gotten out about my arrest or there would be a crowd of reporters, but enough of the public recognized me for there to be inquiries and vicious rumours. I refused to let Alec be the focus of any of them.

When the driver opened the door, I waved Alec forward. "Keep your head down."

Frowning, Alec glanced around, but Luther put a firm hand on his shoulder, using his big body to block any onlookers from getting a clear shot. "Do it. Quickly. He's more worried about you and if we stand here arguing you'll both end up on the evening news."

Alec nodded and slid into the backseat, moving so I could join him. Luther climbed into the front passenger seat while Mr. Briere walked briskly to his own car, parked behind the town car. Without waiting for instructions, the driver pulled onto the road and started back home.

Through the deafening silence I scrambled for some way to explain my idiotic decisions to Luther. And came up blank. He'd have been hurt and angry simply learning of all I'd kept from him. Now he'd be furious.

A soft touch on my hand brought my attention to Alec. He laced his fingers with mine as I met his eyes, his lips slightly curved. "We suck as criminals. Let's not quit our day jobs."

The driver snorted, eyes fixed on the road.

Luther shot him a dirty look, then glared at me and Alec through the rear-view mirror. "This isn't funny."

"I agree." I kept my expression neutral, but it was hard not to laugh when Alec nervously kept going.

Eyes sparkling, he leaned forward and put his hand on the side of Luther's seat. "Xavier thinking he could use YouTube for grand theft auto is *kinda* funny."

"I had no intention of stealing the car." I pulled Alec back as Luther's eyes narrowed. "The hotwiring videos were much too long."

Alec burst out laughing. "You're supposed to practice first."

"There wasn't time. In the future—"

"Are you two fucking serious?" The second the car pulled up in front of the house Luther got out, strode to the back of the car, and jerked the door open. "I had to take a red-eye flight to come bail you out of jail and this is all a big joke to you?"

I stepped out of the car, holding my hands up and shaking my head. "No. But it was a long night and we're both exhausted. I'm well aware that I fucked up and I'm sorry. Don't be angry with Alec. I've put him through enough."

Scrambling to my side, Alec let out a rough, irritated sound. "I—"

Lifting one hand, Luther cut our man off, bringing his focus back to me. "Why though? What the fuck did you think you'd accomplish breaking into some guy's car? Why didn't you talk to Brendon? The only reason I even knew something was wrong was because *he* called me."

"This isn't his fault either. I hadn't notified him that we were coming in yesterday."

"Oh, I know it's not his fault. I had to convince him not to quit." Luther inhaled slowly as Mr. Briere's car pulled in. "Let's handle things with the lawyer. Then the three of us need to talk."

Thankfully, the meeting with Mr. Briere didn't take long. His brow rose when I confessed that I'd been trying to get to Joel's phone and that I'd likely been set up. From his expression, he could tell I was leaving something out.

And didn't particularly care. He finished jotting down a few notes, then gave a sharp nod as he rose from the table in the main dining room, the scrape of his chair echoing in the immense space. "I'm going to be frank with you, Mr. Ashburne. This all sounds like a ridiculous prank between old friends." His brow shot to his receding hairline when I fisted my hand on the table. "You knew the man previously, did you not?"

"Yes. However—"

"The 'however' could drag this out much longer than necessary. You did no damage to the car and your only crime is intent. The judge won't be interested in pursuing this unless this man, Joel…" Mr. Briere's lips thinned as my jaw ticked. "Unless he carries through with these trumped up charges. Which would be a waste of all our time." He held my gaze for a moment, then stuffed his notes in his briefcase. "I recommend you avoid him or, if you can't, keep things *very* cordial."

"Of course." I stood and walked over to shake his hand. "Thank you, Mr. Briere. I appreciate all your help."

"It's what you pay me for." Mr. Briere gave my hand a firm shake, nodding to Alec and Luther before making his way across the room. He hesitated when the butler opened the door for him. "Alec, all charges against you have been dropped. I should have mentioned that earlier, but I'm accustomed to only representing Mr. Ashburne. I apologize."

The color left Alec's face. He lowered his gaze, not saying a word as Briere inclined his head and quietly slipped out.

Luther pushed his chair away from the table and went to stand by Alec's side, resting a hand on Alec's shoulder. His eyes met mine. "Tell me what's going on, Xavier. *Now*."

Dragging out a chair at the other side of the table, I sat down slowly and placed my hands on the table, ignoring the cold that settled on every inch of my skin, as though it would never leave. Luther was back. Alec would be safe.

No thanks to me, but he would be safe.

If Luther decided he'd put in too much time and effort already, decided he wasn't willing to deal with my detached, workaholic, omissive bullshit anymore, I would let him go. Without a fight. With the man we both loved. They deserved much better than I'd ever been able to give.

But first, I did the one thing I should have years ago.

I told Luther everything.

My throat tightened as I reached the part when Joel had brought up the game with Alec as a prize. I couldn't look at Luther right away. I had no right to expect anything but disgust from him after all that I'd done.

He came around the table and jerked me to my feet. Held my head against his chest, his fingers in my hair. "Damn you. You're a stubborn fool, Xavier. Do you have any idea how much I love you?"

"Luther, I—"

"No, I heard you out. Now you listen to me." Luther curved a hand under my jaw. "Nothing you've told me changes how I feel about you. Yes, I'm pissed. I'm disappointed. But I'm right where I've always been. Just waiting for you to see that love isn't supposed to be conditional, it's not supposed to be demanding. I'm not your parents. I won't stop loving you because you're not who I decide you should be."

I shook my head and let out a shallow laugh. "Being a man who's honest with you isn't an unreasonable demand."

"No, but you weren't ready to give me that truth before. You never lied to me, Xavier. You held back. You were still healing." He tipped my chin up and brought his lips to mine. "Now it's time to let me help you."

Could it be that simple? I leaned into the kiss, latching my fingers behind Luther's neck and losing myself to the heat of his mouth. To the strength of his body, his strong arms around me, keeping the broken pieces I'd tried to hide for so long from falling apart.

As he'd always done, though neither of us had acknowledged it. The fear and the pain weren't gone, but he was right. Neither were strong enough to come between us anymore.

Sitting on the edge of the table, Alec caught my eye and gave me a soft smile, a hint of 'I told you so,' in it. I smiled back, then held out my hand for him to join us.

Shouts from the hall had him spinning around just as the door was thrown open. Mr. Mathews struggled to shove the door closed in someone's face, but the butler wasn't a young man and he'd always been slight. A shove sent him flying.

Launching himself forward, Alec caught Mr. Mathews before he could hit the floor. Then lifted his head to glare at Joel.

Who let out a cold laugh. "Ah, I see Luther is home and you've decided to break our agreement. A shame. I was looking forward to keeping things light between myself and Alec." Joel straightened his dark grey suit jacket, his predatory gaze sliding over Alec in a way that made me want to cut across the room and wrap my hands around the bastard's neck. "I suppose we could come to some...*other* arrangement."

With a firm grip on my arm to keep me by his side, Luther watched Joel step into the room. Jaw hard, Luther kept his tone deceptively calm. "Why are you here?"

"To speak to Alec, of course. As a show of good faith, I made sure he wouldn't face any charges, regardless of how things proceed. But I'll need some convincing to do the same for Xavier." Joel gave Alec one of his cutting smiles, the one he used when he was sure he'd won. "I'm curious to see if you love this man as much as he seems to think."

"I do. Enough not to let you back into his life. Xavier has good lawyers." Alec fisted his hands by his sides. "You've got nothing. Give it up and get the fuck out of my house."

Crazy as it was, I had to fight not to smile, seeing Alec stand up to the older man like that. To hear him call this his house. Whatever he believed, he was *much* stronger than I'd been at his age.

Joel didn't seem the least bit fazed. "You owe me. If not for me, your brothers would be here, leeching every bit of money possible out of Xavier because he's too weak to—"

One punch and Joel crashed back into the door, collapsing to the floor as Alec moved in to hit him again. Luther bolted across the room and grabbed Alec, hauling him back, his firm grip keeping our man from taking another swing.

Blood dripped over Joel's lip he let out another laugh, this one shaky. He pulled a light blue kerchief from his breast pocket and held it to his lip. "That was stupid, boy. Both Luther and Xavier will do *anything* to keep you out of prison. Maybe I should stop trying to play with their toy and get to know the man Xavier was so eager to leave me for a little better."

Luther's jaw ticked. "Would that get you out of here? If I was willing to entertain you? That's why this is happening, isn't it? Because you're fucking bored?"

Hissing in a sharp breath, I grabbed Luther's arm. "*No.*"

He ignored me.

Rising slowly, Joel inclined his head. "To put it simply, yes. I wouldn't have let Xavier go so easily if I'd known he'd establish such a fascinating life for himself. I'm pleased we've reacquainted." He dabbed at his lip again and winced. "I'm sure there were easier ways to reach this point, but it has been rather exciting. I haven't had this kind of a rush in far too long."

"I bet." Luther nudged Alec toward me, shook his head at Alec's snarled protest, and approached Joel. "So what exactly are you asking of me? Are you looking for another sex slave?"

Joel smirked. "Among other things."

The door creaked behind Joel, revealing Brendon. He exchanged a look with Luther, waiting until Luther had backed off before opening the door wider and letting the police in. Crossing the room at a relaxed pace, he moved past Joel as the officers arrested the pathetic fucker. Stood in front of us, expression blank as Joel shouted incoherent curses before the police dragged him away.

My lips parted. I shook my head. "What's happening? Have they been here all along?"

"We were already on our way when Luther texted to let me know the fucker had shown up. They were originally going to question you about his possible location." Brendon glanced down at Alec's hand. "Let's go to the kitchen and get some ice for your man. Have you taught him nothing, Luther?"

Hooking his arm around the back of Alec's neck, Luther chuckled. "No, but I probably should." He reached back with his free hand and pulled me to his other side. "Telling Brendon about Joel was smart, Xavier. Despite how messed up this seemed, he'd made progress."

"Yes, progress which would have been executed smoothly if these two hadn't come up with the dumbass idea to go after his phone. What about that scenario didn't scream 'This is a trap'?"

In the kitchen, Luther got Alec to sit at the table and grabbed a cold gel pack from the freezer. After using a clean rag to clean the small cuts on Alec's knuckles, Luther gently placed the gel pack over his hand.

Pacing the kitchen, too restless to sit, I started when Brendon grabbed my shoulder. "Stop that, you're annoying the fuck out of me. Grab a beer and stay put so I can tell you why you've got nothing to worry about anymore."

"How in the world have you come to the conclusion that we have nothing to worry about?" I ground my teeth, inhaling slowly when Luther handed me a beer. "On top of everything else, Alec could be charged with assault."

Brendon smirked. "That's not going to happen. Joel was evading possible charges for running several illegal sex clubs. He had it tied up in court for almost two years until one of his victims came forward, exposing him for using manipulation and blackmail to acquire all his sex workers."

"Jesus. Was that what he wanted from…" Alec's skin took on a grey cast. "I'm gonna be sick." He looked at his hand as blood trailed beneath the pack. "I'm fucking glad I punched him."

"You should be." Luther moved the pack to compress the cut with the rag again. "But you're lucky you didn't break anything. I'm serious about those lessons."

Luther's soothing voice calmed Alec and the color slowly returned to his cheeks. I brought Alec a beer and pressed my lips to his forehead, needing to be close to him. Close to them both, whether I deserved it or not.

Brendon took himself a beer and let out a long sigh. "The man had enough money to keep his shit under the radar for a long time. When that girl spoke up his lawyers did everything they could to discredit her. It didn't take long to get the details, but I needed to know if there was any point to bringing in the police. The prosecutor has been looking for more victims to come forward. Denise agreed to. Her statement is the reason he was arrested."

And probably the reason she'd been nervous and distracted enough to fall for Joel's trap. Still, I was damn grateful that she'd been strong enough to come forward. Because of her and the other woman who'd exposed Joel, this whole ordeal would finally come to an end.

"Would it help…" I leaned against the counter and rubbed the back of my hand over my lips. "Should I testify as well?"

Brendon gave me a look that held understanding, but thankfully no pity. He nodded slowly. "It might. I'll have my contact get in touch with your lawyer tomorrow. Work it out with him to make your statement in a way that you're comfortable with."

"I will. Thank you." I took another sip of my beer, inclining my head when Luther's gaze settled on me with concern.

The situation was unpleasant, and rehashing my past to a stranger would be even more so, but the sense of closure was a relief. The events of my life that had kept me from truly moving forward no longer had that power. I could continue to build toward my future with Luther and Alec, knowing I was giving them every part of me. There'd be no more holding back.

Smiling, Brendon finished his beer, then excused himself, assuring Luther he'd resume his duties on Monday, once he'd finalized the details of the case. He'd been angry that I'd made his job impossible to perform to his usual standard, but his loyalty to Luther made him uncharacteristically forgiving.

With that settled, I assumed Luther would want to continue our earlier conversation, but he simply motioned for me and Alec to follow him and went straight to my room. Hands on his hips, he stood by the bed for a moment, turning as he took in every inch of the space.

Alec wrapped his arm around mine and rested his head on my shoulder, speaking under his breath. "What is he doing?"

My brow furrowed as Luther walked from one end of the room to the other. "Taking measurements to see how many torture devises he can fit in here?"

Luther stopped and shot me a droll look. "Tempting, but no. There are some things I want to bring from my room if I'll be staying in here. I'm sure Alec has things as well that he'd like to have close. Once we've painted the room a more welcoming color, we can start placing everything. Maybe buy a few paintings we all like."

"Absolutely. Once we agree on a color, I'll hire a —"

"No. We're not hiring anyone for this. We're painting the room ourselves." Luther grinned, crossing the room and cupping the back of my neck in his big, warm hand. "I want us to be involved in making this house a home. To do the work, no matter how long it takes. I don't think you remember how amazing it feels to accomplish something that really matters to you with nothing but your own two hands. Hell, when's the last time you designed a dress and then made it yourself?"

"I..." I tried to recall handling fabric for longer than it took to approve of the color and quality and came up blank. Yes, I still made most of the designs for the company, but managing the business had eaten away at so much of my time the part I'd once loved most was delegated to those I hired with the skills to make my vision a reality.

There was no way to return to handling only the creative aspects, but there were a few of my favorite pieces I'd love to be able to say were entirely made by me. And the atmosphere around the office would be much different if people could see me as more than the boss. As a man who was passionate about the creation.

Maybe, if I could find that passion again, I'd be satisfied at the end of each day. Not be so obsessed with putting in more hours than anyone else. I could do more than live for the job.

I met Luther's eyes. "It's been too long. I want to paint the room. And make dresses. But I need to know what you want too. Not just the furniture, I need to know what you want in our life. Vacations, children, friends and family visiting or —"

"I want you to marry me, Xavier."

Chapter Ten

My heart tripped over the next few beats. I swallowed hard as Luther pulled something out of his pocket and took a knee.

"We can make it a private thing—don't answer on that yet, I want you to think about it. I don't want you forced to face the public and answer questions you're not ready to answer. My loving you doesn't need an audience." He held up the thick, white gold band, inlaid with small diamonds in a single row. "We're more than partners. We've struggled for so long, never sure what we meant to one another, but I think we both know. I want you to be my husband. To see you smiling like you are now whenever you look down and realize we're finally where we belong."

My smile grew with his every word and I had to blink fast because…well obviously it was dusty in the room. I hadn't allowed a maid in here in days. Chest tightening with emotion, I tried to come up with the right reply, the words to tell Luther how much I wanted this.

But I could only nod.

Then look over at Alec as Luther slipped the ring on my finger. "Alec needs to be part of this. I know we can't all legally marry, but as far as I'm concerned, this relationship is a bond between the three of us."

Luther kissed my finger, over the ring, and nodded. "Way ahead of you, my man. Alec, come here."

Red staining his cheeks, eyes wide, Alec released my arm and stepped forward.

Taking his hand, Luther pulled out another ring. This one was a pale rose gold, the design matching mine, which made me love Luther even more. He was right. As always, he'd considered everything.

"Alec, you haven't been with us very long, so this may seem fast. If you need more time, I understand." Luther hesitated, smiling when Alec shook his head. "You came to us with so much energy and strength and such an amazing view of what love and trust really is, it was impossible to continue accepting any less from ourselves. The second you walk into a room it gets brighter. The jaded bullshit of our world can't touch me when I consider that I somehow got lucky enough to not only earn the love of one amazing man, but someone like you."

Tears trailed down Alec's cheeks. He didn't bother to wipe them away as he dropped to his knees in front of Luther. "I'm fucking lucky too. And I don't care if I get punished for swearing. I'm not as good at saying the right things, the right way, but I love you. I love you so fucking much and not just because you saved me. Because *you* taught me what love is. I didn't know. I knew what I wanted it to be, but I wasn't sure until I finally had two amazing men in my life who believed in me. Who I could be happy with, and sad, and scared. Who let me be who I am and let me know, in so many ways, that I was enough."

Once he'd placed the ring on Alec's finger, Luther stood while lifting Alec up against him, kissing him as he carried him to the bed. I joined them, laying on my side and simply enjoying the way Luther claimed Alec with that kiss, soft at first, then harder, pinning Alec's arms to the head of his bed with one hand and laughing when Alec tried to press up against him.

"Soon. But I need to know something first." Luther nipped Alec's bottom lip when he gave a little pout. "Very cute, but I'm serious. Xavier and I have discussed children. Changing the house. Work. You've been part of these discussions, but you haven't asked for anything for yourself. I need to know you're part of this, in every way."

Cocking his head, Alec considered silently for a moment. Then grinned. "I want a kitten."

I blinked at him, leaning forward to make it easier for him to see me while Luther had him restrained beneath him. "A kitten?"

"Yeah...when I was on the streets I saw so many cats. Fed a few and then...some of them just disappeared. The city would pick them up and bring them to a shelter, or sometimes..." He bit his bottom lip and lowered his gaze. "I mean, I'd love to adopt an older cat too, give them a good life. And a kitten so they never end up that way. I'm not sure which I want more."

"With a house this big, I don't see any reason you'd have to choose." I shrugged when he gave me a surprised look. "An older cat who deserves to spend the last of their days with all the love and attention they need, a kitten who will grow up knowing nothing else. Really, if you think about it, we're in a very good position to provide for several without depriving any. And if I'll be home more often, working on dresses—"

"You're not going to want a kitten around while you're sewing." Luther chuckled at my blank look. "Pets take a lot of work, and you've never had one. But you do have a point. We've been working on being home more often and this is good motivation. Personally, I've always wanted a dog, but I wasn't sure I had the time."

"We can *make* the time." I must be insane, but both Alec and Luther looked so happy, I was ready to agree to anything. And several members of the staff had hinted to wanting pets around the house, so why not? I could only see one issue. "I assume cats and dogs can cohabitate?"

Both of my men laughed as though I'd told a very funny joke.

One I didn't get.

"Yes, and we can discuss that with the shelter. Find a dog who's been around cats before. Or who's young enough to adapt." He let out a low groan. "Alec, I'm glad you're excited, but if you keep wiggling like that we're not going to be discussing your kitten for much longer."

Leaning up and nipping Luther's chin, Alec laughed. "Good. We can talk about this tomorrow. I want my fiancés to fuck me until I can't think about anything."

"I am not fucking *anyone* until I take a shower." Suddenly, even lying on the bed felt wrong. I pushed up and off, then unbuttoned my shirt. "Would it be pushing it to complain about how filthy that prison was? It's inhumane to have any living creature contained in that space."

Lowering his head, shoulders shaking, Luther muttered a prayer.

Alec's expression turned thoughtful. "Will you do that before or after you bribe the cops?"

I huffed at that and tossed my shirt in the laundry basket tucked away beside my dresser. "I was not bribing them. I was trying to show them that there were no hard feelings."

"There is only one thing hard right now and I'm going to forget about it if either one of you bring up being in jail again. I really should beat both your asses for that." His eyes narrowed at Alec's laugh. "I still might."

"Doing it in the shower would be hot." Alec shifted his hips, smirking when Luther groaned again. "Think of how red my ass will get when it's all wet. Me on my knees, sucking both your dicks before you fuck me and—"

"Let's go before I decide to fuck you right here, dirty and smelling like...fuck, I didn't realize how bad you smelled until just now." Luther rose and pulled Alec to his feet. "Xavier's right. Shower."

The bathroom attached to my room had a shower big enough for the three of us, but in the six months Alec had been with us, we still hadn't used it together. Even Luther had been in here with me no more than half a dozen times. And never for long.

I'd made my room, my part of the house, into little more than an extension of my work. A place I came because having a bed at the office seemed a bit much, even to me. Not that I'd never been tempted, but I'd tried to manage a routine that was at least outwardly acceptable.

Unlike the bedroom, the bathroom had a nice, calming allure that I'd never appreciated as much as I should have. The bath looked like a large, smooth white bowl, set in front of a massive fireplace I hadn't bothered to light since I'd lived here. Luther went to it and flicked a switch, bringing a small fire to life that immediately gave the room a soft, golden glow, flickering against the light grey stone wall around it.

The walls were all a pale grey that matched the stone, and inlaid lighting kept the room just bright enough not to be harsh. Two sinks rested on a floating, black marble counter, my toiletries all tucked away in the two shelves beneath. The floors were made up of large marble tiles, warmed from beneath so no matter what the temperature was in the rest of the house, walking on them barefoot was always nice.

I stripped off my clothes as Luther turned on the shower, which had two large square showerheads that mimicked a heavy rain above, and several inlaid in the three stone walls that had shelves for soaps and shampoo. Luther preferred the rain setting, which I enjoyed as well when I wasn't in a rush. The jets were good for soothing tired muscles and washing quickly, before and after work.

Since I wouldn't be returning to work for the next few days, maybe I'd take advantage of the more luxurious parts of this room. Maybe even the bath. It was big enough for the three of us, like the shower, but I wasn't in the mood to soak at the moment. Even though I could imagine Alec trying to see how long he could hold his breath, dipping his head under the water and slipping his lips over my dick…

Tomorrow. I would have him in here again tomorrow.

And maybe the day after that.

Not maybe. You'll have them both. In here, in your room, in every space you've isolated yourself. No matter how badly you fucked up, you get to keep them both. Forever.

"Come, Xavier." Luther held out his hand, already naked in the steamy shower with Alec. "I know you. You're looking back, wondering why we haven't done this before. That doesn't matter. We're doing it now."

I hesitated when I looked down at the ring on my left hand. I didn't want to take it off, but I didn't want to damage it either.

"Leave it. It'll be fine." Luther grabbed my wrist and pulled me to him, raking the fingers of his other hand into my hair as the hot water hit me in large, rapid drops. "Look at me. Look at him." Luther released my wrist and placed his hand on the top of Alec's head as our man slid his lips over Luther's dick. "There's nothing else to think about. To worry about. We're here. Together. There've been challenges, but we overcame them."

"And always will." I sucked in a breath when Alec turned his attention from Luther, to me. His mouth was hotter than the water, the pressure of his lips sliding over me fucking decadent. Between the water raining down on me, Luther's grip on my hair, and Alec's mouth, thinking at all was becoming difficult. But there was one thing I needed to say. "I'm sorry I forced you to cut the visit with your brother short. That wasn't what I intended, but I was foolish."

"You were, but it's all right. And I don't want to talk about my brother now." Luther's whole body jerked as Alec stroked me and sucked him. "I think our pet is trying to distract us."

"I think he's very good at it." I placed my hand over Luther's on Alec's head, moaning as I watched him try to get both our dicks in his mouth. I cupped the back of his head, tugging at his hair to hold him still as I worked my dick in deeper, then pulled out so Luther could thrust in.

Alec tipped his head back, relaxing his throat, eyes pressed shut as Luther fucked his face until he gagged. I let Alec take a deep breath before pressing my dick in and gripping his hair, forcing him to swallow around my dick.

His hands, which had been clasped behind his back, moved to his dick, one gripping tight as though to stop him from coming, the other giving desperate tugs.

I tightened my grip on his hair. "Hands behind your back as they were. You don't get to come until we let you." I glanced over at the stone shelves and grabbed the silicone lube I'd used with Luther. "How much do you think he can take?"

Luther's lips curved. "Not as much as you can."

Arching a brow, I considered his words. He was right. Alec enjoyed being fucked, but we'd only begun playing with larger toys and he still had moments when he had a hard time relaxing enough to take more. When Luther fucked me, I enjoyed a bit of a challenge.

But would Alec be comfortable with fucking me? He'd never topped. This would be something new.

If he was willing, I was eager to try it.

I looked down at him, easing my dick in and out of his mouth at a slower pace. "Would you like that? Me riding your dick while Luther stretches me open and makes us both come so fucking hard, we won't be able to move after? We'll stay here until the water gets cold. Maybe longer."

Alec stared up at me, his eyes hot with lust. He liked the idea.

"Not here. It'll be easier in your bed." Luther reached out and grabbed the soap. "Wash him while I wash you. Holy fuck, this is gonna be hot."

Pulling out of Alec's mouth and dragging him to his feet, I pressed him against the wall, rubbing my body against his as Luther began to smooth his hands over my back. I fumbled with the body wash, pouring too much in my hands, forming a lather on Alec's flesh, making sure I didn't miss a single inch of his skin.

When I grabbed the shampoo and began washing his hair, he wrapped his hand around my dick.

"Hurry. I don't think I'll last much longer. You're both driving me insane." He shuddered when Luther reached out and began stroking him with his soapy hand, already done with my hair. "Please. Oh fuck, this is too much."

After washing himself and letting us both rinse, Luther shut off the water. "Bed. And I'm getting the cock ring for our boy. We're not rushing this."

Back in my room, Alec dried himself quickly, then dropped onto the bed, his whole body shaking as I climbed over him. He gasped as Luther clipped the tight leather cock ring around his dick and under his balls, his lips parting as I slicked him up with the lube.

"I don't know how to do this, Xavier." His whole body stiffened when I straddled him, rising up and reaching back to position his dick against my ass. "It's always you taking me."

"I'm still taking you, Alec." I lowered onto him slowly, hissing in a breath as his dick filled me. "Oh fuck, you feel good. So fucking good." I rose up, tightening around him, then settled back down. "Luther's the only other person I've let fuck me since… None of the boys we played with did. It was too personal, but I love feeling you inside me."

"Holy fuck, this is…" Alec tipped his head back into the pillow, eyes pressed shut. "Is this how it feels when you're inside me?"

"Yes. It's amazing, pet. Move for me. I want to feel how much you need to have me before Luther takes over." I gave him enough room to lift his hips, cursing as he hit the right spot and angled himself to hit it again and again. "Good. So good. I want to take you like this one day. When you're ready. That tight little ass stretched open…" I slammed down on him, reaching back so I could press my fingers into him. "You like that idea, don't you?"

"Oh god…I do. I want you to. But it's…it's a lot. And you're doing it now and I don't want to hurt you."

"You won't." Luther settled behind me, his fingers tracing where Alec was buried deep inside me. "Hold still and just feel me opening him up. You have him so fucking ready for me."

I expected Luther to start with his fingers, but he knew my body well. I was ready and the pressure of his slicked up dick pressing above Alec's was all I needed to let myself relax completely. The burn intensified as the head of his dick stretched me and I fisted my hands in the sheets by Alec's shoulders, holding still as Luther shifted back, then continued to ease in.

My mind went blank as his dick penetrated me, sliding along Alec's, so slick with lube I could sense him fighting the easy glide as he let me adjust to having both their dicks inside me. He stroked my thigh, holding me in place with his other hand as he gave a few slow thrusts.

I panted against the side of Alec's neck. The burn brought the pleasure to the edge of pain, but it was good. So fucking good.

"Alec is slipping out, so I'm going to help him get in deep. You have no idea how amazing it feels to be wrecking your amazing ass. Nothing else anyone has done to you matches this, does it?"

A rough sound escaped me as Luther pulled out and I was suddenly empty. Then Alec thrust up. And the stretching returned.

Luther latched onto my hips and drove in hard. "Oh fuck, yes. Look at you, taking us both. So fucking hot."

It was hot. The movement inside me, a still pressure, and deep, grinding movement, trapped all my senses to the relentless glide that triggered every nerve inside me. I cried out, leaning back, taking them both as much as I could. I couldn't control my body. I wanted to move, but I couldn't.

"Fuck. Yes, *fuck*!" Alec grabbed my shoulders, thrusting up hard. "Luther, fuck him. Fuck him, please! I can't...you're both..."

Luther let out a low growl and wrapped his hand around my neck. "Hold him and I'll take off the ring. I want to feel you come inside him. And you come on him, Alec. I won't stop until you both beg me to."

Slamming in, Luther reached down and removed Alec's cock ring. And all I could do was lose myself to the sensation of Alec mindlessly grinding into me while Luther dragged his dick in and out. The entire core of me lit up until I couldn't tell them apart.

The entirety of my body was fixated on the erotic feel of being stretched and filled, hot breaths and sweat everywhere. Everything slick and wet and hot. I couldn't follow the motions. They came to me.

Harder. Faster. All over.

And something within shattered. I shuddered as the rip of light flashing from the purest flame took form inside me, bursting out in an endless wave of pure energy. An overwhelming rush drowned out my rapid pulse and I bit into Alec's shoulder as I came.

His body bowed beneath me and he stopped breathing for a moment, jerking and digging his nails into my shoulder. Neither of us moved until Luther slammed in one last time. Then there was a trembling aftershock that turned me into a boneless thing, laying over Alec and kissing him, needing his breaths to remind me how to breathe myself.

Luther pulled out and dropped hard on the bed, stroking my back as he dropped one arm over his eyes. "As soon as you can move, I need to hold you. I need you to tell me I didn't hurt you."

My arms shook as I braced my arms by Alec's shoulders and looked down at him. He lay there, completely drained, but his hand was on my side, holding me close. As though he wasn't ready to let go.

I let him slip from my body and kissed his parted lips. "Are you all right?"

"Better than. But please don't ask me to do anything."

"I won't." I kissed the top of his head, then let myself collapse on the bed between him and Luther. A slick sensation inside me brought a weary chuckle to my lips. "I should probably go clean up again, but you've both destroyed me. Any complaints about the wet spot will get you shoved off the bed."

Tipping his head in my direction, Luther smirked. "You'll hear no complaints from me. But if you're going to leave yourself all nice and wet, don't be surprised if you wake up in the morning with me fucking you."

"If you think that will bother me, you don't understand why I want you in my bed."

From the soft breaths coming from Alec, he was already asleep, but Luther never let go that easily. He cupped my cheek in his hand, rising up to look down at me, his eyes filled with love.

"Ours, Xavier. Our bed. Our life." He pressed his lips to mine. "This is all ours. Finally."

I nodded, kissing him back before resting my head on the pillow. "Ours. But there's still something I need to do."

"I expected as much." He brushed his lips over mine. "I'll be by your side. No matter what. And so will he."

Smiling, I pulled Alec over so his head was on my shoulder and rested my own on Luther's chest. Again and again these two amazing men had proved their love for me. And I'd tried to do the same, but I hadn't known how. Hadn't known what that kind of commitment really meant.

It wasn't about money, or gifts, or even amazing sex.

There were two things I'd struggled to give them, but not anymore. The limits were gone.

I'd accomplished everything I'd ever wanted, but never let it be enough. Because I'd been so determined to define myself by my accomplishments. I always had something to prove. And now, I could finally accept I'd reached my goal. And enjoying it meant trusting those who loved me didn't need me to prove anything.

And I wasn't running out of time anymore. Life only gave so much, but living as though it had a limited value meant not taking chances. Not using the minutes and hours and days for what really mattered.

Not my career. Not making sure I left my mark on the world.

But making sure I made time to enjoy all I had. All that didn't have a price.

Laughter. Dreams.

And love.

Chapter Eleven

A week after Joel had been arrested, I finally had a moment to breathe before I turned my whole world upside-down. As much as I'd wanted to shift my focus to my relationships and my art, offering to make a statement in the case against him meant several meetings with lawyers, and then appointments with my therapist, because reliving what Joel had done to me wasn't easy.

No…'wasn't easy' was my way of dismissing my own pain. It was pure hell. I'd never dealt with the impact he'd had on my life and as often as I tried to convince myself it was over, I knew it wasn't. I spoke to Denise and the girl who'd first exposed Joel, Colleen, and returned home feeling completely gutted.

Alec and Luther were patient, and loving, but they wouldn't let me hide like I would have once. Which was comforting. Some days I went to my office and pulled out a book covering one of my favorite artists and just stared at it. Alec would slip in, take another book, and just sit near me, waiting until I was ready to tell him that ripping open all those old scars was tearing me apart.

Other days I'd start rearranging the house, moving heavy furniture from one room to another, asking the staff to let me handle it and not caring that I looked ridiculous, shoving huge cabinets down the hall.

Luther would come to me, give me one of his patient looks, and help me move whatever it was. Or if I decided a room needed a fresh coat of paint in a bright color, he'd just show up with a paint-brush and work with me until I stopped and told him what was on my mind.

My therapist told me I was desperate to regain control, and that there was nothing wrong with me trying to find it in changing my surroundings, but I should be patient with myself. I'd sold half of the things in my house, replacing the paintings and knickknacks and such with items I found that Luther and Alec liked, before I finally realized it wasn't the house that was bringing me down.

Yes, the loss of control was messing with my head, but it was the secrets I kept from the world, the side of me I never let them see, that made me feel like I was trapped in the life I'd lived before.

My lawyer came to me after work on Friday and showed me a piece written by someone Joel had paid off, trying to make me seem like a cold-hearted, selfish asshole who'd risen to the top in the most mercenary way possible. And I'd only joined the effort to expose him to make myself seem more sympathetic.

"You've changed so much, Mr. Ashburne. And I know you enjoy your privacy, but you were planning on adopting several pets. Why not let the media see you there, picking out a puppy. It will change the way they look at you."

"I'm not adopting a pet to appease the masses."

"Maybe not, but I agreed to you adding your testimony because I thought it would help. And I know this is important to you." Mr. Briere crossed my office and stared out the window. "The woman who originally testified was a porn star. Denise's girlfriend's record of social activism through street art is contro-versial. That she'd written some ugly things as a teen on a few walls has people divided on whether they want to support her. The media is using that to lessen the impact of their statements. Since all charges against you were dismissed, you come off as someone who has nothing to gain from this. More to lose, if anything."

"I'm aware of that. Which is why I told you we're giving the prosecutor anything he needs."

"He *needs* someone who won't be condemned by the public."

"And me holding a puppy will do that?"

"It couldn't hurt."

Luther, Alec, and I had been waiting until all the changes in the house were done before we went to the shelter, but when I told them what Mr. Briere had said, they agreed. The next day, we went to the local shelter.

As expected, Alec fell in love with every single animal in the place. He found a cat with one eye and one ear, fur a patchy grey, and named him Sir Nevsky after a historical figure he'd been reading about. He also found a black kitten with three legs who he named Morticia. And her brother, who he named Wednesday.

I didn't ask. The cats were cute and even though we'd agreed to two, three wouldn't be too difficult. The staff was ready and had already brought in enough toys and treats for a dozen animals. I had a feeling they'd been eager for a little more work than three men and the rare guest typically gave them.

Maybe I should have been throwing more parties.

Wait…no. The cats would be fine.

What was difficult was Luther falling in love with a puppy who'd been diagnosed with cancer and surrendered because the owner couldn't afford his treatment. No surprise, Luther immediately asked which animals were on the list to be euthanized.

Thankfully, the puppy was the only one.

And there was hope for him, with the right treatment. But the shelter didn't have the resources. The dog was nine months old, lethargic, and had been given three extra months with the care he'd been given so far.

Seeing Luther holding the undersized, skinny mastiff was heartbreaking. But the second the puppy licked Luther's nose I decided I would find a way to make sure the puppy lived a long life.

As if my money could somehow guarantee that.

Maybe I was a fool, but there were two options. The puppy was put down in two days or had an amazing life for the next month. More if we could find the right vet. No one else could afford to do what I could and my man seemed willing to do anything to keep that little fluffball alive.

We were at the shelter for most of the day, with more privacy than expected because the reporters crowded outside where scaring everyone away. I finished signing all the necessary paperwork and took one of the cat carriers from Alec, thinking my words over carefully.

My lawyer wanted me to present myself as someone who could avoid all the scrutiny of the other victims. As though my life was somehow cleaner. Better. Easier to digest.

I turned the ring on my finger with my thumb.

No matter what had changed, people still saw me as a mystery. They'd like the idea of animals being saved, but...using that sympathy to make them believe in me over Joel's other victims was fucked up. I couldn't do it. Joel's crimes were clear. I wasn't more or less important than anyone he'd hurt. And I wouldn't hide who I was to somehow shift the narrative.

Stepping out in front of the crowd of reporters, I glanced over at Alec and Luther. The two men who'd stood by me through everything. Who would be there long after the trial was over and people forgot something that would stay with me for the rest of my life.

I squared my shoulders and stared into the closest camera.

"We've adopted several pets, but that's not why you're here. You want to know who I am. And I'm ready to tell you." I took a deep breath. "I am bisexual. And I'm about to marry one of the two men I love."

Damasked

Chapter One

Scraps of leather covered the worktable like a miniature war had gone down between the fabric and all the tools, small droplets of blood adding to the realism. Shaking my head, I crossed the room, snatching up the medkit I'd left on a shelf the other day for this very purpose. Why it surprised me that the new project had quickly become an obsession, I had no idea, but I hadn't expected casualties.

Head bent over a spread of diagrams, Xavier Ashburne's expression held a hint of betrayal, as though all those lines and numbers were intentionally trying to make a fool of him. One elbow on the edge of the table, he held his bloody finger away from his work like it was nothing but an inconvenience to be dealt with later.

Over the past few months, Xavier had mellowed out in so many ways, which pleased me. His sleek, black hair, held back from his face with a loose leather cord, softened his features, and he was wearing dark blue jeans and a snug, faded blue T-shirt— clothing he hadn't even owned for years. And damn it, it suited him.

This 'remembering I'm human' thing is sexy as hell.

But the driven perfectionist hadn't gone far. This new passion project was threatening to put him in the same volatile mood that still had his employees scrambling for cover at the office.

Thankfully, I'd never let that mood chase me away.

And I'm not about to start now.

Pulling one of the padded leather chairs shoved against the wall close, I sat and set the medkit on Xavier's desk. Wrapped my hand around his wrist, tightening my grip when he made an irritated sound and tried to pull away. "I'm taking care of this, my man." To keep things a bit light, I shot him a slanted smile when he glowered at me. "Don't make me call Alec in here to hold you down."

That got a laugh, though it was a bit strained. Xavier relaxed, turning his chair to face me as I tended to the cut on his finger. "Luther, unless our boy deserves a punishment, you should keep him far *far* away from me." He cast a miserable look at whatever it was he was trying to put together. "I know what you're thinking, but I can't stop until I get this vision out of my head. My staff has attempted a few prototypes, but... Damn it, they're all dull as fuck. This new line needs..."

"Perfection." I lifted my gaze from where I'd finished cleaning off the blood. "I can't fault you for that, you're putting your name on it. But you've only started learning how to work with leather. Did you really think you'd pull off runway-ready shoes overnight?"

The question only had Xavier looking more dejected. He rubbed his uninjured hand over his face. "It's a purse. Damn it, I need to go back to the drawing board. There's no way I can make it to brunch in the morning. You'd make a better date for Alec anyway."

All right, this was not like Xavier at all. The relentless drive? Yes, that was familiar after all these years. But the hopelessness wasn't something I could tease out of him.

I pressed some gauze against the length of his elegant finger, routine manicures the only thing keeping the calluses at bay with how much he used his hands. Let the silence stretch between us until he shifted and stared at me, as though to force the words out of me by will alone.

A strand of black hair slipped from its leather tie, trailing down his cheek. I reached up to tuck it behind his ear. "What's really bothering you, Xavier? The company is doing well. Your designs are more popular than ever. The new junior line is a success and—"

"And it could be more!" Xavier clamped his lips shut, shaking his head when he tried to pull away again and I kept a firm hold on him. For the most part, Xavier was a Dom, but in times like this he needed to give that control to me before it swallowed him whole.

Of course, he always had to resist a bit, just on principle. A game I was used to, and enjoyed more now that the lines were clear.

My steady gaze was met with challenge for a few beats before Xavier lowered his eyes, huffing out a laugh. "Are you going to beat my ass for raising my voice at you?"

He was changing the subject, but I'd allow it. For the moment. "Do you need me to? I'll have to finish with your finger so you don't get blood all over your desk when I bend you over it..." A slow smile curved my lips at the flash of heat in his eyes. Yes, this was much better. I touched my engagement ring on his left hand, loving how the gold looked against his lightly tanned flesh. "This means you are mine. Every part of you, which means I will care for you when you can't or *won't* care for yourself."

"It was an unwanted distraction, but I won't fight you on this." Xavier held still as I got out the skin glue and used it to repair the damage he'd done before bandaging the wound. "I would appreciate it if you'd go with Alec, though. He'll enjoy himself with you and I'd simply be distracted by what I'm hoping to accomplish."

"Hm." Rising from my seat, I went over to study the purse he'd been working on. The lines, the stitches, were more complicated than the skill level he'd reached with his private lessons. From the sketches on the pad nearby, I could see what he was going for. Something sleek, streamlined, with intricate details and the elegance of one of his favourite luxury vehicles. Like all of his designs, he wouldn't be able to relax until he was finished.

Except he needed to hand over more control than he could to anyone besides me to accomplish that. It had taken him years to trust other designers and seamstresses to make dresses and suits for his lines. That had expanded to the junior line, with Alec assisting at the helm, but this new project seemed to have brought them right back where they'd started.

Not a great place to be.

"I'll go with him, but on one condition." I motioned for Xavier to stand so I could hold his gaze as I spoke. Hopefully make the decision easier by taking the choice away. There was no guarantee it would work, the man could be stubborn as hell, but damn it, I had to do something. "Bring in one of the leatherworkers to help you with this. You said a few showed potential. I don't care if you hover over their shoulder the whole time. Pick one who won't care either. You will stop torturing yourself." I brushed my fingers over his lips to smooth away the dark frown. "That pleasure belongs to me."

A small shudder, one I could feel with my fingertips as Xavier closed his eyes and nodded. He inhaled roughly, his voice barely audible on his exhale. "I need this, Luther. I can't...let all I've built become stale. Stop growing. I've become too comfortable, too...tame." His throat worked. "I need to know the changes in my life won't leave me with barely a memory of that passion I used to have."

That word, 'tame', told me everything I needed to know. As much as Xavier was enjoying our home more now that it actually *looked* like a home, as much as he soaked in the affection he shared with me and Alec, it was taking him away from that single-mindedness of always being the best at what he did. The first to start a new trend among the socialites, the one who earned a spot on the front page of every fashion magazine so often it was practically reserved for him.

He didn't see how he could have both.

And maybe he was right. Maybe one would have to give, in some ways.

I wouldn't force him to choose, but there was a small voice in my mind whispering.

Please choose me. Choose us.

It would never be that simple. He'd been erased by his family and those scars were too deep for him to ignore. I understood. I supported his need to scream out to the world 'I'm here and I'm not going anywhere!'

The problem was, it put us right back where we'd been for too damn long. Me standing back while he tried to prove himself, over and over again. Waiting for the moment when he needed more. When he realized he didn't have to prove himself to me.

There was one change that seemed to have brought back those old feelings more than anything, though. Our relationship.

So I cupped his cheek, keeping my voice level to avoid any misunderstandings. This wasn't an accusation. It wasn't going to make me love him any less. But I needed to know. "Do you still want to marry me?"

Xavier blinked like the words didn't quite make sense to him. He lifted his hand to the back of mine. "God, yes, Luther. More than anything. And we'll continue with the planning as soon as…" He blew out a breath. "I can see why you would have your doubts, but I will take your advice. I'll bring on someone with adequate skills and stop being such a control-freak."

My brow lifted at that. "This I have to see."

"And you will. But don't gloat, or I'm not bending over that goddamn desk." The edge of his lips quirked. "Take your win, my man. The next one won't be so easy."

The next big win would be standing at the end of the aisle, with Alec by my side, watching Xavier walk toward me. And I didn't expect it to be easy. But it would be worth it. Worth whatever I had to do to show Xavier he didn't have to sacrifice who he was, all his goals, to have me standing by his side, promising forever.

Tonight, I'd focus on the ground we'd gained. Patting his

cheek, I jutted my chin toward the desk. "Get yourself comfortable. I want to make sure this lesson sticks."

A bit of tightness along his jaw, a flash of defiance in his eyes, but Xavier simply nodded before turning away from me. The moments of submission he gave me were often like this. Grudgingly accepting what he needed until we got started and he finally surrendered.

It was beautiful to watch, so I took my time going to him as he braced his hands on the edge of the antique desk he'd gotten at a little shop in one of the beachside towns we'd visited with Alec last summer. Our boy was exploring his tastes in everything from clothes to furniture, and he loved things that were a bit different. Handcrafted pieces with a history, a contrast from the sharp modern style Xavier had leaned toward for the longest time.

I wasn't sure what made this desk appeal to Xavier more. That it was solid enough to fuck our boy on, or that he could picture the look on Alec's face the moment he'd seen it every time he came into this room.

Probably the latter, but the thing had gotten a lot of use.

Spine straight, toned muscles tight along his arms and back, visible even under the T-shirt, feet a precise shoulder-width apart, Xavier had the look of a man who'd lay his head on the chopping block without losing an ounce of dignity. The only thing that really ruined the image was that nice round ass, sticking out, ready for me to enjoy in *every* way.

Moving up behind him, I reached around him to unbuckle his belt, speaking low, close to his ear. "I'll use this. And when I'm done beating you, I'm going to fuck you. Make sure you feel me when I'm gone and don't forget to care for my property again."

When I pressed my already hard length against him, Xavier hissed. His arms shook as he visibly struggled to maintain his perfect position. "Would you like that included in the prenup?"

"Yes." I wouldn't take the bait. He was still trying to cling to control, push me off balance—likely unsure why he was doing it, just knowing he couldn't give in just yet. I'd broken through all his walls before and I had no problem doing it again as I bared his ass and warmed the flesh with the palms of my hands. "I want it all in writing. That you'll belong to me. That you'll take my name. That I can have you, like this, whenever the fuck I want."

Another shudder, followed by a moan. "You're going to traumatize my lawyer."

"Probably." Laughing, I undid the tie holding Xavier's hair, letting it flow loose. The sleek length spilled over his shoulders and I gathered it to lay it over one so it wouldn't hide his face. Made sure there was nowhere for him to hide from me. "Would you like me to amend any of my demands?"

There was a brief pause. Then the moment I'd been waiting for came. A small smile curved his lips as he shook his head. The tension left his body and he shifted, like he was impatient for what came next.

"No. Not a single fucking one."

Chapter Two

With the experience I'd gained at local clubs over the years, dealing with submissives wasn't difficult. Alec stumbled at times, but it came so naturally, all he really needed was guidance. And he thrived under a caring, but firm hand.

Xavier craved some of the same, but his own Dominant side was too strong to even really call him a switch. I couldn't imagine him letting go of the control he held onto so tight with anyone else. But our relationship gave him that space where he could. Where he'd finally seen the satisfaction he got from helping someone else escape for a time was something he could have for himself.

The pressure he was putting on himself to produce something extraordinary had to be released before it consumed him, and I was just the man to get him there. Years ago, I would've faced more of a fight trying to make him see that, but our relationship had evolved.

And I would use that progress for all it was worth.

Folding his belt in half, I took a step back to give myself some room, eyeing the smooth flesh I hadn't marked in far too long. Despite Xavier's never-ending projects, things around here were going smoothly, with a comfortable familiarity that had one day flowing into the next. We were all busy, had fulfilling careers, so the time apart—within reason—didn't put a strain on our relationship. It only made the time together more special.

But the balance could easily shift if Xavier went back into his old mindset of leaving nothing outside of work to spare. That had been our normal once. Something I'd accepted.

I couldn't go back there.

No more conversation was needed, so I laid the belt across his ass without warning, smiling at the way that perfect stance shifted, Xavier hissing out air through his teeth. The second was harder, the *Crack!* of impact filling the large office and reverberating back to me like the base beat of my favorite song. I put my whole arm into the next three strikes, controlling the strength of them, swinging the belt from side to side to land them on his upper thighs.

The steady pulse of the sting and the deep ache was changing for him. His shoulders relaxed, his head bowed, and he was subconsciously leaning into the blows from the thick leather.

Now my words would be heard. I leaned over him again, digging my fingers into the rising welts. "Fuck, you needed that, didn't you? To feel yourself again. To feel me. This is a horrible punishment because of how much you want it, but the real penalty comes after. When we're not having so much fun."

Xavier let out a breathless laugh, squirming under me. "I love it when you get nice and twisted. But if you want this to linger, you'll have to keep going."

Still too much in his head, but that wasn't a problem. I didn't mind a little Topping from the bottom, not with him. It reminded me of exactly who I was dealing with. That submitting to me wasn't Xavier sinking into a headspace he usually craved. It was somewhere he let me bring him. A path we walked together until I tipped him over the edge.

His words told me he was still hanging on, but not too tightly.

So I gave him that final push.

Five more strikes, then six to catch him off guard. As he gasped in air, pressing back against me, I threw the belt onto the desk in front of him and undid my own. Lowered the zipper of my jeans, freeing my dick. I let him feel my length against his ass as I reached out to open the drawer where he kept the lube, breathing a laugh against the side of his neck when I found one bottle, almost empty. Thankfully, there was more.

"Our sub is such an accommodating pet. He's gotten better at coming to you when he needs you." I poured the lube over his hole, then into my palm to slick some over my dick. "And you've gotten much better at showing how much you need him."

Xavier glanced at me over his shoulder, his eyes a bit glazed. His knuckles were white as he gripped the edge of the desk. "What can I say? He's spoiled and I don't mind taking a quick break to fill that greedy hole."

The crude words were hot, but also made it obvious Xavier was avoiding anything too emotional. I'd be worried if I didn't see how happy Alec was whenever he left the office, riding on a high that sometimes had me keeping an eye on him for hours to make sure he didn't crash. Our boy had come to us not expecting much from anyone, so even crumbs of affection would satisfy him.

But Xavier had learned to give him more, whether he wanted to admit it out loud or not.

I wouldn't force him to delve into his feelings now, though. Sometimes, he still saw them as a weakness when they were spelled out. He showed his love in his own way, that was all that mattered.

Positioning myself against him, I pressed in slowly, gripping his hip with one hand when he tried to thrust back and take me in all the way. I brought my other hand to the back of his neck, a reminder of who was in control. One he desperately needed.

Lips against the curve of his shoulder, I breathed out a laugh. "He's not the only one with a greedy hole. Keep that up and I won't let you come."

"Fuck you, Luther. Don't toy with me."

Another laugh as I dragged out, then eased back in. "You mean 'fuck me, Luther'. And it should sound more like begging."

The growl he let out was cut off when I slammed into him, replaced by a low moan. I didn't quicken my pace, but taking him deep and hard stopped any more attempts to take over. The grip around my dick made it hard to restrain myself, my whole body ached to go faster, claim my release in his hot body, but I wanted to draw this out as long as possible. Indulge in the brief time when I could feel he was completely mine.

Panting, Xavier lowered his forehead to the desk, not even bracing against the impact. Simply accepting the pleasure until I withdrew again, teasing his hole with the head of my dick, rising up so I could watch it stretch around me. Precum spilled over the tip of my dick as I moved back enough to deny him the pressure and he let out a rough sound.

"Damn it, Luther. Please…" His arms trembled as he lifted his head, but he didn't look back at me. "Please fuck me. Please don't fucking stop."

I ran my hand up and down his spine, soothing him as familiar footsteps approached and the door opened. Without looking, I knew who it was. "Alec, your Dom is suffering. Come help him."

Without a second of hesitation, Alec crossed the room and slipped under the desk. Xavier cursed under his breath, moving away from the desk to give our boy more space. He supported himself with only one hand, using the other to grip Alec's hair.

Filling him again, I latched onto his hips, controlling the motion, fucking him, making him fuck Alec's mouth, leaving no room for him to escape the onslaught of pleasure.

"Oh fuck! There. Right there!" Xavier tipped his head back, muscles tightening around me, a whimper escaping Alec as the grip on his hair clearly became painful. But he didn't stop bobbing his head, swallowing down every last drop of Xavier's release.

Ramming in deep, I found my own, riding the violent tide of bliss until my vision spotted. I drew out to leave a bit of a mess on my man, the white sheen on his skin, contrasting with the red welts, so fucking beautiful all I could do was stare at it as I slowly came down from the rush of ecstasy.

Alec crawled out from under the desk as Xavier pulled up his jeans with a huff and a slight curve of his lips. The mess would force him to take a much needed break. Not my original intention, but one of the benefits to the days he worked from home.

If I'd done this to him at the office, he'd be tearing me a new one.

Still on his knees, Alec swept his thumb over his bottom lip, sucking on it and looking very pleased with himself. He gazed up at Xavier, then me, expression softening with the love he always put right out there for both of us to see.

"I didn't mean to interrupt, but dinner is served. I'm gonna crash right after so I'm fresh in the morning." Alec smiled, resting his head on Xavier's knee. "The brunch was making me a bit nervous, I haven't been to one before and the formal stuff still makes me feel out of place. But it'll be better with you there, sir. You set me right when I mess up without embarrassing me."

Guilt shadowed Xavier's eyes, but he masked it quickly as he stroked Alec's hair. "Luther is just as good at that, pet. He'll be joining you in my place."

Rather than look upset, Alec lifted his head and gave Xavier a reassuring smile. "He really is. And Judy is great at managing the investors, so all we have to do is go there and look pretty."

Combing his fingers into Alec's hair, only the tick of Xavier's jaw betrayed his feelings about the woman. He respected her, or she wouldn't be part of his upper management, but he was not a fan of the trial by fire she often put Alec through. As tough a Dom as Xavier could be, Alec had latched onto a softer side of him that had continued to grow.

His growly, protective side was sexy as hell. Even more so now when he wrapped it around our boy and leaned in for a soft kiss. "You are that, but don't you dare forget what you bring to the table. Your sketches still need some work, but you communicate your ideas with the designers even better than me. The junior line wouldn't be so successful without you."

Glowing under the praise, Alec rose up on his knees for

another kiss. "I've learned from the best, sir. And I'm *still* learning. Candace is teaching me how to sew. I've been spending my lunches and any time I have after work practicing."

Taking out a wipe from the drawer where I'd grabbed the lube, I cleaned my hands and chuckled. "We've created another monster. What am I going to do with you two?"

"Keep dinner waiting while I go clean up." Xavier rose to his feet, drawing Alec with him. "You, pet, will tend to me while I do. If you're good, maybe I'll do something about that needy dick. You held back for me. I am pleased."

"Mmm, well I was kinda distracted watching the two of you." Alec grinned at me when I cupped his cheek, feeling his smile against my lips as I kissed him. "I'm glad you came in here, sir. I thought about it a few times, but I always feel bad about distracting him from his vision. You seem to know when it won't be a bad thing."

I kissed him again, appreciating the honesty. "It took years to get here. I think you'd surprise yourself, though, love. You're not nearly as disruptive as I am. I know how much he likes having you close."

"This is true, but don't let our man corrupt you. I enjoy you coming when I call." Xavier wrapped his arm around Alec's shoulders, holding him close to his side. "Speaking of which. Shower. Now."

Watching them leave the office, I couldn't keep the goofy smile off my lips. Sure, there were still things to work out, but the uncertainty I'd had in my relationship with Xavier for so long had loosened its grip. In moments like this, I stopped doubting asking him to be my husband. Stopped wondering if the timing had been all wrong. If it felt too much like asking him to decide what was more important. Me or his life's work.

Something I would never do.

Dinner was pleasant, most of the silence filled by Alec name dropping all the famous people who'd be at the brunch. Talking about the well known orchestra that would be playing music, the chef that he'd met last week with Judy to sample food that was 'almost as good as Ms. Lacey's', which got him a warm look from the cook. And an extra slice of lemon meringue pie. Our boy was so open and loving with his praise, and a horrible liar, so it was clear he meant every word.

Ms. Lacey *was* an excellent cook, but I had a feeling it was how much she cared for Alec, the time he spent with her and the almost motherly role she'd taken in his life that made every bite taste even better.

I could relate in some ways. My relationship with my family was strained. Having someone genuinely care about me was special.

Alec had no one for so long, he soaked in every bit of attention, all Ms. Lacey's fussing, like a sponge. This lavish lifestyle could have easily overwhelmed him, or ruined the best parts of him, but a lot like jumping into design and his own little taste of fame, he somehow managed to stay grateful, humble, and eager to learn as much as he could so he had something to offer in return.

Watching him thrive in everything Xavier and I had given him was a treat.

The end of the day had gone so well, I wasn't sure why I wasn't prepared for something to go wrong to steal away all those good feelings. In the bedroom, I took out the cotton onesie I loved dressing Alec in, enjoying how it eased him into a more vulnerable headspace, how he trusted me enough to really dive into it. I'd learned a lot about 'little play', but I didn't think we needed anything so official. Tucking Alec into bed, giving him a teddy bear, and holding him close as he drifted off was enough.

And he was adorable on those mornings, still slipping into that role effortlessly as I carried him to the kitchen and gave him a cup of chocolate milk and some cereal. A rare indulgence—the play, not the hot chocolate, the boy was addicted—but something special just for me and him. Xavier tended to stand back a little, a soft smile on his lips, as though he wasn't sure how to join in. Or if he even should.

I'd work on that. I knew very well Xavier had never had this kind of softness as a child. He didn't have anything to draw from for roleplay.

Head on the pillow, Alec's quiet breaths telling me he'd already fallen asleep, I waited until the digital clock by the bed became a bright red warning that I wouldn't be in my best form tomorrow if I didn't get some sleep myself.

I held out a little longer, hoping to hear the door creak open, any moment.

But the darkness took me. And it was a good thing.

Because Xavier never came to our bed.

In the power exchange, in reaching out to him, giving him that release, I must have missed something.

The problem was…

I had no idea what.

Chapter Three

The steel blue suit I put on Alec after he chose it, coming together piece by piece, made him look sophisticated. Polished. A complete stranger to the half starved young man I'd first caught stealing one of Xavier's cars. Smoothing his tie down his chest, I looked into his eyes and saw what I had then. The thing that had kept me from turning him in to the cops.

A fighting spirit. A love of life, even when it was cruel to him. And that was something he hadn't lost, despite all the luxury he'd acquired, being with me and Xavier.

The wealth hadn't ruined him. Hadn't stolen away that love, or the passion finally given room to grow now that he wasn't struggling to survive. I hadn't cared all that much about money before, but seeing what it could do for someone like him? I was grateful for what I had. What I could offer. Both to him and to others who weren't so fortunate.

He blinked up at me, studying my face, the blush spreading over his cheeks making it clear he still wasn't *quite* past his discomfort with being the center of attention. "Do I look all right? Everyone's used to seeing me in flashier outfits, but that didn't seem right for brunch. I've never...been to a brunch like this. Just the small ones with you and Xavier when he throws one for the company."

"You'll do fine, my boy. Follow my lead and you'll get through this without a hitch." I gave his tie one last tug. "Just don't let those fancy bastards intimidate you. Remember, you and Judy are the ones in control of something they want. Make them impress *you*."

Some confusion filled Alec's eyes. "But...aren't we supposed to tempt them to invest? Tell them what they can get out of it? How much the line is growing and...all that?"

He had a point, most of the time it was, but this was a different opportunity. Investors were competing with one another for a buy in on the line. To own a portion and be invited to join the board of directors. Money alone wouldn't guarantee them a spot. Alec and Judy would judge them on what they had to offer. Capital, experience, connections, even whether or not they'd be a good fit with the rest of the board.

It was a game rich people got a thrill out of. One Alec had never participated in.

But he'd have to learn if he was going to secure his place in the fashion industry. Because all those in power around him would continuously play it.

Either he learned how to join in or get eaten alive.

With Xavier by his side, it would have been much easier on him. Few really had the balls to challenge my man, with all the power he'd gained over the years. He knew each and every one of these people, their strengths and weaknesses. The brunch would've been almost a formality. He'd have made his decision before walking through the doors, simply testing Alec to see if he'd come to the same conclusions.

Judy was damn good at sussing out the most potential herself, but she took the equal partnership with Alec very seriously. She'd never overrule him or hold his hand. As much as she loved working with Alec, she understood she'd always have to prove herself for her position, while his was pretty secure.

Unless he messed up in a way Xavier couldn't ignore.

I'd make damn sure that wouldn't happen.

"These people will be investing more than money into the line, my boy. I know Judy discussed this with you, but it can be difficult to really nail down the implications." I held my finger to my lips as we passed Xavier's room on the way out, glancing in to find him getting some much needed sleep. Anything we had to discuss, we could when I got back. I continued down the hall, not speaking again until we were outside. "Put the wrong person on the board and you have instability. Anyone too entitled, or coming in with their own agenda, could create serious problems."

Alec quietly thanked the driver who held the back door of the town car open for him. He put his hand over mine when I slid in beside him. "So that's why it's a more intimate setting. But I still have to remember to use the right fork."

"Exactly." I squeezed his fingers lightly, then brought my hand to the back of his neck, massaging lightly. "You'll do fine. Just be yourself."

The edge of Alec's lips curved. "People always say that, but everyone acts differently, depending on the situation. At home I wouldn't have to worry about a fork. I'd be kneeling at your feet while you feed me."

Something I often did when Alec came home from a rough day and he needed to give up control. Get out of his head for a bit. His nerves were still getting to him.

Unfortunately, it would be a few hours before either of us could indulge in what had become a comfortable part of our everyday lives. He had to take charge. And he would.

At least until I got him alone again.

The town car pulled up in front of the large hotel, where a number of the investors were staying. A private space had been set up with an elaborate buffet, the subtle decorations adding to the light, airy atmosphere Judy had been going for. The patio beyond the glass doors would give everyone a space to step out and enjoy the weather, which was looking to be perfect for the brunch meeting, not a single cloud in sight.

As soon as we stepped into the venue, Judy looked up from

where she was fussing with one of the orchids set in crystal vases along the white runner. She was wearing a flowy white off-the-shoulder dress with tiny blue flowers on it, her brown hair in a half up-do, curls spilling over her shoulders. Her smile was warm, but her own nerves were showing in the way she rushed over, gave Alec a quick hug, then darted back to the table to straighten a few napkins.

"Everything looks good, right? Would you mind checking with the kitchen and seeing if the food will be ready on time, Alec?" She plucked her phone from her purse. "We only have half an hour and the investor from Eclipse Fabrics is notorious for being early. Do you think we should have some food ready for them? At least some coffee. Definitely coffee."

Giving Alec's waist a pat to get him moving, I crossed the room to stand in front of Judy. "Coffee will be good, but you are paying people to handle this. This hotel has dealt with Xavier's clients and investors in the past, they know what they're doing." I caught her eye when she looked ready to dash away again. "Breathe, Judy. You're both going to do just fine."

Judy closed her eyes, inhaling and exhaling slowly. "I know that, but this is...there's no clothes to distract them. No spread-sheets. And...look at us." She pointed at herself, then Alec as he slipped back in through the swinging doors—probably having done nothing more than say good morning to the kitchen staff. One thing he was very good at was trusting people to do their jobs.

But Judy had somewhat of a controlling nature, which wasn't a bad thing. It balanced things out nicely with how easygoing Alec was once he was in his element.

"We *look* too young. They're going to try to take advantage of that." She eyed Alec, groaning as he came over and rubbed her arm. "Did you have to shave? The suit is perfect, but a bit of scruff would've aged you up a bit." She lifted her hand to her hair. "And what was I thinking? Curls?"

Biting back the urge to laugh, I motioned to one of the head waiters who came in, a knowing smile on his lips. He held a tray with a bottle of prosecco, some orange juice, and three tall champagne flutes. "If you would, ma'am, sirs, I'd appreciate it if you could let me know if the taste is to your liking?"

"Oh please yes." Judy stopped fidgeting, taking the glass the waiter served her, sipping with a sigh of pleasure. "That's very nice. One of my favorite things about brunch."

Looking a bit uncertain, Alec eyed his own glass. "These are all really rich people...shouldn't we be using champagne?"

The waiter shook his head, not seeming at all surprised by the question. While the staff here could handle everyone from politicians to royalty, they treated every one of their guests with respect and compassion—one of the many reasons Xavier liked booking events here. "Try a sip. Some try to impress by using champagne, but the flavor suffers for it."

"Ah, that makes sense." Alec's cheeks reddened, like he felt foolish for not knowing that. He took a sip, letting out a surprised sound. "I'm not usually into wine and I find champagne a bit...well, it's not my thing. But this is really good."

A glass each would have both Judy and Alec relaxed before the investors got here. I didn't need it, but I brought my own glass to my lips, savoring the citrusy depth of flavor and enjoying the warmth from the sun bathing my skin through the large picture windows around the room.

Before long, the first investor arrived, the two representatives from Eclipse Fabrics, who'd been trying to get into business with Xavier for years. Both were young, close to Alec and Judy's ages, the children of a third generation textile mogul. The company had been infamous for shady business practices and labor violations until the twin's father, Georgio Castle, staged a takeover from his parents and turned things around. While profits hadn't been too severely damaged, the company's reputation was still being repaired.

Nena and Ryan Castle had taken the company in the right direction with their focus on climate awareness and ethical production. Xavier was considering a contract for some of their more sustainable fabrics, made from bamboo, or recycled material. Getting them on the board and working with the junior line would be a bit of a testrun.

Skin a few shades lighter than my dark brown, both with long, reddish brown hair and light brown eyes, the twins didn't make any effort to hide their excitement as they shook Judy's hand, then Alec's.

Nena hesitated before offering her hand to me as well. "I apologize, I'm not sure if you're a bodyguard, but I'd feel rude just ignoring you."

"She's right, where are my manners?" Ryan stuck his hand out. "It's a pleasure to meet you all."

Stepping closer to me, Alec took my free hand as I accepted the greetings from both of the twins. "This is one of my partners, Luther Cross. He is the head of security for Ashburne Style and Media, but today he's here in an unofficial capacity."

"In other words, I'm just here for the food." Now that Alec had decided to put our relationship out in the open from the get-go—which was an unexpected, but damn welcome surprise—I didn't hesitate to put my hand on the small of his back as we made our way to the head of the table.

Thanking a waiter who came quietly to her side to offer a mimosa, Nena gave me a shrewd look. "Maybe, but you're also Xavier Ashburne's fiance. I love that you've got a special kind of relationship between the three of you, and I'm surprised you've managed to keep it a secret for so long. But I'm a business woman and I won't miss this opportunity to make sure he has plenty of incentive to use our fabrics for his clothing line as well."

She certainly didn't intend to waste any time getting right to the point, but I could respect that. The twins' habit of showing up early had gone a long way in keeping their father's company at the top of the game. They were personable, but sharp. Their knowledge of the industry and innovative methods of production made it easy to ignore how young they were.

Dealing with them would be the perfect warmup for Judy and Alec.

But I noticed Nena had redirected the focus to me, likely assuming I had more power. I smiled, taking a slow sip of my drink as I sat back in my chair. "Xavier does discuss things like that with me, but I never have much to add. He trusts Alec and Judy explicitly, so if they decide to bring you in, you're set."

Without missing a beat, Ryan turned a charming smile on Judy. "We're grateful to have been invited to brunch...and you mentioned a tour later this week? I'm looking forward to that. No one expected Ashburne Style to be a real contender with more 'urban' customers, but ever since one of your pieces made it to the Teen Choice Awards, it's all anyone can talk about."

The conversation flowed effortlessly, Nena opening her purse at one point and pulling out a few samples for Alec to examine. By the time the rest of the investors began coming in, he was completely at ease, greeting each representative with the confidence he'd grown into over the past year.

While everyone was helping themselves to the food that had been laid out on tables along the side of the room, I stepped outside to check my phone and see if Xavier had called to check in.

Nothing from him, but there was a message from Ms. Lacey, asking if she should bring his lunch to his office. He'd missed breakfast.

A heavy sigh escaped me. Me and my man were going to have to have another talk. Beating his ass for this too might be fun, but it wouldn't fix the problem. I could order him to take care of himself all I wanted, but that didn't mean he'd obey. Or even think of it when he got too wrapped up in his work.

Luther: I'm sure he'd appreciate that, Ms. Lacey. Thank you.

Ms. Lacey: It's no trouble, my dear. If he gets grumpy with me, I'll just smack some sense into him.

Chuckling, I put my phone away, knowing full well she wouldn't lay a hand on my man. If anything, she'd mother him if he let her. Which might help.

"Hey, is everything okay?" Alec bumped against my side, giving me an impish smile around the muffin he was munching on. "Judy let Mr. Rothchild talk her into showing off a few pieces in production for next season, so I have a few minutes. Or more if you need? They're talking makeup and I don't know anything about that."

Lips twitching, I glanced over to where Mr. Rothchild—also known as Kitty DeVamp for his drag persona—had gone from a stiff, proper demeanor to letting Kitty out to play. I turned my attention back to Alec. "Yes, it's just our man, being himself. You'll have to go back to being sneaky about getting him to eat lunch with you at work. Use that adorable pout, he can't resist it."

"I can do that, sir. But...there's something more." Alec held my gaze, concern in his eyes. "You two seem good, but...not. Or maybe I'm imagining things."

"You're not, but it's nothing to worry about. We tend to get a bit distant when there's a lot on Xavier's plate." I hadn't been expecting it this time and I wished I knew how to avoid it. What I did know was our relationship had been through worse. It would survive this as well.

I just wasn't sure if it would thrive.

Alec's brow furrowed, like he'd caught what I hadn't said. "Like the wedding? Shouldn't you be planning that together?"

Inhaling a slow, measured breath, I lifted my shoulders. "I'm sure we will. Eventually. I didn't propose to put more pressure on him, though. If and when he's ready, we'll start planning."

"Wait, what do you mean 'if'? He said 'yes'." Alec held up his hand for Judy to wait when she called to him. "Are you afraid the wedding won't happen? He's excited about it. He ordered all that fabric and he's been making these gorgeous suits for—" He clapped his hand over his mouth, eyes going wide. "Forget I said that."

There had been some fear. A hopeless feeling, gathering deep in my chest, that the future I wanted with Xavier was nothing more than a foolish dream. That it wouldn't fit in with the drive and ambition that were an important part of the man I loved.

Alec's words released it. I laughed as I exhaled, shaking my head. "No, but I won't ruin the surprise." I pulled him in for a hug. "Thank you, my boy. I fucking needed that."

Arms around me, Alec spoke quietly. "You'd spank me if I swore like that. Especially somewhere fancy like this."

Tipping his chin up to claim a discrete kiss, I grinned. "Are you thinking of spanking me, pet?"

"No, sir. That would feel all backwards." Alec blushed, ducking his head. "I'm glad you're feeling better, though. And I won't tell you about how I've been shopping around for florists on Xavier's orders. He doesn't know what kind of flowers he likes best, so I've been bringing some to the office every day. The wedding is happening, the two of you just need to, like...sit down and set a date."

"Agreed, and I have the whole event calendar I can send over to you so you can pick the best one. The season is crazy, but nothing could be more perfect to display all the designs than a huge, romantic event." Judy latched onto Alec's arm, giving it a little tug. "Now, if you don't mind, I need my business partner. Please don't make me deal with our celebrity guests alone."

Taking a few more minutes to myself, I watched Alec move through the crowd, smiling at the way everyone relaxed around him, setting down their false fronts. He was still learning everything he needed to know about the industry, but the good thing about him being so approachable was that almost everyone was willing to share their experience and he soaked in every bit of knowledge.

I didn't have to worry about him, not here.

And I shouldn't have worried about Xavier. I should have trusted him when he said he really did want to get married. My man wasn't a liar, and he didn't sugar-coat things. Sure, he might have to be *reminded* about the wedding now and then to put it on his schedule before he filled it to the brim. But he had to be reminded there were three meals in a day sometimes, so I wouldn't take that personally.

He was working on our suits. Picking out flowers. Taking the first steps to what—as Judy not so subtly implied—would be one of the biggest events of the season.

Maybe he wasn't the one who had to step up.

For this wedding to happen? I had to take action.

And I will.

Pulling out my phone again, I searched out a number I hadn't used in a while. "I hope this isn't too last minute, but any chance you could set something up for me for tomorrow? Great, I'll email you a list."

Starting now.

Chapter Four

A dent in a pillow had never made me so happy. Granted, Xavier had come to bed after both Alec and I fell asleep, and was out before Alec's alarm sounded, but I vaguely recalled the feeling of him in my arms. The brush of his kiss on my cheek. Spending the nights in another room wasn't going to start over again.

Thank the higher powers, because I wouldn't have put up with that for long and I didn't want to start a war between me and Xavier before the wedding.

No matter how hot the makeup sex could be.

Humming to myself, I pulled into the underground parking. A car cut in front of me and I snapped my arm out to keep the boxes at my side from tipping over. Frowned as one of the new interns sped off, barely clearing the barrier as it rose. Either someone was riding them too hard, the intern was reckless, or both.

Either way, as head of security, I'd be sending them a warning before someone got hurt.

That pinned on my to-do list for the day, I parked in my reserved spot next to Xavier's, then got out and grabbed the boxes. I was running a bit late, but I'd called in to my second-in-command and best friend, Brendon Hyles, to cover for me. The times I'd even taken a sick day were rare—and I was never late—so I didn't feel bad about using some of my privilege here for something special. I could have saved this for tonight, but getting the text that it was ready this morning? There was no way I could wait that long.

Boxes balanced in one arm, I swiped my passcard and headed up to the top floor. Greeted a few of the managers on my way to Xavier's office, dodged a few interns and designers, and took note of how harried everyone seemed.

Xavier was in a mood. It happened less often, but the possibility still kept everyone on their toes. It didn't sound like he was throwing anything...that wasn't his go-to, though. When something went wrong, his tone sharpened and his micromanaging became a bit extreme. One seam being misaligned in an order could have him inspecting every single piece before it was sent out, the seamstresses lining up in the hall, intimidated by the idea of having to present their work to the 'big boss'.

No matter what the rumors were, Xavier wasn't cruel. He was exacting. Sometimes brutally honest. Unlike Alec, he wasn't easily approachable, but he had been trying to fix that.

His demands for quality would never change. It was his reputation on the line, so I couldn't really fault him for that.

Setting the boxes on the edge of an empty desk, I pulled out my phone to text Alec.

Luther: You may have to do some damage control, love.

Alec: Believe me, I know. People are all stressed because he's not taking any calls and he kinda growled at the last person who knocked on his door, asking not to be disturbed. I'm gonna check on him when I finish going over these orders.

Trust Alec to have his ear to the ground during a 'catastrophe'. If nothing else, he'd get everyone calmed down.

Luther: I'm going in to see him now. Hopefully this surprise will cheer him up.

I didn't bother knocking. Xavier wouldn't expect me to, we had an understanding when it came to situations like this. He might not want company at the moment, and I'd respect that, but I would leave no doubt that I was here if he needed me.

Jaw ticking, he didn't bother looking up from the magazine laid out in front of him. "This is not a good time, Luther. I am not a goddamn child, if I wanted something to eat, I'd go get it."

Inhaling slowly, I put the boxes on one of the two leather chairs in front of his desk. "I don't think I've ever treated you like a child, Xavier. But I have made it clear I won't accept that tone. Take a few deep breaths and tell me what's wrong."

Xavier lifted his gaze, his dark forest-green eyes flashing before he closed them. Breathed as I'd instructed, then let out a bitter laugh. "All I asked for was some peace. Perhaps that was unreasonable of me. What do you want?"

This tone wasn't much of an improvement, but I could deal with a bit detached much better than outright hostility. I studied his face for a moment, trying to decide whether or not now was a good time to show him what was in those boxes.

Might be best to find the source of the problem first. "Alec and Judy would have sent you their picks for the board by now. Do you have an issue with one of them?"

"No, Luther. They are all choices I would have made myself. And I'm not so much of a control freak that I'd throw a fit over decisions the two make over the division I gave them to run." He slammed the magazine down and stood. "The worst thing is, I didn't throw a fucking fit. I didn't speak to a goddamn person besides my secretary when I asked her to hold my calls. Did I not ask sweetly enough? Send Alec in here, perhaps he can instruct me on how to be kind and gentle enough to be left the fuck alone when I ask!"

Blinking at him, I couldn't think of a single thing to say for a few moments. I could count on one hand the amount of times he'd raised his voice at me since we'd known one another. The first time was when he'd been kicked out of his house by his father.

"Hey, it's okay. It's gonna be okay." Wrapping my arms around Xavier, *sitting on the sofa Mom had fixed up for him, I held him close when he*

finally broke down in the middle of the night. His quiet sobs had been muffled by his pillow, but I'd laid awake for hours, listening for them. "Parents can be jerks sometimes, but then they cool down and figure things out. Your father loves you. He'll change his mind and ask you to come home."

Stiffening, Xavier lifted his head and stared at me. "How could you say that?"

The comfort I was trying to offer was all wrong. Chewing on my bottom lip, I glanced over to where my mother stood quietly in the doorway. There was the faint sound of my father in the kitchen, probably putting on tea.

They'd both struggled with me coming out, but made sure I knew they'd always love and accept me, no matter what. It was my little brother who gave me the looks of disgust I'd been so afraid of. The one who acted like I was dead to him now.

It fucking hurt, but Mom said he'd eventually get past the fear of being judged at school by his friends because of me. She'd keep talking to him, make him understand.

That was what grownups did. And Xavier's father didn't really care about him being bi. He just had this whole plan for him, even though he was only sixteen. Marriage, kids, and a side-piece of ass if he wanted it. But that side-piece couldn't be me, because I was all wrong for the 'heir' or some shit. It pissed me off, but this wasn't about me.

Xavier needed his family. Needed his father to be a father.

And it didn't make any sense that the man wouldn't get there eventually, right?

"I'm just saying it because it's true, man." I stroked his hair away from his face, ruining the perfect style it seemed stuck in whenever I didn't see him for a few days. "I bet he'll call in the morning and say he's sorry. That he made a mistake."

Jerking away from me, Xavier pushed to his feet. "He won't because he hates me! I'm nothing to him, I might as well be dead! And my mom..." He let out a broken sound and my own mother rushed across the room, catching him before he dropped to his knees. "She packed up all my stuff. I thought...I thought at least she loved me... Now I have no one."

"Hush, baby. You have us, and you have a place to stay, for as long as you need." My mother gave me a firm look when my lips parted, then led

Xavier back to the sofa. "It was a really hard day and I'm so sorry you went through all that. Why don't you have some tea with me, then try to get some rest? We'll see what we can figure out in the morning."

My father patted my shoulder as he passed, setting the tea tray down on the coffee table. I didn't understand what Xavier was going through, because I knew my own parents would never do that to me.

But I would try harder to get it. Support him like Mom and Dad were.

Until he really believed he'd never be alone. He'd always have me.

So many promises I'd made to myself, and I'd done my best, but I'd been a foolish child at the time. I'd lacked the skills to give Xavier all I'd wanted to.

But I wasn't that boy anymore.

"Is being alone what you really want right now, Xavier?" I kept my own tone calm, which almost seemed to frustrate him more. As though he was looking for a fight. Whatever he was dealing with hurt him. And I was starting to get an idea of what it might be. "It might help to talk about it."

Standing, Xavier paced away from his desk, shaking his head. "Talking doesn't always fucking help, my man. Yes, I want to be alone. I want to get my damn head on straight and do my job." He shot me a cold look. "As you should be doing yours."

Now *this* was the man so many were intimidated by. How many of the staff still saw him, even though he hadn't retreated into his ice shell for almost a year. There was no way in hell I'd wait long to crack it open again, but now was not the time.

So I gave him a sharp nod. "Understood. I'll get out of your way."

Picking up the boxes, I started toward the door.

"Wait." Xavier turned to face me, his gaze going to the boxes. His tone was quieter, like all the rage had seeped out of him, leaving him completely drained. "What is that?"

As calm as I was trying to be, as patient and understanding, the reminder of how excited I'd been to share this with him clenched in my guts and left a bitter taste in my mouth. I rolled my neck from side to side, forcing a stiff smile. "They're samples. For our wedding cake."

His lips parted. Regret, shame, emotions I couldn't deal with at the moment flashed through his eyes. He cleared his throat. "That was thoughtful of you. Would you still like to try them with me?"

"No, Xavier, I wouldn't." Fuck being reasonable. I strode up to his desk and dropped the boxes onto it. "But if you would? Go for it. You've been planning everything else on your own, just add this to the fucking list."

My reaction definitely wasn't improving the situation, but I wasn't the man I used to be anymore either. I refused to take the blunt of his anger when I hadn't done a damn thing to him. I wouldn't put on a professional mask and pretend the man I planned to marry, the one I hoped to spend the rest of my life with, hadn't fucking hurt me in ways I'd never believed he would again. I could take a lot, but treating me like nothing more than an employee?

No. Not again. *Never* again.

So I crossed the room without looking back.

And slammed the door behind me.

Chapter Five

By the time lunch hit, I didn't want to throw things anymore. I was too damn old to start slamming my fists into walls—I had more control than that—but I wouldn't have minded a bag in the control room to blow off some steam.

It took about five seconds of me walking in the door for Brendon to catch on that something was up. And get me minding my own tone. The man was a retired soldier and had two modes. Commanding or friendly. If I wanted the latter, I gave him the respect he'd more than earned.

Putting in his earpiece, Brendon rose from where he'd been monitoring the screens for the design and cutting rooms, both empty and locked while everyone went out to eat. He paused by my side. "Do you want me to pick you up something?"

"That won't be necessary." Xavier stepped into the control room, awkwardly carrying a few paper bags on top of the white boxes I'd left on his desk. "But I would appreciate some privacy with my fiance, Brendon, if that's all right?"

Brendon smirked, nodding as he continued out. "Be my guest. But this better be the last time your relationship drama ends up in my office, you hear me?"

He didn't wait for an answer, closing the door firmly behind him.

Brow creasing, Xavier set everything down on the folding table in the corner, beside the coffee machine and the minifridge kept filled with water bottles. He wiped his hands on his slacks as he turned to face me. "You are the head of security. This would be considered *your* office, would it not?"

Again, reminding me of my job. And that he was technically my employer. This unexpected lunch date was off to a *wonderful* start. "Is there something I can help you with, Mr. Ashburne?"

Yes, it was petty. But I found it hard to give a damn when it didn't seem like a thing had changed.

Xavier winced, then shook his head slowly. "Please don't call me that, Luther. Even though I deserve it. I was a complete asshole. I'm sorry. The question wasn't intended as a reminder of your 'place'."

"Is that what you're sorry for?" Sighing, I rubbed my hand over my face. "This is a bad idea. We have a lot to discuss, but not here. We'll talk when we get home."

For a second, it looked like Xavier agreed with my suggestion. He took a step toward the door. Stopped and came to me instead, throat working as he swallowed. His shoulders relaxed, that stiff bearing he held around the office—highlighted by the crisp lines of his suit and the sharpness of his features with his hair tightly bound—completely gone.

Then he did something that always caught me off guard when he did it in the building.

He lowered to his knees.

"That's not all I'm sorry for. The way I spoke to you was unacceptable. You've loved and supported me through the most difficult times in my life and you don't deserve to become a target when I'm hurt or angry." He lifted his gaze. "No one does, but you least of all. I thought I'd become better at managing my emotions, but I still have much work to do. And I will do it."

The whole mess in his office wouldn't be easy to set aside, but it made a huge difference that he actually understood what he'd done wrong. Back when we'd had a relationship that barely earned the title, a lot of things *had* been acceptable. There'd been some hard lines between what we shared and our professional lives.

Then, I would have been the one keeping the staff away from his office, not going in myself. I wouldn't have asked questions he didn't want to answer. I hadn't seen a point in pushing for more.

Alec had crossed those lines without seeming to notice they were there. He'd shown me a side of Xavier I'd almost given up on.

I wouldn't let us go back there.

Sighing, I brushed my hand over his hair, tugging at the tie holding it so tight. Letting it flow loose, I smiled when Xavier's lips twitched downward, pleased that he didn't object, even though he hated looking anything but perfectly put together at work.

That he let me get this far showed how sorry he really was. Such a small thing, but it meant a lot. I needed to see my man was still in there. That he wasn't out of reach. Curving my hand under his jaw, I tilted his head back. "Don't *ever* talk to me like that again. If you can't talk about something right away? Fine. If you need to be alone, say so. Say so as though I'm someone you love and I'm not to blame for whatever you're feeling. Unless I am, then there's a whole different set of rules."

His brows lifted slightly. "Such as?"

"I haven't decided yet." I held out my hand and he placed his in it, letting me help him to his feet. "We've gotten better at communicating. What changed?"

Xavier blew out a breath. "The subject. I came across a magazine that did an incredible exposé on my father. Revealed things that should have him liable for a string of workforce and production violations. The more research I did about how he was avoiding responsibility for any of it, the more frustrated I became. I couldn't focus on anything else. Part of me wants to see him brought as low as...as he brought me. I was reading over the exposé again when you came in."

That explained a lot. I pulled him in for a hug, stroking his back until the tightness under my hand relaxed. "Do you want me to team up with Brendon and see what we can dig up? If he's breaking any laws…"

Already shaking his head, Xavier drew back, going to the table and taking out the containers of food like he needed the distraction. "He isn't. No more than most big companies do, in any case. He'll use his lawyers to explore how far he can push the rules before they snap. His employees are miserable, but…" He bowed his head. "I really am no better than him."

"Hey, enough of that. There's a huge difference between being tough to work for because you demand quality—paying damn well for it, mind you—and what he likely does. I can imagine his wages and work hours are *exactly* like the businesses you refuse to work with." I stepped up behind him, rubbing his arms. "You do have things to work on, but don't erase how far you've come. Or who you became despite his efforts to turn you into another heartless tycoon."

Xavier glanced at me over his shoulder, serving spoon posed over the steaming Cajun rice. "You have a way with words, my man. Have you ever considered a career as a poet?"

His sarcasm was more tolerable than his earlier behavior, but still a way to deflect actually dealing with his feelings. And I wasn't going to let that slide.

So I landed a solid smack on his ass, knowing the impact would reawaken the lingering marks from the belt I'd used on him the other night. Before he could turn to say something regrettable, I smacked him again, then barred my arm across his chest, growling in his ear. "Careful, Xavier. You've already pushed me far enough today. We could enjoy our lunch and continue with a pleasant day, or I could just punish you and send you back to your shiny office. You may be my boss here, but I'm off the clock."

Sucking in air through his teeth, Xavier let out a soft laugh. "You're going to make me forget there *is* a clock. And lunch will get cold."

True. And I wanted to see him eating a proper meal, which he'd probably guessed. Motioning for him to continue serving up the food from our favorite Cajun restaurant, I dragged both mine and Brendon's chairs closer so we could get comfortable.

Halfway through the meal, I decided to ask the question that was nagging at me. Hopefully, Xavier was in the right mindframe to take it for concern, rather than criticism. "Why were you reading that article about your father? I thought you'd gotten out of the habit of keeping tabs on what he's doing. It's a lot better for you."

Using a cloth napkin he'd pulled out of God knew where, Xavier wiped his mouth before he replied. "I tend to avoid anything involving him, but I enjoy the magazine. Alec brought it to me, loving the variety of it. Everything from fashion to business to entertainment. Most magazines cater to a niche audience, unless they're tabloids just throwing incendiary trash together. I've been considering putting something similar together for our 'media' branch, but so far the board seems to think print is on its way out."

"It's definitely not what it used to be, but there are people who enjoy holding something physical in their hands." I finished off my last bite of spicy chicken, then set my plate aside to wash later. "That magazine you like probably has a blog, too. How's it doing? That would give you a better idea of what to expect."

Xavier gave me a blank look. This side project hadn't caught enough of his interest to really dive into. His 'presentation' to the board had likely been an offhand suggestion easily brushed aside, both by himself and the members.

Chuckling, I let it be. He already had more than enough to keep him busy. And we had a wedding to plan. Standing, I placed his mostly empty plate by my own and picked up the first box. Opening it, I admired the delicate decorations on the miniature cakes, having kept the box closed so I could enjoy the reveal with Xavier.

I leaned close to him, balancing the box on my thigh. "They really went all out. The owners were old friends of my mother's, so they were my first choice. Their work has always been exquisite, but now that their daughter joined in the family business, the artistry is on a whole different level. She's won a few awards. I wasn't sure they'd have time to make these, but they stayed up all night."

"I'd feel guilty, but they'll be paid handsomely, as well as get some coveted exposure at our wedding." Xavier smiled softly, his gaze going over the cakes. "I suspect Alec let something slip about me beginning the initial planning." His smile faded as he looked over at me. "That wasn't intended to cut you out. I wanted to surprise you. Show you I'm fully invested in spending the rest of my life with you. I know you've had your doubts."

Not something I could deny, so I inclined my head. "Yes, because you've been so busy lately—doing this with Alec probably didn't help. We keep him from overworking, but we still haven't managed that with you. I thought it was the new shoe and clothing line you're obsessing over that was stealing all your time."

Red spread over the sharp curves of Xavier's cheeks. "Yes, well, it has stolen a great deal of it. I wasn't aware of how much, but I've taken your advice. I brought in *two* skilled leatherworkers. I still want to learn, but perhaps I can keep it as a hobby, rather than try to master it overnight."

"Hallelujah, he can be taught!" I nudged Xavier's shoulder with my own when his expression darkened. "Relax, I'm teasing you. I was upset when you didn't come to bed the other night. When it seemed like you were pulling away again. I realized I wasn't doing my part in finding out why. And I was resentful about not starting the wedding plans, but I'd made no effort to fix that. I'm sorry I assumed the worst."

"I've given you plenty of reasons to, but I'm happy that we've finally discussed this. It gives us both something to improve on." Xavier studied the cakes. "How will we know what's what? I like the white and silver decorations with the black accents, but I have no idea how that would look on a bigger scale. Maybe I can sketch something and—"

Quickly shaking my head, I plucked out the small cake and

placed it on a clean plate. "Hell no. There's a list of all the flavors on a card under each of the boxes. I asked for all their best options. You're to taste, choose your top three favorites, tell me what decorations you like best, and that's it. You are not taking on *more* work than necessary. We are going to trust the people we hire to do their jobs."

The kind of control Xavier didn't like to give up, but too bad. I'd already started to regret not insisting on getting a wedding planner. It would be fine if we could enjoy the process—so long as I set some limits.

Sighing, Xavier selected a fork from the stash on the table, wiping it with the edge of his napkin before taking a bite of the cake. Then sighed again as he savored it. "Raspberry truffle. This is definitely going on my list." He licked his lips, swiping his thumb under his bottom lip in a way that had my blood pulsing low. "I'm happy to be doing this alone with you, but we should save some for Alec. I don't want him feeling excluded."

"I agree. Even though it won't be official, he's as much a part of this relationship as either of us. We've already made promises to him, but I plan to make a few more." I used another fork to cut into the cake, bringing it to my lips. Groaned as the flavor of rich chocolate and tart berry burst over my tongue. Sweet, but not overwhelmingly so. Setting what was left back in the box, I picked out another cake, this one with gold leaf accents. "The boy has a healthy appetite, so none of this will go to waste. I want you to eat with him more often. Let him set a good example."

Xavier's lips curved. "Always finding a way to slip in your own agenda." He dipped his fork into the cake, lifting a large piece to my mouth. "I will agree, so long as you take at least a few of your lunches outside of this cave with us."

"Deal." I finished off what was in my mouth, not a huge fan of the texture. Pulling out the card taped under the box, I checked for the flavor. "Baci mousse. I'm not a fan."

Taking his time tasting this one, Xavier cocked his head. "I like it, but I don't believe it will be a favorite."

Going through the rest of the samples took up our entire lunch break and then some. Brendon returned to find us writing down our top picks and took out a fresh fork to try a bit of each to see if he could help narrow down the choices from the eight between us we'd ended up with, completely abandoning the three choice rule.

In the end, he shook his head with a laugh. "Sorry, guys, I'm useless with this. They're all delicious. You should have more than one cake."

"Naturally, there will be one at the rehearsal, and another for the reception, along with a variety of desserts for those who like a bit of everything." Xavier looked over the box I'd moved our choices to, sounding a bit frustrated. He seriously disliked not having an immediate answer to any dilemma. "We should have Alec meet us in my office so we can resolve this."

Shaking my head, I packed up the boxes and handed them to Xavier. "Not right now, he's got a full day with his own projects. And I need to get back to work. Bring these up to the staff kitchen and put them in the fridge. Tonight will be soon enough."

"Of course." Xavier gave his head a subtle shake, then laughed. "It's so easy to get caught up in this. I have plenty of my own to take care of, especially after my...*setback* this morning. But I'm glad you did this, Luther. I'm sorry it wasn't apparent at first."

"All is forgiven." I held open the door for him. "Judy's sending me your and Alec's calendars. I'll pick a few dates for us to choose from. Get that settled so we can start on all the other details. Whatever those are."

Xavier leaned in for a kiss as he passed, his lips still sweet from the cake. "Alec's already made a list. It's a good thing you keep our boy disciplined or he'd have the whole thing arranged for us already."

That made me smile, excited to end the day and get home so we could share this step in the wedding prep with him. I'd also give my mother's friends, Dan and Emmy Keirsten, another call and see if we could swing by and watch them decorate one of the cakes. Alec would get a kick out of that.

Unfortunately, the day decided to run longer than usual, 'the twins' showing up minutes before most of the staff was set to head home. They had their own bodyguards, but I wasn't a fan of having strangers with guns strolling around my building. I left Brendon to watch the cameras, heading up to shadow the group as Alec gave Nena and Ryan a tour of the junior line's floor.

He declined an invitation to go out for drinks once they'd seen everything, promising to schedule something later that week — saving Judy from declining herself when she struggled to come up with an excuse. The young woman was a hard worker, well on her way to having no life outside of this building until she'd hooked up with a bartender who worked at the place where she often brought clients.

The woman wouldn't be working tonight. She understood Judy's dedication to her job, but it would be good for them to spend more time together. Prioritize their relationship.

Like Xavier and I were finally learning to do.

Once I'd turned over the keys to the night shift, I headed down to the parking garage with Alec, pleased to see Xavier's car was already gone. A rare occurrence, but despite how the day had begun, it was turning out to be a damn good one.

"You're smiling a lot. I like that." Alec glanced at me sideways as I drove us home. "That surprise you planned...it turned out okay? I wasn't sure when people started texting me about the yelling in Xavier's office."

Putting my hand over his, I nodded. "Better than okay. We removed a few obstacles."

"Did you pick a date?"

"Not yet." Lacing our fingers together, I broadened my smile even more. "But we've got cake."

Chapter Six

The sun sank toward the horizon, painting the sky in brilliant hues, gold and red fading into a rich purple, all colors I'd seen Xavier try to capture again and again for different designs. Parking the car, I stepped out to gaze across the expanse of the neatly manicured grounds and drink in the sight, breathing in the air that held a hint of coming rain and freshly cut grass.

At my side, Alec snapped a few pictures, giving me a lopsided grin when I arched a brow at him. "Sorry, sir, but Xavier's not the only one who gets inspiration from everything. I learned from the best." Tongue between his teeth, he lowered his gaze to his screen. "I need to ask Judy if denim can be bleached and dyed to these exact colors, I think —"

Swooping my boy off his feet, I threw him over my shoulder and strode up to the front door, grinning at Ms. Lacey when she opened the door for me. "Thank you, Ma'am. How would you feel about taking the night off? I'm thinking you deserve to be pampered at your favorite hotel, my treat. I'll schedule you a massage from that guy you're sweet on over there."

Ms. Lacey smacked the center of my chest lightly, clucking her tongue. "You, sir, need to stay out of my business." Her cheeks were a bit pink as she went to the closet off the entryway to grab her coat. "But you don't need to tell me twice."

As the door closed behind me, I carried Alec down the hall, checking the kitchen, the dining room, then the bedrooms for Xavier. I finally found him in the new sunroom he'd had built this past summer, placing each piece of leftover cake on china plates, spread out on the low table in front of the antique chaise lounge Alec had found at another of his favorite little shops.

Plunking Alec down on the lounge, I caught Xavier's eye. "After all this trouble we've been going through to find a good work/life balance, *your* boy ruined a sunset for me by making it all about an idea for a new design. I think he should be punished."

Unlike Xavier, Alec didn't get defensive when he was called out on things, especially when he knew I was teasing. But sometimes he'd use it as an opportunity to be a bit of a brat.

Like he was doing right now, reclining on the lounge like the biggest diva in existence. "Xavier, he doesn't understand. The muse must be fed or I shall parish!"

Xavier snorted, rising to stand over our boy. "Is that so? Very well, I'll just throw out all this cake we saved for you. You know very well I understand your dedication. I encouraged it, in fact. Why don't you use my office to find those colors?" He licked off some icing he'd gotten on his thumb. "I'm sure Luther and I can make a decision on the wedding cake without you."

"No, sir. I'd like to help." Alec sat up, looking over the cake as Xavier sat a bit behind him, tugging off his suit jacket, then undoing his tie. Chewing on his bottom lip, Alec held still as Xavier undressed him. "I'm not sure I can focus on cake while you're doing that, though."

"Hmm." Xavier lifted the tie to cover Alec's eyes, tying it in place. "Perhaps this will help?"

Lips curving, I stood back for a moment, enjoying the sight of Xavier toying with our boy. The flush that spread from Alec's cheeks, down to his chest as his shirt was taken from him. How he laid back with only a little urging so Xavier could remove his slacks. His breath was coming in little pants, his dick already nice and hard under the confines of the snug white boxer briefs.

"This way, you won't be influenced by the decorations, or either of our reactions. You're so good at reading your Masters, pet. Figuring out what they want from you." Xavier curved his fingers at the waistband of Alec's boxers, easing them over his dick, then down his thighs. "This decision will be made on taste alone."

Hissing through his teeth, Alec shifted restlessly on the lounge. "I like that idea very much, sir. Thank you."

Xavier leaned in to brush a soft kiss over Alec's lips. "Don't thank me yet. I didn't say the choice would be easy."

Moving to the end of the lounge, I shackled Alec's wrists in my hands, drawing them up over his head. He tipped his head back, as though trying to see me, but his ties were very efficient blindfolds—Xavier made sure of that. Fingers curving into his palms, he gave a light tug, his way of telling me he needed the restraint to feel real. To feel my power over him, and Xavier's, in every way.

"I've got you, my boy." Tightening my grip just enough that it would be almost impossible for him to jerk free, I pressed my lips to his knuckles. "Now relax and enjoy."

A small piece of cake between his fingers, this one the salted caramel that was at the top of my list, Xavier fed it to Alec, not moving until our boy had licked off every crumb. He spoke softly as Alec groaned his appreciation. "You like that one?"

"Yes, sir, it's...the perfect balance of sweet and salty. The icing isn't overwhelming." He tipped his head to the side. "Is this your choice?"

Xavier chuckled. "No, but I did enjoy it. Maybe I need to try it again."

Usually, Xavier preferred things neat and tidy. Sex was the one exception, but even then, he had his limits.

Tonight the limits seemed to go out the window as he smeared the rest of the salted caramel cake and icing over Alec's chest.

Bending down, he used his tongue to clean a bit off, lingering over Alec's nipples.

He made a thoughtful sound. "Yes, I think I'll move this to my list now. I find it's even more delicious than I'd originally thought. But we still have seven more options to explore."

Evil man. I smirked as Alec squirmed, precum already trailing from the tip of his dick to his stomach. My mouth watered and I shifted to ease some of the pressure from my zipper on my own length.

As though he didn't notice either of our suffering, Xavier turned his attention to the table, selecting another piece of cake. He let Alec taste it, covering his lips with the chocolate icing. The moan Alec let out was positively erotic.

"That's...that's it. You have to go with that one." He licked away the icing, his tongue touching Xavier's fingertip as he trailed it along his bottom lip. "It's very rich, but it's like a fucking orgasm in my mouth. God, sir, I'm gonna come."

"Not yet, you naughty boy. You have a job to do. It wouldn't be right to choose one without tasting them all." Xavier slicked the cake and icing along Alec's neck, bending down to suck it off, leaving little teeth marks behind. "Besides, we've decided we need at least two cakes."

There was no way I could stay back, not getting my hands and mouth on our boy for the rest of the samples. Tugging off my tie, I looped it around Alec's wrists, securing the end to the leg of the lounge so he couldn't move. Then I shifted over to Xavier's side, picking the next piece of cake.

I offered Alec the barest taste, teasing his lips with it as his tongue darted out.

"More...please, sir?" Alec pouted at me, his glistening bottom lip sticking out in a way that had me wanting to slide my dick right over it. And he knew *exactly* what this kind of begging did to me. "I need more to decide."

Taking another piece, I fed it to him. Let him finish it, but didn't let him speak. Slipping my fingers past his lips, I languidly fucked his mouth with them, torturing myself a little as I toyed with him. "So much more, my boy. Look at that pretty mouth. You'd make the perfect party favor for our guests. I think we should have a second reception for our special friends, don't you, Xavier? With all we've been given, it's only fair that we be...*generous* from time to time."

"Mhm. I've been considering breaking him in for some new games." Xavier licked his way down Alec's chest, cleaning off the cake and icing with his tongue. He palmed our boy's dick, stroking it idly as he smiled at me. "Do you think he's ready?"

Bringing my lips down to Alec's ear, I spoke softly. "I think he'll love anything we decide to do with him. I think this mouth being fucked over and over until it's red and swollen, slick with cum, would make him feel like the luckiest boy in the world."

Breaths coming in a rush, Alec shivered. "I...I trust you. I want you to know...I mean it when I say I'm yours, for whatever you want to do with me. If...if you want to let someone you trust use me, it would be...fucking hot. Knowing you're watching. That...that I can be a dirty little slut for you."

"Fuck, you say the dirtiest things so sweetly. Good boy." I kissed him in reward, smiling against his lips. Sharing like that hadn't really been on my radar, but it appealed to me, trying something different. Pushing the boundaries of what might be acceptable to anyone else. "Were you paying any attention to that cake, or did you get completely distracted, imagining how many people we'll let fuck you."

"Umm..." Alec's cheeks went red. "That, and...sirs, I'm kind of hoping *you'll* fuck me before I lose my mind."

Xavier eased onto the lounge, pressing Alec's thighs apart. Raising his hips up to expose his hole. "Since you've impressed us so much, I think we can arrange that." He slicked his fingers with icing and spit and pressed them in, a bit at a time until Alec was whimpering. Incoherently begging. "Will you make us proud, show whoever uses you how much you can take?"

"Yes, sir. Anything." Alec gasped as Xavier stretched him with his fingers. Two, then three, never going deep enough to give him any relief. "Oh God...God...please!"

"Greedy sub. Hush, I want to get my fill of this beautiful hole before I let anyone else near it." Xavier reached behind the lounge cushion and pulled out a tube of lube, showing he'd been well prepared before we'd even walked in the front door. "You'll be able to take Luther and I both before you get another dick pounding into you, pet. I think we should start preparing you now."

Covered in icing and cake, every bit of the well-put-together young businessman of not even an hour ago replaced by complete abandon, Alec writhed as Xavier poured the lube over him. Dipping my fingers back in his mouth as he cried out, I muffled the sound while using my other hand to smooth his sweat slicked hair back.

He pressed his eyes shut when Xavier began to work three fingers in, easing in and out, adding more lube as he pressed in deeper. With the fourth finger he slowed, his gaze assessing as Alec jerked and pressed his eyes shut tight.

"A bit too much, isn't it, pet? It's okay, you can tell me." The tenderness in his voice had Alec's muscles relaxing, When he nodded, I gave him an approving smile, kissing his still so fucking sweet lips. Xavier spoke quietly. "Next time, I want you to try to tell me before I have to ask, but I will always pay attention. So will Luther. We have you, my boy."

This man, this caring, attentive man was the one who'd stolen my heart so many years ago. Needing him back was part of why I'd invited Alec into our lives. I knew someone Xavier could care for, who needed him in a raw, honest way, who might be able to give in return in ways my man never expected, would keep him from straying too on the path of his ambition.

I hadn't expected to learn a few things myself. To fall so hard— for Xavier all over again, and for Alec without any of the reserve I'd clung to.

There was so much for us to all experience together, but no rush.

We had a lifetime for it all.

"Sir, don't stop. I can do it. Just...just…" Alec made a desperate sound as Xavier slid his hand free. "I can…"

"And you will, but I'm feeling very greedy myself." Xavier rose up to kneel between Alec's thighs. He undid his slacks, palming his dick and tapping it against Alec's glistening hole. "Beg Luther for his dick and I'll give you mine as well. You know how much he loves hearing us beg."

Alec's eyes met mine, his voice breathy. "I need you. I need to taste you, sir. Can you please fuck my mouth like you own it?"

"I don't know when the two of you started talking like porn stars, but I can't say I don't enjoy it." I kissed Alec again, then undid my own slacks, positioning him with his head slightly off the lounge, undoing the tie restraining him to take the pressure off his arms. The position was more challenging for him, but this way I could take his mouth while watching Xavier claim his body. "Tap my thigh if you need me to stop. Otherwise, I won't be gentle on you, my sweet boy. I'll give you exactly what you asked for."

There was some relief in Alec's nod, as though he'd been nervous not being able to take everything Xavier had been giving him would somehow spoil our fun. He moaned as Xavier's dick sunk into him in an unrelenting glide, the sound cut off by my length passing his lips.

His tongue against the top of my dick was a smooth, hot pleasure. I caressed his throat, encouraging him to relax as I slid in all the way. Hands against my thighs, pulling a bit to urge me on, Alec swallowed around me. The jarring of Xavier's thrusts added to the sensation and I had to draw back to stop myself from coming right then.

In and out, controlling Alec's breaths, fucking his throat while Xavier fucked his ass so hard the sound of flesh slapping flesh, and harsh breaths, filled the room like the most erotic beat. Muscles tightening as the pressure built up at the base of my spine, I hit the back of Alec's throat, letting him swallow down every drop of my release.

He was enough of a mess already. My dick twitched when I left his mouth, all red and glistening. Aftershocks stole the last of my strength, waves of bliss slamming into a ship barely surviving the storm, but there was the urge to continue. I wanted every bit of both these men that I could take.

Dropping down over Alec without pulling out, Xavier gathered our boy in his arms. Huffed even as he kissed Alec's lips. "I forgot about all these crumbs. They were much more enjoyable when I was making a mess of you with them."

Alec snickered, wrapping himself around Xavier even more. "They don't bother me at all, sir. But I've made my decisions."

"Have you? There are still a few more to try." I sat on the lounge, reclining on it as both Alec and Xavier rested their heads on my lap. Xavier's hair draped over Alec's shoulder and I idly stroked the silken strands.

Nodding, Alec tipped his head slightly to look up at me. "The raspberry chocolate one and the salted caramel. But I think you should have a whole cupcake display too so all the guests can try them all too..." His brow furrowed. "Unless that's asking too much from the bakery?"

"Oh, my precious boy. No business complains about *more* orders, so long as they're within a reasonable timeframe." Xavier trailed his fingers along Alec's arm. "The only issue will be picking a date."

"I'd like it to still be in the fall. And the bakery is prepared for it, I was told they didn't need more than a month's advance notice since there aren't as many orders now." A smile tugged at my lips. "They'll be invited to the wedding and I think they were looking forward to it, because they kept suggesting dates in November."

Xavier cocked his head. "November would be nice. The temperature will be ideal, the different colors on all the leaves would make a stunning backdrop. I've considered a few different venues, but...I'd like to do it here." He took a deep breath, staring off into the distance. "I created this place almost as a way to compete with my father. Both of you have helped me turn it into something more. I'd like to keep building on the memories here...have guests who aren't coming just for business."

Eyes closed, Alec's lips curved. "None of us have anything planned for the twentieth. It's not long after our last fashion show of the season."

"The twentieth it is, then." Xavier chuckled when I blinked at him, saying the first words that came to my mind before I could get them out. "Yes, that easy. I've spent years earning your doubt in my commitment to us. I will spend the rest of my life, if that's what it takes, until you're absolutely certain you are my priority. You and Alec and...perhaps a few children, as we've discussed."

I wrapped his hair around my hand, tugging lightly and bending down to give him a soft kiss. "I'm loving every step we're taking, but let's stick to one at a time."

A huge one was what we'd done today. Sharing some of our concerns, delving into issues we still had to work through, and communicating on a level we'd been striving for ever since our relationship became more important than Xavier's need to one-up his father.

The man would always be something of a shadow, creeping around the edges of Xavier's happiness. The damage he'd done would never be completely erased.

But just Xavier sitting here, discussing plans for the future as though he had nowhere else he'd rather be?

It proved he could see beyond the shadow that used to cut off all the light.

Because the light was pushing it back, right in the center of his world, growing stronger every day. Alec adding to it almost effortlessly...

And me finally seeing I could.

Chapter Seven

A dopting a kitten over lunch break had been a horrible idea. Shaking his head as sharp claws dug into his calf, Xavier picked up the calico kitten and sat it on his desk. Rambunctious little beast. She'd had his heart from the moment he'd seen her alone in that cage, apparently the runt of the litter and not as sweet and plump and fluffy as the rest had been.

Alec was going to love the tiny thing.

The older cat they'd adopted a while back, a one-eyed gray cat named Sir Nevsky, had passed peacefully months ago, and the two younger black cats seemed a little lost without him. Luther's mastiff, Chance, was gaining strength after his last round of cancer treatments, but the puppy still couldn't keep up with them. Hopefully, the new kitten would bring some balance back to the household.

Which hadn't been Xavier's initial reason for visiting the shelter, he'd offered to stop by with Alec's monthly donation and ensure the volunteers had everything they needed. Most of the animals there were waiting to be picked up by owners who'd lost them, or new families excited to give them a good home.

All except for this little rascal.

"Rascal is the perfect name for you." Xavier saved his pen from the kitten, but not his keyboard, which she raced across to pounce on his hand. "You're making it difficult to work. Please be still."

Luther would be laughing his ass off at you right now.

Perhaps, but Xavier was positive their black kittens, Morticia and Wednesday, had been much better behaved at this age.

Purring, the kitten stepped to the edge of his desk, pawing at his tie. He petted it, glancing over as his phone chimed. One of the alerts he had for 'The Depths', a magazine he'd become a bit obsessed with. Luther's questions on how the magazine's blog fared had him diving into every bit of information he could find. On the business side, it needed some work, but it was profitable. Run by a man who'd come up from nothing as a journalist, made several smart investments, then launched something fresh and innovative with a drive Xavier respected.

Expecting a new deep dive into the questionable practices of business tycoons, Xavier frowned when he saw the mention was from an article in the New York Times. Odin Gail was being accused of being an unstable deviant. Pictures of him at a BDSM club, surrounded by naked submissives, all men, were shown with all the 'naughty bits' blurred out. He'd kept his life fairly private, even being voted Bachelor of the Year several times, but the article tore down all the walls he'd built around himself.

Unlike Xavier, the man didn't have a secure foundation to fall back on. Even though Xavier didn't tell his board much, he had made sure to carefully select people who were open-minded. Who wouldn't be shocked when photos were leaked of him and Luther, or him and Alec. Or both. He prefered not dragging them into the spotlight, but shining a light on who he was wouldn't destroy him.

Odin didn't have that kind of support.

Reading on, Xavier's grip on his phone tightened until the damn thing was about ready to snap. With all the details in the article, one thing was clear. Someone had been digging into Odin's life. And since nothing had come out before now? Gathering intel for the smear campaign had been initiated after the exposé about his father.

One more thing for the man to destroy because God forbid, his ego take a hit. That he might admit he was wrong. That those who worked for him, who he continued to use, ever get out from under the soles of his ugly leather shoes.

Stocks in the magazine had plummeted. Several of the events where it had been headlining were making statements to distance themselves. Within the week, the magazine would be obsolete. Barely worth snide whispers in dark corners by the elite.

Shoving to his feet, Xavier slammed his phone on his desk. Stepped out of his office, not wanting to risk having this conversation over the phone. Odin was in town, so it was the perfect opportunity to meet in person. Maybe he was being paranoid, but it had just become very clear that there were no limits to his father's reach.

And he needed to make some moves before the man flexed his power even more.

"Stephanie, I need you to send someone over to Odin Gail's hotel." Xavier wrote down a note with a time and place for them to meet. If Odin knew anything about him, he might be hesitant to show up, but it was a chance Xavier was willing to take. Hopefully, the man would be curious enough to hear him out. "This is to be placed in his hands. And cancel all my meetings for the rest of the day."

Holding his gaze for a split second as though to gauge the importance of the assignment, Stephanie gave a quick nod. "Yes, sir. If I won't be needed for the rest of the day, I'll bring it to him myself."

"That would be perfect, there's few I trust as much as I do you." Nothing but the truth, but Xavier's words seemed to surprise Stephanie. He smiled at her when she blushed. "You're due for a nice bonus. Take the rest of the day off after this to celebrate."

"I will, sir. Thank you." Stephanie grabbed her jacket from the back of her chair, rushing toward the elevator.

Xavier returned to his office, his focus locked on writing up a proposal over the next few hours, the kitten fast asleep on his knee.

He still had much to learn about the industry he was determined to immerse himself in. Who better to guide him than someone who'd been fighting to make his mark in it for years?

Slipping the kitten into its carrier to cuddle up on the blanket within, Xavier carried it along with the proposal for Odin, closing his office early. Not surprisingly, no one had disturbed him with Stephanie away from her desk—and Luther off hovering over Alec while the twins were on the junior line's floor. The sky was a bit cloudy, but the bar wasn't far, so he'd have his driver pick him up when he was done.

His luck held, keeping the rain at bay as he made his way down the few blocks to the upscale bar where he entertained his favorite clients. Something as simple as a walk shouldn't feel so liberating, but he couldn't forget the times he'd kept himself so busy, this would've been considered a waste of time.

Luther will be so proud of me.

That Xavier wasn't uncomfortable with how good the thought made him feel was another change. He shook his head with a soft laugh as he dodged a few of those trailing out of the various high rises in the business section, reaching the bar with moments to spare.

Inside the space held the rich aroma of cigars and leather, the ambient lighting a relaxing blue, music quiet enough to encourage conversation. The decor was a mix of classic and modern Alec absolutely loved. The last time they'd come together, he'd spent hours talking to the owner about the design.

Xavier and Luther's boy appreciated beauty in all forms. It was amazing, looking through the world in his eyes.

But when he spotted Odin, sitting at the bar, sipping from an expensive bottle of whiskey he'd had the bartender leave out for him, Xavier's assessment was all his own. His boy's biggest strength was also his greatest weakness. He always wanted to see the best in people, which had been very dangerous when he'd met Xavier's old...'mentor', Joel.

That kind of mistake was one Xavier hadn't made in a very long time.

The man was about Luther's height, well over six feet, but without his muscular build. His skin had a healthy pink undertone under a light tan, which would give him a beach-boy look with that wavy dark blond hair touching the collar of his shirt, except for the neatly trimmed beard outlining his sharp jawline and cheekbones. A very handsome man, with good tastes to match. His cobalt chevron blazer and trousers was Brunello Cucinelli, a designer Xavier had admired for years.

As much as 'do not judge a book by its cover' might sound good, in Xavier's line of work, it was difficult not to, to some extent. So far, Odin was off to a good start.

Walking over to the bar, Xavier held out his hand. "Mr. Gail, it's a pleasure to meet you. Thank you for coming on such short notice."

"I was curious why you—of all people—would reach out today of all days." Standing, Odin shook his hand. He held up the bottle, waving over the bartender for another glass when Xavier nodded. Settling back onto his stool, he waited for Xavier to join him before continuing. "From what I've read about you, I doubt you're here to defend your father. But if I'm wrong? Save it."

From anyone else, even *suggesting* he might be aligned with his father in *any* way would get his hackles up. But with what the bastard had just put Odin through, he couldn't blame the man. He set the carrier by his stool and the proposal on the bartop before he sat. Took a sip of his whiskey, curious at the choice of such an expensive bottle when Odin's finances must be in ruins.

There was one of two explanations. Either Odin had prepared better for the hit than reports indicated, or he was enjoying the lifestyle he'd worked so hard for, one last time.

Xavier hoped it was the former, for Odin's sake, but he sincerely doubted it. His father was too damn good at destroying those who got in his way.

The only one he'd ever failed with was Xavier himself. And it wasn't for lack of trying.

"I'm not here to defend him. I'm dead to the man." Xavier gave Odin a level look. "I'm here to help save your magazine. I happen to enjoy the whole concept—I was toying with the idea of becoming your competitor, but my board turned down my very uninformed proposal."

Brow raised, Odin held his glass to his lips. "You want *The Depths* to become part of Ashburne Style and Media? No offense, Mr. Ashburne—"

"Call me Xavier."

"Very well, then please call me Odin." The man polished off his whiskey, then refilled his glass. "I don't think you have the slightest clue how bad the damage is. There's no coming back from this. Most of my best writers are jumping ship. I can't *give away* stocks. I'd expected some backlash, but this…" He lowered his gaze to his glass. "I was a fool not to have prepared for this."

There was no way Odin could have, unless he had a truly depraved mind, but Xavier didn't need to point that out. What he intended was to give the man some hope. "There will need to be a rebrand." He slid the folder holding the proposal closer to the man so he could look it over when he was ready. "Talk to the people you can and want to keep. We'll get together with my PR staff and work out some suggestions for how to present this to the public. If you're interested, go radio silent while we create an airtight plan that will survive anything he can throw at us."

The edge of Odin's lips twitched. He drew the folder closer, but didn't open it. "Maybe I've had too much whiskey, but I'm not hating this 'us' talk. How much power do I have to give up for you to make this investment?"

A very good question. Xavier wanted Odin to run the new magazine much like he had his old one, and he respected what the man had built, but he'd be a fool not to demand controlling interest with how much money he'd have to put into this venture.

If Odin was as proud as Xavier suspected, he would be resistant at first, but it wouldn't take much to get him to see the benefits. "I'll have my lawyers draw up an official contract, but I'm aiming for sixty percent."

Closing his eyes, Odin exhaled slowly. "Fuck…" He shook his head, letting out a soft laugh. "I can't say it's unreasonable, but I managed over a decade building up this magazine on my own using nothing but the money I earned off a few books, articles, and some timely snapped pictures." Opening his eyes, he tipped his glass from side to side, staring into the amber liquid. "If I do this, I'd be working for you."

"No." Xavier set his own glass down and leaned forward, waiting until Odin lifted his gaze before continuing. "You will remain the CEO and you will run everything. I don't have the experience to even attempt taking over, and even if I did I have my own business to run. Once a significant portion of my investment is repaid, I will sell you back eleven percent. I may decide to split my remaining shares if we find people who could help the magazine thrive. You lost most of your upper management. From now on, we will expect more loyalty than that, and personal investment is a good incentiviser."

That got him another of those barely there smiles, but Odin seemed to be warming to the idea. "I can see that. I'd want the final say in who I'd be working with, but if you've put all this in writing?" He tapped the folder. "I'm in."

All right, that had gone much smoother than Xavier expected. He frowned, picking up his glass to polish off the whiskey. Set it down and sat back as Odin refilled his own glass. "Just like that?"

"Mhm. I'm a writer, not a businessman, Xavier—that much should be clear by how my company just collapsed like a house of cards. You have the money for the lawyers, all I have is my experience in reading contracts. And an idea you want." Elbow on the bartop, Odin's gaze followed a pair of men as they passed, as though noticing for the first time that they weren't alone in there. "It will take a while to rebuild and I want to get started as soon as possible. If you're fucking with me, I don't have anything else to lose. If you're not?" He lifted his shoulders. "This could turn out to be the start of the perfect partnership."

The mention of his not being able to afford lawyers to go over the contracts with him was discomforting, but that couldn't be helped. Xavier's lawyers had strong ethics, despite being pitbulls in the courtroom. Since they were on retainer, he'd have them spend some time with Odin, answering any questions he might have. They'd be working for the magazine as well until it gained some independence.

Offering anything else right now might be seen as *too* charitable, so Xavier sidelined that discussion for later. "Is there anything you expect from me? I feel like I'm the one making all the demands. I don't intend to bully you into agreeing to all my terms."

Odin snorted, lifting his brow slightly as he held Xavier's gaze. There was something in those rich blue depths that told him the man hadn't been *playing* at being a Dom in that club. "You couldn't bully me, Xavier. But there is something I want." He tapped his fingers on the bartop. "Let me write your biography. You've led a very interesting life. Telling your side of the story your father tried to erase you from will do more than my exposé ever could. Having my name on the cover would be the perfect 'fuck you' to the old man, and I could use some revenge."

Inhaling slowly, Xavier went over the repercussions of taking on his father on that level. Granted, his business was much better protected than Odin's had been—he'd expected some covert attacks from his father since the very beginning—but there were still some risks.

Of course, there were risks to just getting married in what would be a very public affair. His father could choose any reason to lash out at him. And Xavier refused to cower from the bastard.

"Deal." Xavier shook his head, laughing at his own recklessness. "My boy has certainly had an interesting influence on me. If we'd had this conversation a couple of years ago, I would have said you were out of your mind."

Odin chuckled, pushing away the bottle as though deciding he didn't need to drown his sorrows in it any longer. "I may be. I'm assuming you're talking about Alec and not Luther?"

The man had done his research. Xavier inclined his head. "He has a brilliant mind that almost went to waste, a way of looking at life that...I was sorely lacking. Between the two of them? This may sound overly sentimental, but they saved my soul."

"You're talking to a writer. And also someone who was just buried by your father's wrath. I don't think it's 'overly sentimental'. I believe it's true." Odin's gaze went down to the carrier when the kitten let out a plaintive *Meow*. "You've been sitting here all this time with something alive in there?"

Xavier huffed, reaching down to pick up the carrier. "She's had the run of my office for half the day, she needed a nap. And the cage she was in at the shelter wasn't much bigger, I'm sure she's fine."

Some humor lit Odin's eyes. "I'm sure she is, I just wasn't expecting the great Xavier Ashburne to be strolling around town with a kitten." Odin stood, latching his fingers behind his neck and stretching out his back like he'd been sitting for too long. "I appreciate you reaching out like this and I'm honestly looking forward to working with you. Let me know when you have the contracts ready—and when you can fit me in to begin discussions about the book."

"I'll be in touch." Xavier gave the man a firm handshake, surprised when he was pulled in for a back-slapping hug.

Chuckling, Odin drew back. "I believe we're going to become very good friends, my man. It might be the liquor talking, but you just offered me a way out of the mess I'd made. I won't soon forget that."

"It wasn't a mess. You brought something to light that still needs to be addressed. I don't know what will come of it, but when your magazine is up and running again? You'll get another chance to make sure he can't bury his treatment of his workers. It might empower them enough to take action." Xavier knew it might not, but he'd learned how powerful hope could be. And the man in front of him needed that. "If nothing else, failing to take you down for good? Will piss him off. He's used to getting his way and can be downright ruthless."

Odin smirked. "Which is one of the qualities he's going to wish he didn't pass down to his son."

There was *no* part of his father Xavier wanted to claim. His eyes narrowed slightly, several replies on the tip of his tongue that would make this whole meeting a waste.

But Odin put his hands up, shaking his head. "It was a compliment, my man. You've used your powers for good—I've done my homework. If you didn't have that kind of strength, you wouldn't be able to offer me what you have. I'd just rather not be on the wrong side of it."

"I knew you were a smart man." Xavier relaxed, paying off their tab and ignoring Odin's objection. "Save your money to buy a suit for my wedding. I'm putting you on the guest list."

File in hand, Odin walked with him to the door, eyeing the kitten who was meowing louder now. "Send me an invitation and I'll be there. I'm looking forward to meeting the two men who found the chink in the Ashburne armor. They're a very big part of your story."

"Yes, they are." Xavier said farewell to the man before texting his driver to meet him, speaking softly to himself. "The most important part."

Rain pelted the town car on the drive home and Xavier took off his jacket to cover the carrier before getting out, hurrying to the front door, which Ms. Lacey opened for him. After handing Xavier a towel to dry his hair, she took the kitten out of the carrier, cooing at it and giving him a smile like he'd impressed her.

Cheeks heating, Xavier retrieved the furry little thing that was purring like a small motor. "I'm fulfilling a promise, that is all."

"You're a sweet man giving one of the men you love a precious gift." Ms. Lacey gave him a gentle nudge toward the hall. "They took their dinner in the den, where I believe they're still watching a movie. Go on, I'll bring you a plate shortly."

Nodding, Xavier crossed the hall, keeping one hand on the kitten as it crawled up to his shoulder. As he opened the door to the den, the kitten moved around the back of his neck, forcing him to bow forward so the silly thing wouldn't fall.

"Xavier, what in the world…?" Luther let out a rough laugh as Alec scrambled off the sofa, coming over to save Xavier from the wicked claws the little creature was digging into his neck and back to show its dominance. Untangling it from his hair took Luther joining in the efforts. "I was wondering what was taking you so long. The last thing I expected was for you to be looking for a new master."

Bringing his hand to the back of his neck, Xavier came away with blood. He frowned at the deceptively cute bundle now in Alec's arms. His expression softened as Alec buried his face in the multi-colored fur. "I got her earlier today. I feel betrayed by the attack, but I deserve some punishment for keeping her in the carrier so long at the bar." He sat on the sofa while Luther stepped out of the room, returning seconds later with a small medkit.

The sofa creaked as Luther slid in beside him, dabbing at the scratches with some gauze. "There was nothing scheduled away from the office that I was aware of? Did you check in with Brendon before leaving?"

"No, I didn't think of it. I hope I didn't worry you, it was…a rather spontaneous decision." Xavier held still, breathing through the sting of the alcohol Luther used to clean the small wounds. "I am buying a magazine."

Curling up at his other side, wearing one of the onesies Luther loved dressing him up in, Alec cuddled the kitten while giving Xavier a surprised look. "*The Depths*? I saw a few things about the closure online, but I hadn't gotten a chance to find out what happened. I know you were really into it, and you were thinking about starting your own magazine, so…this is kinda perfect?"

"It's complicated, but let's just say my father had a hand in its demise, so it's only natural that I play a part in its resurrection. It will be under a new name, but the concept will be the same." In the past, Xavier wouldn't have bothered discussing any kind of business like this in a personal way, and Luther wouldn't have asked, but Alec never hesitated. It felt good to have someone to share it with. "Odin Gail is a victim of my father's ego—I doubt he would have let it hold him down for long, but I made him an offer to expedite the process."

Luther nodded slowly, stroking the undamaged part of Xavier's neck. "It sounds like you like the man. I hope he's going to be doing most of the work, though. You have enough on your plate."

"I do. And he will, once the contracts are signed." Xavier didn't mind Luther setting some boundaries with this, they both knew he needed them. It would be much too easy for him to get caught up in another project and their wedding was the priority. Speaking of which... "I also invited him to our wedding."

"Oh you did, did you?" Luther's lips brushed over the flesh warmed by his touch, his voice low. "Should I be concerned about your interest in this man?"

Brow raised, Xavier shot Luther a sideways look. "Why in the world would you be concerned? This is business, nothing more."

Plucking out his phone, Alec tapped on it, then held it up so they could both see the screen. "Because he's hot. And kinky as fuck."

"Language, pet." Luther smacked Alec's thigh, then gave him a thoughtful look. "Maybe we should extend this invitation to the afterparty. Mixing business and pleasure can have its advantages."

The way Alec blushed at the implication in Luther's words was adorable. And had Xavier's mind shifting to how he could secure this new partnership with Odin in a way that would be beneficial to them all.

His father had tried to use the man's *extracurricular* activities to destroy him.

Why not let them be part of celebrating his comeback?

Reached over Luther, Xavier curved his hand under Alec's jaw. "Or sooner. I can think of a signing bonus that would be perfect for welcoming Mr. Gail into the fold. Would you enjoy that, pet?"

Alec shivered, wetting his bottom lip with his tongue. "I've never played that way, sir, but...if it would get you and Luther off? Yeah, I totally would."

"That man doesn't know what he's in for." Luther folded his arms behind his head on the sofa, a crooked smile on his lips. "Let's invite him to the bachelor party Alec's been secretly planning as well. He can get to know everyone in a more...intimate setting."

That got a bit of a pout from Alec. "How did you know about that? It's supposed to be a surprise."

"I like keeping myself well informed. You'll have to follow Xavier's lead if you want to keep secrets, my boy. Tell no one what you're doing until it's done." Luther brought his hand down to Xavier's thigh, stroking it lightly in a way that made it clear he wasn't upset. "I like this. Exploring something new. Discussing different plans—the tame and the more carnal. I didn't know what our life would look like after we got married, but if this is any indication? I can't fucking wait."

Xavier took Luther's hand in his, lacing their fingers together. Part of him, a part he hadn't truly faced, had been afraid taking this step would mean giving up many of the things they'd enjoyed sharing. Not Alec—he would always belong in their lives—but the kind of indulgence that would have his father damning him to hell a thousand times over.

Instead, it felt like their relationship had become strong enough to have a taste of the forbidden together. They could communicate any desires they had without fear of judgment. He could trust these two men with all of himself and that, above all else...

Was part of a future he'd never dared hope for.

Now I just have to make sure not to fuck it up.

Chapter Eight

"The invitation is very...fancy, Luther. It will make a nice keepsake."

Shaking my head, I smiled a little at my father's attempt to find something nice to say about what he likely saw as an extravagant waste of money. Phone to my ear, I checked the schedule for the weekend security shift one last time. "The gold leaf was a bit much, but Alec was charmed by the artist and wanted to support her work, rather than go through a regular printing company."

The only response I got to that was a grunt. Then my father changed the subject. "I'm incredibly happy for you, son, but...don't you think your brother would make a better best man? He's closer to your age and less likely to misstep in this unique...lifestyle of yours. No, wait. That's the wrong thing to say, isn't it? You see? I'm too old to be all 'woke'."

"Dad, even when you didn't understand what I was going through, you supported me. Rezz and I are doing better, but we're not quite there yet." Guilt nagged at me to admit it out loud, but the ugly shit my younger brother had said to and about me for years still stung. To my brother's credit, he didn't push for me to just forget it all. He'd apologized and he'd give me however long it took to rebuild our relationship, welcoming me to be part of his children's lives with zero expectations. "If you're not comfortable with it, I understand."

My father went silent. Cleared his throat. "I will be at your wedding, Luther. Sitting with the rest of your family."

Throat tight, I nodded, keeping my tone neutral as I ended the call. Hearing Brendon behind me, I forced a smile and turned.

His expression told me he wasn't buying it. The deep scars on his light brown face grew more pronounced as his lips thinned. "We're about to head to your bachelor party and your boy's been working his ass off, planning this for weeks. Don't let family bull-shit ruin it for you."

"It's nothing like that, my man. There are some things my father can't do. He accepts me." I shrugged, grabbing my jacket and the rucksack I'd brought with a change of clothes before we left the control room to the night shift. "That's all I can ask."

Brendon shook his head, shoving his hands in his pockets and glowering at one of the young interns, who'd gotten on his bad side by forgetting his clearance pass every morning this week. The young man yelped and ducked into the closest storage closet. "Accepting you is the bare minimum, but it's none of my fucking business."

"You clearly have an opinion."

"And I just gave it to you." Brendon shrugged as he led the way onto the elevator. "It's your special day. Whoever stands by your side should be someone you want there, who wants to be there. Far as I'm concerned, it's pretty damn simple. You're a popular guy. You have friends. Choose one of them."

Even with his blunt attitude, and his unwillingness to get close to people in general, Brendon had been one of the few I could count on during one of the hardest times in my life. He was more than family. When I'd been at my lowest, he'd built me back up. Gave me a purpose. His support had always been unconditional, and I needed that right now.

Probably not what he'd intended with his observations, but he'd just solved the issue of my standing by the altar alone.

Taking a deep breath, I faced him. "Would you do me the honor of being my best man?"

Brendon blinked, then rubbed his hand over his mouth. The flesh around his eyes crinkled as he lowered his hand, revealing a big grin. "Hell, I'll probably scare half your guests, but yeah. I'd like that."

"Then it's settled. There's still time for a fitting, I'll have Alec get your measurements this weekend." I laughed at the panic in his eyes, which he quickly hid. "Don't worry, the tux will be a classic style. Nothing flashy. And if you tell him the size of your gun, he'll make sure there's space for it."

Pressing the button on his keyfob to start his SUV, Brendon nodded slowly, his gaze a little suspicious. "So long as your boy doesn't get handsy. He's easy on the eyes, but he's too soft for me. I'd break him. I like my men and women with a lot more padding."

Somehow, in all the time I'd known Brendon, I'd never been clear on his preferences. I'd had a bit of a crush on him when he'd been helping me get into top form for my security training, but he'd shut that down real quick. He didn't get involved with those he mentored.

Looking back, I was grateful he'd set those limits. His friendship was too important to have blurred those lines, and I'd have lost him when I'd gone back to Xavier.

Life had a way of leading you exactly where you needed to be. Even if it was on the rockiest road possible. In a junker. With four flat tires.

In the passenger side of Brendon's SUV, I settled in for the ride out to the club where Alec had reserved tables for a group that kept getting larger, every time I snuck a peek at the guest list. There were a lot more kinky people in Ashburne's Design and Media than I would've guessed. Checking my phone, I sighed at a text from Xavier, letting me know he was running late. He'd scheduled some time with Odin to discuss the book the man was apparently writing about him.

If I knew Xavier as well as I thought I did, the whole thing would be another exposé about his father, only with more pages. And details that had remained private. Until now.

I had no problem with my man handling his father however he needed to, but the book would take months, if not years. Our wedding was in a week. This was our time to celebrate the life we were building together—something he'd seemed fully invested in.

This is a distraction, don't make a big deal about it. He always shows up when it counts.

True, but the closer we got to the wedding date, the more his Redstone past seemed to haunt him. Almost as though he believed the right move could cut all ties for good. Like the steps he'd taken years ago, changing his name and eliminating all connections with Edmund Redstone The Second, hadn't been enough.

He was still letting the man have power over him, and I didn't know how to help him take it back.

Maybe this was something he needed to face on his own. Like I'd had to deal with my family drama. Brendon had been there to support me, but Xavier didn't have any close friends he could turn to.

If Odin became one?

I could put up with my man being delayed. Within reason.

But I wasn't the only one he had to worry about.

Standing on the curb, wearing a long black trench coat, black liner framing his blue eyes, Alec practically bounced in place as I climbed out of the SUV, Brendon continuing to the large parking lot to pick the perfect spot. I held out my arms, catching my boy and lifting him against my chest to claim a deep kiss.

Arms wrapped around my neck, Alec looked around, his brilliant smile fading at the edges. "Where's Xavier? I thought he'd be right behind you."

"He's running a bit late, my boy. Didn't he text you?" I lowered Alec carefully to the walkway, taking note of the platforms on the shiny black boots that stretched up to his thighs.

Patting the fake pockets on the trench coat, Alec gave me a sheepish look. "I left my phone in the changing room. He probably did. And I bet he won't be long." He grabbed my hand, tugging me along with him as Brandon joined us. "This place is incredible, I've been dying for you to get a chance to check it out. They'll give us a discount if we host the afterparty here too. There's a really nice private room in the back that would be perfect and the head Pro Domme runs the flower shop I ordered all the flowers from for the wedding."

"You do know my *father* will be at the reception?" I took in the gothic decor and the high mirrored ceilings, the deep purple lighting casting an ethereal glow over the mingling crowd already filling up the space and congregating to the tables around the large stage. "I thought we were going for something a bit more...traditional."

Alec nodded, leading me and Brendon to a table front and center. "We are, but this is for the party after that, remember? When we can all let loose and stop posing for the media swarm."

Although Alec had gained more confidence dealing with the press before and after events, he still prefered to let Judy take the spotlight. And she'd gotten better at catching on when he was uncomfortable. The two made good business partners, and she'd been amazing at helping him with the parts of the wedding planning Xavier and I let him take over.

This must be part of some compromise between them. It would be a waste not to use the publicity the wedding would bring the company, but none of us wanted the whole thing to be a performance.

Of course, it seemed like there *would* be a performance of some sort tonight. I picked Alec up and sat him on my knee, wrapping my arms around him, enjoying the feel of the toned muscles he'd developed after countless morning runs and workouts with me.

Nuzzling his neck, I spoke softly. "What have you got planned for us tonight, pet?"

"You'll have to wait and see, sir." Excitement lit Alec's eyes, flushing his cheeks as he relaxed against me. "Let's just say, it's part of something I've been preparing for months and...I think you and Xavier are going to love it."

Once everyone was settled, the stage lights were turned up and those around us were lowered. Voices quieted as a tall woman in a crimson corset walked to center stage, holding a whip. She surveyed the crowd, a wicked smile on her red lips.

When she cracked the whip, a few people jumped and gasped, letting out nervous laughter as a man in a crisp black suit and tie rushed over to her with a mic.

"Good evening, my good people. For those who don't know me, my name is Mistress Grace and I'll be your hostess for the night. As always, Friday nights begin a weekend of sin and debauchery, where we put all your desires on display before you explore each and every one in rooms designed to serve your pleasures. Or, if you prefer to watch, our entertainers will be putting on shows all night." Mistress Grace ran her hand down her assistant's chest, tugging open the buttons of his shirt. "Tonight, we have some special guests, celebrating for the last time as bachelors before they shackle themselves for life. Let's show some love for Luther Cross and Xavier Ashburne!"

The spotlight hit our table. Brendon leaned his chair back, giving me a wry look as he folded his arms over his chest. Alec's eyes went wide, red blotching his cheeks as he frantically shook his head with embarrassment.

Laughing to cover my own humiliation, I hugged him tight and spoke loud enough for everyone to hear. "Xavier is on his way, but please, continue! I'll just have to torture him with all the erotic details later."

Mistress Grace didn't look too impressed, but she made a sharp motion with her hand, bringing the spotlight back to the stage. "You heard the man. Let's make the other groom-to-be sorry he missed this, boys!"

Five more men in suits joined the first and a dark version of the song, *Crazy in Love*, came on. Slow and sultry, the dance began. The men ripped open their shirts, revealing tanned, muscular chests, abs that undultated as their bodies flowed to the music. Jackets hit the stage, the men pairing up, pressing together, skin glistening with sweat.

Shifting on my lap, Alec's breaths came in little bursts, and he was shivering like he was nervous. Or maybe so turned on he didn't know what to do with himself.

Shoving aside the disappointment of Xavier not being here for this, I slid my hand under the bottom of the trenchcoat, stroking Alec's inner thigh. It didn't help with the squirming, but the shivering stopped. He let out a needy sound, leaning back against me and turning his head to brush soft kisses along my jaw.

If he kept it up, both of us would miss the show, too.

The music changed to a song I'd heard so many times at home I'd lost count because Alec seemed obsessed with it. *Montero* by Lil Nas X. As the first verse finished, the now shirtless dancers jumped off the stage, surrounding our table, two of them lifting Alec from my arms.

Shoving to my feet, I started forward. Brendon grabbed my arm, chuckling as he forced me back into my seat and held me there. "Down, boy. This is his show."

At center stage, Alec caught my eye, winking and blowing me a kiss as he was lowered to his feet. He joined the clearly choreographed dance that he must have started practicing before he'd even booked the venue. The trench coat covered most of him, but some of the hip thrusting moves revealed teases of what I'd felt when I'd touched him. Besides the boots, he wasn't wearing much underneath.

Relaxing in my seat, I let my gaze tell him how fucking impressed I was, how much I wanted him as I drank in his movements. A rough sound escaped me as the two men who'd taken him to the stage stripped off his trenchcoat, revealing a harness crossing his chest and leather booty shorts with red accents, matching the red slashes along the tops of the thigh high boots. Caressing his chest, then the outline of his dick through the leather,

Alec used his body to tempt every single person in the room. But his gaze held mine, as if they'd all disappeared.

He danced out of reach when the other dancers reached for him. Dropped to his knees, hands on the floor, gyrating like he was being fucked.

There was no way I was getting up on that stage, but the urge was there. My own dick was straining against the confines of my leathers, despite them having been comfortable not even ten minutes ago. As I shifted to relieve some pressure, Alec's smile turned wicked.

This man...this wonderful, sexy man, knows exactly what he's doing to me.

And in that moment, he was all mine.

The original six dancers came around to the floor in front of the stage, forming stairs with their bodies. Alec walked down, almost stumbling halfway, but Mistress Grace stepped forward to steady him. Released him as he got closer to me.

Straddling my thighs, Alec ground against me, hissing in a breath when I latched onto the harness to jerk him close and claim his lips. Sweat slicked the kiss, salty and hot as my tongue touched his. All around us, people were clapping and cheering, but I blocked them out. My entire world narrowed to my boy, to holding him, marking him with my teeth against his throat, leaving no doubt to anyone watching that he belonged to me.

Lost in the moment, I barely noticed when the song changed and the dancers continued the show. Whatever else Alec might've planned—there couldn't possibly be more, could there?—I hoped he didn't mind me spoiling it by dragging him off somewhere. My self-restraint had gone out the fucking window.

A smile curved my lips as I brought my gaze to Alec's.

He went still, looking past me.

Glancing over, I frowned as Xavier settled in the chair that had been left empty for him. He gave Alec an appreciative once over. "I apologize for being late, but it appears I arrived just in time for the best part."

Jesus Christ, Xavier. Read the fucking room.

Eyes narrowing, Alec glared at Xavier. Stepped away from me and straightened, hands fisted at his sides. "Of course, *sir*. You're just in time." He grabbed the trench coat Mistress Grace had laid over the back of Brendon's chair at some point. "To go fuck yourself."

Before I had a chance to move, Alec stormed off, disappearing into the darkness beyond the stage. I stood, turning slowly to face Xavier as he rose, confusion and hurt warring in his eyes. I cut off whatever he was about to say. "Save it. You don't get to make this about you. He did this for *us*. He's been working so hard to make it special for the three of us because that's what it was supposed to be. It might officially be *our* wedding, but he was never meant to feel less important."

"He's not, Luther." Xavier kept pace with me as I strode across the club, finding a door by the stage and shoving through it. He spoke in a rush. "I was doing something to let him know how important he is to me."

"You just *showed* him otherwise. All you had to do was be here, Xavier. It wasn't too much to fucking ask." All around us were different props, lining a long hall with half a dozen doors on either side. Alec could be behind any one of them. "He was magnificent up there and you missed it because you were too focused on your own plans. What you did was unspeakably fucking selfish, do you understand that?"

Slowing, Xavier lowered his gaze. The large brown envelope in his hand hit the floor with a thunk as he nodded. "Yes. I do, Luther. And I will do anything in my power to make this up to him. I was wrong. So fucking wrong."

The acknowledgment was something, but it wouldn't erase how much hurt Xavier had caused. I stopped a few feet ahead of him, closing my eyes to get a hold on my anger. It wouldn't serve any of us. The most important thing was finding Alec. Making sure the entire night he'd planned wasn't completely ruined.

"You will tell him that when you see him. You'll tell him *why* you made the choices you did, but if he's not feeling fucking forgiving, you'll give him the space he needs." My guts twisted as I held Xavier's gaze, feeling torn in two.

I loved him so damn much. I knew this side of him, I'd accepted it long ago. There were times when his decisions revolved around what he thought was right at the time, and his intentions might be good, but he didn't consider the full impact. How someone needing him, *just* him, might be more important than whatever he wanted to give.

"Would it..." Xavier stared down at the envelope. "Would it be better if I left?"

Grinding my teeth together, I said a silent prayer, resisting the urge to grab him and shake him. "No. You stay and face this. Be the man I know you can be when you get out of your own goddamn way."

"I'm sorry, Luther." Xavier glanced down the hall. His throat worked. "Alec..."

Hugging himself, Alec watched us as we approached, looking half ready to bolt again. Tears trailed down his cheeks and his black liner was smudged. He didn't speak as I put my arm around his shoulders, drawing him close to my side.

Pressing my lips to his hair, I kept my voice low. "You know this place pretty well, right? Is there somewhere private where we can talk?"

Alec jutted his chin toward a partially open door. "Mistress Grace was letting me use this changing room for rehearsals. Two of the other guys shared it with me, but they won't be back here for a while."

Inside, the changing room was fairly standard. Four vanities with lit up mirrors, makeup bags open with their contents spread haphazardly, a few racks with various costumes, the scent of cologne and baby oil hanging in the air. The corner of the room had a small gray loveseat, with two mismatched armchairs around a sturdy wood coffee table. With Alec's hand in mine, I crossed over to the loveseat, sitting with him and leaving Xavier to his own devices.

Rather than choose one of the chairs, he sat on the table, facing us. Holding the envelope he must've picked up off the floor at one point.

He placed it beside him on the coffee table, then braced his hands on his knees, loose strands of hair framing either side of his face. "Luther is right. What I did...it was thoughtless. I should have made you a priority in the way you'd asked me to. You trusted me to show up when I said I would. I broke that trust."

"This was really important to me. Maybe I didn't make that clear enough, but..." Alec irritably swiped away a tear with the side of his fist. "I didn't think I had to. You *knew* I'd put a lot of work into a special surprise."

"I did. And no, you shouldn't have had to spell it out." Xavier met Alec's gaze, his own shadowed with regret. "I cut it too close. I should have been here early, instead of pushing things to the last minute."

Alec groaned, tipping his head back against my shoulder. "*Why?* Seriously, what was so fucking important? The book? I support you wanting to get it written, show the world what a bastard your father is. I really do, but...did it have to be tonight?"

For a moment, Xavier was silent. He shook his head, lifting the envelope and holding it out to Alec. "No, it didn't have to be tonight. But the part we started with wasn't about my father. It was about you."

"What...?" Alec opened the envelope, carefully pulling out the pages within. Several tears hit the paper as he read over the words. His hand found mine as I leaned in to read it over myself.

My lips curved slightly. "This is the day you met Alec."

"Yes. Odin only intended to discuss a brief outline, but when we got to the part where Alec had come into our lives, I could see it so clearly..." Xavier lifted a hand to brush his hair away from his face. "He started taking it all down, fleshing it out, giving me the words for all I felt, looking back on what that day meant to all of us. You brought him to me, and then he brought out a side of me that finally deserved you. I wanted him...I wanted you to know, Alec. I finally had a way to tell you what you mean to me." He held up his hand when Alec's lips parted. "This doesn't take away how much I hurt you. I'm sorry, my boy. So fucking sorry."

Laying the pages carefully on the arm of the loveseat, Alec eased off the loveseat and stood in front of Xavier. A shaky smile spread across his lips. "I forgive you. I'm still really upset, but...I love you too much to hang onto that. Just...please don't ever do it again?"

"I won't. I swear it to you, unless I physically *can't* get to you, I will always be there when you need me. That goes for both of you." Xavier let out a sigh of relief when Alec dropped down to his knees and wrapped his arms around Xavier's waist. Hugging our boy, Xavier whispered into Alec's hair. "Tell me how to make this up to you. I'll do anything."

Sitting back on his heels, lips slanted, Alec peered up at his other Dom. "Anything?"

Oh boy, this should be interesting. Chuckling, I stroked Alec's back, happy that the two men who owned my heart had worked things out, but not wanting to risk opening up a whole new can of worms. "Within reason, pet."

"No, I mean it. I need to make things right for him." Xavier cupped Alec's cheek. "There are no limits."

Gazing up at him, Alec inhaled slowly. "Dance with me. On stage."

For a split second, Xavier looked like he might be regretting his offer. He tugged at his tie, loosening it. "Ah...of course, but I have to warn you, I am not much of a dancer."

Hopping up like the six inches of his platform boots were the most comfortable things in the world, Alec grabbed Xavier's hands and tugged him to his feet. "I know exactly how well you can move, sir. All you have to do is follow my lead."

Not Xavier's strength in general, but he clearly *was* willing to do anything, because he took a deep breath and nodded. "Very well. But no one better damn well be recording this."

Lifting my brow, I pulled out my phone. "No one except for me." My lips twitched when he cursed under his breath. "Come, my man. Let's make some memories."

As angry as I'd been with Xavier's absence, I couldn't be happier with him at that moment. Before leaving the dressing room, he brought Alec to one of the vanities and wiped away the black smears from his tears. Then he touched up Alec's eyeliner, his micromanaging everything before the models hit the catwalk in his designs paying off for once.

Not that the makeup artists would agree, but that was an issue for another day.

Returning to the table alone got me a concerned look from Brendon. He leaned forward, voice low. "Is the wedding off or did Mistress Grace lend Alec her whip?"

"Neither." I grinned, nodding toward the stage as the spotlight was flicked back on. "Even better."

Brow furrowed as I began recording, Brendon finally just shrugged and lifted his beer bottle to his lips. He tilted his head to one side as the song Alec had danced to earlier came back on, but didn't comment.

Xavier had found the words to express his love to our boy, but he was about to do something even more important.

Prove it. With his actions.

Chapter Nine

The night hadn't been ruined, but I didn't know what to expect when Xavier stepped onto that stage. Absently sipping the beer Brendon had ordered for me, I tensed as Xavier walked to the center of the stage alone. Shoulders squared, hands fisted at his side, I could sense the discomfort radiating off him as if it was my own.

Alec deserved this from him, their relationship needed this, but it still took everything in my power to stay in my seat and not pull Xavier off the stage. Find another way.

Soft murmurs around me from those who hadn't left to use the club's many playrooms didn't help matters. I caught Xavier's eye, nodding my encouragement.

He visibly braced himself, bringing his hand to his chest and mouthing *'I'm all right. I love you.'*

The atmosphere changed as his gaze shifted to the side of the stage, where Alec sauntered into view, his provocative dance a bit different from the choreographed one earlier, but still showing all he'd learned during what must have been months of dance classes while he'd been 'Out grabbing a drink with a few coworkers' or 'Helping Judy with something.'

Knowing my boy, he likely *had* done those things before or after the classes, so it wouldn't be a lie. Sneaky sub. I'd have to talk to him about making sure he was careful when he did things like that. Now that our relationship with Xavier was becoming more common knowledge, he'd make a tempting target for ransom demands.

Or revenge.

Except...he already knew that.

Tearing my gaze from where Alec had moved behind Xavier to tug off his suit jacket, I glared at Brendon. "You knew about all this. The dance lessons?"

"Who do you think brought him?" Brendon smirked over the rim of his bottle. "You might have a bit of a brat on your hands, but he's an intelligent young man. After the mess with Joel, and the issues with his brothers, he didn't want to worry you if you found out he wasn't always where he said he'd be. I hoped you'd check in with me before panicking."

I would have. And it was reassuring to know Alec had made his own safety a priority.

With that settled, I was able to focus on his seductive little dance around Xavier. The way he trailed his hands over our man's chest as though worshiping every inch of him. His hands went to Xavier's hips, guiding him to the rhythm of the song.

Laughing, Xavier tossed his hair back, putting his arms around Alec and taking the lead. A few observers let out wolf whistles as he brought his hands down to take a firm hold of Alec's ass. Grinding together, lost in one another, they were the picture of lust and love, the connection they shared clear to one and all.

And suddenly, I felt too separated from it. There was absolutely no reason for me to keep my distance. I didn't have to just sit here and watch.

Draining the last of my beer, I shoved to my feet. With a few strides I was at the stage, vaulting onto it to a few cheers. I moved in behind Alec, hands on his waist, trapping him against Xavier.

"This is good practice for our first dance on our wedding night." I brushed my lips along the length of Alec's neck, then kissed Xavier over his shoulder. "I'm not sure I'd last through the full reception before needing to drag you both off somewhere private."

Xavier hooked his fingers to the pockets of my slacks, bringing me even closer, so my hard length was pressed firmly between Alec's ass cheeks. "The DJ's proposed song list is less likely to traumatize your father and brother. We still have time to add a few suggestions...maybe we can save this one for closer to the end of the night."

"You need something romantic for the first song." Alec's voice was breathless, but the excitement he'd shown for every detail of the wedding prep returned with a ferver. Brow furrowing, he shook his head, twisting around to loop his arms around my neck and grinding back against Xavier. "But tonight is about fulfilling all your dirty fantasies. For the last time, because you'll be married men after. Have to do things all...proper or something."

"Ha!" Reaching between us, I stroked him over his leathers. "The only thing that will change is Xavier's last name. And yours."

"Mine?" Alec lost the beat as he stared up at me. His eyes shone as he jumped up, pressing his lips to mine. "Yes. Fuck yes, I thought you'd never ask."

There hadn't really been time with my two men taking on their own roles as different versions of groomzillas, but seeing it all come together was worth it. And I was grateful I still had something to offer.

Tightening my grip on Alec's dick to still him, I nudged my chin toward the side of the stage as the song ended. "I think we've given everyone enough of a show. Did you have any other plans for our bachelor party, my boy?"

Nodding, then shaking his head, Alec groaned as I moved my hand. Xavier steadied him as we made our way off the stage and Alec seemed to forget that easy saunter he'd been doing in those boots most of the night. "I planned the dance, then basically just enjoying ourselves with some of our favorite people and giving you...anything you wanted."

"That sounds perfect, pet." Xavier swept Alec off his feet when he stumbled again. "But first, let's get those off you before you break something. I won't have you limping down the aisle with me."

Ordering a round of shots, I stood by the table, accepting handshakes and congratulations from several of the upper management from the company, along with a few strangers who seemed caught up in the excitement. Xavier sat Alec on the table to strip off his boots, gently stroking his thighs over the red marks left by the leather.

Shot glass in hand, I tipped it to Alec's lips, licking away the bit that spilled when Xavier's fingers traced the hem of his booty shorts. Tipping his head back, Alec let out a happy sigh. "Mmm, this is more like what I pictured when I was putting everything together."

"Oh?" Tossing back my own shot after handing Xavier one, I gave Alec a hooded look. "You laid out on the table like a party favor for all our guests?"

Licking his lips, Alec glanced over at Brendon, who moved the shots to a nearby table, where he pulled out a chair. A clear sign that he didn't mind watching, but didn't intend to participate. Which had Alec relaxing a bit. He liked how their relationship was and didn't want it to change.

Good to know.

His cheeks reddened a bit as Odin approached and I chuckled, leaning down to whisper in his ear. "Do you think he still needs incentive to give Xavier everything he wants?"

Making a face, Alec shook his head. "He already made him late. Fuck that dude."

Xavier frowned as he laid Alec on the table. "Alec, that was not his fault. He's going to be working closely with me for quite some time. We don't need to include him in our play, but you will be civil."

"Yes, sir." Alec schooled his features, but the look he gave Odin wasn't friendly.

Odin's brow lifted as he glanced over at Xavier. "Am I missing something? You left in such a hurry to show him what I'd written, we didn't get to discuss any details about the bachelor party. I assumed I was still invited?"

"You are." Xavier smacked Alec's thigh. "By the way, Odin is a Dom. If you want to go to more clubs like this, you're going to learn to show the proper amount of respect, pet."

This would be a good opportunity to see how Alec behaved in a more formal setting, without getting more strict with him than he was used to. I gave him a level look when his eyes met mine, biting back a laugh when he rolled his eyes.

You're not off to a very good start, my boy.

"Did you not like what I wrote, Alec?" Odin braced one hand on the table, leaning in a bit so Alec couldn't avoid his gaze without turning away. "Or is there something else I've done to piss you off?"

Alec huffed, staring up at him. "This was supposed to be a special night for *us*. It's...not really your fault, but Xavier spent a lot of it with you." He bit his bottom lip as though absorbing his own words and realizing how they sounded. "I'm sorry, I'm being a jerk. I loved what you wrote. You're the perfect choice for showing the world who Xavier really is."

"Thank you. And apology accepted." Odin patted Xavier's shoulder. "You're a lucky man. He's a sweet boy, if a little wild."

"Just a little." Xavier undid Alec's shorts, revealing his dick, which bobbed against his smooth stomach as though just the touch of the air was almost too much for Alec to take. The way he writhed on the table proved it. "We haven't played with him in public like this before, but tonight will be his introduction to a different kind of pleasure."

At first, Odin kept his eyes on Alec's face, as though to read his reactions before shifting his attention to Xavier. One brow arched, he folded his arms over his chest. "Mistress Grace would be ideal for helping with any training."

"I agree." Xavier stroked Alec in a loose grip, his tone conversational. "What do you think, my boy? Shall we ask the Mistress to assist us?"

Catching on to the game, I moved to the other side of the table, latching on to Alec's wrist so he could slip into the mindset that would make this all much more enjoyable for him. He'd taken on a lot of control to pull this party together. All around us, our friends and acquaintances were having fun. This wasn't a traditional bachelor party—like with our wedding, all gifts were made in donations to the three charities we'd chosen, and none of us were the type to drink to excess or fool around with random strippers.

Anything we did would be together.

But I would be paying very close attention to what Alec was ready for. So far, Xavier had eased him into some exhibitionism. After his performance on stage, this seemed comfortable enough for him.

And as much as he'd resented Odin's presence at first, he didn't seem to mind it at all anymore. Actually, he kept glancing at him, then at Xavier, shifting his hips as though something on his mind was heightening the pleasure to the point it was almost unbearable.

Blood pulsing low, I recalled his reaction to talk of being shared. There was only so much of him I was willing to let anyone besides Xavier and myself touch, but seeing those sweet lips wrapped around another man's dick, controlling how much they could have of him?

Yes, that appealed to me very much. And I wouldn't mind seeing Xavier's new friend Odin come undone a little. He looked a bit too contained at the moment for a party.

"The Mistress is busy. But Odin, you seem familiar with this club and proper submissive behavior." I stroked Alec's inner wrist with my thumb, making sure he knew he wasn't in trouble. And giving Odin the opportunity to either accept the invitation, or excuse himself. "We were discussing you the other night. What was it you said about him, my boy?"

Drawing in a sharp breath, Alec visibly struggled not to thrust up into Xavier's loose grip. "That he was fucking hot, sir."

"Why thank you, sub. But if you'd like my assistance in learning how to be a boy who will make your Doms proud?" Odin lowered his lips close to Alec's ear, speaking softly. "Good boys don't swear."

Alec shuddered, nodding quickly. "Yes, sir. Luther tries to get me not to swear, but sometimes I forget."

With the wedding plans, I'd slacked somewhat in the training I'd started with him. Seeing how another Dom would handle it would be interesting, so I inclined my head at Odin's questioning gaze, giving him permission to touch my boy.

Fingers tracing Alec's lips, Odin clucked his tongue. "We'll have to come up with a way to help you remember. I find gags the best way to start. A ring gag ensures this pretty mouth can still be used. Do you trust your Doms?"

No hesitation, Alec nodded again. "Yes, sir. But I don't know you that well...they'll be here, though."

That caught Odin off guard. He tilted his head to one side. "Is there a reason I'd be using something that hasn't been offered to me?"

"*Yet.* I mean..." Alec blushed, ducking his head. "Nevermind. It's not...mine to offer?"

"Apparently there was more to this conversation." Odin slipped his thumb into Alec's mouth, giving him a hooded look. "And no, if that's the arrangement you have with your Doms, it's a gift for them to give. Is that something you want, sub?"

This time, Alec looked unsure, which had Odin immediately drawing back. He didn't know Alec well enough to test his limits. But I knew that expression. The conversation was awkward for my boy. He was responding well to Odin's attentions, but he wanted to give up control.

There was only so much he'd give up to someone he didn't know. Which might be a bit twisted with what he *was* willing to do, but it was part of his submission to myself and Xavier.

Still, as a responsible Dom, Odin would need to hear that Alec was consenting to the scene. Stroking my hand over Alec's hair, I brought his focus up to me. "Do you want to give Odin the gift we discussed? To welcome him properly to our company?"

"Yes, sir." Alec breathed out a laugh. "But that probably won't be appropriate for every new person we bring in."

Xavier chuckled, exchanging a look with Odin. "It would certainly make offering any other perks unnecessary."

"I'd say." Odin raked his fingers through his shoulder length blond hair, the edge of his lips twitching. "And not one I expected from you, but I'm not about to complain. If you'll give me a moment, I'll go grab my bag from behind the bar. I'd planned on choosing a sub for the night, but I wasn't expecting it to be yours."

"Yeah, well Xavier really wanted to get his hands on your magazine." Alec snickered, then hissed when Xavier gave his dick a sharp tap. "Oh, fuck...that wasn't...horrible."

That got Odin's brow raised before he continued toward the bar. "We are definitely going to need that gag."

The stage remained empty, the next show likely coming later tonight, and most of those in the main area had either moved to the bar or gathered in small groups to drink and chat. No one seemed to find it odd that this scene was taking place right here, so it probably happened often.

I wasn't sure how Alec had found the club, but I had a feeling we were going to become regular members.

Lifting him up to sit on the edge of the table and preparing him for the next step, I checked his harness, running my fingers under the leather to make sure it wasn't too tight. "Do you have any questions before we continue?"

"No, sir. We talked about it already and I...like that we're trying something different together." His brow creased slightly. "Do you think things will be weird after? With him?"

Xavier shook his head, coming to Alec's side and stroking his arm. "Not at all. He mentioned before I left that he frequented this club, as do several others who will be sticking with the magazine during the rebranding. From the sounds of it, there's an understanding between them all to keep whatever happens here out of the workplace. It's a policy I'd like to adopt as well."

"Which means no more giving him blowjobs under his desk." I laughed at the stuttered protest that escaped Alec. Lowering my brow, I tapped his nose. "Naughty sub, who makes the rules around here?"

"In my damn office? I do." Xavier wrapped his arms around Alec like he might steal him away, and Alec burst out laughing as I gripped his thighs to pull him back, making him the center of a playful game of tug-o-war.

Which was what Odin returned to, shaking his head like he thought the both of us were out of our minds. "This is not what I'd recommend to teach your sub some discipline."

It wasn't how Xavier and I usually handled Alec at all, but tonight something was different. Lighter, filled with a kind of newness I was more than ready to embrace. I wanted to see Xavier's teasing smile, hear Alec's laughter, know there wasn't anything we needed to hold back from one another.

Without this, involving another man, even briefly, would feel wrong. But with Alec this happy and relaxed? It would be a new experience for him. One he looked more eager for as he eyed the leather bag in Odin's hand. What was likely a small part of the man's extensive collection.

All my toys were stuffed in a drawer in our bedroom.

I need to up my game.

Dropping the bag on a chair, Odin unzipped it and handed me one pair of leather cuffs, giving Xavier another, along with some leather straps. "Is he familiar with restraints? I figured that harness should be put to good use."

"We usually use whatever's on hand, but he's familiar with it." Snapping my fingers to show Alec wasn't completely untrained, I motioned for him to lay on the table, facedown.

He moved into position, pausing halfway to brush his hand over the harness. "Put to use how, sir?"

To him, the garment had been nothing more than an accessory.

The information seemed to amuse Odin. "If you'll obey your Dom, I'm sure he'll show you."

Chewing on his bottom lip and shooting me an apologetic look, Alec lowered the rest of the way to the table. He brought his wrist to his sides, holding still as I secured the cuffs on each one.

Then I gently folded his elbows so his wrists aligned with the center of the cuffs. "The back of your harness has rings meant for the cuffs to clip onto." I attached the cuffs into place, making sure his shoulders weren't overly strained. "How does that feel?"

Giving his wrists a light tug, Alec nodded. "I like that. It's secure and...I don't feel like it will let me go when I don't want it to."

"You'll love this, then." After putting on the ankle cuffs, Xavier clipped them to the straps, attached the straps to the lower rings on the harness, and shortened the straps until Alec's knees were bent and parted. "You have no idea how fucking sexy you look, my boy. Once we have the gag in, you'll be spread open in every way for us to play with, however we choose."

Gaze trailing over Alec's naked body, up on the table, wrapped up in leather, his pink flesh glistening under the dim lights, my dick hardened at how vulnerable he'd let us make him. How he kept testing the restraints, sinking deeper into that headspace where surrender became his whole existence, the satisfaction in the pleasure he offered more important than his own.

Taking out the ring, Odin studied Alec's face, his expression softening as though seeing how naturally Alec slipped into his submission pleased him. He waited for a nod from both myself and Xavier before bringing the ring to Alec's lips. "This will stretch a bit, but it shouldn't be unbearable. One of your Doms is going to have two fingers against your palm at all times. Squeeze twice if you need to stop."

I might've gone with a squeaky toy in this instance, but I liked this method even better. It was more intimate, with less chance of cutting the scene short unintentionally. Whether it was myself or

Xavier, one of us would always be attending to our boy on a different level, his symbolic lifeline if he needed it.

Though, with the way our relationship worked, both of us would always be that for him. I inclined my head when Xavier put two fingers against Alec's palm. After what had happened earlier tonight, it would be good for them to share this, to reaffirm their bond, which was stronger than ever.

And it left me standing close to Odin, watching for any signs of distress as the ring stretched his lips into a wide out and the straps were secured behind his head.

Odin stroked his cheek. "Such a very good boy. Thank you for the gift of your submission. As raw as it might be, it's absolutely exquisite."

Blinking fast, Alec wrinkled his nose a little, as though adjusting to the sensation and losing the ability to express himself with words, or even a smile. He tilted his head in Odin's direction, a small acknowledgement. Then his gaze flicked to me like he needed to reaffirm that I was near.

"My beautiful boy. You're making me very proud." I stroked his hair back, then leaned in to kiss his cheek. "Would you like to taste this man who's been so very kind, lending us his tools?"

Another head tilt.

Undoing his slacks, Odin freed his dick, long and dark red with his arousal, the pronounced head wide enough that it would barely clear the ring. He positioned himself easing in slowly, groaning as he drew back and Alec flicked out his tongue.

"Naughty, pet. Don't take more than you're given." The gentle reprimand was followed by another shallow thrust, so the head of his dick disappeared into Alec's mouth. "Now you may lick me. Just like that. Fuck, you've got a wicked tongue."

Alec made a needy sound and I lifted my gaze to where Xavier had helped himself to some lube from Odin's bag, opening it one-handed to drizzle over Alec's exposed hole. He set the bottle by our boy's hip, then pressed two fingers of his free hand into him, two still pressed to his palm.

Stroking Alec's hair again, I delved my fingers into it, holding his gaze as Xavier began to fuck him harder with his fingers, while Odin fucked his mouth, gliding further and further past the ring. Breathing like I'd taught him, my boy did me proud, not gagging when Odin reached the back of his throat, then a bit more, his dick disappearing into my boy's mouth.

"God, he's perfect." Easing back, Odin stroked himself as I unzipped my slacks.

Palming my dick, I moved into position to enjoy my boy's mouth myself. The ring was a unique experience for me. I both missed the feel of Alec's soft lips, but enjoying the stroke of his tongue, the lack of resistance as I drove forward, more used to his limits than Odin was. Heat surrounded me, the pressure of Alec's throat muscles, the slickness around me pure fucking heaven. I met Xavier's eyes across our boy's body, timing my thrust with the slap of Xavier's palm hitting his ass with the intense finger fucking.

Precum stretched from my dick to Alec's lips as I pulled out, letting Odin sink into his mouth again. I wrapped my hand around the base of my cock to contain myself, catching Xavier's eye. His lips curved and he withdrew his hand, not moving his fingers from Alec's palm until I replaced them with mine as I stepped up behind Alec.

The lube was spread liberally, slicking him up so much that all I had to do was position my dick and drive in deep. Aware of several people watching, I angled my hips so they could see how my dick stretched him, keeping my thrusts long. Part of the experience was having him on display, and I soaked in the pure satisfaction of knowing a few of the onlookers were jerking off to the sight of me fucking him.

Apparently I was more of an exhibitionist than I'd thought.

Latching onto the leather straps with my free hand, I pulled Alec into me with each jarring thrust, the slap of my skin connecting with his, the wet sound of Xavier, then Odin fucking his mouth, drowning out the music in the distance. The grip of

Alec's ass had me groaning as I angled my dick to hit his prostate, adding his soft whimpers to the mix.

An erotic symphony, the table dragging across the floor to the beat, not screwed in like I'd first assumed, but nice and heavy. It took a lot to move it and I used that as a challenge, pistoning into Alec as hard as he could tolerate, pushing him to the very limit.

Recalling Xavier's desire to continue stretching him until he could take us both, I slowed my motions, bringing my free hand down to where my dick filled him. The excessive lube made it easy to slick my fingers, and I brushed them over his pinned down balls, along his taint, then traced the ring of muscles surrounding me. Easing out, I gave a few shallow thrust with the tips of my fingers opening him a bit more, until I got one in all the way while filling him with my dick.

Voice a bit hoarse, Odin stroked himself, while stepping to my side. "I have a narrow prostate stimulator he might enjoy."

"Fuck, yes." I pulled out again, pressing my lips to Alec's hips when he let out a low, keening sound. He was definitely being put through his paces tonight. "It's all right, my boy. You're going to let me show Odin what a special sub you are and take everything we want to do to you."

Xavier stroked Alec's cheek as he eased back to let him nod. Then he drove back in hard. "I would come watch, but I'm loving being greedy with this hot mouth for a bit."

Laughing softly, Odin took the slender prostate massager out of its packaging, the thing the perfect length, with a ring to place around the base of Alec's dick to hold it in place. He used a wipe to clean it. "I'm grateful for what you've shared with me already. I don't mind joining the observers for the remainder of your scene."

"Then I won't be able to watch you come all over his face." Xavier gave his new friend a sly smile. "I'm a man who is never satisfied doing anything halfway. Luther won't let you fuck our boy's ass this time, but he might once he knows you better."

When this had started, I would've said 'Hell no'. But after

seeing how well Odin handled Alec, it would be a good payment for the training he'd be assisting in.

But Xavier was right. Not tonight.

Lips slanted, Odin met my eyes as he positioned the tip of the prostate massager against Alec's hole. The challenge in his gaze as he sank it in brought a kick of arousal to the base of my spine. I stroked Alec's inner thigh to still him as he shifted restlessly against the new sensation. I helped lift Alec slightly as Odin pulled the massager out so he could ease the ring over Alec's cock, then settle the length inside him.

The width of the thing was a bit less than the size of two of my fingers, but still, I took my time stretching him with my dick. With how aroused he was, it didn't take long before I was slamming into him again.

And Odin returned to fucking his mouth with Xavier, the men taking turns, one in, then the other. Then Odin spoke softly to Xavier, a wicked smile on his lips as he removed the ring gag. He wrapped his hand around his dick and Xavier's, guiding both into Alec's mouth. He could only take them in shallow thrusts, but what I could see of them stretching his lips was hot as fuck.

"Good boy. A little more." Sweat slicked Xavier's skin as he circled his hips, his voice rough as he moved in the grip of his friend' hand and the heat of our boy's mouth. "Jesus, Odin. This is the start of the second best friendship I've ever had. It's a good thing I don't have many of them."

Odin chuckled, stroking himself and Xavier faster. "If this is what you enjoy, it won't take long for you to make a few more here. Especially with this tempting little thing... God, his mouth was made for this."

Their talk was not helping me hold back. Shaking my head, I imagined the sexual tension that would be between them the next time they worked on Xavier's book. Which gave me the perfect opportunity to let Odin know who had all the power in this relationship.

I caught his eye as I drove into Alec hard enough to draw a

whimper. "You don't play with either of them without my permission. Since I like you, I just might give it."

Xavier groaned, his pace faltering. "I think we've created a monster."

With a feral grin, I continued fucking Alec. "Or I've simply unleashed him. But Odin knows exactly what I'm saying."

"I do." Odin gave me a lazy smile, leaning closer to Xavier, an edge to his tone. "Come with me."

Every muscle in Xavier's body tensed and he let out a rough sound. His cum hit Alec's parted lips, Odin's strokes dragging out every last shudder until it was clear Xavier was struggling to remain standing with the intensity of his release.

Then Odin let out a deep moan and came, bracing his hand on the edge of the table as his movements slowed.

Alec's grip around me tightened and I followed him over the edge, my vision spotting with white as the pleasure rocked through me, stealing the last of my control. I held my body tight against his, grinding in, pressing kisses to the small of his back as he trembled. The rush of adrenaline, endorphins, and the all encompassing submission had him floating high, which I could see in his eyes as I withdrew. I immediately turned my attention to removing the massager, then releasing his restraints with Xavier and Odin.

Wipes were passed around, each one of us adjusting our clothes as Mistress Grace came over and handed me a blanket. She nodded to a dark corner, where there were plush leather sofas and a coffee table that had a tray already set up.

"There's water. And some chocolate for him." She gave Alec a fond look as I wrapped him in the blanket and lifted him into my arms. "He's a sweetheart. I'm glad to see he's found good men to care for him."

I smiled at her, then pressed a kiss to Alec's temple. "He deserves every bit of it and more. Thank you for looking out for him when he came here."

"It was my pleasure." With that, Mistress Grace continued

across the club, checking on a few other members who'd decided to play in here.

Carrying Alec to the sofa, I settled in while Xavier uncapped a bottle and brought it to his lips. Odin remained at the table, cleaning his toys and the table. His part in the scene was over and I was grateful for the way he stepped back without needing any more reassurances. He was clearly an experienced Dom and he didn't need my attention.

So I brought my focus fully to Alec. And Xavier, who took a few gulps of water, then set it aside and picked up one of the chocolate bars. "How are you, my man?"

Xavier blinked at me. "Why do you ask? I wasn't the one on the table."

"I like tables." Alec rubbed his cheek against my chest, sounding a bit sleepy. And drunk, even though he'd only had one shot tonight. "We should get one."

Laughing, I stroked his back. "That's a very good idea, my boy." I looked at Xavier again. "I never would have suggested this kind of play after what you've been through in the past. But since it was something you wanted, I was willing to give it a try. It only continues if it doesn't bring up any triggers."

"Ah…" Xavier nodded slowly. "It really doesn't—I hadn't thought of what Joel put me through at all. I believe feeling enough in control to know Alec is safe with us, and anyone else we choose to play with, made it very different. And the control I don't have, you do. It was…comforting, when you let Odin know everything needs to go through you. It took the pressure off me when I wasn't in any condition to handle it."

That he opened up without my having to pry every thought and emotion out of him was an added benefit to this experience. One I would encourage so I could give him the security he needed from me. "Will you be able to keep that in mind when you're alone with him?"

Head cocked, Xavier seemed to think that over. The edge of his lips twitched. "I don't think you'll be asking that once you see how we work together. He's just as bad as I am, getting so involved in what he's doing, the rest of the world ceases to exist."

"Another workaholic. *Fun.*" I put my arm around his shoulders as he fed Alec the chocolate, my gaze drifting to the stage as another show began, in front of a crowd that looked as wrung out and satisfied as we probably did. "Speaking of, how are you going to handle the next two weeks away from work? I don't think you've taken more than a day off in all the time I've known you."

Xavier lifted his shoulders, his eyes half closed. "I assumed you didn't mean *full* days off. And it will give me some free time to work on a few new designs. Maybe go on a relaxing trip with you and Alec to inspect the textile production of our new business associates."

In other words, his idea of a 'break' wasn't much different than any other day. It would be interesting to disabuse him of that notion. I leaned over to brush my lips over his, speaking against them. "I changed my mind about a honeymoon in Milan. Let's give the tickets to Judy and her girlfriend. I'm taking you and Alec somewhere remote. With no internet access."

That Xavier simply laughed told me how out of it he was. He rested his head on my shoulder. "I'll go wherever you want me to, Luther, but I don't think such a place exists."

"It does. And it makes me very happy to hear you say that. Because we're going to have that place, just for us, for the rest of our lives." I had a few ideas in mind, but I'd wait until he was a bit more clear-headed to suggest them. Right now, in this moment, I already had everything I'd ever wanted from him.

No distractions, no interruptions, nothing that would keep him out of reach for hours, if not days at a time. With who Xavier was, I accepted that times like this would be rare. I could deal with sharing him with his passions, so long as he found space for me and Alec among them.

Years ago, I wouldn't have even asked for that much. It had been enough to stand on the sidelines. To be there when he needed me, even though the love had seemed so damn one-sided, sometimes I felt like a fool to keep giving it.

I hadn't realized I'd protected half of my heart from him, holding back from commiting completely until Alec came in and knocked down all the walls between us. While I might still have some lingering reservations, our boy had none. I smiled as I pictured him once his tears had dried, telling Xavier *exactly* what he expected from him. How to repair the damage done between them before it had a chance to become permanent.

There was a lot I could learn from our boy. I didn't want to demand too much, from either of them, outside of the control they gave me. Still, it wouldn't hurt to ask for more, to make sure my own needs were met. Expecting them to be open about theirs wouldn't be fair if I couldn't do so myself.

I loved who my man was.

But I was looking forward to finding out who we could be. Together.

Chapter Ten

Mother nature didn't give a fuck about carefully laid plans. Thunder sounded loud enough to make a few people jump as the staff rushed around the ballroom, rain slashing against the windows. I shook my head as Alec paced, every once in a while glaring out like he could shame the clouds into clearing out of the sky so the day would be 'perfect'.

That seemed to be his favorite word today as he'd rushed around, offering to help the decorators make sure the silver and cream paper lanterns were *perfectly* spaced, that all the balloons were the *perfect* size and were they sure all the gift bags had the *perfect* items for each guest?

The only thing he didn't dare question was the flower arrangements. Not after the first time Mistress Grace—who was just 'Grace' outside of the club—whispered something in his ear that had him looking a little afraid of her for the rest of the morning.

I almost felt bad for him, except he was making *me* nervous. The backup plan to move the ceremony into the ballroom had been executed perfectly, so there was nothing to worry about. The mansion was more than big enough to accommodate all our guests. Brendon had set up security around the house to make sure no one unwelcome got in, and those who were there didn't end up where they weren't supposed to be.

There was absolutely *nothing* to worry about. The cakes had been delivered on time, the food was being made under Ms. Lacey's supervision, and the only difference from when we'd had the rehearsal last night would be the lack of birds for Chance to chase around when he was supposed to be sitting by my side at the altar, the small pillow for the ring attached to his collar.

"Maybe I should see if I can find more umbrellas? People are going to be miserable if they have to sit around, soaking wet." Alec laced his fingers behind his neck, letting out a heavy sigh. "But that won't help with their shoes... Do we have any slippers we could hand out?"

Blinking at him, I tried to picture some of the distinguished guests who'd been invited, wearing tuxes, elegant gowns, and...padding around in slippers. It would definitely keep things from getting too serious.

The press would have a field day.

And Xavier would lose his damn mind.

Stepping up behind Alec, I wrapped my arms around him to stop his pacing. "They will be met at their cars, all of ten steps from the entrance, with umbrellas. The valets will be parking the cars—and I made sure all of them were covered, so they wouldn't get soaked walking back. The maids will give anyone who needs it towels. Some people are waiting until they get here to get changed and there's rooms for all of them to do so. Ms. Lacey has been managing events here for Xavier for a long time, my boy. There's not a single thing that could come up that she doesn't already have a plan for."

"I know, and she's amazing, but...I asked to help prepare everything for the wedding. It was my gift to you and Xavier." Alec pressed his eyes shut, tears from all the stress he'd been putting on himself wetting his lashes. "You both have *everything*. It's all I had to offer."

How in the world had I not figured out *that* was why he'd been so obsessed with every little detail? Turning him to face me, I cupped his face in my hands. "You are offering *you*, my boy. I've been trying to make sure this wedding didn't feel like it was only mine and Xavier's, that it was just as much yours, but I failed if planning it was something you were doing for *us*."

Alec worried his bottom lip with his teeth. "You didn't fail. I just want everything to be—"

"Perfect. Yes, I know." I silenced him with a kiss. "It is. At the end of the day, the three of us are making vows to one another. I couldn't care less if it was out in that rain. Or at the office. Or if there was a single person there to witness it. All this window dressing is because you and Xavier like things pretty."

That got a smile tugging at Alec's lips. "You don't want to know how much it cost to just 'make things pretty'. I think the decorators who've worked for freakin' royalty would take offense."

"Royalty. Well, if we're paying them that kind of money, let them be offended." I chuckled as he glanced over at one of the staff from the decorating company, like he was afraid they might trash all the decorations in response to my words. "I'd say you're being silly, but I know how important this is to you. Why don't you go find Xavier and make sure he's not inspecting the stitches on his tux. I'm going to let Chance run around outside to burn off all that energy, so he's not overly excited by everyone at the ceremony. Last night showed me *one* thing we hadn't planned for, which is animals having absolutely no respect for what a solemn occasion a wedding is supposed to be."

Alec snickered, shaking his head. "It's not supposed to be 'solemn', it's supposed to be fun. And everyone loves him." He wrinkled his nose as I drew away. "But you'll get soaked out there and you still need to get ready."

"I guess it's a good thing I won't be wearing my tux to take the dog for a run."

I patted his cheek, then jogged past a group of photographers who were vying for the best spots around the room, needing a break from the invasion of my home. I headed to the blocked off wing of the mansion, where Chance was curled up on a sofa in the rec room. The new kitten, who Alec had named Mosaic, was fast asleep between his paws.

Lifting his head as I came into the room, Chance wagged his tail, stepping gingerly off the sofa like he was afraid to disturb the kitten. He'd gained some weight since his treatments had ended, the smooth dark brown and beige fur filling in the patches and making him look so much healthier. His energy was also way up, so I'd been able to start taking him on runs with me and Alec in the morning without being afraid of tiring him out.

Last night had proved adding a second or third long run a day might be a good idea, but I'd have to clear it with his vet. For now, I'd keep it short. I didn't mind the rain, and neither did he, but I didn't want to push it. And there was only a bit more than an hour before all the guests would arrive. An hour and a half before the ceremony.

Which meant Xavier was likely already getting ready. And Alec would start soon.

I'd shaved that morning, so all I needed to do was put my tux on. Would take me about ten minutes, if that.

The second I opened the side door, Chance raced ahead of me, turning and barking at me as he bounced around. I laughed, grabbing a stick I'd left near the door and tossing it for him. Catching up at a slow jog as the rain pelted down on me, I was soaked to the skin in seconds, but damn, it felt good. I could deal with the press, with the formality of the wedding, with the 'perfection' Alec thought was so important, but it got a bit stifling after a while.

As much as I was looking forward to making those vows, and celebrating with the two men I loved, part of me couldn't wait for it to be over with.

Playing in the rain with Chance gave me the break I needed to get through everything else.

Back inside about an hour later, I dried off in my room and got dressed, smiling at Brendon in the mirror as he came in to fulfill his duties as my best man. He looked me over, giving a satisfied nod before pinning the small boutonniere to my lapel, a tiny rosebud with tiny green leaves, the kind of detail I never would've considered, but was important to Alec.

Or had been once Grace mentioned them. I couldn't fault the woman's business sense, I was just grateful she hadn't taken advantage of Alec's enthusiasm.

Unlike the person who'd sold him on the idea of personalized gift bags for all the guests, that were comparable to those given out at some award shows. I hadn't expected our wedding to have sponsors.

The look Alec had exchanged with Xavier when I'd jokingly made the comment yesterday told me I really didn't want to know how many it *did* have. Hopefully, the ceremony didn't have to cut to commercials.

"How do I look?" I turned from side to side, fussing with my tie just to fuck with Brendon and lighten the mood before I had to go out and face the crowd. "I thought I'd go traditional with the black tie, but...there's one Alec really likes, with tiny little sail boats. Maybe I should change it."

Brendon shook his head, his brow furrowing. "You look fine. Sail boats? I thought the boy was known for his good taste in…" He shoved my shoulder when I burst out laughing. "Very funny. Let's get this shit over with. The guests are starting to get restless. I think someone let it slip that Xavier isn't here."

I stopped short in the doorway, almost slamming into Brendon as I spun around. "What do you mean, he's not here?"

"He left a note. He had to go pick something up." Brendon shrugged, propelling me into the hall. "I'm sure he won't be long. Between him and your boy, I think they even have a schedule for bathroom breaks. You better not get divorced, I'm never doing this again."

Forcing another laugh, I nodded slowly, thanking one of the guards who met us in the hall with Chance, his fur dry and gleaming from his time with the groomer, the pillow on his collar ready for the rings to be tied onto it.

In the ballroom, I looked around at the seated crowd. My father was with my brother in the front row. Most of the management from Ashburne Style and Media was there, along with some high profile guests, investors, favored clients, and others I didn't recognize. Classical music was being played in the background by the orchestra, the soothing melody drowning out the quiet conversation, but it couldn't hide the concerned glances coming my way as I took my place at the altar with Chance sitting beside me, Brendon tying the rings on his collar before moving to my other side.

The minister didn't appear to realize anything was off. He came over and shook my hands before getting in position. Taking his cue, the band began playing the song I'd chosen for Xavier to walk down the aisle to with Alec, the one thing that had been most important to me because the song just felt...so fitting. *Grow as We Go* by Ben Platt. But hearing the orchestra playing the melody and the door opening to show Alec, standing there alone, made my heart clench.

When Alec stared at me from across the room, shaking his head, the words to the song came to me, even though no one was singing them.

The meaning behind them, the promises Xavier and I had already made when he'd come back to me the first time.

Maybe this was one of those times I had to show him I'd never ask for more than he was willing to give. Maybe, he'd realized he just wasn't ready. I didn't care if it was embarrassing to be standing here, left at the altar, with all those eyes on me. What hurt was that he'd been too afraid to tell me how he was feeling.

After everything we'd been through, I'd really believed we'd at least gotten past that.

Running down the aisle, Alec grabbed my hands, speaking in a rush. "He wouldn't do this, Luther. Not again. There's something wrong."

"Alec, it's all right. This doesn't change anything." I put on a brave face for our boy. This whole event had meant the most to him. "I love him. And he loves both of us. We'll figure out what happened. We don't need all this to—"

Grabbing my lapels, Alec let out a frustrated sound. "You're not listening. Xavier does fucked up things sometimes, but never twice. He would have at least called, even if he got cold feet or whatever. But he didn't. I saw him before he left, he was excited. He wants this."

How messed up was it that it was easier to believe Xavier would just not show up to our wedding than even consider something *had* gone wrong? Alec was right, Xavier did his best to learn from his mistakes. More now than ever before. He'd worked so hard to change from the closed off young man he'd once been, acting on nothing but ambition and self-preservation.

It shouldn't have taken me this long to see it.

"Brendon, go check with your men. See if one of them went with him. If not, I'm going to beat his ass after the reception." Motioning for Alec to follow me, I strode down the aisle, sparing a glance for my brother as he raced to catch up. "Rezz, I need you to do me a favor. Talk to Ms. Lacey. Ask her if she can take over until I get back, keep the guests entertained. Tell them if they leave, they don't get to come back when this whole thing restarts."

Rezz called after me as I threw open the front door. "Where the hell are you going?"

I glanced back at him over my shoulder.

"I'm going to find my man."

Chapter Eleven

I f ever there had been a series of events to test Xavier on how serious he was about getting married, some higher power appeared to have saved them all for today. All he'd had to do was stay home, in his perfectly fitted tux, his hair left loose as a surprise for Luther, glistening from the special treatment his stylist had spent two hours on.

All ruined now by the mud and rain he was absolutely fucking covered in.

The text he'd gotten had spurred him to acting without damn well thinking, something he'd promised Alec he wouldn't do again. But he needed to have all the pieces in place for both of his men for the wedding to have any meaning.

And the gift he'd gotten Alec was at the other side of the city. The metalworker who'd made the custom piece had been called away for a family emergency. All Xavier had to do was pick it up.

Which he had. The drive was no more than twenty minutes. The random security guard he'd brought with him joked he could make it half that if Xavier didn't mind covering the speeding ticket.

Except, when Xavier came out, the man with the easy smile and ready laughter was bent over behind the car, losing his lunch —which he'd thankfully had *before* getting to Xavier's place, so at least he didn't have to worry that all the guests would end up with food poisoning.

After dropping the man off at the hospital and making sure he was in good hands, Xavier started the drive home. Swerved to avoid hitting a deer and landed the car in a ditch. His phone was somewhere in the crushed front of the car. Which meant he couldn't call a tow truck. Or Luther.

Who is going to fucking strangle me for being a damn fool.

Other than being a bit disoriented from slamming into the air bag, Xavier felt fine. And the walk couldn't possibly be that long.

Or that's what he'd told himself. An hour ago.

The 'shortcuts' he'd taken through the woods did nothing but make him absolutely filthy. His shoes had become torture devises made of italian leather. His tux jacket was useless at keeping him warm, doing nothing but weighing him down as he trudged through another ditch to climb back up onto the road.

He hadn't wanted to risk hitchhiking, but at this rate, he was fairly certain he'd miss not only the wedding...he'd come home to find all his things covering the lawn.

Not something Luther would do, but Alec? Yes, his boy would show his displeasure with the same passion he did everything. Strangely enough, the thought made Xavier smile. As much as he hated disappointing Alec again, he loved that his boy had gained the confidence to speak his mind. Or show Xavier exactly how he felt.

Only once besides the bachelor party had he pissed Alec off that much. When he'd cancelled a show for the junior line without telling him. One of the models had been involved in the kind of controversy that needed an immediate response, and there was no other way to distance the company from her.

Something Xavier had been through before, so he didn't think twice.

Until he walked into his office and found every single piece that had been prepared for the runway strewn over every available surface, Alec standing in the middle of the room, glaring at him.

"How could you? Everything was in place. You knew I was handling this alone while Judy's taking care of her mother." Alec strode up to him, jabbing his finger in the center of Xavier's chest. "You had no fucking right!"

Keeping calm only seemed to upset Alec more, but Xavier wasn't sure how else to react. He caught Alec's wrist when his boy poked him again. "This is my company. I had every right."

Frustrated tears filled Alec's eyes. "The junior line...you told me it was mine and Judy's. I thought…" He tried to jerk away. "This was a mistake. I fucking quit."

Shaking his head, Xavier pulled Alec into his arms. "These things happen, Alec. I don't understand why you're so upset."

"Because this didn't matter to you! But it was important to me and I don't know how you can say you love me and...act like this." Alec twisted away from him. "The only reason I give a damn about the designs, the runway, any of it, is because I love being part of this world with you. I'm not really, though, am I?"

It hit Xavier then, what his boy saw in that moment. Not his lover. Not someone who loved him unconditionally, but someone cold. Someone Xavier didn't want to be.

But he had no idea how to fix this. Except he couldn't let Alec leave, believing he didn't care. "I should have handled this better. You are part of my world, my boy. Such an important part. I am not good at handling my personal life and my business at the same time, but with you...I need to find a way."

Hand on the door, Alec paused. Looked back at him. "You could start by saying you're sorry."

Xavier blinked. Motioned to his office. "You've already made me very sorry."

"That's not what I mean." Alec sighed, turning and leaning against the door. "Nevermind. I appreciate you hearing me out. And I'm sorry for making a mess."

Crossing the room, Xavier stepped over the various scarves and shoes littering his floor. He stopped in front of Alec. Framed his jaw with his hand until his boy met his eyes. "Do you still want to quit?"

"No, but I kinda want to throw something at you."

"Would that help?"

"No."

"Alec, I'm sorry." Xavier hadn't said those words often. He was so used to simply dealing with any problem that came up. Delegating the task of mending fences to PR or his assistant when it became necessary. Luther seemed satisfied with any effort he made, but Alec needed more from him. And he wanted to give it to him. Even if it was just two words that seemed meaningless.

Right then, the way Alec looked at him, he realized they weren't.

"Thank you." Alec's voice was little more than a whisper. He closed his eyes, letting out a shaky laugh. "I'll find a better way to communicate when you do something that pisses me off."

Xavier smiled, shaking his head. "Don't. I am not very good at subtleties. And I appreciate the dramatics of the display. It's actually very fitting."

Lifting his brows, Alec smiled a little as he wrapped his arms around Xavier's neck. "You're going to regret telling me that one day."

"Never. Because I won't stop trying to get this right. And I don't mind a bit of a mess when I get it wrong." Xavier pressed his lips to Alec's. "So long as you're willing to stick around while I clean it up."

The mess he'd made today was on a whole different level. His suit was ruined. He was late for his own wedding. Luther would be so fucking hurt.

An apology wasn't going to cut it. And his excuses seemed absolutely ridiculous. He could have sent someone else. He *should* have been exactly where Luther and Alec expected him to be. If nothing else, he tried not to fuck up the same way twice—at least be a bit original about it.

But he'd failed both his men again when they were counting on him.

On the edge of the road, rain pouring down his face, he glanced over as he heard a car approaching. Sweeping his hair away from his face, he stuck out his thumb.

The car screeched to a stop.

"What in God's name do you think you're doing?" Luther

threw the door open, rushing to his side, taking off his jacket to wrap it around Xavier's shoulders. "Where's Cody?"

Xavier blew out a breath as Luther guided him to the back seat of the very nice, warm car. "The poor man got very sick. I dropped him off at the hospital."

Climbing between the seats, Alec snatched up a blanket, using it to dry Xavier's hair. "Did you leave him the car? Where's your jacket?" He patted Xavier's pockets. "And your phone?"

None of that mattered now. Xavier reached out to take Luther's hand. Cupped Alec's cheek. And said the words he knew they needed to hear. "I'm sorry. I ruined the wedding and I hurt both of you again. If it's not too late—"

"Stop." Nudging him over so he could get out of the rain, Luther slid into the backseat beside him. "I don't care about the wedding right now, Xavier. You scared us. Tell us what happened."

Repeating the whole thing was embarrassing, but Xavier didn't hold back, telling them everything except for what the gift was. If he could preserve anything, he hoped it would be the surprise he'd risked so much for.

Wrapping his arms around Xavier from behind, Alec spoke softly. "I knew you wouldn't do something like that again. This wasn't your fault. I'm glad you're okay."

Xavier frowned, shaking his head. "Of course it was my fault. I can't very well blame the driver."

Lips slanting with amusement, Luther smoothed his hair back. "Then maybe the deer?"

"Don't be ridiculous."

"Why not? Things happen, my man. You left two hours before the wedding. There was plenty of time to get where you were going and back, but a whole lot of shit happened that was out of your control." Luther touched their foreheads together. "Do you think Alec and I are completely unreasonable?"

"I left you standing at the altar. I...wouldn't have done that on purpose." Xavier studied Luther's face. His man knew. He believed him. And that was all that mattered. "But it's not too late."

Lips hot against his, Luther kissed him, then shook his head. "No, it's not too late. But are you sure you're all right?" His lips twitched when Xavier nodded. "Good. Then listen to me very carefully. You attempted to walk over forty miles in the rain to get back to me. If that doesn't prove how much you love me? Nothing ever will."

Put that way, Xavier had to admit his man had a point.

Alec cuddled against Xavier's side as Luther left the backseat and climbed in behind the wheel. Lacing his fingers with Xavier's, Alec let out a soft sigh. "If you think about it, this whole thing was like the most romantic tragedy. Except...with a happy ending."

There were times Xavier wondered if he understood people at all. This was one of them.

The two men who owned his heart were crazy, that was all there was to it.

But no sane person would have done what he just had to try to get to his wedding. The more he thought about it, the more he saw why Luther was so amused. Why Alec was being all...poetic.

Maybe I'm a little crazy myself.

Chapter Twelve

With all the planning, with all the obsession over every detail, the *imperfection* of the wedding was what ended up making it so special. Raindrops all over my tux, I stood at the altar as the music played, watching Xavier come down the aisle.

In a pair of slippers Alec had grabbed for him, the only things that wouldn't hurt his feet with all the cuts and blisters on them. He was also wearing a thick black robe over flannel pajamas, which had gotten him to stop shivering.

I'd expected him to object to coming out here like that. Had been more than willing to put off the wedding for another day so it could be everything he and Alec had pictured.

But Xavier had been determined to follow through.

And Alec couldn't stop smiling and whispering to anyone who stopped him to ask about how romantic what Xavier had done was.

And I couldn't agree more.

Even in the robe, his hair still damp, pulled loosely away from his face, Xavier managed to look dignified as he walked toward me. By his side, Alec looked a bit more rumpled, but the happiness practically glowing off him outdid the most well pressed suit in the room. Not that I really saw anyone else.

I couldn't look anywhere but at the two men who made up everything I could ever want, ever need, in this life. Holding out my hands, I took Xavier's in mine, rubbing them a little to warm them up as the minister began his sermon.

Cameras flashed and Xavier rolled his neck, letting me know he was a little self-conscious about how he'd be seen by the world. But when his eyes met mine, they told me something else.

None of it mattered to him. He'd fought to be here with me. And even if it had taken a few false starts?

He'd found his way in the end. I'd just had to meet him somewhere in the middle.

The rings were taken off the pillow on Chance's collar. Brendon handed me one, and Xavier the other.

Xavier took a deep breath as he began his vows. "You saved me, from the very beginning. I would say you have something of a hero complex, but you don't see it in yourself. It's just who you are. A man who doesn't give up, who takes what everyone else would consider a lost cause and becomes the safe space where it can heal. And grow. I didn't know that kind of strength existed until I met you. I didn't believe I deserved love until you gave it to me, expecting nothing in return." Holding up the ring, he shook his head with a quiet laugh. "This is such a small thing, with so much meaning behind it. And that's what I will give you, Luther Cross. My heart, my life, all the best of who I am. who I'm becoming. Because I was the first lost cause. And the love I'm capable of? It's because of you." He slid the ring on my finger. "I've accomplished many things in my life. But nothing comes close to somehow being the man you want as your husband."

The minister smiled, then nodded for me to say my own vows.

I winked at Alec before I began. "For a long time, I was waiting for some sign that we could have this. Today, in the pouring rain, it was there. The man I loved for so long, who'd spent years focused on beauty and image and prestige—obviously all very important—covered in mud." My voice grew rough as I pictured him, at the side of the road. Despite the teasing, I needed him to know the impact it had on me. "You showed the kind of grit and determination that was always behind all the glamor, that was part of building your empire, but...it was there for me. I knew you loved me, Xavier. I knew I wanted you in my life, in whatever way I could have you." I slid the ring on his finger. "It wasn't until that moment that I really understood the love I had for you was returned, every bit as powerful. There's still so many things we're still getting to know about one another. I can't wait to keep doing that, with you as my husband. Saving you as often as you need to be saved, because you saved me, too."

Holding Xavier's hands again, I inclined my head for the minister to continue with his part.

But Xavier cut him off. "Wait."

Reaching into the large pocket of his robe, he motioned Alec to join us as he took out a flat box. Inside was a platinum collar, with an infinity knot in the center, a small lock at the clasp, and two small keys.

Xavier took out the collar and the keys, handing me one. "I was going to wait until we were alone, but I almost missed my own wedding for this, so I think it's fitting we do it now." He gave the hand signal for Alec to kneel. "You brought Alec to me and he changed our whole lives. He forced us to face all the distance we'd let come between us. He is part of everything we have now, all we will have in the future." Tipping Alec's chin up with two fingers, he smiled down at our boy. "Will you wear our collar, Alec? Will you let me keep working to become even half as good a man as I see in your eyes when you look at me? Earn that love you keep giving me, no matter how many times I fuck up?"

"Yes, sir. But only if you let me keep working on making you believe, you already have." Alec brought his hand up to the collar as Xavier put it around his neck and I locked it in place. "That last minute thing you went to get...it was for me?"

Nodding, Xavier touched Alec's cheek. "Yes. Luther and I came up with the design together."

"But you're the one who made sure he had it today." I hadn't been sure how to include Alec in the ceremony, aside from having him stand with us. There'd been words I'd wanted to say, but none of them told our boy exactly what he meant to me, to Xavier, as clearly as the delicate metal circling his neck. I stroked Alec's hair and smiled at Xavier. "Thank you."

A warm smile on his own lips, Xavier inclined his head, then faced the minister. "I apologize for the interruption. You may continue."

Once we were pronounced husband and husband, the minister stumbling a bit over adding Alec as an unofficial 'And partner?' we walked back down the aisle together, hand in hand while the guest tossed flower petals and the orchestra played.

Leading my men to our bedroom, I claimed a bit of time alone with them while everyone else was led to the large dining hall for the reception.

Collapsing on the bed, Alec brought his hand to his collar again as though to make sure it was still there. He gave his head a little shake. "I feel like I'm dreaming. Did that just happen?"

"It did." Xavier sat beside him, patting his ass. "Now make yourself useful, pet. I am not spending the entire night in my robe."

Scrambling to his feet, Alec rushed to the closet and began pulling out suits. "If you want to make an impact—"

"No, not that one, I didn't invite him for a reason."

"But, sir, it would make a great headline."

"I just got married in a robe. Do you really think I give a damn?"

"Yes." Alec gave him an impish grin. "How about this one? It brings out the color of your eyes."

Standing by the door, arms folded over my chest, I watched them argue fashion and shook my head. Some things didn't change.

But the important things did. Maybe not right away, but when it counted, when there was someone who mattered enough to make those changes?

Every single one of us had for one another. Not because of any demands, not because it was expected, but because love brought out the best in us. I knew, looking back, that loving these men had given me the strength to become more than I'd ever thought I could be.

I hadn't been ready for that love, even when Xavier had come back to me.

When I'd met Alec, I'd accepted the little I could get. That it would have to be enough.

There were a lot of times in my life that I'd been wrong, I wasn't ashamed to admit it.

But this was my favorite one.

Chapter Thirteen

There were consequences to the little adventure of Xavier's on our wedding day. After the reception, I noticed how flushed he was. I got him to bed and called the doctor, who said he just needed some rest.

When Xavier woke with a retching cough, I brought him to the hospital with Alec. Fired the doctor who'd been my man's personal physician for a few years. Xavier had pneumonia. Which meant the afterparty, and the honeymoon, had to be delayed.

Three weeks later, he was back to full strength, sitting at the breakfast table in the sunroom with Odin, going over some notes for his book. Sitting on my lap, Alec researched destinations for our honeymoon with my specifications in mind. Remote. With no internet access. Where Xavier would be forced to relax.

"I don't see why you're insisting on those rules, I've been resting for long enough." Xavier sipped his coffee, ignoring the amused look Odin gave him. "And Alec would love Paris."

Looking up from his phone, Alec shook his head. "Nope. Sir, you are not using me to go somewhere that you're going to be spending all your time going from one runway to another between meetings. How about Madagascar?"

"So we can be one of those fools who's eaten by a lion?" Xavier shook his head, then turned his attention back to Odin. "I don't mind something brief about the trial, but I don't want too much focus on it. Joel was convicted without my having to appear in court, there was enough damning evidence against him and the judge didn't want the trial turned into a media circus. That bastard will rot in jail. The end."

Odin nodded slowly. "All right, but are you comfortable including some of what happened to you with him when you were younger?"

Reaching across the table, I put my hand over Xavier's as his throat worked. Therapy had helped him deal with that time in his life, to some extent, but it didn't erase the scars that had been left behind. Reliving that would be hard for him.

"If he wants to include it, I'll tell you what I know." I gave Odin a level look, letting him know it was time to change the subject. "How is the rebranding going for the magazine?"

A broad smile spread across Odin's lips. "Better than expected. Your boy came up with a new name that we've been using to build interest. It has just the defiant edge to use the takedown to our advantage. We're calling it the 'IrrePRESSed' magazine. The buzz online promises to make our launch a huge success."

"That's my clever boy." I ruffled Alec's hair as he peered up at me. "Have you considered turning in your color palette for a typewriter?"

Alec snorted. "Yeah, no thank you, sir. I'm about as good at writing articles as I am at stitching."

"You can sketch and you know how to put together a cover worthy outfit." Xavier gave Alec a warm smile over the rim of his mug. "We'll be keeping your talents for Ashburne Designs, Alec Cross."

Climbing off my lap, Alec straddled Xavier's thighs, stealing a kiss when the mug was out of the way. "I'm all yours, Xavier Cross."

After taking a few more notes, Odin closed his notepad and stood. "That's my cue. I think I have enough to start the first few chapters. My plan is to have the book done in time for the launch of IrrePRESSed, so we can include it in the marketing."

Distracted by Alec, Xavier nodded absently. "Tomorrow morning would be perfect. Thank you, Odin."

Shaking my head, I walked Odin to the door. "Don't mind them. Alec's been worried about him."

"So have I, but I'm happy to see him looking so much better." Odin clasped his hand to mine and gave me a one-armed hug. "Go enjoy your men. From what I know already of your journey, it hasn't been easy. For any of you. You deserve a break. And make sure he takes one too."

"Oh, believe me, he's not getting a choice." I held the door for him to pass, waving him off before closing it and returning to the sunroom.

Where Alec had found another way to make sure Xavier couldn't focus on anything remotely resembling work. On his knees, his onesie undone and open to his waist, he slid his lips over Xavier's dick while Xavier fisted his hands in Alec's hair.

Grinning, I opened the bottom drawer on the nearby cabinet to grab some lube. My boy had the right idea. Keep Xavier exhausted enough with pleasure and the last thing he'd be thinking about would be the book, or his next design.

Who said we had to go anywhere for our honeymoon anyway? We had all we needed, right here.

"Don't let him come, my boy." I put my hand over Xavier's, urging Alec to take him in deeper. "He'll come once he's inside you. With me."

Xavier hissed in a breath, shaking his head. "He's not ready for that, my man. I still need to work on getting him to take more."

"Your fist is very different than him taking both of us..." I studied Xavier's face, catching the flash of heat in his eyes. The preparation was part of what aroused him. I could work with that. "Of course, if he can take it, there's so much more we'd be able to do to him."

Groaning, Alec tipped his head back. "Yes, please."

I grinned, lifting him off the floor and laying him on the table, in front of Xavier. "I do believe this is becoming one of my new favorite places for you. You're so fun to serve up to our man."

Tugging the onesie off Alec's legs, Xavier tossed it aside. "This is one meal I'll never refuse." Palming Alec's ass cheeks, he spread him open, licking over his taint and teasing his hole with the tip of his tongue. He made a soft sound of pleasure. "Fuck, thank you, Luther. You keep this pretty hole so nice for me. I know he whines about the waxing, but don't listen to him."

A sharp gasp escaped Alec as he searched for something to hold onto, finally latching on to the other end of the table. "I don't whine, I just...please...please..."

"Needy pet." I opened the lube, waiting for Xavier to fuck Alec with his tongue until our boy was incoherant. When he moved back, I poured the lube over Alec's already glistening hole. "You're going to get everything you want, my boy. And more...so much more."

Slicking up two fingers, Xavier pressed them past the snug ring of muscle, adding a third without much delay. He'd taken to finger fucking Alec in the shower almost every morning, leaving him on edge most of the day, so he was more than ready for pleasure whenever we chose to give it to him. Fingers tight together, he worked in a fourth, testing Alec's limits.

Usually, this was when Alec either safeworded or the resistance of his body made things too painful for him to even try hiding. But this time, the glide was smooth. Alec pressed back, panting as Xavier slid in deeper.

"There we go. Such a good boy." Xavier tucked his thumb in, standing as he pushed until his knuckles were against the ring of muscle. "Deep breath, you're almost there."

Stroking Alec's thigh, I helped him relax as much as I could, whispering my own praises to him as Xavier's hand slid in to the wrist. Precum spilled from the tip of Alec's dick as Xavier fisted him, groaning as though reaching the point hit every one of his erotic triggers.

He kissed Alec's stomach. "Don't come yet, let me feel you. Fuck, you're so hot. So fucking hot. My perfect boy."

Head tipped back, Alec panted. "I don't know if I can hold back much longer, sir. I...I'm trying."

"Let him come." Taking a knee, I slid my lips over Xavier's dick, giving him more incentive to let our boy finally have his release. As much as I wanted to take him with Xavier, there was something about this step that was special.

That symbolism Xavier brought up sometimes, like with our wedding rings. Alec's collar.

From the day I'd brought Alec to him, Xavier had been working toward being able to care for him, to feel like he could handle someone so much more vulnerable than himself. He earned Alec's trust long before he'd trusted himself.

This time, he hadn't waited for me to take the lead with our boy. To decide how much he could take. There would still be times when Xavier would need or want my control, but not because he didn't believe his own was enough.

What I tasted on my tongue as he came down my throat was my man accepting his own power. And it was fucking sweet.

There would be plenty of chances for me to enjoy that tight little ass. And a thousand different experiences I wanted us to share. Today, tomorrow, and every day after that.

Our story had just begun.

About Bianca Sommerland

Tell you about me? Hmm, well, there's not much to say. I love hockey and cars and my kids...not in that order, of course! Lol! When I'm not writing—which isn't often—I'm usually watching a game or a car show while networking. Going out with my kids is my only downtime. I get to clear my head and forget everything.

As for when and why I first started writing, I guess I thought I'd get extra cookies if I was quiet for a while—that's how young I was. I used to bring my grandmother barely legible pages filled with tales of evil unicorns. She told me then that I would be a famous author.

I hope one day to prove her right.

For more of my work, please visit: www.Im-No-Angel.com

facebook.com/BSommerland

twitter.com/BSommerland

instagram.com/biancasommerland

amazon.com/Bianca-Sommerland

bookbub.com/authors/bianca-sommerland

goodreads.com/Bianca_Sommerland

youtube.com/biancasommerland

Also by Bianca Sommerland

UNTAMED (FERAL BONDS)

SOLID EDUCATION

STREET SMARTS

UPPER CLASS

Excerpt from Solid Education

Chapter One

Strong winds blew snow across the campus, rattling the windows as the storm raged; yet all but one of the seats in the classroom were filled. Professor Derek Paulson smiled at his students as he prepared to begin the day's lesson. He started off by asking random questions from the required reading, pleased by how quickly answers were shouted out. During his brief stint as a professor at Cathia University, he'd gained the reputation as a hard, uncompromising teacher, but most of his students were thriving.

At the end of the day, he still preferred the company of the animals he worked with in his veterinary clinic, but he didn't regret accepting the position teaching his future peers. His tough course load had weeded out those who weren't serious about a future in animal care.

Which was why the one empty seat kept distracting him.

Three days a week he looked over at the seat by the window to see Gage Tackett, one of the few students he hadn't pegged from day one as either a dropout or completely dedicated. Gage turned in papers that were thoughtful, well-researched, and showed promise, but he never voluntarily answered questions in front of the class. He always seemed distracted, yet, when called upon, replied in a way that proved he was listening.

Derek knew Gage didn't live on campus, so perhaps the storm had delayed him, but the young man was religiously prompt. Gage dressed like a biker, but he sat up straight in class and his manner didn't fit his delinquent appearance. He was the ultimate contradiction, and Derek didn't know what to make of him.

But he had almost thirty other students who were present and deserved his full attention. So he forced himself to focus on them and forget the empty chair.

A soft knock at the door made focus a little more difficult when Derek saw Gage through the small window. He gave the front row of students worksheets to hand back before going to the door. He braced himself to address Gage as he would any other student who couldn't show up on time. His policy had been made clear from the start. There was no excuse for tardiness. Gage had already been marked absent.

The young man stepped aside as Derek opened the door. Gage's coal black hair was weighed down with melting snow, and there were patches of white on his leather jacket. His clean-shaven cheeks were red with windburn.

Gage lifted his broad chin, standing stiff with his arms at his sides. "I apologize for interrupting, sir, but there were extenuating circumstances—"

"Perhaps, but I have no time to hear about them. You're disrupting my lesson, Mr. Tackett." Derek gave Gage a hard look as his lips parted. "I hope to see you Wednesday. On time."

There really wasn't much more to say, but Derek wasn't surprised when Gage inched forward, his evergreen eyes darkening with rage. "Listen, you—"

Holding up a finger, Derek pulled the classroom door shut. At the beginning of the semester he'd dealt with several students who thought they were entitled to special treatment. He'd never considered Gage to be one of those, but if he was, Derek wouldn't allow him to make a scene.

"No, you listen. Missing class will affect your grade, but not as much as being dismissed from this course will. I'd consider carefully before continuing on this path, Mr. Tackett. Perhaps this behavior worked in high school, but it's time to grow up." Derek wasn't even sure how old Gage was, but he could picture him as a star quarterback who'd had the world in the palm of his hand until reality showed him he wasn't such a special little snowflake. He hadn't made the cut in his dream job, and this was just his second choice.

Not a fair judgment when Derek knew very little about him, but the undertone of aggression in Gage's stance was much like that of the muscle-heads Derek had dealt with in school. He was well aware of the fact that Gage could break him in two without much effort. Derek was in pretty good shape; he swam laps almost every morning and watched what he ate, but Gage was huge. No more than an inch taller than Derek's six feet but much wider. Easily intimidating if Derek forgot who was in charge.

Moving a little closer, Gage met Derek's unblinking stare. From the corner of his eye, Derek caught the man's fists clenching. He braced himself, positive he couldn't move fast enough to protect himself if Gage was going to punch him.

Then Gage shook his head and took a step back. "I thought you were one of the good ones. I apologize again, *sir*. I'll see you on Wednesday."

Seeing Gage turn away, shoulders slumped as he made his way down the empty hall, was much worse than a punch. Derek was tempted to call him back. Give him the chance to explain, maybe let him off with a warning. But how could the students respect him if he started slacking on the rules? If he let one rule slide, then the others would be tested as well.

He was a good teacher and didn't mind the extra work, but this was a part of the job he hated. He plastered on a smile and returned to the classroom, diving into the lesson and dismissing the urge to let the situation with Gage distract him any longer. The man wasn't one of Derek's wounded dogs at the clinic whom he could get through to with affection and special treats.

But, later that day as Derek tended to a young beagle who'd lost a leg and was bravely learning to function with the impairment, he couldn't help but think how much he preferred working with animals. The rules were simple—he never felt like he was kicking one when they were down.

And he still couldn't help feeling like that was exactly what he'd done to the young man who'd just needed to be heard.

Back in the snow, Gage cursed out the professor. Not so much for keeping him out of class, but for proving that going to class at all was a waste of precious time. He found the tracks of the emaciated dog he'd spotted out in the snow. Followed them into the alley where he'd lost sight of the poor thing. He'd grabbed a bag of dog food at the corner store and had a handful in his pocket in case he needed to tempt the mutt close enough to get him off the streets.

As he trudged through the snow, the cold seeped through his jeans, but he hardly noticed. The dog had probably been sleeping out here, and who knew how much longer the poor pup would survive as the temperature continued to drop? At least the wind had calmed down a bit, making it easier to follow the tracks, though most of them were filled in.

He heard laughter in the distance, past where the alley between the old apartments forked. A dog's pain-filled whine quickened his pace. He ran around the corner and saw three young teenage boys surrounding the dog, pelting it with snowballs. He wasn't sure why the dog couldn't seem to get away. All he knew was he needed to get the little shits to stop.

"What the fuck do you think you're doing? Get out of here!" Gage lunged at the closest boy, who dove out of reach and scrambled to his feet, taking off without waiting for his friends. The other two boys dropped their snowballs and bolted after him.

Cowering in the snow, the dog stiffened as Gage approached. Tried to stand and dropped hard as though his legs just couldn't support him any longer. Gage stuffed his hand in his pocket, moving slowly as he offered the food to the dog. The dog sniffed the food. Whimpered and took a little bit, but most of the hard pellets spilled into the snow.

"It's all right, pal. I've got you." The dog wasn't small—Gage was pretty sure he was a German Shepherd—but he was frighteningly light as Gage carefully picked him up. Despite the boys' attacking him, the dog didn't growl or struggle as Gage carried him to his car. His cold, wet nose pressed against Gage's neck. He let out a soft whine as Gage lowered him onto the backseat and used his jacket as a makeshift blanket. "I know. We're gonna get you all warmed up, buddy. Maybe get you something to eat? I got some leftovers. Might be easier than that hard stuff."

Getting to his apartment took longer than usual since not all the roads were clear, and plows slowed the progress on the bigger streets. He finally pulled into the outdoor parking lot, parked, and got out to lift the shivering dog into his arms. He'd had the heat blasting, so hopefully the shivering was a good sign. He kept his jacket around the dog and brought him inside.

He made it to his apartment before a new problem arose. His nosy neighbor had opened her door just as he was unlocking his. He knew from when he'd first moved in that she would call the landlord over anything—he'd gotten a knock on the door within minutes of unpacking for a noise complaint. Middle of the day and he'd been tuning his guitar without speakers or anything. He never had friends here anymore because he'd gotten warnings just for them talking in the hall.

No animals allowed meant he could expect another pleasant visit from the super. This place fucking sucked, but he couldn't afford to find another apartment. He'd find the dog a good home after he made sure the poor thing would be all right. He settled the dog on his worn, brown, second-hand sofa and covered him with a few blankets before going to the kitchen to see what he could feed him. He had some leftover chicken, so he put a few slices on a plate. Filled a bowl of water and brought both to the living room.

The dog weakly climbed off the sofa as he came in. Laid on his belly and sniffed the chicken Gage set in front of him. He ate slowly, his gaze darting to Gage every time he moved. It took a while, but the dog cleaned the plate.

"Good boy." Gage sat on the sofa and scratched behind the dog's ears. The dog had thick fur, which had probably helped him survive out there, but it was dirty and matted. "Gonna get you to a vet before I worry about cleaning you up, but until then, just looking at you, I've got the perfect name. What do you think of 'Matty'?"

Tipping his head back, the dog grunted then licked Gage's hand.

"I'll take that as a yes. All right, Matty, here's the deal. I can't keep you here, but I'm gonna find you a real good family. After we make sure you ain't just lost." He chuckled as Matty plunked down next to the sofa and closed his eyes. The dog needed to get looked at, but no harm in letting him rest for a bit.

Gage took out a few of his course books and decided to make a dent in the assignments. He was comfortable with most of his subjects, but he'd put off starting the midterm chemistry paper because he was struggling with some of the basics and refused to turn in anything substandard. The professor was a soft-spoken old man who appeared as bored with the work as most of the students, which meant Gage was doing most of his learning on his own.

And sucking royally at it.

He was good at biology though, so he finished his latest assignment and closed the books a couple of hours later with a sense of accomplishment. Quiet while he studied usually made him jumpy, but he hadn't even noticed the silence. He grinned at the dog. Having him here had probably helped. Matty lifted his head as

Gage stood. His wagging tail began thumping against the sofa when Gage knelt beside him.

"Time to go, Matty. Maybe the road will be cleared and this won't take too long." Gage sighed as he wrapped Matty in a thick, gray flannel blanket. The dog was great company, but if he kept Matty too long, he'd get attached. Getting attached would be bad. And not just because he wasn't allowed to have a pet in the apartment. "You remind me of my dog, Gunner. He was meaner than you, though. Those stupid punks would have been sorry if they messed with him." He laughed as he held Matty against his chest and the dog licked his cheek. "He didn't like being picked up, but you're a cuddly thing, aren't you? You'd probably do great with kids."

Matty sneezed and rested his head on Gage's shoulder. His eyes looked sad. Almost as though he knew this was gonna be goodbye.

"I can't hardly take care of myself, pal. You need a family with a big house, a huge backyard—maybe that organic food that will keep you healthy and fatten you up." He had to believe letting Matty go was the best thing for the dog. His life was empty without Gunner, but he didn't have it in him to love and care for a pet when he'd spent so long with a dog as his partner.

A partner he'd lost after serving by his side for three years.

His steps faltered as he pictured Gunner, wagging his tail and hunting for IEDs like finding bombs was a game. Gunner would go still and his posture would change when he'd catch the scent of the explosives. With the last one…he hadn't had a chance.

Shaking his head, Gage quickly brought Matty back to the car to take him to the closest vet. On the drive, he caught himself rubbing the tattoo on his wrist. H916—the same tattoo Gunner had inside his ear. His chest ached as the memories haunted him. He knew his best bet would be to drop Matty off at the vet and forget about him. He'd spent the last nine months trying to figure out how to rebuild his life. He couldn't afford to get all sentimental and fuck up his progress.

A tiny receptionist with big brown eyes and a warm smile looked up as he walked into the Cathia veterinary clinic. Her smile faltered as she looked at Matty. "Oh, the poor baby. How long has it been sick?"

"Not sure he's sick. Found him." Gage would never let a dog get sick enough to be in this condition. Of course, the girl didn't know that. "Fed him, but I think he needs a vet to look him over, ma'am."

She pursed her lips. "Well, I can make you an appointment for later in the week, but unless it's an emergency, I'm afraid Dr. Paulson is booked solid."

"Dr. Paulson?" Couldn't be the professor, could it? Gage frowned, adjusting Matty when he squirmed in his arms. "Listen, he can hardly walk, he was out in the cold for who knows how long, and he's underweight." He tried to stay calm, but he couldn't help the anger that slipped into his tone. He didn't care who the vet was. Matty needed to be taken care of now. "I'll wait."

Blinking at him, the receptionist stood and watched him take a seat with Matty in his lap. She huffed and then spun on her heel, disappearing down the hall and behind one of the wood doors. He rolled his eyes and scratched behind Matty's ear as he looked around the room. There were six chairs on one side, a large window at the front, and the desk. All clean and smelling a bit like a hospital. Smaller than he'd expected looking at it from outside. The rest of the clinic must take up most of the space.

Only a few minutes passed before the receptionist returned. With Derek Paulson, Gage's animal science professor, striding behind her then past as she took her place behind her desk. He stopped in front of Gage, his blue eyes narrowed and his bearing so like Gage's Sarge that he had the urge to stand at attention.

But he wasn't going to disturb Matty unless he was gonna be taken care of. For all he knew, they'd have to find another vet.

"I shouldn't be surprised. This is twice in one day that you're demanding attention, Mr. Tackett." Dr. Paulson folded his arms over his chest, the same disapproval in his eyes and his tone that had been there in the hall of the university. Only instead of a stuffy suit, the man was wearing a white jacket over a pale blue shirt and dark blue tie. There was no one else in the waiting area, but the man acted like he was too busy to deal with Gage. "Britney tells me you refused to take an appointment?"

Inhaling slowly, Gage stroked Matty's head as the dog whimpered and snuggled closer. He didn't want to deal with Paulson either, but he wouldn't let Matty suffer for his pride. He lowered his gaze and swallowed. "Not trying to be pushy, Doctor. He was out in the cold for a long time. You can see his ribs and his spine. I want to make sure there's nothing else wrong with him."

Paulson's eyes softened as he glanced down at Matty. "Is he the reason you were late for class?"

"Yeah." Gage looked up, not sure what to make of the sudden understanding in Paulson's gaze. The professor hadn't cared to listen to his "excuses" before. No point in dwelling on that now. He stared up at Paulson, relieved when the man simply nodded.

"Follow me." Paulson turned, leading the way to one of the doors, revealing an exam room larger than the reception area. He patted a metal table in the center of the room and went to pull on some rubber gloves as Gage carefully placed Matty on the table. Paulson's tone was low, soothing as he petted the dog, then began his cursory exam. "Definitely needs to be fattened up, but I suspect that's not your biggest concern."

Gage jutted his chin at the dog. "He can't walk right."

"And you have much better vocabulary. Proper sentences please, Mr. Tackett." The hint of a smile played at Paulson's lips. He gently checked Matty's paws, his brow furrowing when he reached the right hind leg. "She's got frostbite on all her pads, but there's serious tissue damage on this one. I may have to remove some of it. We'll start her on antibiotics and see if we can get the infection down. I'll run a battery of blood tests and give her some painkillers." He left Gage standing with Matty and started collecting supplies on a metal rolling tray. "You'll be able to take her home tonight, but make sure she doesn't aggravate the wounds."

"She…" Gage's cheeks heated at Paulson's amused look. Then continued before the professor could comment on his not checking the sex of the dog. "I can't take her to my place—no animals allowed."

Lips in a hard line, Paulson put his hand on Matty's back in a way that Gage could only define as protective. "So you intended to just leave her with whatever vet you found?"

"Of course not. But I can't keep her." The patronizing stare was gonna get the asshole punched, but Matty still needed treatment—which would be difficult for Paulson to administer with two black eyes. So Gage forced himself to calm down. "I planned to find Matty a good home."

"You clearly don't see that as your responsibility any longer."

"I didn't fucking say that!" Gage strode away from the table, returning quickly at Matty's sharp cry. He put a comforting hand between her shoulders to hold her down as she tried to stand. "Shh, baby. It's all right." He was going about this all wrong. He sighed, focusing on Matty as he spoke to the professor. "Can you take her home with you? Just until she's well and I can get someone to adopt her?"

Brow furrowed, Paulson shook his head. "Between my hours at the clinic and teaching, I don't have time to—"

"I'll watch her when you're busy."

This time, Paulson's brow lifted. He let out a soft laugh. "Are you inviting yourself to my house, Mr. Tackett?"

"I'm taking responsibility for my dog."

"She's not your dog, remember?" Paulson prepared a syringe. "Very well. When we are done here, I will keep her overnight. I will give you directions, and you will arrive at my door no later than seven a.m. Are we clear?"

"Yes, sir." *Fuck, I hate this guy.* But Gage reeled in his animosity and spent the next hour comforting Matty, relaxing even more as she stopped whimpering and jerking every time Paulson came near her. She didn't even budge when Paulson shaved some of the fur on her leg to reveal an infected cut that had to be cleaned and bandaged. Brave girl.

Took a while, but the hatred faded back to the initial grudging respect Gage had held for the professor. He chanced a smile once Paulson had Matty loaded in a large travel crate with a few blankets. Held out his hand.

The professor glanced at his hand, and then jutted his chin toward the front door. "I have to lock up. I will see you in the morning. Don't be late."

Cheeks heating with embarrassment, Gage nodded. "Yes, sir. And thank you."

Alone in his car, Gage let out a curse under his breath. He'd been right about Paulson.

The man was a complete asshole.